The Master Butchers Singing Club

Also by Louise Erdrich

NOVELS

Love Medicine
The Beet Queen
Tracks
The Bingo Palace
Tales of Burning Love
The Antelope Wife
The Last Report on the Miracles at Little No Horse

WITH MICHAEL DORRIS

The Crown of Columbus

POETRY

Jacklight
Baptism of Desire

FOR CHILDREN

Grandmother's Pigeon
The Birchbark House
The Range Eternal

NONFICTION

The Blue Jay's Dance

The Master Butchers Singing Club

Louise Erdrich

HarperCollins*Publishers*

HarperCollins books may be purchased for educational, business, or sales promotional use. For information, please write: Special Markets Department, HarperCollins Publishers Inc., 10 East 53rd Street, New York, NY 10022.

Grateful acknowledgment is made to the editors of *The New Yorker*, where portions of chapters 5 and 6 appeared in slightly different form as "The Butcher's Wife."

Nothing in this book is true of anyone alive or dead.

FIRST EDITION

Designed by Elliott Beard

Library of Congress Cataloging-in-Publication Data
    Erdrich, Louise.
        The Master Butchers Singing Club : a novel / Louise Erdrich.—1st ed.
            p.   cm.
        ISBN 0-06-620977-3
        1.Triangles (Interpersonal relations)—Fiction. 2. World War 1914–1918—Veterans—Fiction. 3. German Americans—Fiction. 4. Married people—Fiction. 5. North Dakota—Fiction. 6. Immigrants—Fiction. 7. Butchers—Fiction. 8. Singers—Fiction. I. Title.
PS3555.R42 M37 2002
813'.54—dc21
                                                            2002068501

03 04 05 06 07   ❖/RRD   10 9 8 7 6 5 4 3 2 1

To my father,
who sang to me.

Die Gedanken sind frei
Wer kann sie erraten
Sie fliehen vorbei
Wie nächtliche Schatten
Kein mensch kann sie wissen
Kein Jäger erschiessen
Es bleibet dabei
Die Gedanken sind frei.

—"Thoughts Are Free" (German song)

The Master Butchers Singing Club

ONE

The
Last Link

$\mathcal{F}$IDELIS WALKED home from the
great war in twelve days and slept thirty-eight hours once he crawled
into his childhood bed. When he woke in Germany in late November of
the year 1918, he was only a few centimeters away from becoming
French on Clemenceau and Wilson's redrawn map, a fact that mattered
nothing compared to what there might be to eat. He pushed aside the
white eiderdown that his mother had aired and restuffed every spring
since he was six years old. Although she had tried with repeated scrub-
bings to remove from its cover the stains of a bloody nose he'd suffered
at thirteen, the faint spot was still there, faded to a pale tea-brown and
shaped like a jagged nest. He smelled food cooking—just a paltry steam
but enough to inspire optimism. Potatoes maybe. A bit of soft cheese.
An egg? He hoped for an egg. The bed was commodious, soft, and after
his many strange and miserable beds of the past three years, it was of
such perfect comfort that he'd shuddered when first lying down. Fidelis

had fallen asleep to the sound of his mother's quiet, full, joyous weeping. He thought he still heard her now, but it was the sunlight. The light pouring through the curtains made a liquid sound, he thought, an emotional and female sound as it moved across the ivory wall.

After a while he decided that he heard the light because he was clean. Disorientingly clean. Two nights ago, before he'd entered the house, he begged to bathe in a washtub out in the tiny roofed courtyard, beneath the grape arbor. They built a fire to warm the water. His sister, Maria Theresa, picked the lice from his hair and his father brought fresh clothing. In order to endure all that the war necessitated, including his own filth, Fidelis had shut down his senses. As he opened to the world again, everything around him was distressingly intense and all things were possessed of feeling, alive, as in a powerful dream.

Quietness reverberated in his head. Ordinary sounds, people outside in the streets, seemed marvelous as the chatter of rare monkeys. A thrill of delight crashed through him. Even to put on his clean and vermin-free clothing was a task so full of meaning that the fastening of his grandfather's gold boar's-head cuff-links nearly made him weep. Breathing low, he collected himself, and stilled his tears with the power of his quietness. Ever since he was a child, when sorrow had come down upon him, he'd breathed lightly and gone motionless. As a young soldier, he'd known from the first that in his talent for stillness lay the key to his survival. It had carried him through the war as a pitifully green recruit of whom it was soon discovered that, from a sniping post, he could drill a man's eye at 100 meters and make three of five shots. Now that he was home, he understood, he must still be vigilant. Memories would creep up on him, emotions sabotage his thinking brain. To come alive after dying to himself was dangerous. There was far too much to feel, so he must seek, he thought, only shallow sensations. Now he tried to adjust. He must slowly awaken even to this childhood room he knew so well.

He sat down at the edge of the bed. On a thick shelf set into the wall, his books stood in lines, or stacked as he'd left them, marked with thin strips of paper. For a time, though his occupation was assured, he'd cherished the vision of himself as a poet. Therefore his shelves were stacked with volumes of his heroes, Goethe, Heine, Rilke, and even Trakl, hidden behind the others. He looked at them now with dull curiosity. How could he ever have cared what such men said? What did their words matter? His childhood history was also in this room, his toy soldiers still arranged on the sill. And his young man's pride: his diplomas and his guild papers framed on the wall. These things did matter. These papers represented his future. His survival. In the closet, his bleached, starched, and pressed white shirts hung ready to embrace him. His polished shoes waited on the shelf beneath for the old Fidelis to put his feet into them. Gingerly, Fidelis tried to slide his feet into the open maws of the stiff shoes, but they wouldn't go. His feet were swollen, tender from frostbite, peeling, painful. Only his hobnailed boots fit, and they were green inside and stank of rot.

Slowly, he turned to contemplate the day. His bedroom window was a long, golden rectangle. He rose and opened the window, using the ram's-horn curl of its handle, and looked out, over Ludwigsruhe's slow, brown river, over the roofs and dead late-fall gardens on its opposite bank, across a patchwork of tender, gray fields, and then a tiny complex of roofs and chimneys beyond. Somewhere in that next town's maze lived the woman he had never met before, but had promised to visit. He found himself thinking about her with a complex intensity. His thoughts formed questions. What was she doing now? Had she a garden? Was she gathering the final few dusty potatoes from a small, raised, straw-covered berm? Was she hanging out her laundry fresh and white on a piece of icy rope? Was she talking, over tea, to her sister, her mother? Was she singing to herself? And his own presence, what he had promised to tell her. How could he go through with it, and also, how could he not?

EVA KALB, 17 Eulenstrasse. Fidelis stood before the blond-brick walkway, frowning at the frail cast-iron arbor that marked the entrance. The ironwork was threaded with the tough overgrowth of climbing rose stalks, leafless and almost black, huge thorns white at the tip. The walk wasn't swept and papers littered the front entry. The rest of the block was neatly, fanatically well-kept even in the chaos of defeat. Fidelis found the neglect of Eva Kalb's house disturbing, perhaps indicating a death in the family already. His eyes filled with tears and he pinched the bridge of his nose—the readiness of his emotions, even in public, horrified him. There was some movement behind a sheer curtain in the front window of the house. Fidelis knew he had been seen, and so, breathing deeply and shrugging himself into a tougher shell, he stepped forward, onto the bricks of the walkway.

She opened the door almost immediately at his knock, so he knew she had been the one at the window, watching him. He knew this was Eva from the picture in his best friend's locket, which he'd kept. Even now, in the tiny breast pocket of his jacket, the cheap vermeil keepsake made a hot oval lump. Inside the miniature frame was set the hand-colored picture of a woman who looked both capable and delicate, her mouth a sensitive line grooved at the corners by sensuality and shrewdness. Of deepest green, her slanted, indecipherable Magyar eyes now shocked Fidelis with their open, searching gaze. The trained immobility that had helped him to survive the last few years cracked when she looked straight at him. *Schnell, die Wahrheit*, she said with a preemptive hostility that caused him to obey her directly and to state what he had come to tell: Her lover, her betrothed, her husband-to-be, Johannes, with whom Fidelis had endured all that could be endured, was dead.

Directly afterward, Fidelis wasn't sure whether he thought or actually said these words, but it did seem to him that sounds had come from his mouth. Although he didn't hear them, Eva understood—she took the meaning of the sounds into herself with a huge, unsteady breath. That cruel air seemed to dizzy her and her intelligent face lost focus, her expression snapped away, so that Fidelis saw her, for one moment, in the state of a naked being accepting pain. Then Eva Kalb slumped toward him, hands clasped, face calm, in an attitude of prayer. As he caught her and folded her carefully against himself, he understood with a visceral surprise that she was pregnant. Later, privately, Fidelis came to believe that the child had actually knocked from her womb at that moment, its motion touching the helping palm of his hand.

Fidelis lifted his best friend's fiancée into his arms and stood in the doorway of the house, holding the woman effortlessly, as he would have held a sleeping child. He could have stood there with her for hours. The strength required to hold her was a minute portion of the strength he actually possessed. For he was one of those born in the phenomenon of strength. He'd always had it, from the beginning, and each year it increased.

It is said that some people absorb the cellular essence of a twin while still in the womb—perhaps Fidelis was one of those. Maybe he was simply of that old Germanic stock who roamed the forests and hung their god from the tree of life. There is also in some parts of Germany a belief that one who kills is at the moment of the other's death entered by that victim's essence. If so, that explained both the lightness and the gravity of Fidelis. He had seen the flash of a man's smile through telescopic sights in the instant before his sniper's bullet shattered the distant face. He had watched the blood pump through a man's fingers on the throat he'd neatly creased. He'd dealt death out so accurately from his sandbagged and reinforced turret that the French and the British tried to clock his watches. They hated him, and they tried with near success to capture him, for they had planned how slowly they would kill him. Between him and them, the war was very personal. He accepted this. And he had not turned away from his task. He simply continued with a raptor's perseverant ease to pluck men from that too shallow rift in the earth.

They'd dug down deeper to escape him, and yet he caught them anyway in a moment of foolish ease, pure tiredness, or fatal exuberance. Perhaps it was true that those souls flew unerringly across the drenched slime to lodge within him, for the quiet in Fidelis had deepened to a serene violence undisturbed by the roar of the big night guns. His fellow soldiers began to fear and then detest him as their misery increased. He drew enemy fire, so he was avoided. He slept, and slept. Shells fell near him, men shrieked in his ear. Fidelis only frowned a little, sighed with childish irritation, and kept on sleeping. He dreamed black dreams from which he woke with no memory. He meticulously oiled and cleaned the workings of his rifle. He ate the brot and wurst, the little packages of dried peaches and apples he'd brought from home, and he dipped the finger he would set on the trigger, every morning, into a small pot of honey from his mother. He licked that finger and tasted the bee-sugar dark with forest bitterness. A childhood taste, sucked from the hidden blossoms of the densest stands of silver fir. He never licked all the honey quite off, and once he took the rifle up his finger never slipped.

Now, in the doorway, Fidelis waited until Eva's mother came to investigate. When he brought Eva into her house and laid her down upon a faded rose pink sofa, he decided what he'd known already, what he'd promised his friend Johannes, who had died on the walk home from the war and in a shimmer of fractured musical notes. Fidelis would marry Eva. Later, when she agreed to his plan and when she kissed him, he tasted on her tongue and on the skin of her throat several layers of meaning. He tasted Johannes, whose forehead he'd kissed in death as though he were putting a little brother to sleep. That taste was the salt grief. Eva's taste was different, and familiar. Hers was the bitter edge to the sweetness of forest honey, and her fragrance, as he lifted his face away from hers, possessed the fading sharp persistence of the secret flowers of the blackest pines.

Their wedding was a poor and scrabbled-together affair, she enormous with the child fathered in the war's last insane and desperate season. But the priest, knowing all, blessed them, and they spent their first night together in Fidelis's tiny bedroom, where he'd left his lead soldiers to patrol the sills. That night, she lay naked in the trembling light of a candle, her body covering the childish stain on the flannel-covered eiderdown. Her gold hair, shot with the same red as his, sprayed across the pillow. Her breasts were veined with blue fire, her nipples chapped and dark. He knelt before her, between her legs, put his hands on her, and felt the hot movement of the child. The powerful emotions that had accompanied his return had faded slowly, at last, to a sense of embarrassment at his survival. He now had no idea what to do about his life, but upon entering Eva's body, clasping her hips to him, winding her legs behind his back, he moved from the dangerous quiet where he lived, into the unacceptable knowledge that in spite of the dead weight of killed souls and what he'd learned in the last three years about the monstrous ground of existence and his own murderous efficiency, he was meant to love.

FIDELIS SOON FOUND that he was also meant to travel. He became convinced that he should go to America because he saw, from that place, a slice of bread. This sighting occurred in the public square of Ludwigsruhe. Crossing it one day shortly after he married Eva, he noticed people grouped around a neighbor well-known to his parents. This man held something white and square in his hand that Fidelis took at first to be a picture of some sort, but it was blank. When he saw that it was bread, shaped with a precision that could only be the work of fanatics, Fidelis entered the circle of men to examine it. The thing was sent in a package from distant relatives, from a far coastal city, as an example of what such a commonplace item as a bread loaf became in the hands of inventive people. Machines had kneaded and baked and then sliced it. Or were these everyday American bakers? That was the argument. Fidelis inspected the bread when, passed hand to hand, it came around to him. He noted the fine texture and wondered at the treatment of the yeast, observed the sharp edge of the cut, shook his head at the strangely even gold brown of the crust. It seemed an impossible thing, to him, an artifact from some place that must adhere to an impossibly rigid order. Later that day, visiting the neighbor, he got the name of the place it was sent from, spelled it out on a scrap of paper, and kept it with him through the next months, until it changed from being the source of a small marvel to an actual destination.

STEPPING OFF THE RMS *Mauretania* into the harbor chaos of New York City with a suitcase full of his father's miraculous smoked sausage, Fidelis was directed through the swirl of massed arrival by his power of quiet. It was 1922 and Eva's baby was three years old. His talent for stillness had carried Fidelis through the war's aftermath of want, in which he'd been forced to enter a treacherous black market. Now, in the suitcase that Fidelis carried was massed the wealth of his entire family. All of their remaining trinkets, including the cuff-links, and their best woolens had bought his ticket and kept him from selling his knives. His own carefully hoarded bullets and hidden-away rifle had poached the wild boar from which were made the sausages that would carry him across this new country. He spoke only the English that he had learned on the ship, words specific to his intent—*train, train station, west, best sausage, master butcher, work, money, land*. His family's fortunes now lay solely with him and, as he saw it, his ability to maintain a watchful silence.

In his calm immobility, it was true, there was a power. But that was complicated by the restless sweep of his eyes, which were of a blue so transparent that his skull seemed lighted from within. His thick roan-blond hair, crushed underneath his father's prewar dress hat, needed cutting. He was clean shaven, though, and he wore clean underwear. The inside pockets of his father's suit held all he needed. The suit was of the fine Bavarian quality of the hat. His family, who were emphatically not Bavarian, in fact distrusted people from the south and believed them of a coarser quality than their woolens.

Although they were tradesmen and master butchers, his family also prided themselves on acquiring a degree of learning and on a talent for producing male voices of special beauty that skipped from son to son. His older brother hadn't much voice at all, for instance, but Fidelis had a singing tenor of such natural clarity and freshness that his last name, Waldvogel, might have been invented just for him. Waldvogel was such a common name in his town that he'd never thought of it, but in this new country, where Germans were Germans regardless of their regional origins, more than one person would remark upon it, and also note that Forestbird was an oddly gentle name for one whose profession was based in slaughter.

That was not how his family viewed it, of course; there was an art to a proper killing. The profession, acquired only through painstaking study and examination from a young age, was one of extraordinary precision and timing. A Metzgermeister's diploma required working knowledge of every spice known to humankind, the arcane preparation of hundreds of varieties of wurst, and the ability to commit one's knife edge to the animal's created bulk and grain with a dreamlike intuition. His father, having practiced all his life, hardly seemed to move his hands as the animal fell into increasingly civilized circles and predictable shapes. On a block set before him, its creatureliness disappeared and it entered, as Fidelis saw it, a higher and more satisfactory form of being.

Fidelis thought of his father's working grace as he stood for hours in lines, endured inspections, stamps, paperwork, the crush of impatient humans, and his own hunger. That he also managed, with that internal discipline of quiet he had learned at the rifle's sights. For the smoked sausages in his suitcase were not for him to eat; they were his ticket west.

Walking toward the train station through milling throngs of people, those who had acquired a foothold in this place, Fidelis gave in to an extravagant loneliness. Those who passed him saw an erect and powerfully carved man, high-cheekboned, fair, with a straight and jutting nose and a mouth as perfectly shaped, though who around him knew, as the voice that could pour from it. That he was afflicted by the riptide of a recent and unexpected love was, of course, not apparent to those who noticed him in the crowd. He tapped his heart, which from time to time beat too anxiously behind the lapels of his suitcoat. The locket that Eva had given to Johannes, and which Fidelis had secretly kept, was lodged there, for Fidelis was both thrilled and terrified to find that, although he'd married Eva on the strength of a promise to his dying friend, he'd fallen through a trapdoor into blackness—a midnight of love that had grown like a bower of inky twigs over the baby's defenseless beauty, over Eva's prickly loveliness, her trim fortitude, her bullheaded, forthright, stubborn grace.

The train station's massive brass-trimmed doors swallowed Fidelis with all the others. Easily, the current of people pulled him to the windows of the ticket counter. He waited again in line until he stood before a sharp-mouthed girl whose jaws moved in a rhythm peculiar to people in this city. Fidelis was unfamiliar with chewing gum and the motion of so many jaws made him uneasy. Her eyes brightened with an automatic greed, though, and the chewing stopped when he came before her.

"I wish to Seattle," he said, gathering the words in his mouth, "to go."

She told him the price of the ticket. He did not understand the click of numbers on her tongue, and mimed writing down her answer. She did so, and then, with a glance to one side, added her name and the words *Come see me if you're ever in town.* Her lacquer-nailed fingertips presented the slip of paper to him. She made him tug just a little to get it. He thanked her, in German, and she replied with a manufactured tragic pout that he was too weary to notice. The amount was legible, anyway. He understood it, knew how much money he would have to add to the meager amount he still possessed. He put the paper in his pocket and then found a pillar against which to stand.

He took up this position, the back brim of his father's hat just touching the grooved stone behind, and then he lifted the suitcase in his arms, unlatched the lid, and lowered it enough so that he could see just over the opened top. For the remaining hours of the day and then on into the dusk, during which the smoky radiance through the high windows intensified and then diminished to a feeble gray, he stood. Motionless, he seemed not so much rooted as suspended, as though he'd been lowered by strings that still held him poised. That was perhaps the visual effect of his hunger. For it crawled in him to lighten him, opened him from the inside. His gut yawned. Yet he remained impassive and somehow buoyant in the dark. He had rehearsed on the boat across the price he would ask for the sausages, and at once he sold seven, not perhaps because they were so irresistible but because, even in that city of every possible sight the image of the man holding open in his tireless arms the sausage-filled suitcase, which looked heavy by the way, arrested quite a few. From time to time, a shaft of the fading light plucked his calm and idealized features from the gloom. So he sold, just as he'd known he would, out of his depth of silence as much as the quality of what he carried, though he believed most certainly, and with a firm drama, that his father's were, no argument, the best sausages upon the earth.

Maybe they were. The next morning some who bought one the day before came back for two. And more people that same afternoon. Other than sleeping on a platform bench with the closed suitcase in his lap, visiting the washroom, or drinking the surprisingly cold, sweet city water, Fidelis had remained at his post. Those who noticed, and there were a few among the swirling crowd, wondered at his endurance. How did his arms support that open suitcase hour after hour? The suitcase, which also contained his treasured knives, was heavier than it looked, yet he held it lightly. As the day went on, his stillness seemed an un-questionable form of self-torture. But it wasn't, for Fidelis, the way it seemed to an observer. Standing there was not so difficult. It was almost a relief, after the constant motion of the sea. And the strength required to hold the suitcase in one position all that time was nothing to him, even though he was weakened by not eating.

Hunger had been with him forever, it seemed, and hunger was with him now. He'd learned its routine and knew, on the second day, not having eaten since the scrap of a last meal on the boat, that he must have food. No matter how reluctant he was to spend his money, the time had come. Fidelis shut the suitcase, from which sausages had no-ticeably disappeared, and he walked straight across the station, the fa-miliar, famished buzz in his ears, to a small diner set into the side of a wall. There, at a stool, the suitcase clasped between his feet, he chose three bowls of the cheapest stew—tough beef, potatoes, carrots, gravy—and ate with the intent patience he'd developed when relieving a period of starvation. The waitress brought him extra bread, and when he indi-cated that he couldn't pay for it and she insisted that he keep the bread, he thanked her with a gulp of surprise. The goodwill of most of the people here amazed him, but then, he reminded himself, they were nei-ther starving in the main nor recently and thoroughly defeated and de-tested outside their diminished borders. So they could afford, he decided, the ordinary kindnesses, the gift of bread.

He paid, recalculating the slight diminishment toward his goal, and he went to the public washroom for his morning shave. He unwrapped a scrap of stolen soap that had grown almost transparent, and had a sur-reptitious wash using one of his two pocket handkerchiefs. If he'd had the chance, he would have rinsed out his other pair of undershorts, tucked into the back pocket of his pants, but there were other men in the room and he was embarrassed. From a breast pocket he removed a carved ivory toothbrush, the boar's bristles softened and mashed with use. He'd had this with him all through the war. And the razor, too, thinned with years of stropping, the tiny comb, and the clever silver ear cleaner. All fit neatly back upon his person when he was finished. He lifted his suitcase and went back to his post.

By the time dusk began to throb in the windows again, he'd made more than half of what he needed. Now, as he counted his money, an idea occurred to him. Why not board the train with what he had, ride as far as he could get, and sell the sausages to the other passengers captured in the train cars? He went back to the ticket booth, encountered this time an impatient and elderly gentleman, and bought a ticket that would take him somewhere into the beginning of the Middle West. Then he went back to his post, sold one more sausage, closed his suitcase, and walked to the numbered platform with his ticket in his inside breast pocket. Among the boarding passengers wallowing in long good-byes or traveling with others, he entered the coach, settled himself, and waited patiently until the train began to rock, away from the hateful ocean, away from New York.

THE SAUSAGES TOOK HIM through Minneapolis and rolling prairie country into the sudden sweep of plains, vast sky, into North Dakota, where he sold the last link. He left the train and walked along the edge of a small town railroad platform. The town was a huddle of cheerful squat buildings, some framed with false half-story fronts on top of awnings and display windows, one or two of limestone and at least three of sturdy brick. Against the appalling flatness, the whole place looked defenseless and foolish, he thought, completely open to attack and, with its back against a river, nowhere to flee. It looked to him like a temporary place, almost a camp, that one great storm or war could level. He read the sign Argus aloud and memorized the sound. He turned in a circle to get his bearings, brushed off his father's suit, assessed the fact that he'd arrived with thirty-five cents and a suitcase, now empty of sausages, that contained six knives, a sharpening steel, and graduated whetstones. There was horizon to the west and horizon to the south. There were streets of half-grown trees and solid-looking houses to the north. A new limestone bank building and a block of ornately bricked stores on the principal street stretched down to the east. The wind boomed around Fidelis with a vast indifference he found both unbearable and comforting.

He didn't know that he would never leave. Fidelis simply thought that he would have to stay here, and work here, using the tools of his trade, until he made enough money to travel on to the destination he'd picked out for the severity of its bread. Now he wondered where the bread was made in this town, where the beer might come from, where the milk and the butter were kept cold, where the sausages were stuffed and the pork chops sliced and cleaved and the meat killed. Nothing gave him a clue. All directions looked the same. So he adjusted his father's hat, shrugged down his pants cuffs, picked up the suitcase.

TWO

The Balancing Expert

IN A SMALL TOWN on the headwaters of the Mississippi River and in a room rented solely for the purpose of making love, a man and woman, unclothed and in bed, paused in apprehension. For several months before this hour, they had been comfortably well acquainted, even friends. They had met doing town theater in Argus, North Dakota. Inevitably, they both became curious whether there was more and they set off together. Could they make a living with a traveling act? Were they in love? The man reached out and the woman, Delphine Watzka, raised her penciled eyebrows as though to judge. His hand swerved. "You have," he said, "very strong stomach muscles." He swept her torso lightly with his knuckles, then the tips of his fingers. With a thump, Delphine turned over onto her back, threw the covers off, and pounded herself on the stomach. "My arms are strong, my legs are strong. My stomach's tough. Why not? I am not ashamed I grew up on a goddamn farm. I'm strong all over. Not that I know what to do with it . . ."

"I have an idea," said the man.

She thought for a moment that the man, whose name was Cyprian Lazarre, and who was of a tremendous tensile strength, would put his idea into immediate action. She hoped that his purpose would over-come lack of nerve. That did not exactly happen. Enthusiasm for the plan in his brain gripped him, but instead of leaping passionately upon Delphine, he knelt, upright, on the sagging mattress and regarded her thoughtfully. Welts of soldered skin fanned across his shoulders. He was thirty-two years old, and his body was flint hard, perfectly muscled be-cause of his gymnastic practice. She thought that he looked just like one of those statues dug out of the wrecked ancient city of Troy, even to the damage of war and time.

Along with a cousin and a buddy, Cyprian had enlisted in the U.S. Marine Corps, survived his training and perhaps the most dangerous part of the war, exposure to Spanish flu, to find himself plunging ahead in the fourth wave at Belleau Wood, where he was burned in the wheat. Dur-ing that last year of the Great War, chlorine gas blinded him, the split barrel of a machine gun nearly took his hand off, dysentery unmanned him, his sense of humor failed, and he very much regretted his zeal. He came home before it even occurred to him that, as an Ojibwe, he was not yet a U.S. citizen. During his slow recuperation, he couldn't vote.

With a slight bounce, he went from his knees to standing and then hopped off the bed. There was a chair in the tiny room. Eyes flashing with performance fire, he gripped the bowed back, twisted the balls of his feet for purchase on the wooden boards, and then kicked up into a handstand. The chair wobbled just a bit, then steadied. "Bravo!" he breathed to himself. With his back to her, head down, sculptured but-tocks and pointed toes, he was an ideal picture of manliness. Delphine was glad she couldn't see around to the front of him. She was also hoping that no one outside in the street opposite this rooming house happened to glance up into the curtainless second-floor window, when she heard a scream from outside. Cyprian ignored it.

"This will be the finale," he said, "I'll be ten feet in the air, and you'll be holding me up here with your stomach muscles!"

Another scream outside was followed by a shudder of voices in the street below.

"Oh, will I?"

Delphine's voice was muffled by the neck of her blouse. One of Delphine's talents was to dress very quickly. She had learned it changing costumes in the repertory theater, where they'd all played two or three roles at once. She was dressed, even to her stockings and shoes, and the covers were pulled up on the bed before Cyprian even grasped what was happening in the street below. He was, in fact, still talking and planning as he practiced the handstand, when she slipped out the door and hurried down the stairs. She stopped at the very bottom, cooled her thoughts. With a composed air she stepped out the door and went straight up to the landlady, who was already purple.

"Mrs. Watzka!"

"I know," Delphine sighed, her face a mask of resigned calm. "Back in the war, you know, he was *gassed*." She tapped her temple as the landlady's mouth made an O. Delphine then walked straight into the cluster of people on the street. "Please! Please! Don't you have any respect for a man who fought the Hun?" She dispersed people with sharp waves and claps, the way she used to scare her chickens. The people staring upward suddenly were staring downward, pretending to examine their purchases. One of the ladies, cheeks delicately wrinkled, her eyes very round and her mouth a little beak of flesh, bent close to Delphine's ear. "You had really best persuade him to rest, dear! He is in a state of *male indiscretion!*"

That Delphine did not turn to look up at the window proved her both quick thinking and self-disciplined, although she did decide to hurry back into the room. "Oh dear," she said in the tone of a resigned wife, "and to think, standing on his hands is the only way he can maintain his readiness. And we've managed to have two darling children!"

Turning away she spoke to the crowd sweetly, as though nothing out of the ordinary had occurred at all, as though she hadn't just thrown them into a state of startled conjecture. "Don't forget, the show is at five o'clock this evening! Second stage at the fairgrounds!"

From the quality of the silence behind her, she knew it would be packed.

THAT NIGHT, Cyprian spun plates on the top of poles balanced two on each arm, one on each shoulder, one on his forehead, and one between his teeth. He set up a long line of poles and plates that he twirled as he ran back and forth, while Delphine took bets from the crowd on how long he could keep the plates going. That was where they made most of their money. He stacked things on his head, whatever the audience came up with—crates of chickens, more dishes. He declined the washing machine. While the stack mounted up, he jigged. He rode a bicycle over wires strung across the fairgrounds. For the finale, as the night was windless, he climbed the flagpole and balanced, did a handstand gripping the ball on top. The sight of him—tiny, perfect, a human pin against the wild black Minnesota sky—made Delphine start with a thrill of sympathy. At that moment, she forgave him for his lack of sexual heat, and decided that his desperate need for her was enough.

A STOCKY POLISH girl from off a scrap of farm is not supposed to attract men so easily, but Delphine was compelling. Her mind was very quick—too quick, maybe. Things came out of her mouth that often surprised her, but then, she'd had to deal with a lot of unpredictable drunks in her life and this had sharpened her reflexes. She had small, even, very white teeth, a clever dimple on one side of her mouth. Extremely light brown eyes, honey gold in direct sunlight, narrow and bold in a tan face. Her nose was strong, straight, but her ears were rakishly lopsided. She often wore her hair in what she imagined was the style of a Spanish contessa—one spit curl midforehead, two before either off-center ear, the rest in an elaborate bun. If she stared sharply into a man's eyes, he was immediately filled with unrest, looked away, could not help looking back. Just because she was magnetic, though, it did not make life easy.

At the age of three or four months, she had lost her mother. Her extreme affection for her dipsomaniacal father was unappreciated, even misplaced, and yet she was helpless before the onslaught of his self-pity. They would have lost even their tiny wedge of land and homestead many years ago, but for the fact that the farmer to whom her father leased his land refused to buy it outright and sewed that up in a contract. Therefore, they had a tiny income month to month, which went to hooch unless she swiped it. To escape a miserable home life, Delphine had sewed bright outfits, practiced the fabulous speeches of tragic heroines, and thrown herself into local dramatic productions. She'd met Cyprian when he was honing his act with the congenial town troupe. She left North Dakota with him, headed back into the hills and trees of Minnesota, where the towns were closer together and less dependent on the brutally strapped farmers. He'd said that there would be excitement, and that commenced with the all-revealing handstand before the window. He also said there would be money, which she hadn't seen much of yet. Delphine had joined the show because she hoped she'd become infatuated with Cyprian, who was the only other person in the show and was, although this became quite incidental, handsome.

Cyprian called himself a balancing expert. Delphine soon found that balancing was really the only thing he could do. Literally, the *only* thing he could do—he couldn't wash his own socks, hold a regular job, sew a seam back together, roll a cigarette, sing, or even drink. He couldn't sit still long enough to read an entire newspaper article. He couldn't hold much of a conversation, tell a story beyond the lines of a joke. He seemed too lazy even to pick a fight. He couldn't play long card games like cribbage or pinochle. Even if they ever stayed in one place long enough, he probably couldn't grow a plant! She did begin to love him, though, for three reasons: first, he claimed he was crazy about her, secondly, although they had still not made love with decisive lust, he was very sweet and affectionate, and lastly, his feelings were easily hurt. Delphine could never bear to hurt a man's feelings because she was so attached to her own father. In spite of his destructive idiocy when in his cups, she harbored an undying fondness for Roy Watzka that became, unfortunately, a kind of paradigm.

For instance, she expected nothing much of Cyprian, except that he not fall off the chair. For his part, after only one week, Cyprian grew attached to belonging to Delphine. He curled in the cheap rooming house beds, under covers that Delphine had requested be relaundered, as she was picky about bugs. While he nursed his sore muscles, Delphine busied herself with their survival. She mended what they'd torn during their act, planned how long to stay in each town and which to hit next, counted money, if there was any, wrote letters and advertisements to newspapers, decided what they'd eat.

The morning after the flagpole balance, she proclaimed that they had the wherewithal to eat sausage with their eggs and oatmeal. It was necessary, anyway, to fortify themselves for the long practice session they had decided to hold in a cow pasture. They ate slowly, luxuriously, from thick scarred plates. The café owner knew them now and brought extra sugar and a leftover pancake. Cyprian drew a diagram. A stick man standing on his hands on a chair, a random-looking but really very carefully balanced stack of chairs, the bottom chair on the stomach of a woman whose stick arms and legs were supports, whose balloon face smiled out off the scrap of a playbill.

"This will make our fortune," said Cyprian, solemn.

Delphine looked at the tower of chairs, the line that represented her gut beneath, and forked up another sausage.

NO COWS WERE IN the pasture and the patties on the ground were dry circles. She flung them off like plates and did some stretches, a couple dozen toe touches. Flexed. Hard to begin with, her stomach muscles would soon be phenomenal. Cyprian showed her how to develop them using a series of scientific exercises. Now, as he had to fall hundreds of times before he perfected an act, Delphine calmly yawned as the weight left her stomach. An instant later he crashed beside her. She didn't move until all of the chairs had fallen away, battering him. He set the chairs up so that if she just held her position beneath she could not be harmed. Time after time, as he fell and fell, memorizing each piece of the balancing trick in his body, she felt the edifice collapse and strike the earth around her. She stayed still. A few times a chair leg came close enough so that her hair was disarranged a bit, but beyond that she was never touched.

THE DAY WAS SPECTACULAR, and Delphine was dressed in a long elegant red skirt that swirled as she walked before the crowd. She did four cartwheels, and ended up sitting on a low, broad table. Cross-legged, she closed her eyes, folded her hands, and meditated to draw out the suspense. Just as the audience began to shift, impatient, she flipped over and became a human table. Cyprian then approached, holding a large wooden tray set up with tea things. On his head and his shoulders he carried an arrangement of six chairs, which he shrugged off, one by one. He sat upon the last chair, put the tray on Delphine's torso, nodded pleasantly to her. He drew a fork, a knife, a napkin, a herring from his sleeve, and then proceeded to lay out the plate and eat the herring, which he cut into tiny bites and chewed rapidly. When he was finished, he dabbed his mouth, stretched, appeared ready to relax with a smoke and a good book.

At that point, he frowned, he did not look comfortable. He sat in each chair, frowning harder, until he came to the last chair. "Do you mind?" he politely asked Delphine. "I suppose not," she answered. He then cleared off the tea things and set the first chair on the tea tray on her stomach. Now they needed a helpful member of the audience to pass the chairs up. One by one, leg upon wooden seat, Cyprian balanced the chairs. Climbed higher, higher. Finally, he had the sixth chair balanced and he sat down on it and took a cigarette from his pocket.

That was always when he noticed that he had forgotten his matches on the table, or rather, upon Delphine. (Someone in the audience always hollered the information, proud to make such a discovery.) Someone always offered to throw the matches up, but Cyprian politely declined any help, for already he had taken from his shirt collar a little collapsible fishing rod and unreeled the line. The end was fitted with a bobber, an ostentatious hook, and a sinker that was really a magnet and easily attracted the fixed matchbox.

Once Cyprian had possession of the matches, he slowly and luxuriously lighted his cigarette. Then with many flourishes he pulled out a book, and pretended to regale the assembled crowd with its contents—more or less off-color jokes, which he laughed at, too, and even kicked up his heels, so that the chairs swayed alarmingly and drew gratifying whoops of anxiety from the crowd. Cyprian did not fall, of course. Once he finished his book, he tossed it. Did a handstand, on the topmost chair. Everyone applauded until, most amazingly—and here is where Delphine wished for an accomplice to produce a drum roll—he came down the chairs, headfirst, dismantling his tower by piling each chair onto his feet, hooking one to the next, until he stood on his hands under the chairs, on Delphine's stomach.

Let us not forget that all of this time she was beneath, wrists locked, neck in a vise, gut clenched, legs solidly planted underneath the feminine red skirt!

Balancing on her torso, with the chairs on his feet, Cyprian craned his neck until his lips met hers. His kiss was falsely passionate, which got a roar from the crowd and had already started a slow burn of resentment in Delphine. The chairs were still balanced above them. They looked into each other's eyes, and that to Delphine was at first intriguing. But what do you really see in the eyes of a man doing a handstand with six chairs balanced on his feet? You see that he is worried he will drop the chairs.

THEY HOOKED UP with a vaudeville group and traveling circus from Illinois in the town of Shotwell, by the North Dakota border. "This is more my kind of place," said Delphine to Cyprian, comforted by the horizon all around them. At the end of every street the sky loomed. There had been too many trees surrounding the towns before. The open sky was homey. As well, they met carousing friends. Cyprian knew a few of these people from fairs and other shows, and the first evening, he brought her along with him to the local saloon. The place was a low, dank sty. They sat in a booth in the corner, packed in with three other couples, and were immediately served hard liquor. Up until then, Delphine had never witnessed Cyprian drinking, though at times she detected a whiff on his breath. Presented with a shot glass and a beer, he tried to slug the first back, and choked. Delphine said nothing, just nursed her beer and quietly tipped the shot onto the floor. She was almost ashamed of her fierce contempt for alcohol.

After the first round, two of the other couples got up and danced. That left Delphine and Cyprian, and another two. The men were involved in some deep topic, though, and since Delphine and the other girl were at their men's left elbows they could not really make an impact on the conversation or start talking to each other. Delphine pretended to watch the other dancers for a while. Bored, she went to visit the powder room, which was anything but a place to powder your nose, then she stepped outside to marvel at the sunset. The sky was roiling, the edges of the clouds were a startling green, and the light behind them an appalling threatful yellow. A man who passed by in the road said that it looked like a goddamn storm.

"What's it to you?" said Delphine, smiling just because she always smiled at a man, and because she was happy to see a sky that reminded her of home.

"I'm a farmer, that's what."

"Well you should come and see our show," said Delphine. "You should bring your whole family."

"Does anybody take their clothes off in it?"

"Sure!" said Delphine. "We all do!"

"Oh mama," said the man.

When Delphine stepped back into the saloon, the other girl was smoking grumpily in the booth and the men were gone.

"Where are they?" said Delphine.

"How the hell should I know?" said the girl. Her lips moved nervously, drinking and smoking, like two limp ropes. Painted with a glossy purple red, those lips gave Delphine a shiver up her back. The girl was ugly, Delphine decided, and that made her mean. Plus, she'd ordered two more drinks and Delphine thought at first she'd ordered one for her. But the girl drank both, one after the other, right in front of her.

"What's wrong with you?" Delphine asked.

"How the hell should I know?" said the girl.

Delphine left the saloon and walked back out into the road, where the sky was changing as fast as Delphine herself used to when she was an actress. Not for the first time since she'd left her father, she felt lonely and out of sorts. Perhaps all that space was making her homesick. Maybe it was the beer, but the absence of Cyprian was certainly part of it as well. He was very attentive to her moods, and when she felt blue, she told him. He usually came up with some way to cheer her. For instance, the last time she'd entered one of these slumps he'd picked her pocket, for she always kept some money in an easily unbuttoned side vent of her jacket, and he'd bought her a spray of red hothouse roses. That was a thing she'd never had before, roses. She had dried them and kept the petals in a handkerchief just to remember. Then there was another time he'd bought her a little jar of peanut butter to eat with a spoon. That was a treat. He'd bought her an ice cream on a stick, and he'd also done little things for her that did not require money. He'd picked up pretty stones by the lake, and once a tiny black arrowhead that he said an old-time Ojibwe probably used to shoot a bird. She had tied it on a tiny cord, and still wore it around her neck. Now, Delphine decided that he probably had gone somewhere to buy her a gift. It cheered her to find two dollars missing from the stash.

They were staying in a tent this time. She went back to the camp cot, rolled herself in her blanket, and woke before morning because the storm had indeed come and blown through the tent's unwaxed canvas walls and gotten her soaking wet. Luckily, the stuff in the middle was hardly damp, and she was able to string up a line between two trees in order to dry it all. Cyprian had not slept in the tent. Irritation pinched the back of her neck. But when he showed up he was so dear, so sweet to her, so fawning and anxious for her affection and, indeed, he had brought her the gift of a daisy cleverly carved of pure chocolate, that her annoyance collapsed. She smiled into his face and he held her to his chest, which was hard as a piece of armor.

"I love you," she said. It was not the first time she had said it, but there was in her a great tearful lump of emotion that the words unblocked. Tears stung and she reared back, energized.

23

"Where the hell were you!"

"Nowhere," he said.

He did not say this to her smoothly or in a manipulating way, but painfully, as though he really had been *nowhere*. Smoothing her hair back from her face, he kissed her forehead, right below the middle parting. Her hair was braided to either side. She looked, and felt, like a child. Cyprian's voice was so astonishingly sad that she forgot her need to know and molded to him in a melt of sympathy. His arms tightened, to the point that she had to take tiny little breaths. That was all right. They were sitting underneath a tree. Delphine was always to remember that. Without her knowing what had happened, they were close, so close, and she could sense every fiber of his doubtless love for her singing through his skin and in his thoughts. She felt entirely safe. She did not want to move. He fell asleep, beneath the tree, but his arm stayed tightly flexed. Delphine was content to watch the world wake up around them, the earth brighten, the fields beyond fields of green wheat thrash to life underneath a powerful mirror.

THEY MADE IT ALL the way to Gorefield, Manitoba, before she found out what the nowhere was and why it pained him to have told her about it. This time, at a fancy hotel, they stayed in the bridal suite. The furniture was elaborate, all spindles and spools, and the upholstery looked like tapestries right out of a museum. The rugs were deep and probably Persian, but what did Delphine know. She had splurged on this room because she was curious, once and for all, whether they could fall in love. In a way, they did. Not at first. He kept his eyes shut while they were rolling around, and seemed to be in a state of deep concentration. Though it all felt mechanical, she did not want to disturb him. She was alert, a little bored. His hands sprang off her breasts or he tweaked her nipples in a way that was unthinking, even painful. She wanted to bat him on the head, and was about to give up, when, with a happy groan, he climaxed, or at least pretended to.

Immediately, he eyed her for approval like a dog.

She patted his head. After a while, she turned him to face her. That was when they looked into each other's eyes and there commenced a mysterious bonding—something that Delphine had never felt before with anybody else on earth. They left time, left space, and just existed in the calm power of their eyes. They did not let go. Delphine felt loving energy rise in her and without any effort Cyprian went hard. She rolled on top of him and then they started moving again. The deeper they stared into each other's eyes the more each wanted to make use of the other body, the more they loved. The whole thing went on and on until they were exhausted. Still, every time they looked into each other's eyes, they started again to move, found themselves doing another thing, finding out something new. It was a strange experience, one they didn't talk about afterward, or, unfortunately, manage to repeat.

TWO DAYS LATER, Delphine went down to the river on a walk. Cyprian had skipped out on her after their performance and had not told her where he was bound. That left her alone to amuse herself, and because she was good at that she didn't sulk or mope but went to the town's one point of interest. Delphine sat down on a low bench by the river and watched the river move on by. It was heading north, rapidly, she could hear the current lapping shore, dragging little sticks into it, moving dirt and leaves and fish along.

The night was peaceful, and a few steady lights shone just across on the other shore, enough to see a few feet ahead. Annoyed to hear voices, footsteps, Delphine slipped into the tall brush just beside the bench. She wanted her bench back, and not to have to talk to anybody. Soon, two men walked into the clearing. Once they got to the bench they shut up and then one sat down and the other knelt before him. Delphine was hidden slightly behind the bench off to one side. Although she was immediately intrigued, she couldn't see what was taking place. Later, when she put it all together in her mind, she realized it was probably good she hadn't seen it all at once. It would have been too much of a shock. She hadn't known that men could get together like that.

"Oh my dear fucking God," groaned the man on the bench. He put a period stop between each word and moaned the last one. His hands flopped out and his legs sprawled. The man on his knees was utterly silent. There was some movement. The man who spoke was wearing a suit, Delphine saw, because now he turned and held the backrest of the bench as he bent over. The kneeling man then stood behind him, white shirt glowing. There was something about that white blaze of shirt. Delphine peered into the smudge of air. The shirt was suddenly gone, the men were half naked, one was moving across the other with a fluid eagerness.

The men kept changing and dissolving. They rolled over each other like fish. Sometimes they were frantic with a small animal's alacrity, then they slowed into a tenderer pulse. There was no way, now, that Delphine could leave her hiding place, not that she really wanted to. She could not see exactly how the sex was taking place, but she was curious. She put the mechanics together and nodded when she made each discovery. Suddenly she understood that Cyprian was the man who had thrown off the blaze of shirt, and then she did one of those things she often did that surprised her. She walked out of the bushes and cheerfully said hello.

Panicked, the men rolled away from each other. Her numb shock made her wicked. She sat down on the bench, began to talk.

"I was just out looking for you, honey," she said.

"Delphine, I don't know what—"

"Christ almighty," said the other man, scrambling for his clothes.

Delphine crossed her legs, lighted a cigarette, and blew the smoke out gently. As she continued to speak, to elicit polite answers and draw up neutral topics of conversation, a dreamlike hilarity took hold of her. She made a small joke and when the two men laughed reality skewed. No questions made sense, her mind was operating on too many levels. Layers of dark curiosity. Still, she did not acknowledge what she'd interrupted but, wielding an amused power, continued to make irresistible small talk. The three bantered back and forth as they walked away from the side of the river. The men shook hands and went their separate ways. Side by side and gravely thoughtful, Delphine and Cyprian walked back to their own room.

I wonder what will happen once we're inside, thought Delphine. She had the willful naïveté to imagine that now that this was out in the open she and Cyprian could at last be true lovers. She also had the wit to know this was simpleminded. Nothing at all happened once they got back into the room. It all seemed too exhausting to contemplate. They stripped down to their underwear, got under the covers, and held hands like two mourners, alert and lost, unable to speak.

IN THE NIGHT, deep in the dark, Delphine's brain flickered on and her thoughts woke her. She let the roil of feelings wash over her and then shook Cyprian until he groaned. She meant to say something cutting about his betrayal, to ask didn't he remember how they'd looked into each other's eyes? She meant to ask him why the hell he never told her he was *that way*, to shout in his face or just wail miserably. But in the second before her voice left her lips, other words formed.

"How do you balance?"

Her voice was calm, curious, and once she asked the question she found that she really wanted to know the answer. Cyprian was also wide awake. He'd never really slept. He put his palms over his face and breathed through his fingers.

It was not an easy question to answer. When he balanced, his whole body was a thought. He'd never put the balancing into words before, but perhaps because of the dark, and because she knew about him now, and because her voice wasn't angry, he spoke, tentatively at first.

"Some people think of it as a point, but it isn't a point. There is no balancing point."

She lighted a cigarette and blew the smoke into a white cloud over them. "So?"

Cyprian was as clumsy with words as he was agile in other ways. Attempting to describe what happened when he balanced caused an almost physical hurt. Still, he reached far in his thoughts and made a desperate effort.

"Say you have a dream." He spoke earnestly. "In that dream you know that you are dreaming. If you become too aware of knowing you are dreaming, you wake up. But if you are just enough aware, you can influence your dream."

"So that's balancing?"

"Pretty much."

He breathed out, relieved and empty. She thought for a while.

"And what is it," she asked, at last, "when you fall?"

Cyprian caught his breath back, almost despaired, but again—because, in spite of who he was, he loved Delphine—he dug for an answer. It took so long that Delphine almost fell asleep, but his mind was working furiously, shedding blue sparks.

"When you fall," he said, startling her awake, "you must forget that you exist. Strike the ground as a shadow strikes the ground. Weightless."

"I think I'll leave you," said Delphine.

"Please don't leave me," said Cyprian.

And so they lay balanced on that great wide bed.

THREE

The Bones

THE TOWN OF ARGUS was the creation of the railroad, and the railroad had no right to be there. Yet once it crossed the river there was no stopping it from going on into the emptiness. What was hauled into the Argus elevators left on the train, going east or west, and what stayed became the town. First, there were the stores to supply the farmers with equipment and food, and then the banks to hold their money, and then more stores where bankers and store owners, too, could shop. Houses for the town people to live in were constructed. One church was raised, another. A school. More houses for the teachers and the railroad workers and the people who built houses. Taverns for their vices. A drugstore for their pains, and so on, until Argus became the county seat. After the courthouse was built, it looked as though Argus was as up-and-coming a place as anywhere in North Dakota.

Fidelis found work at once with the local butcher, Kozka, and he hired out as well to concerns in surrounding small towns. Not only that, but he custom butchered right at people's farms, as long as he was fetched. He hadn't a car at first, though he was later to own a succession of delivery trucks. When he started working for the Kozkas, their trade increased, for Fidelis had his father's talent for making sausage and he'd learned his father's secrets. He was given them, in fact, on the eve before he left. The secret was extremely simple, said his father. There is no ingredient too humble. Use the finest of everything. Even the grade of salt matters. The garlic must be perfectly fresh, never dried out. The meat of course, and the casings, the transparent guts of sheep. Clean. They must be exquisitely fresh as well. Fidelis, following his father's dictum when he made up his first batch of Swedish sausages for the Scandinavian trade, did not use just any potato in the filling, but sought the finest in the area. He triumphed. On Thursdays, his sausage-making days, customers began to gather in order to buy links hot from the kettle, before they were even smoked, which made Kozka happy because the sausages weighed more then. As for Fidelis, he lived off sausage ends and bruised fruit, stale cookies and suspect trimmings. He made his own beer, washed his own shirts and aprons, and lived altogether sparingly until he'd saved enough to rent a bigger place. With the rest of his hoard, plus a windfall from his parents, he brought Eva over the empty sea into the emptiness of sky and earth.

She arrived on a wild spring day, along with the little boy, Franz, who walked off the train proud to carry his mother's purse. Since the week Fidelis had come home from the war and heard the silky music of sunlight, he had not been afflicted with any similar confusion of the senses. And yet, as the result of extremely hard work at two jobs or even three at once, Fidelis had undergone the effects of sleep deprivation and found himself talking out loud when he thought he was merely thinking. In the excitement of their meeting, Fidelis spoke into the swirl of Eva's hair. *Alles, alles,* he muttered without thinking, and Eva, knowing what he meant but appalled at her surroundings, could not help thinking, What "everything"? What was there? Even with the houses and shops, the land seemed barren as a moonscape. On the way to Argus, as the train took them cross-country, she had watched the signs of human presence diminish and felt a combination of horror and grief. Around dusk she had even thought that she saw, from the train window, wolves melting into the faltering shadows of small trees. She couldn't be sure. But she did think that her husband's offer of *alles*, everything, was farcical. Even in that moment that should have been sublime— their meeting, at last—her lips curled in disbelief. Yet she didn't understand his meaning.

Once more in her presence, Fidelis felt the emotion of love move through his body like a great, rough, startling beast. It came out of him and then its power wrapped them both. In its grip, he surrendered and gave everything he was or could possibly be to the woman in his arms. When a man of such strength lets himself be overcome, the earth of his being shudders. He is immensely alone. Eva might have understood Fidelis then, if he'd had the courage to elaborate, but since he didn't, she merely smiled into his face, kissed him, and decided with a certain bravado that although there was not a damn thing of interest or value in sight, there would be. And she, Eva Waldvogel, would see to it.

THE MAN WHO FIRST hired Fidelis Waldvogel became his chief and then only competitor in Argus. Pete Kozka was a good-natured but humorless block of a man, always in need of help since his ways were cheap and men quit. A tornado had touched down at his shop, once. Pennies from the change drawer had been driven neatly into the plaster wall. People came by just to see that. As rivalries go, that between the two butchers was amicable enough, based chiefly on pranks and boasts. Sometimes, though, things turned more serious. An ongoing joke that got out of control did a great deal, in fact, to sour relations between the two. This occurred after Fidelis left Kozka's meat market and set up his own operation at the other end of town. Since Fidelis had never hidden his intention to do just that, Kozka suffered the move with a stoic shrug. At the time, too, it looked as though Argus might grow forever, even possibly become a major metropolis if the county itself continued to boom in land sales. Although it did not work out that way, when Fidelis made his move there was plenty of business to go around.

With a bank loan and the money from the sale of his share of a building that the Waldvogel family owned back in Ludwigsruhe, Fidelis bought up an old farmstead on the opposite side of town, as far from the Kozkas as it was possible to be and still live in Argus. This mark of consideration also did a great deal to ameliorate any potential hard feelings, at first. Of course, Fidelis could not have anticipated that, when the main highway was rerouted to take the pressure of traffic off the town's clogged main street, it would pass directly by the new storefront that he tacked on to the sturdy farmhouse. Yet it wasn't even the jealousy over business gained, however inadvertently, that made things go bad. It was a different sort of jealousy entirely, and one more primary even than money.

A dog's love is something more or less complicated, according to the owner of the dog. Fidelis, for example, was faintly contemptuous of canine adoration, believing that it was based mostly on the dog's stomach rather than the dog's heart. Pete Kozka, on the other hand, held to the conviction that dogs, his own especially, were creatures of an unsurpassed fealty and that their loyalty was based on a personal love. Pete and his wife, Fritzie, raised purebred chow dogs with coal-black tongues and bitter temperaments. The progenitor of their line, the father of them all, was a snuff brown champion named Hottentot. He bred alternately with his first dog wife, Nancy, and his second mate, Zig, short for Ziguenerin, named for her passion for music—she slept near Fritzie's piano, and had a musical howl any child could prompt by singing nursery rhymes in a minor key.

After Fidelis moved, what should have been an insignificant difference of opinion became another thing entirely when Hottentot began turning up at the back loading plank of Waldvogel's Meats, where there were sometimes scraps. In addition to their differences over such things as the motivations of dogs, Pete and Fidelis also had a fundamental difference over the disposal of the waste, the odd bits, the offal and guts that are an important part of the butchering trade. While Pete kept every tiniest bit down to the tail's tips in a barrel that he locked in the freezer and sold to a guts dealer each month, Fidelis's way was to distribute the wastage, and he had, therefore, a commodious following of those who lived lightly on the earth—from dogs to itinerants and the hard-hit poor of Argus. The visitors at the back of his shop, as mentioned, included Hottentot.

The dog was a greedy, suspicious, evil-minded stud whose character amused Fidelis, as it proved his point about the heartless opportunism of dogs. Hottentot would fawn over anyone who held a bone or the hope of a tidbit, and he regarded the rest of humanity, those who didn't feed him, with an ancient contempt. He had the tendency to snap, and even bite, and those who'd felt the splendor of his teeth detested him. He would have been poisoned, as happened often to offensive dogs in Argus, except that Pete and Fritzie were themselves so friendly. In spite of the fact that they gave no credit and charged money for their soup bones, they were well-liked people and had no enemies.

Fidelis took satisfaction in the fact that the dog, doted on by the Kozkas, made his way across the town to visit him. One day he showed up at the Waldvogels' killing chute, his black eyes clever in a ball of bristling rust brown fur, a sneer on his velvet muzzle. Hottentot was granted all the scraps he could gulp, and then Fidelis gave him a huge cow bone and sent him back to Pete. That would have been all right if that was as far as Fidelis had taken it, but Fidelis had a teasing streak and did not know when to quit. Day after day the dog showed up, and Fidelis amused himself by providing it ever more gruesome skeletal remains—skulls, femurs, ribs. The spinal column of a heifer, trimmed out meticulously to allow the ligaments to maintain articulation, was the pièce de résistance that overthrew the Kozkas' patience. When Hottentot dragged it proudly through the Argus streets, pausing here and there to gnaw a bit or improve his grip on the thing, everybody in the town got wind of what was going on—literally. The bones were ripe, and the warm and sunny entrance of the shop, where Hottentot brought it to chew on for half the morning, reeked by the time Pete discovered it.

Swearing, he bent over the dog to grab away its prize. When Hottentot growled menacingly, Pete grabbed the dog's ears and forced his head back. "Just you try that," he warned. "You'll be a skin on the wall."

"Save that thing," said Fritzie, her arms folded in the doorway, "I've got an idea what to do with them. And tie up the dog."

The dog was attached with a rope to the clothesline pole, but Hottentot was of a studied cleverness that made him impossible to control. By midafternoon, he chewed through the rope and returned to Fidelis to beg an evening meal. He was home by dark with a set of hooves roped together with tasty sinew. Pete chained him next, but Hottentot wound the chain until the links popped and was back at the Waldvogels' place by morning. When Pete found his dog on the front stoop again slavering over an oozing boar's skull, he was enraged past good sense. Grabbing for the skull, he put his arm in the way of Hottentot's teeth. His arm was torn so savagely that Doctor Heech had to see him and closed the gash with no less than ten stitches. Heech also advised him to shoot the dog right on the spot. Most men would have walked home and done so, but Pete Kozka did not blame Hottentot. He believed that his dog's loyalty had been corrupted by Fidelis.

"We'll see, we'll just see about it," he muttered to himself that night, planning what he would do to get even with the man he'd taken in right off the street and hired and who now, as he decided to see it, had turned against him and even stolen the affections of his dog.

FIDELIS WAS NOT a religious man, except when it came to his knives. First thing every morning, after he'd taken his strong coffee from Eva's hand and eaten his breakfast of cheese and bread and stewed prunes, he visited the slotted wooden block where his knives were kept. He took them out one by one and laid them in strict order on a flannel cloth. These were the same knives he'd brought in the suitcase with the sausages, from Germany, and they were of the finest quality—forged from the blade to the tang in a mold and then worked from spine to cutting edge to create a perfectly balanced tool. Fidelis kept them ferociously clean. He examined each for any minute sign of rust. Then he made what for him were the day's most important decisions: which blades needed only to visit his sharpening steel, and which, if any, were in need of the graver attention of the stones. Most often, the knives required only the steel.

Fidelis's long sharpening steel, now kept on an iron wall hook, was the same one that hung from his belt in the portrait that his parents had paid the finest photographer in Ludwigsruhe to take when he mastered the family trade. With a musical alacrity, he swiped across the steel the knives whose edges needed minimal attention, and then he set them back into the block. Fidelis was conservative. He never oversharpened, never wasted good steel by grinding it away. But a dull blade would mash the fibers of the meat and slip dangerously in the hand, so when a knife needed a fresh edge, he was ready. He removed the set of stones from a drawer beneath the wooden block, and then he arranged them in order next to the knife that waited on the flannel. The coarse black stone was first, to set the cut right, and then the stones became finer. There were six in all. The last was fine as paper. By the time Fidelis finished, his blade could split an eyelash.

Every morning, after the boys had left for school and after his ritual with the knives was accomplished, Eva opened up the store and went over the day's schedule. While she was doing this, Fidelis habitually retired to the toilet at the back of the house, where he parted his hair with a surgical precision, combed it back, shaved meticulously, obeyed the prompting of the stewed prunes, and drank another cup of hot coffee. He had enlarged this toilet room, or bathroom, and made it comfortable in the German way. His family had always kept soft rugs and cheerful plants near the plumbing, as well as ashtrays and tobacco, books and newspapers on a shelf within easy reach. Over the tub, there hung an array of cleaning implements: a brush with a handle of polished maple wood to scrub the back, a smaller and brisker brush for the fingers, a large pumice stone for callused feet, and a tiny, hair-soft, blue-handled brush for the face. There was also a stash of soaps, from the harshest lye soap to the French-milled lilac ovals that Eva used. These soaps were kept in a square cedar box with a slatted floor to drain away excess water, so the soaps would last. Next to the tub on another wooden shelf, behind curtains made of ticking material, towels were stacked—the cloth worn thin, but bleached to a sunny whiteness. The entire room was painted a pleasant yellow, and, as its wide glass block window faced southeast, it caught the morning light. It was the comfortable and generous sort of room that would lead a person to think the Waldvogels were wealthy. They were not. It was Eva's doing. She had a knack for saving money and making a good effect out of nothing.

One summer morning after all of these small but essential rituals were accomplished, Fidelis began the primary business of that day—he was to kill a prize sow belonging to the Mecklenbergs and de-create her into rib chops, tenderloin, hams, hocks, pickled feet, fatback, bacon, and sausages. The sow had spent the night in the holding pen and was at present in a rage of hunger. For the first time in her life her morning squeals did not bring a bucket of slops. Instead, of course, she would be killed. The pig was more intelligent than the dog, Hottentot, who waited just beyond the fence to snatch whatever of her was left after the humans took her apart. The pig would certainly have learned a great deal from the coming encounter, but pigs get only one chance to experience the great perfidy of humans. And the betrayal is so swift and final that it comes upon each one of them as though it were the first ever to suffer such a surprising fate. Still, as this sow was perhaps smarter than most, she had more than an inkling that things were not right. Perhaps other sows and boars before her had written final messages in scent. Perhaps she read the avid air of Hottentot. Or maybe the entire unprecedented situation made her uneasy and then more belligerent than usual, because, when Fidelis entered the pen with his 32-20 rifle, which he intended to press directly to her skull, she trotted, huge on tiny legs but still surprisingly agile, to the opposite side of the pen.

From there, she eyed the man, who carried no food, with bleak suspicion. Fidelis cursed in exasperation, and called Franz to help him drive the pig up the chute, where she would be confined, killed, winched into a tub for scalding, scraped, cooled, split, and eviscerated. Knowing all that was to come, Hottentot began a maddened, frenzied barking that set the pig into a rage of horror to escape. Poked through the fence by Franz's stick, she minced forward a few nervous steps. Fidelis jumped behind her and let out an awful bellow that was meant to drive her into the narrow confinement of the chute. She didn't go there, but cleverly circled all the way around the pen to a place, this time, where no stick from behind would reach. There she stood her ground, shuddering, understanding now that something was very wrong. The comfortable life she'd led so far had not prepared her for the strangeness of the situation, but her prize-winning heritage made her cunning. Fidelis prodded sideways at her, but she moaned savagely back at him, and evaded his kick. He spent his breath chasing her through the muck. He slipped, covered himself in slime, swore viciously, recovered. Fidelis rushed at the pig, flapping his apron. Startled, she sidled away. He got the upper hand by continuing to flourish the cloth, mystifying her, driving her where he wanted her to go. Then suddenly she entered the chute and he slammed down the gate.

Fidelis then made the mistake of clambering over the side of the chute, carrying his rifle, and dropping into the confined area along with the pig. He touched down lightly on the other side. As he turned to face the sow, meaning simply to walk up to her and kill her as he'd done with so many others, she charged him. Screaming, she bolted down the narrow incline, broke his kneecap with her crooked brow, and sank her teeth into the flesh just above. As she ripped down, shredding Fidelis's canvas trousers, and skin to bone, Fidelis gave an anguished roar that, along with the shrill, keening attack shrieks of the pig, brought Franz bolting to the side of the chute. For one endless moment he thought that the sow, whose clenched teeth had parted when Fidelis brought the butt of his rifle down upon her head, would close in again and devour his father. She did have the advantage. While Fidelis lurched back trying to turn the rifle around to shoot, the pig charged again, destroying what was left of his knee with another lurching bite. She then repaired to her corner, red-eyed, bleary with hatred, sobbing. And all this time the eager barks of Hottentot, hungry, goaded her, as though the dog were capable of communicating to the pig a twisted fatalism. She tried to charge again, but this time Franz managed to jam a board between her and Fidelis. Temporarily thwarted, she backed off and in that moment of hesitation Fidelis was able to push the barrel of his gun between her eyes and pull the trigger.

There was a huge blast of noise, which delighted Hottentot and dazzled Franz. The sow collapsed with a murmur of sorrow, and straightway Fidelis hobbled over to chain her to the winch and haul her to the iron tub. As he did so, a sudden strangeness boiled up in him, a load of nameless feeling unconnected to his physical pain. This was mental, it was sorrow, he wanted to lie down in the muck and weep. Hot tears poured in a shocking stream from his eyes and dripped down his face. Abruptly, he ordered Franz away. He was bewildered, since he had not cried since he was a boy, and even during the war hadn't broken down like this. But in spite of his attempt to control himself, he wept, angry at his helpless grief, and was all the more horrified to realize that he wept for the sow. How could that be? He had killed men. He had seen them die. His best friend had died beside him. No tears. What sort of man was he to weep, now, for a pig? Angry, he stayed with the creature after that, tending to every detail of her butchering. Although his knee was an agonizing rip of information—he knew it would never be the same—he kept moving. If he stopped to let the knee stiffen, he would be crippled, he thought, and so only late into the afternoon did he quit and then only because Eva forced him. His last act before leaving for Doctor Heech's office was to provide Hottentot with the stomach of the pig and a huge intestinal wad that the dog, unable to eat all at once, dragged back home.

SITTING ON A sheet-covered bench in the examining room, Fidelis absently hummed a mocking song to take his mind off the agony in his knee. *"Ich bin der Doktor Eisenbart."* Heech raised his sleek brows, frowned, and said, "I know that song. *'Ich mache dass die Blinden gehen und dass die Lahmen wieder sehen.'*" Fidelis tried to laugh but the sound came out a gasp. The lame will see, the blind will walk. He'd bound his knee, tight, in an apron and used the strings to secure the improvised bandage.

"Let's see what you've done now," muttered Heech, cutting the knotted strings. Fidelis almost asked Heech to save the apron, but realized that Heech would have ignored him, or even taken it as an insult. With sure hands, the doctor unwound the mutilated fabric, and sighed when a thick flap of Fidelis's flesh stuck to the last fold. "A miracle of engineering," he shook his head. He was prone to lecturing. "Kaput." A favorite word of his. Heech frowned in concentration and began a close examination of the wound. The doctor had beautiful hair, of which he was slightly vain. Thick and glossy curls flopped down over his forehead. He loved anatomy and his walls were decorated with painstaking watercolors of the muscles, bones, and digestive and reproductive systems, pictures that he himself had painted. As he assessed Fidelis's shattered knee and the ripped musculature that had kept the cap in place, he planned how to fix the rips and tears just as a woman does when thrown a half-destroyed pair of boy's pants. Fidelis was looking at his own knee, too. His thoughts were different. They were a butcher's observations. Here, he'd slice. There, he'd skin, use the edge of the knife, the point. In no time he'd have a modest dinner joint with just enough fat to lard the meat. Fidelis banged his skull with his hand to clear it and nearly passed out. The song he'd been singing to himself screamed in his brain. Heech helped him to lie back on the bench.

"Breathe," said Heech, "but do not pass out on me." He fit an india rubber cup over the butcher's face.

Fidelis plunged into a dry, spinning, spark-infested faraway place from which he knew, heard, and even felt all that Heech did with his needle. Nothing bothered him, although he knew in the abstract that Heech's every move was painful. It made things worse that the doctor hummed annoyingly while he sewed, but his bedside manner was unpredictable, the whole town knew it. Sometimes he scolded, sometimes he wept, and sometimes, as now, Heech seemed to enjoy his work in an undoctorly way. As he stitched, he burst into the maudlin "Aura Lee." Fidelis grew intrigued with the tune and began to pick it up. He sang the chorus with Heech, then Heech started over again so that Fidelis could learn the verses. Once he started singing, nothing worried Fidelis, although it was clear from the extent of the damage that he might be crippled. Nothing angered him, either, for he'd taken out his embarrassed and sorrowing rage on the sow by slicing her up with a savage precision. The song did please him, as it pleased Doctor Heech, so that by the last note and stitch they were quite friendly and Heech kept him fifteen minutes longer as he sketched out a brace that would allow Fidelis some range of motion while keeping the knee in place until it healed.

"ENOUGH!" CRIED FRITZIE when she saw the mess that Hottentot guarded at their shop's entrance, a disgusting sight that caused potential customers to veer away from the door and made the Kozkas, most certainly, the butt of town laughter.

She marched her husband to the greening bone pile, stuffed the bones in a gunnysack, and shoved them at him, telling him what he should do. In his turn, Pete took the bones and slung them off the back trunk of his car, and then he drove over to Waldvogel's Meats. He intended only to dump the bones on the front stoop of the shop and then retreat, but when he arrived he was surprised to find the Closed sign up and the place deserted. He was immediately convinced that his rival had such a thriving concern that he could actually afford to take a little vacation. The thought galled him. The outraged envy that he felt, along with the sense of self-righteous pain at his betrayal, caused him to do a thing uncharacteristically vengeful. He took the bones, moldered and stained, the marrow reeking and the knobbed or broken ends foul, and he went around back of the shop and entered the house. Argus was not a place where one locked doors (though for a while afterward Eva set the locks to with an angry click each night and even bought a set of bolts that fastened from inside). Pete Kozka was able to put the bones where he chose—of course he chose unwisely, upped the ante, gave the prank a vengeful twist. He went into Fidelis and Eva's bedroom. There, he ripped down the immaculate white eiderdown, the heavily starched and delicately embroidered sheets that were part of Eva's Old World dowry chest, and dumped in the bones. Then covered up the bones. Bits of the stuff from the bones soaked into the mattress and blended with the fabric and the down inside the comforter.

Ever after that time, Eva had no pity on the Kozkas. If she could drive them out of business entirely, she said she would. Or she would make their lives unhappy. She was not the forgiving sort. What the Kozkas did bothered her beyond the bounds of her husband's ridiculous rivalry, and she would have cause to brood upon it in the future. Eva's household, which she strictly divided off from the butcher shop, was based on order, rich baking scents, cleanliness, and life. Death's rot and stink had now been introduced, and was not easily expunged, though she tried every trick she knew—bleach, lye soap, vinegar, sunlight, and lavender. Essence of orange. Lemon juice. No matter what, no way around it, the faint odor of the bones stayed in the sheets.

ALTHOUGH THE JOKE on the Kozkas had turned ugly, Fidelis did not give up on it. He possessed an implacable loyalty to the joke itself, as though it were a work of art or a story he must finish no matter what. He also blamed the dog's hysteria for the crazed behavior of the sow and wanted to goad the Kozkas, perhaps, into making an escape-proof pen for their dog. The next time Hottentot slipped his leash and waited at the back entrance of the shop, Fidelis threw the dog a braid of chicken feet that he'd been saving and adding to for the past month. The dog, of course, brought the feet directly home. Hottentot trotted proudly past Sal Birdy's drugstore, where those who sat in the wood-paneled booths or at the counter witnessed the gift and wondered just where in the Waldvogel house that scaly, stinking item might turn up. Having desecrated the most intimate place in the Waldvogel house, Pete Kozka was stumped as to what was next. He had done something intended to annihilate the joke and stop the situation, and yet, by treating the joke as though it had not escalated, Fidelis managed to push the Kozkas into a frustrated acceptance. They did build a wire pen, at last, which the dog managed only rarely to escape.

Still, every time Hottentot got away and dragged home some piece of a carcass from Waldvogel's, Pete Kozka swore he'd get even by some means. The dog was such a nuisance that Eva Waldvogel darkly spoke of going to the law. She told a dozen women at least that she personally held the dog responsible for the fact that her husband was forced to wear a brace and undergo painful adjustments for his knee. For a time, the two butcher shops divided the town between them, just as the Catholic and Lutheran churches did.

During this time of estrangement, Fidelis started what was to become a town institution. He missed the old singing club he had belonged to back in Ludwigsruhe. Although the one there was composed solely of master butchers, it dawned upon him shortly after he sang with Doctor Heech that in America there was no need to segregate a singing club by profession.

The first meeting took place in Waldvogel's slaughtering room, which had a high ceiling and walls that bounced the sound back with a gratifying effect. The bank loan officer and one of his clerks, the bootlegger, the town sheriff, the doctor, on occasion, and the town drunk all showed up—a perfect mix. Portland Chavers, the bank employee, and Zumbrugge, the banker, bought the beer from Newhall, the bootlegger, and were happily ignored and excused by the sheriff, Hock. Although Heech disapproved he resigned himself to keeping careful watch on their intake, though his sharp gaze wavered if they happened to persuade him to drink a few drops himself. The town drunk, who happened to be Delphine Watzka's father, Roy, had his fill more than once. And to them all, Fidelis provided crackers, cheese, summer sausage, and a constant supply of good humor, for in song he was a happy man. There was no darkness in him, no heaviness. He was weightless light, all music. That first night, with an air of exquisite discovery, the men drank beer and sang until dawn. They sang their favorites to one another, taught each other the words. Their voices rose singly and then by the second chorus swept in fervent unison through the night. On the more familiar melodies, they instinctively harmonized. Sheriff Hock possessed a heartrending falsetto. Zumbrugge's baritone had a cello-like depth and expression surprising in the author of so many heartless foreclosures. As long as he had a glass of schnapps in one hand, Roy Watzka could sing all parts with equal conviction, but he found that his voice was so similar to Chavers' that they sometimes dueled instead of harmonized. Eva fell asleep, as she would once a week from then on, to the sound of the men's voices. The singing club became the most popular meeting in town and began to include listeners, those of ragged or pitchless voice, who came to sit on the outskirts of the core group and listen.

Sadly, of all the men who lived in Argus, the club probably appealed most to Pete Kozka, who had his own passion for song. He felt left out and moped to Fritzie that he'd start his own club except that all the town's men with good voices were taken by Fidelis. The singing club was one of the reasons that the two butchers resumed their damaged friendship. After some time, Pete simply couldn't bear not to be included, and he showed up one night as though nothing had happened. Fidelis didn't turn a hair. Once the two butchers sang together, the incident was almost set to rest.

People still talked, attempting to keep the interesting rivalry going, but gradually the rancor between the butchers became an old topic and people moved on to newer subjects of absurdity or distress. For of course, every so often the town received a great shock. It seemed that just as people grew into a false assurance, believed for instance that their prayers worked and that evil was kept at bay, or thoughtlessly celebrated the quiet of their community with a street dance, a parade, or any kind of energetic complacence, something happened. Someone turned up dead. A child smothered in a load of grain. There was a pregnant woman, then one day she wasn't pregnant anymore. People knew she killed her baby but there was no proof. A young man, perhaps drunk, was shot and killed in a jealous fit. There was a vicious rape, and the girl was sent to the mental unit while the man walked the streets. Then the man disappeared. A bank robbery. Car wreck. A boy chopped to pieces in a threshing accident. The children's favorite schoolteacher blew his head off. Once again the town would be reminded that even though it was populated by an army of decent people, even though a majority counted themselves pious churchgoers, even though Argus prided itself on civic participation, it was not immune. Strub's Funerary stood flourishing, a testament to the fact that death liked Argus just as much as anywhere else. And evil, though it was not condoned by the city council, flourished nonetheless, here and there, in surprising and secret pockets.

FOUR

The Cellar

$\mathcal{A}$FTER THREE MONTHS on the road, Delphine and Cyprian had milked a startling amount of money from the broke and dusty towns they passed through with their show. Which proved, said Delphine, that even in the summer of 1934, when people were really hard up, they'd pay to get their minds off their misery. Still, even though they were doing good business, Delphine decided that she had to go home. First, though, she went to a second-rate jewelry shop and bought cheap rings for herself and Cyprian. There was no way she could appear back in Argus without at least the pretense of marriage.

"This does not mean crap," she said, slipping on the wedding band, giving him a suspicious look. She waggled her finger.

"To you," he countered.

"You either," she warned. The band seemed tight already, and although it was smooth she'd heard of machines and car doors catching on rings and yanking off or breaking fingers. She'd never worn a ring before.

"Don't get any ideas," she warned. "I don't make breakfast. I'm not ready to be a housewife, yet."

"Fine," said Cyprian. "I'll cook."

Delphine hooted. He'd never so much as buttered a piece of bread in her presence. In cafés, she did it as a little graceful and womanly thing to do for him, but maybe now, she reflected, she should quit taking care of him so much. He'd think she meant to take care of him forever. She twisted the ring around and around, a little piece of armor against the Lutheran ladies who would have their eyes on every move she made. The ring would help, but people would talk about her anyway. Her father always gave them reason. Of course, they didn't know half of what went on in the farmhouse marooned in the tangle of box elders, out of town, where she'd grown up. The only kindness was that her father's misery, thus hers, was usually out of the town's direct line of sight.

She feared the urge to return was a mistake. Not only the fake marriage. Would her father make a drinking friend of Cyprian? Schnapps, he couldn't handle. The stuff would wreck his balance. She had no choice, though, because she truly missed Roy Watzka and she suffered from an annoying intuition. A series of melodramatic pictures nagged her: he was dying, gasping for her like the father in the fairy tale with the beast and the beauty. Plunging headlong drunk into the muscle of the river out behind their house. Drowning himself.

Delphine and Cyprian drove south, toward Argus. The fabulous tall-grass that had once covered all beneath the sky still vigorously waved from the margins of certain fields, from the edges of the sloughs that they passed, and from the banks of the pleasant little river that sometimes flooded all along its length and wrecked half the town. The fields of stunted wheat, bald in patches that year, turned in an endless rush. Army-worms were thick, their nests like gray mesh in the trees. From time to time, they passed an empty-windowed house, or one with a brave and hopeless bit of paint splashed across its padlocked front door. There were gas stations, pumps fixed in front of shaky little stores, here and there a thatch of houses, a lightning-struck cottonwood. And always, there was the friendly monotony, the patient sky rainless and gray as a tarp.

As they passed Waldvogel's butcher shop on the near edge of town, a solid built whitewashed place bounded by two fields, they saw two people running. One was a woman in a flowered wash dress, an apron, and high feminine heels. The other was a boy, maybe fifteen or sixteen years old, with the build of an athlete and a flap of shining dark hair. The two had come from the field and were racing for some finish line just beyond the dusty parking lot in front of the store. They were neck and neck, laughing as they pumped their arms. Then suddenly the woman seemed to leap forward, though her stride actually shortened. She'd gone up on her toes and was bounding to the finish. As the car passed the two, Delphine turned to watch. The woman's hair burst from its twist and floated out behind her, a sudden red-gold banner that announced her triumph, for she'd touched the fence at the end of the lot first and beaten the boy. Delphine turned back to direct Cyprian.

"You should have seen that woman. Can she ever run! Turn there."

They turned down a short and half-overgrown road.

"Slow down," said Delphine.

The road was a ragged track, washed out in several spots, the dirt churned up and dried in pits and snarls. They drove up to the beaten little farmhouse—three dim rooms and a jutting porch—where Delphine had always lived with Roy.

Just as they arrived, Delphine's father happened to be walking out the door. He was a pallid little crooked man with the fat nose of a sinister clown. When he saw Delphine, he removed his slouch hat, jammed it over his face, and began to weep into the crown, his whole body shaking with sobs. Every so often he'd lower the hat to show them his contorted mouth, then smack the hat on his face again. It was a masterly performance. Cyprian had never seen a man weep like that, even in the war, and he was horrified. He offered his hankie, pressed it into Roy's hands, sat down with the old man on the porch. Delphine squared her shoulders, took a deep fortifying breath, and walked into the house.

She ran right out again, gulping air, but she didn't say a word. The men were locked in a blubbering conversation. She ran back in and threw the windows open. Then went back out to the car. She removed a scarf from her suitcase, soaked it with Evening in Paris, and tied it over her mouth and nose. The depth of this horrible odor led her to believe, for the first time, that her father wasn't just a common drunk—he was truly depraved. When she walked past the men she kicked at the leg of her father's chair.

"Don't do that!" said Cyprian.

"Oh shut your mouth," said Delphine from behind her scarf, as she bravely reentered the house.

Bad smells made her angry, they were a personal affront. She had dealt with her father's messes before, but this was of a different order. He had created this one on purpose, she believed, to show her how helpless he was without her. On the floor, there was a layer of must, crumbly and black, for the clothing and food, the vomit and piss, had composted along with the knuckles of pig's trotters and frail chicken bones. Perhaps a dog had crawled in there to die, too. There were layers of husks of insects, foul clumps of rat droppings, and a bushel of rotted, sprouting potatoes some kind neighbor had probably dropped off to keep Roy Watzka from starving. Over it all there had grown arcane scrawls of cheerful and reeking mold. Weak and sick, Delphine staggered out again onto the porch.

"I need a shovel," she said, and she put her face into her hands and began to cry. She wept even harder than her father. Cyprian was completely astonished, for up until that moment she had behaved with a steady cynical kindness and he hadn't known that she was even capable of feeling such intense sorrow. Nothing that Cyprian had done, even getting caught with the hardware store owner in Gorefield, Manitoba, had caused her to so much as mist over. Now the sobs were wrecking her, tossing her like a storm. They built up and died down and then built up again. Her father sat listening to the waves, almost reverent, his head bowed as though he were attentive to a sermon. Cyprian couldn't bear such a show of brutal emotion. He sat down on the porch steps right next to Delphine and carefully, with immense tenderness, put his arms around her shoulders. Until that moment he hadn't realized what enormous respect he had for Delphine—her breaking up like this was very moving to him. He'd seen this in the war sometimes, the moment when the toughest ones go was always hardest. He began to rock Delphine back and forth, crooning to her.

"Don't cry, little sister," he said, and Delphine wept harder because he called her by this sweet name, and although she knew it meant his feelings for her were brotherly, not romantic, she was suddenly as happy as she was nauseated.

"I'll be all right," she heard herself blurt. She couldn't help saying it, though she wasn't all right and wanted to keep soaking up this delicious and unfamiliar male sympathy.

"I know you'll be okay," Cyprian said. "But you need help."

He couldn't have said a more perfect thing, and yet her experience of him so far was that he couldn't do jack shit, except balance. If she depended on him, she was bound for disappointment, she thought, and yet the idea of purging the stink herself made her sob harder.

"I do need help," she wailed.

Cyprian was gratified, and in that sweep of feeling he kissed her tenderly and passionately on her left temple, which throbbed hot red. He had come back lonely from the war and stayed that way, concentrating on his balance. His brothers had all moved far north into Cree country. His parents were drinkers. His grandparents had wandered off in disgust, headed for someplace where they could die in peace. Any uncles and aunts were living their own lives, the sort of lives he didn't want to know about. He really was alone or had been until now. Things had gone past romance. At this moment things went deeper. He now had Delphine Watzka and Delphine's father and also the terrible odor.

The smell emanated from the house as a solid presence. It lived there—an entity, an evil genie. For some reason, it did not cling to Roy Watzka. He smelled all right. Delphine and Cyprian loaded him into the car and drove back to town. They got a room at the hotel on the main street and left Roy there, curled happily around a pint of his favorite schnapps. It was no use trying to keep him away from the stuff, Delphine informed Cyprian. He would just go find it, and the search would put him into worse shape, get him into danger from which he was always difficult to rescue. The two of them bought a couple of shovels and a gallon of kerosene and went back to the house. They began to haul out the horrid junk, both swathing their faces in the scented scarves.

"I never liked this perfume," Cyprian gasped, after he'd carried out the third shovel full of unidentifiable garbage.

"I'll never wear it again, my love," said Delphine. She could use these endearments, because now they both knew the grand passion between them was an affectionate joke. They were something else. They were not-quite-but-more-than family. And together, they stank. As though angry to be disturbed, the odor pounced on them. It wrestled with their stomachs. Every so often, one had to gag, which started the other going too. Delphine was an extremely determined person and Cyprian had been through the bowels of hell, but at one point, having penetrated to some sublimely sickening layer, they both rushed outside and had the same idea.

"Could we burn the whole place down?" Cyprian said, eyeing with longing the gallon of kerosene.

"Maybe we could," said Delphine.

They dragged a couple of beer crates across the yard and had a long smoke. Eventually, they decided that they would persevere. In spite of the woozy atmosphere, Delphine was impressed by Cyprian's ability to shovel and haul. They made a great heap of crud in the yard and set it immediately ablaze. The stuff gave off an acrid smoke and left a stinking ash, but the fire had a purifying effect on their spirits. They went to the work more cheerfully now, hauling, tossing, burning, without stopping to puke. By nightfall, they'd gone through a challenging strata of urine-soaked catalogues and newspapers. It appeared that Roy Watzka had invited his cronies over, and they'd used the pantry off the kitchen as a pissing parlor. One man could not have done so much, said Cyprian, but he got no agreement from Delphine.

"My father could," she said, as they rested before the fire. Mercifully, the odor finally seemed to have blasted out their sense of smell. Nothing bothered them. They had no hunger or thirst. Nor aches or pains. They felt invincible. The house was nearly cleared out—step one.

The next step was more complicated. They believed that the source of the stink was burned to flakes of black tar, but the smell would surely linger in the boards and wallpaper, in the furniture. What substance would remove, not commingle, with such a thing? They had to retreat. After the fire went out, they went back to the hotel, sneaked in because they knew they carried with them the loathsome stench. In the room, Roy was already passed out.

With great foresight, extravagantly, they had rented a room with a private bath. Now Cyprian said gallantly, "You go first."

"I can't," said Delphine.

"Shall we share a hot bath?" said Cyprian. They both felt very kindly toward each other. So Delphine ran the bath and dumped in a little bottle of fragrant hair soap. They got in together and soaped each other up and washed their hair. Cyprian leaned, sighing, against the backrest with Delphine between his legs. Together, they soaked. With her big toe, Delphine occasionally let some water out. Added more hot water. It was erotic, but not sexual, a kind of animal acceptance. Both took comfort in the ease they experienced being naked in the other's presence. Plus, they were very grateful to be clean, though the stink lingered in their memory. They could feel the odor, and were both worried that they'd lost their smell-perspective. Maybe it had somehow entered them. Maybe they'd be kicked out of the breakfast café, where they planned to eat the next morning. Maybe they'd be ostracized in the street. They completely forgot about Roy until they'd dried off, and then Cyprian was startled by the rumbling bray from the next room.

"He snores," said Delphine.

"That too?"

"Oh," said Delphine. She looked at him, worried, and Cyprian looked back at her, standing unashamedly naked before him. Her body was compact, graceful, and tough. Her breasts were very beautiful. As if she was part fox, thought Cyprian, like a woman in one of his grandmother's old stories. Her breasts were perfect golden cones with neat honey-colored nipples. He didn't want to do anything, though—he just enjoyed looking at her.

"I wish I was an artist," he said. "I'd draw you." He began to dry her with a stiff towel. "God, your dad's loud. Maybe I'll sleep outside the door."

"You'll get used to it," Delphine said. "You'll be surprised. Just think of it as something in nature."

"His snoring?"

"Like a storm, a big lake. Trees."

The spluttering and thrashing that Cyprian now heard did not seem natural, and he doubted that he could take Delphine's advice. But once he lay down and curled around her, he fell directly into a fabulous well of sleep in which he dreamed phenomenally. He dreamed of trees with their limbs cracked and creaking in wind, of hopping from ice floe to floe in a roaring torrent, of a sneaky gunpowder booby trap that blew up every time he tried to talk.

In the dream, he spoke freely to Delphine between the blasts of noise.

And what did I say, he wondered, waking slightly before he was sucked again into the black current of unconsciousness. What did I tell her? What does she know? For he hadn't yet dared raise the subject of what she had seen or not seen back by the river in Manitoba. And it had happened so soon after that night—they'd never talked about that either—when they looked into each other's eyes and their bodies had moved together in a way beyond anything they could have wished. Were they in love now, or had things drastically changed? Was she really his little sister, and the noisy drunk next bed over his new father? Perhaps, he thought, bobbing to the surface well before dawn, the smell had addled them all. Perhaps they were affected by the smell's range and power. They would see. They would contend with it come morning.

THE SMELL CAME AT THEM as they slowly approached down the road. It seemed to have settled in a tent about the house. They went inside to battle it and immediately rushed back out. It was as though they hadn't even touched the place yet, or worse, as though they'd only succeeded in lifting the lid off the source of the odor, which still emanated, Cyprian thought, from the cleared-off floor.

"Or maybe the cellar," said Delphine with a childlike shudder.

The cellar was no more than a large pit in the earth, underneath the pantry. There was a hole cut in the floor and a hinged door with a ring that turned to lock it shut, but Delphine never opened it in the first place, if she could help it. She and Roy had hardly ever accumulated a surplus of food to store there, though often enough Roy had stashed his booze on the rough shelves cut into the sides of earth. Once upon a time, she remembered, there were potatoes in a large bin or maybe turnips. Otherwise, it was a ghastly place filled with spiders. It was probably the source of the bugs and rat droppings.

"I don't want to look," said Delphine.

"I don't either," said Cyprian.

"Now is the time to burn the place," she decided.

"Let's have a smoke."

They went back to the beer crates and lighted up. From behind, the house was so small and pathetic looking that it seemed impossible for it to harbor such a fierce animosity of odor. Long ago, Delphine had painted the doors and window frames blue because she'd heard that certain tribes believed that blue scared off ghosts. What she'd really wanted was a color to scare off drunks. But there wasn't such a color. They came anyway, all through her childhood and on into her clever adolescence, during which she'd won a state spelling contest. Her winning word was *syzygy*. She spelled it on instinct and had to look the meaning up afterward.

The truth was, Delphine was smart—in fact, she was the smartest girl in school. She could have had a scholarship to a Catholic college, but she dropped out early. It was the planets, aligned as in her spelling word, casting their shadows indifferently here and there. Malign influence. She slowly became convinced, due to her association with her father's cronies, that at the center of the universe not God but a tremendous deadness reigned. The stillness of a drunk God, passed out cold.

She had learned of it in that house with the blue-framed doors and windows, where the drunks crashed, oblivious to warding-off charms and dizzy indigo. Things had happened to her there. She was neither raped nor robbed, nor did she experience God's absence to any greater degree than other people did. She wasn't threatened or made to harm anyone against her will. She wasn't beaten, either, or deprived of speech or voice. It was, rather, the sad blubbering stories she heard in the house. Delphine witnessed awful things occurring to other humans. Worse than that, she was powerless to alter their fate. It would be that way all her life—disasters, falling like chairs all around her, falling so close they disarranged her hair, but not touching her.

Perhaps the early loss of her mother had caused her to undergo a period of intolerable sensitivity. Although the actual mishaps struck visitors, friends, acquaintances, strangers, Delphine experienced the feelings that accompanied their awful misfortunes. A child down the road was struck blind. For weeks Delphine found herself groping her way through the nightmare in which she was told she was blind as well. Or abandoned by her husband, as was the cheerful and sordid Mrs. Vashon, who tried to kill herself at the prospect of raising nine children alone, did not succeed, but ever after bore the rope's dark scorch mark around her neck. Or her best friend from high school, Clarisse Strub, who was victimized by a secret disease. These things happened with such regularity that Delphine developed a nervous twitch in her brain. A knee-jerk response that rejected hope and light.

Not that she ever railed at God. From the time she'd understood God wouldn't give her her mother back, she knew that was a waste of time. Because it offended her to swallow as many as twenty or thirty lies per day, she quit school in her final year. God was all good. Lie! God was all powerful. All right, maybe. But if so, then clearly not all good, since He let her mother die. All merciful? Lie. Just? Lie. All seeing? Had He really the time to watch what her hands did beneath the covers at night? Did God really invade her brain and weep at her impure thoughts? And if so, why had He concentrated on such trivia rather than curing her mother of her illness? What sort of choice was that? Delphine counted and even wrote the lies down in the margins of her textbooks and library books. Lies! More lies! She wrote so fiercely that for the next five years the nuns would admonish their students both to disregard and to bring to their attention any books bearing handwritten annotations.

Her father was pleased enough. As soon as he learned she'd quit school, he quit life and proceeded to pursue his own serious drinking, while Delphine went to work. Well, maybe she shouldn't have been so smart, she admitted. Maybe better to endure the tyranny of lies than the series of jobs she had then, briefly, held. She had wrapped butter in the Ogg Dairy. She had worked cracking eggs, gasping at the sulfur whiplash of the rotten ones. For a while she had sorted cookies into metal troughs, survived on the crumbs. Ran a buttonholer in a dress shop. She ironed. Blistered her hands in bleach laundering sheets. All these jobs were tedious and low-paying. Besides, since she lived at home, her father tried to appropriate half her money.

The first time she split her pay cash, he quietly used it to drink somewhere else. The next time, he brought his buddies home. She arrived home—lame, dusty, exhausted, from sorting bricks at the brick-works—to find them drinking a case of skin tonic. Although she tried her best to ignore them, they made a ruckus, ate every morsel, even the last bit of the ham, and in a half stupor blundered into her bedroom, which was her only haven. She took a broom to them, cracking the handle against their legs. When they guffawed and refused to leave, a storm of white dots fell across her vision. At long last, she decided to clear them out. She walked out to the woodpile, yanked the ax from its block, strode back into the kitchen.

Hey, Roy's baby . . . , one of them mocked her.

She lifted the ax high overhead and brought it down, split the just dealt ace of diamonds, then tugged the ax from the wood and lifted it again. Her father yelped. She shook the ax and screeched back at him, which caused him to jump backward in boozy dismay, scattering the poker deck, and to declare that she had gone haywire. Mightily affected, he raced out the door, gasping for breath, flanked by his companions. Somewhere in the night he fell through thin ice and from his dousing got pneumonia, almost died, so that Delphine had to quit the brick-works and nurse him. The ax was the first time she had turned on him, and he couldn't get over it. All of his bluster had collapsed at the sight of her, striding through the door in her white rag of a nightgown, *hollering bloody murder*, as he put it, weak and feverish. That had been the gist of Delphine's life, that and more of the same. Still, she could not burn the house. It was the house where she'd grown up and where, according to at least one version of Roy's story, her mother had given birth to her. He said it happened right in the kitchen, by the stove, where it was warm.

"I suppose we should clean out the cellar," she sighed.

"I was hoping you wouldn't say that," said Cyprian, but his voice was cheerful. He stubbed out his cigarette, slapped his pants, and laughed at the puffs of dust that swallowed his hands. Delphine wanted to tell him that she admired his capacity for brute labor. It was a thing people in the town valued, and she herself was proud of her own endurance. If she said as much, though, would she be admitting she'd once thought of him as a useless lug who couldn't so much as grow a plant? Maybe, she revised in her mind as they walked toward the house, she'd had it all wrong to begin with. He was an artist. A balancing artist. Maybe while doing the show his whole being had concentrated on that one thing. Maybe now that he wasn't balancing, he could display his more ordinary talents.

TO GET TO THE RING in the floor, they had to chip away a seal of shattered jars of canned peaches, the turds of some stray locked-up dog, and strange handfuls of spilled red beads mortared into the peach juice. Once they had pried off this layer, they hammered on the stuck ring. Gradually, the sky grew dark and they had to stop, find a lantern. They stalled, took some time filling it with kerosene. Cyprian fussily trimmed the wick, finally lighted it. By now, they were determined to finish what they'd started. They used a crowbar and a can opener to pry up the hinged hatch in the floor.

Thinking back later, Delphine had the sensation that the door had blasted off, but of course, that couldn't have been the case. It was just that they had been mistaken about the mighty odor they'd fought. That smell was only an olfactory shadow. Now came forth the real smell, the djinn, the source. Both of them dived through the back door and rolled, addled, in the scroungy backyard grass.

"What the hell was that?" said Cyprian, once they'd crawled to the beer crates and lighted their cigarettes with rubbery fingers. It was as though they'd been thrown from the house by a poltergeist. They could not even recall exactly whether they had actually lifted off the hatch.

"I think we did," Delphine said.

"I do too," said Cyprian.

"There's someone down there." Delphine breathed out a long smoky sigh.

"Who?"

"Someone dead."

She was right. There was someone, plus another someone, and maybe another person, too. It was hard to tell. They were kind of mixed together, said Cyprian later. Afraid of the consequences of calling up the sheriff—what *had* Roy done?—they gathered every particle of trauma- tized energy and ventured back. They raced in holding their breaths, grabbed the lantern, leaned over the open hatch, looked down, and bolted back outside, all without breathing. Far from the house, they stopped and gasped.

"Did you get a good look?"

"Yeah."

"It was a person, right?"

"Monsters."

Which was exactly what those pitiable bodies had become—huge of tongue and pop-eyed, brain blasted, green, bloated, iridescent with fungal energy, unforgettably inhabited by a vast array of busy creatures. The bodies were stuffed upright in the cellar surrounded by many empty bottles.

What *had* Roy done?

"Now is it time to burn the house?" Delphine was panicked.

"We can't. If we do, it means that we suspected foul play. There's no way if we burn the house the sheriff won't come investigate, or the fire chief. There's no way to burn up the basement—I mean, what if even fire won't destroy what's down there? Then we'll really be in trouble."

Even at such a moment, Delphine was touched by his casual use of *we*. He could have ditched her right then, left her to handle her father and the stinking house and the bodies generating strange life in the cellar. But he stuck with her, uttered not a single word of exasperation with the mess. Besides this new competence, he is even *loyal*, thought Delphine, I would marry him if he did not have to do what he did with other men. It was an odd time to take his measure as a potential husband, perhaps, but as Cyprian faced this great challenge beside her, his brow furrowed in grave thought, Delphine observed that he had never looked more handsome. The planes of his sculpted cheeks were drawn and his eyes were somber. She liked this weighty, serious, considered quality he now displayed. She liked his patience with the problem.

"We will have to go back and tell Roy about the bodies," he stated. "We need more information, Delphine."

ROY BAWLED in a helpless rage at the two of them upon their return. He'd inadvertently rolled himself up tightly in the bedsheets and believed that they had put him into a rudimentary straitjacket. He'd been through the d.t.'s in a sanitarium once, and as part of his treatment the staff had fastened him in a cold wet sheet. They had tightly pinned together the edges seam to seam. He was left to experience whatever he would experience. It had been lonely snaking out in a soundproof padded room. Spiders had leaked from the walls and giant lice had crawled underneath his skin. The experience itself had driven him back to drink, he said, and he never even contemplated quitting again. His mind couldn't take its own power.

"Can you take this?" said Delphine, unrolling him. "There's dead people in your cellar."

"Release me! I implore you!" Roy begged. As usual, his manner was a mixture of pretension, low need, and melodrama. "I need a blast here. Can you get me a good blast?"

With a resigned gesture, Delphine directed Cyprian to offer her father a sip of the whiskey they'd bought for him on the way.

"We're going to let you down slow, Dad," she said. "You're going to have to talk to us. There's dead people in your cellar," she repeated.

"And who might they be?" he asked huffily.

"Well, we don't know who."

"Perhaps you could describe them." Roy's eye gleamed with a mad fire upon the pint of whiskey. He grew slyly meek. "What, may I ask, do they look like?"

"Hard to describe," said Cyprian, with a helpless glance at Delphine. "One had on a porkpie hat, I think. There was a bow tie, or maybe it was something else . . . you know, come to think of it, one was wearing a suit."

"A black suit?" Roy was suddenly alert.

"Delphine, do you think one was wearing a black suit?"

Delphine paced the floor, shut her eyes to recover the hideous picture in her mind. "I do think so. A black suit," she faintly agreed.

Roy jumped up in a sudden fit of energy. He grabbed the whiskey from Cyprian's hand before the other man could react, and he swilled as much as he could before, with a struggle, Delphine and Cyprian wrested the bottle back from him.

"Oh God, oh God!" Roy swiped his sleeve across his mouth and staggered around the room twice before he stood before them, hands thrown wide. "It's Doris and Porky and their little kid, too!"

"What? What?" Delphine grabbed his shoulders and shook him so hard his head snapped back and forth.

"Hold off!" Roy slumped onto the bed, held his hand out for the whiskey bottle, which Cyprian put instead to his own lips. With a feral swift movement Roy tried to grab the flask, but Cyprian plucked it out of his reach and brandished it high.

"Who are Doris and Porky?"

"And their little . . . what . . . boy?" added Delphine. She knew the family, but not that well. Her friend Clarisse was a relative. In fact, Clarisse had told her a few things about Portland "Porky" Chavers,

Delphine now remembered. Things so bad that she couldn't feel sorry for him, at least.

"They were guests," Roy said in a tranced voice. "At the funeral party."

"Whose funeral?"

"Your girlfriend Clarisse's dad. Friend of mine too, of course. He wanted a party, not a funeral, because he's a Strub. I was the only one who would throw him a party instead of your typical funeral proceedings, which he'd attended all his life. I was the only one who would do it." Roy paused, then spoke rather pompously. "You could call it an act of corporeal mercy."

"Only you would think of that," said Delphine.

"I was an extremely gracious host. We had tubs of beer," Roy said in a longing, confessional hush.

"Bought with the rent money," said Delphine in utter fury.

"It doesn't matter about the beer," said Cyprian. "Tell us about Doris and Porky."

Roy gulped like a dutiful and panicked child, nodded, and went on.

"Weeks after, we did notice they were gone."

"We who? Your stinking hobo friends?"

Roy gave Delphine a look of deceitfully gentle reproach, but he was too much in shock to carry out a more detailed act.

"Kozka and Waldvogel, Mannheim and Zumbrugge, all of those. Of course we wondered where they went. Porky wasn't at the singing club. They just left everything. Their house was abandoned. Everything. Even their dog . . . it came back looking for them. It wouldn't leave the pantry. Oh God! Now I know why!"

Roy bent double and began to weep, though with a soft intensity for which he needed no audience. "And here we thought they went down to Arizona," he said softly, over and over.

Delphine and Cyprian felt themselves thump down like wooden beings, right on the bed, felt the breath leave their bodies. They tried to retrieve some sense, but it was too soon. Their nerves were shot. Cyprian went into the hotel bathroom, turned the bathwater on, and motioned to Delphine to enter. He tossed the whiskey bottle out to Roy and then they locked the door shut on him.

"Let's not think," Delphine counseled.

Cyprian didn't even answer. He made the bath very, very hot, and he added some strawberry bubbles that he'd bought at the dime store. While the water was getting good and deep he took off all Delphine's clothes, then he took off his own. As he balled them up and laid them in the corner, he said, "We're going to burn these." They got in and with great care and speechless tenderness they washed each other, then they soaked themselves sitting cupped together for comfort. They kept the water going in and out. Their skin got very soft, then spongy white, wrinkled as a toad's. Once Roy knocked, but then he mumbled some vague apology and went away.

"I never want to leave this tub," said Delphine.

Cyprian added more strawberry bubbles, more hot water, and they sat there and sat there until the water drained out, then they sat there some more.

NOW THEY HAD the problem of who to tell and what to do—there was family, there must be family for Doris and Porky, and, unbearable to contemplate, their child. And there was the infuriating prospect of getting the entire story out of Roy. They questioned him the next morning. He gave out bits and pieces. They learned, for instance, that he'd wandered off during the wake itself and slept in the abandoned coop that once housed the black rosecomb bantams that Delphine used to keep. In his grief over Cornelius Strub, father to Clarisse, he'd gone to live in the bum's jungle down by the railroad tracks. Weeks had passed there, he thought, and when he returned he was so wrecked he was hallucinating. So he may have actually heard pounding, even awful noises coming from the walls and floors of his house, but at the same time, as he was plagued by the usual visions of snakes uncoiling from the lamps and dripping from the walls, he disregarded these noises.

"The noises finally went away," he said in a small, flat voice that trailed off weakly. "As noises will do . . . and I said to myself I must be coming out of the delirium!"

"That's it, we'd better go to the sheriff," said Cyprian, grim-faced.

"Won't they arrest Dad?"

"As long as he didn't lock them in . . . you didn't lock them in the cellar, did you?"

Roy sat bolt upright, rigid. His mouth fell open and he looked so vacant that for a moment Delphine was sure he was falling into a fit. Then he snapped his mouth shut suddenly and stated that he positively knew he had done no such thing.

"I don't think they'll prosecute. It looks to me, anyway, as though the whole thing was an accident. Maybe Doris and Porky got curious and went down there to show the old cellar hole to their"—Cyprian shut his eyes saying it—"little boy. Someone knocked those jars off the shelves and hit the ring in the floor. They got sealed in sometime at the wake."

"I didn't have a drop down there," said Roy. "Not a single drop."

"Well, who knows, then."

The three ate a very tense, morose breakfast before walking over to the sheriff's office.

SHERIFF ALBERT HOCK was a striking combination of fragility and mass. His delicate features were surrounded by great soft rings of flesh plumped into cheeks and chins. The pale brown hair on top of his head was a thin froth but the hair on his face was vigorous. His beard sprouted into stubble as soon as he shaved it. His mouth was grubby as a little boy's and often smeared with juice or chocolate, but he had a precise way of putting things. The spinning hysteria of Roy Watzka caused him to tip away from his desk and go still in the wheeled chair. Impassive, his face was a mask of patient contempt, although when he blinked at Delphine his look was tender as an old dog's.

"I want those bodies out of there!" said Roy in outrage.

From his attitude, one would have imagined the pitiful hulks in his cellar had invaded on purpose and died there to spite him. He glared at the sheriff as if Hock himself were responsible, which was, Cyprian thought, a very bad ploy.

"Here, sit down," Cyprian advised Roy, whispering into his ear that he should also shut up. "We'd best go over this from the beginning."

"Please do," said Sheriff Hock, pulling himself back to the small wooden desk. He drew a brown paper blotter toward himself and folded his beautiful fingers around a pen. He smoothed his left hand over a record book bound in moss green fabric, into which he jotted information that people from the town brought to him. "You may proceed." He nodded, opening the book.

Delphine took up the story. She and Cyprian then alternated the facts, relating everything in as much detail as they could recall, pausing politely as the sheriff copied their words. He seemed prepared to take down every single nuance and waited while they sought the best, most accurate, way to describe each step of their experience. With his hand poised, arrested in the air, and his eyebrows lush as sandy caterpillars, drawn in thought, he listened. The quality of his attention brought things out—the exact time of day, the light sources, the peculiar power of the odor, their own theories, their concern over Roy. By the time they took the sheriff up to the present moment, Delphine and Cyprian felt that they had participated in a monumental task. They were exhausted, and yet there was still so much before them.

As Sheriff Hock rose with tedious majesty, Delphine recalled that prior to his successful bid for the sheriff's position, he had triumphed as King Henry VIII and also played a Falstaff legendary in the town. She regarded him with a complex respect mixed with pity. He was cruelly and hopelessly infatuated with Clarisse Strub, and everyone who knew it also knew she angrily despised him. He had chased her for years and written many a poem of self-pity. His passion had become a stale joke, but as he was the sheriff no one told him.

"We now commence the investigation," he stated, walking to the back of his office. A small room held the signal tools of his status. Pistol, measuring tapes, red flags for stopping traffic, more notebooks and files, a rack bearing several rifles. He carefully grasped a selection of things he needed and then, leaving a copiously worded note for his deputy, ushered them out.

"Roy will ride with me," he stated. Aclatter all at once with a combination of privilege and fear, Roy hopped into the passenger's seat. Cyprian and Delphine followed, at a somber distance. When they reached the house and got out of the car, Delphine was impressed to see that the sheriff had included a quarantine mask in his kit, and that now he donned it as he entered the house. He wasted no energy speaking to them. His bulk passed swiftly and daintily between small rooms, and he soon blotted out the pantry door. Sheriff Hock opened the hatch in the floor. He made some cursory notes, propped the hatch open, and then stepped out the back door into the yard.

He stood there for a long while, either battling his stomach or collecting his wits. The others waited, silent, at a short distance.

"Before I can allow you to reinhabit your house," the sheriff finally said to Roy, "I will have to interview the other guests who attended your house on the fatal night. Since, in your understandable zeal," he now addressed Delphine and Cyprian, "you have probably both seen and destroyed any evidence of foul play, I will have to insist that you remain in town as potential witnesses."

Both agreed, and the sheriff drove off. Roy informed the two that he needed a spot of solitude, and walked down to the bank of the river. Delphine tipped her thumb to her lips to indicate that he always stashed a bottle in the roots of trees near the bank. She and Cyprian proceeded to unload their DeSoto and to pitch their sleeping tent upwind and as far away from the house as possible. Then Delphine directed Cyprian to stay with Roy and make sure he didn't take it into his head to go swimming once he got good and schnockered. She, meanwhile, would drive to town and gather supplies.

HERE'S AN ODD and paradoxical truth: a man's experience of happiness can later kill him. Though he gave every sign of being no more than an everyday drunk, Roy Watzka was more. He was a dangerous romantic. In his life he had loved deeply, even selflessly, with all the profound gratitude of a surprised Pole. The woman he loved was the woman everyone supposed was Delphine's mother, Minnie. No one ever saw her except in Roy's pictures, or knew much about her except from Roy's stories. Those stories, however, made her vivid in town memory. Perhaps she had had a secret self who loved Roy back with a singular passion, for there was little in Minnie's indistinct photographs to indicate a romantic spirit. She was half turned away from the camera in one picture, her mouth clenched in a frown that might have been suspicion or just the shadow cast by direct sun. Another photograph caught her in a sudden movement, so she was blurred, her face trapped within an indistinct gray wash of light. In yet another, a chicken had flapped up and she'd reached suddenly to catch it so that her features were obscured by wings and hair.

Yet after she was gone, Roy indulged in a worship of those pictures. Some nights, he lighted a line of votive candles on the dresser and drank steadily, and spoke to her, until from deep in his cups she answered. Then, as candles played across the old photographs that Roy reverenced and he saw Minnie's face clearly, he remembered her eyes transformed and softened by words he'd spoken. But what could Roy do with bliss remembered? Where could he put such a thing when he could no longer experience its power? During the first years after Minnie took her leave, a sorrow about which Roy would never speak and a time when Delphine was no more than a baby, Roy bounced in and out of drink with the resilience of a man with a healthy liver. He remained remarkably sloshed, even through Prohibition, by becoming ecumenical. Hair tonic, orange flower water, cough syrups of all types, even women's monthly elixirs, fueled his grieving rituals. Gradually, he destroyed the organ he'd mistaken for his heart.

As her father began to drink out of a need produced increasingly by alcohol and less by her mother's memory, Delphine reached her tenth year. After that, she knew her father mainly as a pickled wreck while her mother remained youthful and mysterious in the pictures on the dresser. The blur of movement, the obscuring chicken, made her look so lively. Just what killed her, Roy would never say. Delphine thought it a wonder nobody in the town ever drew her aside and took the satisfaction of whispering that secret in her ear. But since no one did, she concluded that no one knew. In that void of knowledge, Delphine's mind had darted forward constructing fantasies, shaping her mother's story out of common objects, daydreaming her features in shadows of leaves and shapes of clouds.

Delphine was sure, for instance, though Roy had never verified her theory, that the objects in her own tiny closet of a room once belonged to Minnie. The lacquer bureau, the picture of a wave crashing on a rock. Her prize was a wooden box. In it, she kept a small, white stone wrapped in the end of a ripped muslin scarf. Sometimes, when longing gripped her, she opened the cigar box, which still gave off a sweet and fleeting aroma of tobacco and cedar. Ceremoniously, often in the late afternoon when sun slanted through the western window of her tiny room, Delphine wound the scarf around her wrist and put the white stone in her mouth. She lay there sucking on the stone, memorizing its blunt edges with her tongue, wrapping and unwrapping the scarf from her wrist in a white haze of comfort.

When she was twelve years old, she put the stone back in the box and simply quit the habit. She replaced it with a more grown-up awareness of what she'd missed. Watching other girls with their mothers sometimes made her head swim, her neck ache, but she'd borne it. She had always been too stubborn and shy to approach an older woman— a teacher, the mother of a friend—with her need. But it had been there all along, sometimes buried, sometimes urgent, especially in times of difficulty. Now, as Delphine drove the car into town, she was glad that in their desperate struggle with the smell she and Cyprian hadn't burned down the house, because she missed the photographs of her mother that Roy kept stashed in the top drawer of the black lacquer bureau. She wanted to look at them, to sit with the familiar mystery.

She was afflicted with a sudden and almost physical need to open the cigar box, too, and remove the white stone. She stared ahead at the road and wished an old, pure, useless wish: that just once, for a moment, she'd had the gift of a clear look at her mother's face. It was in that fit of longing to see the face of her mother, then, that Delphine entered Waldvogel's Meats, and met Eva Waldvogel.

FIVE

The Butcher's Wife

THE FIRST MEETING of their minds was over lard. Delphine was a faceless customer standing in the entryway of Waldvogel's Meats, breathing the odor of fir sawdust, coriander, pepper, and apple-wood-smoked pork, a rich odor, clean and bloody and delicious. She walked forward eagerly and put her strong fingers on the counter.

"One quarter pound of bacon. I'm going to fry some fish in the grease."

"What kind of fish?" asked Eva pleasantly. Her accent was heavy, but she didn't stumble over words. She always started conversations with new customers, and this young woman, though familiar, was neither a regular customer nor an acquaintance. She stood behind the shining display cooler filled with every mood of red—twenty or thirty cuts of meat, summer sausage, liver sausage, beer sausage, veal, blood, Swedish, Italian and smoked pepper sausage, glistening hearts and liver

and pale calf thymus, sweetbreads, as well as a great box of the deli-
cately spiced, unsmoked, boiled wieners for which people stood in line
on the days Fidelis made them fresh.

"Don't know yet," said Delphine. "They're still swimming in the
river." She immediately recognized the woman behind the counter as
the same woman who'd won the race in the dirt lot two days before. She
felt familiar with her, and spoke with more assurance than she might
have otherwise. "One strip is for bait. Then I figure that if we don't
catch the fish, we at least eat the rest of the bacon."

"This plan is wise," said Eva, weighing out the best pieces of lean
bacon. With a new customer, she was always very careful with quality,
and gave a small present as an enticement to return.

"Try this lard," she insisted. "For fish, it is good. Very cheap and to
save it you let the cracklings settle and pour off the top. Get your bacon
for tomorrow. Now, there is lard and there is lard."

Eva reached into the glass case cooled by an electric fan. "My hus-
band was back in Germany a master butcher—not like Kozka, who no
more than was a war cook—my Fidelis has learned a secret process to
render fat. Taste," she commanded. *"Schmeckt gut!"*

Eva held out a small blue pan of the stuff, and Delphine swiped a bit
on the end of her finger.

"Pure as butter!"

"Hardly no salt," Eva whispered, as though this was not for just
anyone to overhear. "But you must have an icebox to keep it good."

"I don't have one," Delphine admitted. "Well, I did, but while I was
gone my dad sold it."

"I seen you here, I seen you there," said Eva, "but still I cannot
place. If you please, your father's name?"

Delphine liked Eva's direct but polite manners and admired her
thick bun of golden red hair stuck through with two yellow lead pencils.
Eva's eyes were a heated green striated with silver. There was, in one
eye, an odd gleaming streak that would turn to a black line when the life
left her body, like a light going out behind the crack in a door. At pres-
ent, those eyes narrowed as the question of the lard, the icebox, the

father who sold the icebox, were forming a picture in Eva's mind. She waited for more information.

"Roy Watzka," Delphine said slowly.

Eva nodded as she wrapped and secured the package all in one expert sweep, and took Delphine's money. She counted the change into Delphine's hand. The name told her all that she needed to know. "Come with me." Eva swept her arm around back of the counter. "Here I will teach you to make a mincemeat pie better than you ever ate. It's all in the goddamn suet."

"Where did you learn to speak English?" asked Delphine.

"Close listening to the butchers," said Eva.

As Delphine came back around the counter and followed Eva down the hall, she peeked at the office cascading with papers and bills, at the little cupboards that held the men's clothes and who knows what, at the knickknack shelf set into the wall and displaying figures made of German porcelain. These figures were of little children—one picked roses, another led a small white goat. They entered the kitchen, which was full of light from big windows set into thick walls, placed over the sink. Here, for Delphine, all time stopped. She took in the room.

There was a shelf for big clay bread bowls and a pull-out bin containing flour. Wooden cupboards painted an astounding green matched the floor's linoleum. Bolted to the counter was a heavy polished meat grinder. The table, round, was covered with a piece of oilcloth printed with squares. In each red-trimmed square there was printed a bunch of blue grapes, or a fat pink-gold peach, an apple or a delicate green pear. There were no curtains on the window, but pots of geraniums bloomed, scarlet and ferociously cheerful. The whole place smelled generously of fresh rolls.

Upon walking into Eva's kitchen, something profound happened to Delphine. She experienced a fabulous expansion of being. Light-headed, she felt a swooping sensation and then a quiet, as though she'd settled like a bird. She sat in the sort of solid square-backed chair that Cyprian favored for balancing while Eva spooned coffee beans out of a Redwing crock, into a grinder, and then began to turn a little iron hand crank on a set of gears that gnashed the roasted beans. The grinding made a lot of noise, so Eva just raised her eyebrows at Delphine over the little mahogany box as she cranked. A wonderful fragrance emerged. Delphine took a huge breath. Eva, hands quick and certain, dumped the thin wooden drawer full of fresh grounds into a coffeepot made of gray enamel speckled with black and white. She opened a handle on her sink faucet and got the water out of that, not a pump, and then she put the coffeepot on the stove and lighted the burner of a stunning white gas range trimmed with chrome swirled into the title Magic Chef.

"My God," Delphine exhaled. She didn't have a word to say. But that was fine, for Eva had already whipped a pencil out of her hair and grabbed a pad of paper to set down the mincemeat recipe. Eva's writing was of the old, ornate German style, and she was an awful speller, at least in English. The last tiny shortcoming made Delphine grateful—in fact, it was a great help to her, for Eva appeared so fantastically skilled a being, so assured, the mother also (she soon learned) of four sturdy and intelligent sons, the wife of a master butcher, that she would have been an unapproachable paragon to Delphine otherwise. Delphine—who never had a mother, who cleaned up shameful things in her father's house, who toughened on cold and hunger, and whose lover balanced six chairs and himself upon her stomach, Delphine who was regarded as beneath notice by Argus's best society, and yet could spell—stole confidence from the misspelled recipe. At that moment, she made a strategic decision.

Since sooner or later this Eva, whom she already dearly wished to have as a friend, would learn of what happened in the house of Roy Watzka, Delphine decided to tell. True, she would be immediately associated in Eva's mind with a sordid mess, but the older woman would know anyway, soon enough. Delphine understood, moreover, that she was in possession of a valuable thing. A story, a source of gossip, perhaps even the making of town myth, was hers. Hers to give to Eva, who could always say, *First thing the girl came to me half undone, the poor kid, and she told me. . . .* And so, exhausted and dispirited though she was, and still disgusted by what she had been through during the past three days, Delphine related to Eva all she'd just experienced. With the understanding that it was a prime piece of town gossip, she said offhandedly, only, "you're the first to know."

Eva heard the story with a prelate's fearless gaze, and although she was not asked for absolution, provided it in the form of the fresh coffee and a cinnamon bun exquisitely dotted with raisins and sugar and butter. Because the horror was just beginning to seep into Delphine's own mind, it filled her with gratitude to be treated in a very simple, human way. It was only when one of Eva's youngest sons, a strong little boy of five or six years, round-faced with brown curls, ran into the kitchen, asked for and got a roll, and ran back out, that Delphine burst into tears. All along, she had been shielding her mind from the actuality of that child in the cellar. She hoped they'd kept him drunk, or that in some way he'd found comfort in being with his parents at the last. Face to face with his unthinkable end, Delphine felt again the old shocking powerlessness. The little house she'd grown up in seemed determined to teach her just how cruel life was, and always to spare her so that she could ponder.

This is shameful, she thought, her face in her hands as she sobbed, to come to this woman's house and cry my heart out! But Eva seemed used to people crying at her table. That or she was lost in knowledge of the events that Delphine had recounted. Eva murmured, "Shoosh." From time to time she put a hand on Delphine's shoulder and provided more coffee.

"You weep seldom," she said, which made Delphine feel somehow impossibly strong and heroic.

"True," said Delphine, though it was the second time she'd wept since her return to this town, where her father would always be known, now, as the man too drunk to hear three people dying in his cellar.

LEAVING THE BUTCHER SHOP with a chunk of wrapped lard, the bacon, three oranges, six onions, bread, and a stick of summer sausage, Delphine thought it might be possible for her to face her father once again. She drove toward the house, bumping clumsily along, skirting the larger pits and holes. Meeting Eva had put her into a dreamy state—

it was much like being in love but it was also very different. That Eva had taken notice of her, even taken her into the kitchen, that Eva had given every sign of wanting to know Delphine, it was all too sudden a pleasure. By the time Delphine turned down the long, sorry curve and caught first sight of the little house, she decided it was probably a one-time thing, a kindness on Eva's part. Or that her weeping would have surely frightened her off. Even so, she was very grateful that Eva had invited her into her kitchen.

"I'll have a kitchen like that someday," she said out loud.

The sight of the sheriff's car and the gangly boy-deputy, an undertaker's hearse, and a couple of curious neighbors, as well as Cyprian disconsolately juggling in the corner of the far field, reminded her that day would not be coming soon.

THE TOWN FUNERAL DIRECTOR and mortician, Aurelius Strub, was in charge of hauling out the bodies, along with his wife, Benta, and his young niece and apprentice mortuary assistant, Delphine's friend, Clarisse. Clarisse stood to inherit the business, Strub's Funerary, the most advanced and well-respected funeral practice in that part of the state. Her future had complicated her high school relationships, as one by one her classmates realized that if they lived their lives in Argus, they would eventually wind up in the resolute, rubber-gloved hands of Clarisse Strub. Pretty Clarisse, who got an A+ in the dissection of a flatworm. Flirtatious Clarisse, who already knew the art of using makeup in the next life, as well as this one. Clarisse, whose brilliant and mocking glance had dimmed for a time when she suffered a secret and shocking infection, the cause of which was never determined. To cure the disease, which may have originated with a body whose syphilitic condition was unknown, for even then she had assisted in the embalming room from time to time, under her aunt's supervision, Clarisse underwent a complex long-term treatment. Her cure was overseen by Doctor Heech, who insisted that a dead body could not possibly have transmitted the disease and viewed her infection with a sober suspicion. His method of treatment consisted of intravenous salvarsan and deep-tissue mercury injections, both extremely unpleasant. Clarisse was toughened to them, but Delphine had quailed to see her poked. She'd held her friend's hand all through, nonetheless. The only day they'd not minded was the day when the treatments had made Clarisse's gums bleed and Heech had conditioned them with a cocaine rub. Delphine was the only one besides Doctor Heech who knew what had happened, and the only person, other than family members, who was ever admitted into the sanctum of the Strub Funerary basement.

Clarisse wore a sacklike white gown, a green mask, gloves of india rubber, and smoked glasses, but her curly black hair gave her away, and even the hard realities of her vocation hadn't dulled the singular light in her face. The sight of Delphine caused her to rip off her mask and gloves and then, torn between excitement at seeing her friend and the gravity of the situation, she threw out her hands and stepped closer. She looked around to see if anyone was watching, for the Strub family practiced resolute control and reverence in the presence of the dead, and she should not be seen joking about with a friend. Finding that they were alone, Clarisse screwed her face into a mask of hideous intensity. They had acted together in town theater as first and second witch in *Macbeth*.

"When shall we three meet again," she hissed. *"In thunder, lightning, or in rain?"*

"When the hurly-burly's done, When the battle's lost and won," Delphine went on.

The two could have gone on and on like this, for they knew practically the entire play as they'd understudied Lady Macbeth, and everyone else in the cast, but Aurelius appeared with a grim-looking package, and Clarisse made signs for talking later. Delphine mimed sympathy. They could communicate perfectly with facial expressions. Clarisse twisted up her face and from one side of her mouth croaked, *"Like a rat without a tail, I'll do, I'll do, and I'll do."*

Before she returned to her work, with a flash of intrigue, she pointed to Delphine's tent, across the field, and at Cyprian, who with his shirt off was practicing his gymnastic exercises and his balances on a chair dragged from the kitchen. Clarisse winked over the hygienic green mask and then turned to continue with her difficult tasks. They were going to have to vat the bodies right in the yard, Delphine saw. A three-sided canvas screen had been set up just beyond the door and the smell of formalin and rubbing alcohol came from behind it. Jugs of distilled water were neatly lined up on the grass. There was a sense about the scene, now, of efficiency and seriousness. When the Strubs appeared to take charge of the dead, there always was a sense of relief. Clarisse was still regarded as a bit exuberant, but the Strubs generally developed the right temperament for the job, a matter-of-fact sympathy not at all unctuous, oily, or sweet. The town relied upon them. The dead were complicated in their helplessness, and made everyone around them helpless, too, except the Strubs.

As Delphine walked her packages out to the tent, she saw that Cyprian had made a little fireplace out of rocks. He was proving remarkably handy, she thought, in ways odd and wonderful. For instance, the fireplace was not a lazy round circle of rocks, it was carefully fit stone on mortared stone. There was a chimney, a little shelf. A hook set into the mortar. He was fixing up the chicken coop. And, too, there was his beauty.

As Cyprian turned toward her with a gentle sideways glance his profile caught her breath. His eyes were deeply set, a resinous coal, and his nose was a classical line with perfect teardrops of nostrils. There was a slight curve to his lips, and an eerie perfection to his teeth when he smiled. It was that last, the even whiteness of his teeth, she decided now, that might possibly make his face too handsome to be handsome. Yes, she imagined, regarding him more critically, there was something to that. Some imperfection makes a face much stronger looking, gives it points of interest. Or am I just jealous? Protecting my own heart?

She held out the packages. He took them from her and added them to his juggling routine, happily catching and tossing them before him and behind him, in the air, under a leg lifted straight out and pointy-toed like a ballerina's, and then crooked to the side like a pissing dog's.

How could one not love a man who juggled so cleverly? How not love a man who stuck by you while the sheriff and deputies and morticians hauled three bodies out of the cellar of your father's house? She forgot her moment of critical thinking and merely decided to appreciate Cyprian. There was no question, he had done his best to make her comfortable. He had not only erected their own private tent, but rigged up another, a neatly constructed house of tarpaulin and blanket, for her father, and it was near the river. Near Roy Watzka's inevitable rootbound stash. Far away so that they wouldn't hear him snore.

After the three dead bodies were taken away, a traumatized exhaustion descended on Delphine and Cyprian. They sat long, staring in a numb trance, at the fire until it burned down to coals. A gentle snow of darkness fell upon them. There was no moon. Long into the night, they sipped fresh water and ate summer sausage, bread and lard, oranges for dessert, for Cyprian had caught no fish after all. The moonless night brought out the beams of stars. There was a gentle extravagance of light in the heavens. The air was so quiet they could hear the river flowing, and within its low sound Delphine at last shed a little of the horror and experienced a rare comfort.

An urgency to speak gripped her. The darkness covered her face; her father was drinking down in the bushes; Cyprian was sitting beside her. She decided to ask.

"That man by the river. You know what I'm saying."

Cyprian's heart thunked, a jolt of adrenaline buzzed his brain. He had been waiting for this moment, hoping it wouldn't come. Long before, he had decided what his answer would be.

"You're all I want out of life," he said.

Delphine pondered this. In a way, this was exactly what she'd prayed for when much younger, trapped in her room while drunks roared in the yard and kitchen. Here was a good-looking man, very strong and with an odd, but surprisingly proven, source of income that consisted of balancing. A talented man. A man who professed that she was all he wanted out of life—that is, presumably he wanted to marry her. And yet, this man had what she now understood she'd heard referred to as an affliction. That was the polite way she'd heard it. Other than such references, this whole thing was sheer enigma.

"Why do you do it?" she said.

"I don't know."

"I have to know."

As usual, and Cyprian could have predicted this, she would not accept an easy answer or even one that allowed him to keep his dignity. Even an evasion that might ensure their happiness was unacceptable. Nothing he'd heard about his desire matched the feelings that he had when he was experiencing this form of love. Then, at those times, it was simply the most basic joy he'd ever felt. He'd always hoped that he would never, ever, have to explain it, especially to a woman. But, he thought, looking at the ruby firelight on Delphine's face, if he had to tell a woman he was glad it was she. The way he felt about Delphine Watzka was an utter surprise to him, something he'd never expected in his life. He loved the things she said, her amusing directness, the strength she had dismissed until he taught her to develop it, and now, the kindness she showed toward this scroungy old bastard of a father. Even her insistence that he tell her the truth about this hidden side of himself was a part of her true charm.

Still, he didn't know how to put it, and she was determined to obtain the whole truth and nothing less.

"You're not a Pole with a name like Lazarre," she sidetracked.

"I am not," he admitted.

"So then what are you?"

"I'm French."

"Plus what else?"

Cyprian paused. "Well," he said at last. "I'm Chippewa. Ojibwe. The word my grandpa used was Anishinaabeg—the humans. Same thing."

"That makes you an Indian."

It was no small thing to admit this in the town where the two now lived openly together as though married, but he did at last.

"You have light skin."

"My dad was half French and my mom was part French, too. Have you ever heard of michifs or métis?" Cyprian peered at her, then shrugged and looked away. "I guess not, but if you had, you'd have heard of my

77

famous ancestor, Louis Riel, who died a martyr to the great vision of a mixed-blood nation—not a loose band or bunch of hunters. A place with boundaries and an actual government taking up a big chunk of Manitoba. There's lots of us who still do dream about it! I'm descended of a famous man, Delphine, for your information. Riel. You can find him in the books of history."

"Was he a good balancer?"

Cyprian cocked his head to the side and smiled. "He was an excellent balancer, but they hung him anyway. I guess the light side of my relatives came out in me, if not their heroics, though I did fight a decent war. All my cousins, two of my brothers, they're brown."

"But now I see it," said Delphine, softening toward him and his fantasy of lost glory and a hero's inheritance, "in your eyes and all, or maybe in your hair." Still, she was not to be diverted by Cyprian's sudden burst of information. "Tell me about the man beside the river."

Her voice was patient, and Cyprain lost any hope of diverting her. His breath came short and he attempted to find the right words to describe what came over him when he knew it was going to happen with another man. He couldn't, and was relieved when she finally asked him a question.

"Did it start in the war?"

"It started in the war!'

He said this with a surge of hope, for it was an explanation that he hadn't thought of yet. Yes, his thoughts knit quickly. This could be another freak effect of wartime life, a consequence of living so closely with other men, a side effect of getting gassed, or of the other things, septic wounds, a trench disease, a fear-borne germ. As he scrambled about with these explanations in his mind, he knew that they were not enough. During the war he had, in fact, fallen devoutly in love with another man, whose death he still grieved. And the love itself had not been a surprise. For he'd always known. It was perfectly apparent to him that he had the feelings for men that men usually expressed for girls, then women. What could be more obvious? No, the war had done far worse things than deciding whom he could or couldn't love.

Even thinking of it exhausted him.

"Look," he finally said, wearily, "ask yourself the same question. Why you like to do it with men? Your answer is the same as my answer."

Delphine nibbled some bread, poked the fire into a stronger blaze, and considered. After thinking of it for some time, she decided that she now felt a kinship with him that was more female than male. It seemed as though she could tell him anything that went on in her woman's heart, and he would understand it, he would know the truth of it, having felt it in his own. So she was satisfied with his answer although it meant that truly, for good and all, they would not be lovers. She did not know if they would even travel anymore, putting on their show. After all, they were stuck for a time, right here, according to their pledge to Sheriff Hock. What they needed to think about, especially in the face of the money they'd been forced to spend on the hotel, schnapps for Roy, cleaning supplies and new blankets, was work. They had to think just how they would acquire work.

THIS TIME, Delphine walked over to the meat shop, a distance of about four miles. She and Cyprian had decided not to waste gasoline. Also, she needed to exercise her leg muscles in case they did resume their show—perhaps they should put it on here for a weekend or two just to raise enough to purchase a new mattress for Roy, not to mention buy a concoction that would remove the still raging stink from the floor and walls of the house. When Delphine walked into Waldvogel's she noted the jangle of a cheerful shop bell and thought how pleasant it would be to hear it from deep in the house.

Delphine made known the purchases she sought, as before, and as before, Eva asked her to come sit down for a coffee. There was not a product on Eva's household cleaning shelf that would serve as a strong enough cleanser for the job Delphine required, and Eva wanted to concoct something of her own.

"Believe me, I have the experience," she said. "This type of stink is a hell of a problem. Most difficult to destroy.

"First off, a good vinegar and water wash down. Then I should order the industrial strength ammonia for you—only be careful with the fumes of it. Maybe, if that doesn't work good enough yet, raw lye. From the first, Delphine, I suggest to fill that cellar in, not just sprinkling with lime, but packing her up with a good mixture of wood ash and dirt. You will not be going to use it?"

Delphine vigorously shook her head.

"Then good. Fill it up." Eva sipped her coffee. Today, her hair was bound back in a singular knot, the sides rolled in smooth twists, the knot itself in the shape of the figure eight, which Delphine knew was the ancient sign for eternity. Eva rose and turned away, walked across the green squares of linoleum to punch some risen dough and cover it with towels. As Delphine watched, into her head there popped a strange notion: the idea that perhaps strongly experienced moments, as when Eva turned and the sun met her hair and for that one instant the symbol blazed out, those particular moments were eternal. Those moments actually went somewhere. Into a file of moments that existed out of time's range and could not be pilfered by God.

Well, it *was* God, wasn't it, Delphine's thoughts went on stubbornly, who made time and created the end of everything? Tell me this, Delphine wanted to say to her new friend, why are we given the curse of imagining eternity when we know we can't experience it, when we ourselves are so finite? She wanted to say it, but suddenly grew shy, and it was in that state of concentrated inattention that she met Eva's husband, Fidelis Waldvogel, master butcher.

Before she met him, she sensed him, like a surge of electric power in the air when the clouds are low and lightning bounds across the earth. Then she felt a heaviness. A field of gravity moved through her body. She tried to rise, to shake the feeling, when he suddenly filled the doorway. Then entered, and filled the room.

It was not his size. He was not extraordinarily tall, not broad. But he shed power, as though there was a bigger man crammed into him. Or could it have been that he was stuffed with the cries of animals? Maybe it was his muscled shoulders, or his watchful quiet. One thick red and punished hand hung down at his side like a hook; the other balanced on his shoulder a slab of meat. That cow's haunch weighed a hundred pounds or double that. He held it lightly, although the veins in his neck throbbed, heavy-blooded as a bull's. He looked at Delphine and his eyes were white blue. Their stares locked. Delphine's cheeks went fever hot and she looked down first. Clouds flew across the sun. Light shuddered in and out of the room, and the red mouths of the geraniums on the windowsill yawned. The shock of his gaze caused her to pick up one of Eva's cigarettes. To light it. He looked away from her and conversed with his wife.

Then he left without asking to be introduced.

That abruptness, though rude, was more than fine with Delphine. Already, she didn't want to know him. She hoped she could avoid him. It didn't matter, as long as she could still be friends with Eva, or even hold the job that she soon was offered, waiting trade.

"When?"

Delphine was immediately happy with the thought of working in the shop and sitting for her breaks in Eva's kitchen every day.

"Starting tomorrow."

"I'll be right here when you open," said Delphine.

"At six."

From the next day on Delphine used the back door that led past the furnace and washtubs, the shelves of tools, the bleached aprons slowly drying on racks and hooks. Leaving the utility room, she walked down the hallway cluttered with papers and equipment. Lifted from a hook by the shop door Eva's own apron, blue with tiny white flowers. From now on, she would hear the customer bell ring from the other side of the counter. She would know the slaughterhouse, the scalding tub, the tracks and hooks that held unbroken quarters of beef and half hogs. There was a cooler. Open the steel lever and the air lock broke, the thick door sighed open. She gulped the scent of spice and cheese. The deep freeze had a grimmer odor. Both were fitted with tracks, hooks, bins, and shelves. Between the slaughtering room and the store was a small smoking room, and piled beside it logs of hickory or apple wood and buckets of brine. Set to the side of the little smoking room was the busy processing room fitted out with butcher blocks, stubby tables where the quarters were broken. There were steel-sheeted tabletops around the saw where steaks and roasts were cut. The floor of that room was spread with fresh sawdust every morning to soak up blood and absorb the dust of bones that the meat saws spewed and the bits and pieces of gristle and suet that were flung off the blocks when they were cleaned with heavy, rectangular steel brushes. Aprons smeared with blood hung by the doors. It was Delphine's job to assist in the shop laundry. Every day, she collected the stained aprons and rags and brought them back to the concrete-floored laundry room. Eva let her bring her own laundry, too. Not that Eva ever said so, but no matter how hard Delphine washed, it felt to her as though the smell of Roy's house lingered—maybe in the seams of her dress, in the green and gray checks, the vines of the print, the stitched hem. Only gradually would that scent be replaced by the smell of the shop. Raw blood, congealed fat, sharp pepper, and sawdust. Delphine put on a fresh clean dress nearly every day. She washed her hair in the river at night. Still, the smell of meat clung to her, and bothered her until she finally grew used to it and didn't smell it anymore.

ON HER SECOND DAY of work, Delphine was arranging loops of wieners in the cooler when she heard the bell jangle, then jangle again, then jangle with a truly furious commotion. Who was this who could not wait a few seconds? Who was it who entered in a stormy tantrum? Irritated, Delphine stepped out of the cool locker into the presence of a woman known in town as Step-and-a-Half. She was a rangy stray dog of a woman who was probably still young—she looked between thirty and forty—and yet moved with an air of ancient bitterness. Step-and-a-Half lived alone, when she lived in Argus at all, and made her living trading in rags. Roy spoke to her sometimes, and Delphine remembered times as a child when Step-and-a-Half had thrust a stick of candy or a coin into her hands. Times when the woman had appeared, from nowhere, and drunks in the house had melted off as though into the earth. She was intimidating. The name Step-and-a-Half was hers because the length of her stride was phenomenal. She loved the night and could be seen, her beanpole figure in a trance of forward movement, walking the town streets and checking back porches to see whether anyone had left out a worn skirt, a piecemeal assortment of shirts and blouses, or maybe even a coat. Now, since she ate the town's leavings as well as gathered them, she'd come for tripe. Or snouts, though Eva mainly used them in a salad that she believed was especially nutritious for boys. Today bones were also available for Step-and-a-Half. Delphine knew this because already Eva had set them aside.

The bones, cut generously and hung with scraps of meat, lay collected in a pan underneath a towel. Delphine shook them into waxed, white paper, wrapped and secured them in string she pulled down from a roll suspended from the ceiling. She pushed the package impatiently across the counter, expecting Step-and-a-Half to snatch it. But the older woman threw back her racklike shoulders, stood tall, and glared down at the package in quizzical silence. She carefully unwrapped it. Wordless, she smoothed out the white paper between them, and displayed the dull, fat-smeared bones. Step-and-a-Half examined the bones as though they told the future.

"This one's for shit." She pushed a knobbed legbone aside. "And I don't take necks."

Step-and-a-Half inspected the rest, smiled approvingly at an oxtail, exercised over the scraps the meticulous discernment of a banker's wife critically comparing the marbling on expensive steaks. When done, she waved the bones back. Delphine ceremoniously retied the package and gave them to the woman with a respectful flourish. She understood that this was the way Eva did things. Satisfied now with her treatment, Step-and-a-Half reached into an inner pocket of her voluminous man's trench coat and pulled out a neatly cut pile of dust rags.

"Give 'em to Eva," she ordered, as though she thought that Delphine would keep the rags. Her eyes were a brilliant and searching black. Her gaze had at first seemed powered by a sharp, cryptic hatred, but now suddenly she shifted, looked at Delphine with an unreadable expression of melancholy.

"Can I help you with something else?" Delphine asked, uncertain. But Step-and-a-Half only continued to stare, taking Delphine in carefully. For her part, Delphine stared right back. That was when she noticed something new about Step-and-a-Half. Although her face was planed rough, her features, almost noble in their raw strength, could have been beautiful if suspicion had not pulled the corners of her mouth down so tightly that deep lines tied beneath her chin. Her eyes, that surprising color, were constantly narrowed. Suddenly, the older woman slapped the counter sharply with one hand. She grabbed the package with the other and without a word of thanks or gesture of common courtesy, she turned on her heel and swept out. The door jangled shut in that same fury with which she had entered.

That was one of the customers, and there were others. Some paid money and some, like Step-and-a-Half, lived off the scraps. For the shop and the dead animals fed a complex range of beings—from the banker, his steak cooked perfectly and set before him every night, to those who bought the sausages, then the cheapest cuts; from the family of Dakota Sioux who were darker than Cyprian and dressed in old-fashioned calicos, wore strings of rose, blue, coral, and yellow beads, and traded wild meat or berries for flour and tea, to the ones who did not pay at all like Step-and-a-Half, Simpy Benson, the Shimeks, and the out-of-work fathers who had taken to Depression roads; and still on down to the dogs who gnawed the bones that Step-and-a-Half rejected and even further, to the plants that flourished on the crushed bones even the dogs could not chew to bits.

There were also a number of customers who didn't always buy but regularly came in to talk or to plan the meetings of the singing club—the fat bootlegger, Gus Newhall, and the courtly, stone-broke, but immaculate Tensid Bien, who always wore a tie and coat, who took forever to browse through the Sunshine Baking Company rack of cookies, from which he meekly sampled, and who bought one or two slices at a time of minced ham, occasionally an orange, a few cookies, a meager cut of the toughest beef, a turnip, a sparse rind of cheese. There was Pouty Mannheim of the Mannheim brothers, chubby and with rich-boy airs, and his confused perpetual girlfriend, Myrna. There was Chester Zumbrugge, who tried to put the moves on her. There were Scat Wilcomb and Mercedes Fox, Old Doctor Heech and his son, Young Doctor Heech, who was not a doctor at all but a dentist, and was that shocking thing, a vegetarian, and thus suspected to be a Communist. The only one of them all whom Delphine truly dreaded seeing, however, was Eva's spoiled sister-in-law. Everyone just called her Tante because she otherwise insisted on her baptismal name, Maria Theresa, and no one wanted to add to her swellheadedness by using such a queenly title.

Delphine did not call her Tante, she did not call her anything. She carefully did not address the woman who swept in with one clang of the bell, as though the bell itself were subdued by the woman's sense of her own elegance and importance. On Delphine's first day of work, Tante went right around to the sliding panel on the case that held the sausage, opening it with a clatter. She fished out a ring of baloney and put it in her purse. Delphine stood back and watched Maria Theresa—actually, she stood back and envied the woman's shoes. Those shoes were made of a thin, flexible Italian leather, and cleverly buttoned. They fit her long, narrow foot with a winsome precision. Tante might not have a captivating face, for in that she resembled Fidelis, she replicated his most aggressive features—the powerful neck and icy bold demeanor, a too stern chin, thinner lips and eyes of a ghostly blue that gave Delphine the shivers. Still, Tante's feet were slim and pretty. She was vain of them, and all her shoes were of the most expensive leather and make.

"Who are you?" Tante asked, rearing her head back and then swirling off without deigning to accept an answer. The question, insulting in the first place, since Delphine had already been introduced to the butcher's sister, hung in the air. *Who are you* is a question with a long answer or a short answer. When Tante dropped it between them, bounced but did not retrieve it, Delphine was left to consider the larger meaning as she scrubbed down the meat counters and prepared to mop the floor.

Who are you, Delphine Watzka, *you drunkard's child and fairy's whore, you vagabond, you motherless creature with a belly of steel and a lusting heart? Who are you, what are you, born a dirty Pole in a Polack's dirt? You with a household cellar full of human rot and a man in your tent who has done the unimaginable to other men? Who are you, with a father seen sucking his bottle like a baby in its own shit? Who are you and what makes you think you belong anywhere near this house, this shop, and especially my brother, Fidelis, who is the master of all he does?*

DELPHINE WAS NOT CAPABLE of indulging in that sort of self-doubt without resenting the one who had introduced it into her heart. She hated Tante from the first and she imagined the woman's overthrow. She would be ruthless in attaining at least one small eventual victory from which Tante never recovered. Tante even tried to lord it over Eva, for which, in her complicated, loyal heart, Delphine detested her. When Tante swept back out with a loaf of her sister-in-law's fresh bread under her arm, and grabbed a bottle of milk besides without a by-your-leave, Delphine wrote it down on a slip. *Tante took a bottle of milk, a ring of baloney, and a loaf of bread.* And she left it at that. She did not know there would be repercussions for even so slight an accounting, but there were, for Tante didn't take things. By her reckoning, she was owed things. Out of money left by her grandmother, whose favorite she was, Tante once gave her brother five hundred dollars to purchase equipment. Although he had paid her back, she continued to take her interest out in ways that would remind them all of her dutiful generosity.

The boys, in particular Markus and Franz, did not like Tante. Delphine could see that. Not that she knew all that much about children. They were foreign to her. She had not been around them often. Now, things were different. As these boys were children belonging to Eva, she was interested in who they were. She took note of them beginning with the oldest boy, Franz.

At fifteen years he was extremely strong and athletic with a proud, easygoing American temperament perfectly transparent and opaque at the same time. His inner thoughts and moods were either nonexistent or hidden, she couldn't tell. He always smiled at her. He always said hello with only the faintest German accent. He was always cheerful and he was unfailingly polite. As time went on, she would see that he was the product of Fidelis's insuperable patience and also his controlled rage. Franz's strength coupled with his mother's wire-frame tenacity made him a formidable athlete. He played football, basketball, and baseball, all with powerful grace, and was, in fact, something of a town hero.

The next boy was more reclusive. Markus was barely nine but already it was clear that he had a philosophical bent and a monkish nature, though he'd play with tough abandon when he could. His grades were perfect for one year, and abysmal the next, according to his own interests. He had inherited his mother's long hands, her floss of red-gold hair, her thin cheeks and eyes that looked out sometimes with a sad curiosity and amusement, as though to say, *What an idiotic spectacle.* Markus was also polite, though more restrained. He anxiously accomplished errands for his father, but he clearly doted to the last degree upon his mother. He was named after her beloved father. His mother often stroked his hair, so like her own, the curls clipped. She often pulled him close and kissed him. He pulled away, as boys had to, but in a gentle way that showed he didn't want to hurt her feelings.

The two youngest boys, Erich and Emil, were five-year-old twins, bull strong, morose when hungry, perfectly happy once they ate their fill, simple of heart and devoted to their stick guns and homemade sets of clay and twig armies that eternally strove in combat across the floor of their back room. Those armies, which included those that once had belonged to Fidelis, and a few more modern soldiers bought with precious pennies, were just about the only toys in evidence around the house. Once, when Delphine wondered what boys played with, Eva told her that they played with everything around them, inventing it into something else.

"A stick, it becomes a gun. Our meat trays they slide down the hills. Once in a while a bat, a ball. You never know. Delphine, I just leave them out of my interest to see what they build."

Delphine watched and indeed they made surprising things. Out of abandoned springs, wheels, crates, they put together a buggy that the dogs pulled. They rigged up a near lethal tree swing, which flung them from a branch near the road in an arc over the dirt where they could be hit by a passing car. Down near the river, they made rafts out of old lumber scraps. Swords from lathes, forts from packing-crate wood, guns that shot gravel, bombs of cow's bladders filled with water. Yet, in spite of their rowdy play out in the world, they were quiet and subdued in the shop and around their father, especially. They worked hard on slaughtering days. When every hand was needed, even the two youngest pulled gizzards inside out and cleaned them of gravel. Once old enough, the boys learned to use knives without slicing off their hands. Fidelis had determined to train them all in his profession.

There was that—the profession. Delphine didn't mind selling groceries, or even cutting headcheese, but butchering wasn't her kind of work. Not only did she hate the brutish excitement of the killing, but its long and meticulous aftermath. The casings must be washed and rewashed, for sausage, and the gizzards turned inside out and carefully smoothed back together. Each product had an endless procedure and she thought some of the steps unnecessary, though Eva insisted they were not. Maybe, Delphine thought, she wouldn't mind actually mixing the spices up into the ground meat and making the sausages, but that was Fidelis's work and he was jealous of each step he took. Some steps were secret. He brooded over each batch like an alchemist.

Delphine would rather have spent her time on the stage, or even backstage, designing costumes and sewing them. She liked to build sets. She was good at everything that had to do with drama and most of all she liked dressing up in whatever composed a costume: feathers, wreaths, gowns, Victorian shirtwaists. Delphine had always loved making up shows. It was, in fact, their mutual passion for disguise that had first brought Clarisse and Delphine together while they were still in grade school. They had staged complicated shows in Clarisse's backyard, using a sheet draped over a clothesline for a curtain, and playing all parts with complicated costume changes and stage directions, even lighting from an old captain's lamp, the glow of which could be directed onto the grass as a kind of spotlight after dark. Their inventions, and the mingled derision and awe in which other children held them, had made them close as only children can be who are set apart. Their loyalty to each other had saved them. Over time, they had become invulnerable to teasing and gained a complex form of respect. When small towns find they cannot harm the strangest of their members, when eccentrics show resilience, they are eventually embraced and even cherished. So it began to happen with "those two girls"—an acceptance of their peculiar getups and an appreciation of their entertainment value.

Still, in their shared daydreams, Clarisse and Delphine had always seen themselves taking leave of Argus, moving off into the vague wilderness of cities and other people and even bona fide theaters. Although Delphine had, for a short time, pursued some form of their fantasy, she was disappointed that it had only been as a human table, a prop, the base of Cyprian's flamboyant balancing. As for Clarisse, she'd never left at all, since her father and uncle required her in the business directly after high school. It was her fate to stay and to assist the town's dead on their short journey into the earth. She didn't mind, she told Delphine, she had accepted it. She had always known that she would step into her parents' spot, but once she lost them the luxury of going to school or playing at drama was at an end. Besides, her aunt Benta said she had a natural aptitude for embalming, which was an art that went back to the Egyptians but was only now catching on in the Dakotas. Aurelius Strub had taken the course and earned his diploma from one of the first itinerant embalmers to enter the state. Since then, he had made steady technical improvements. Strub's was getting first calls from people in towns at quite a distance, from people who had seen and found comfort in the serenity of the bodies that Strub's prepared and displayed.

Clarisse moved her own grocery trade from Kozka's market to Waldvogel's, as soon as Delphine began to work there. She had inherited her parents' house and often unwound from her day by cooking elaborate meals for herself in her mother's kitchen. She was very finicky about her diet, and Delphine now saved the leanest cuts of meat for her. They were alone in the shop one afternoon, regarding a lavender-pink pork chop that Delphine had just laid on a piece of waxed paper.

"Trim off the fat, will you?" said Clarisse.

"There's no fat on it," said Delphine.

"Just that corner," said Clarisse, pointing.

Delphine removed a bit of translucent flesh no bigger than a fingernail.

Clarisse nodded for her friend to wrap the rest. Her pinch-waisted brown suit of summer-weight wool and her crisp white blouse and white piped leather pumps looked good enough for city wear. Her philosophy, she'd informed Delphine, was not only to prepare the deceased as the guest of honor at a party, but to dress herself with an elegance that befit the grand going-away occasion. She had just come from the funeral of a thirty-four-year-old drowning victim, a man, and was pleased, though she merely hinted of this and only whispered the disagreeable term "floater," that she had managed to nearly eliminate the awful red and purple blotches from his face and halt its typical rapid degradation.

"I would never have let him go out in front of people looking like that drowned boy who purged, right in the church, up in Fargo," she said. "Sloppy work. Those poor parents. The wife of mine—you don't know them, they're new in town—anyway, his wife told me that she couldn't believe the work we'd done. She thanked me. The family tried to give Benta extra money. We wouldn't take it. How do you like this jacket?"

The two were the same size and Clarisse was generous with her clothing, so Delphine always took a possessive interest in her friend's wardrobe. Even now, Clarise said pleasantly, "This would look swell on you."

"I can't think where I would actually wear it," said Delphine.

"You and Cyprian go out, don't you?"

"We're living in a *tent*, Clarisse," said Delphine, and then she laughed. So did Clarisse. Her sweet, fresh voice bubbled over the rumble of generators and the clash of meat grinders out in back. While they were laughing, Eva walked into the shop with a new roll of string for the spool that hung above the cash register. She gave Clarisse the smile Delphine knew as her formal smile, the one she used with customers she did not particularly know or like. Delphine wasn't sure which category her friend fell into, and she experienced a sudden anxiety, a confusion of loyalties in which she wanted to please them both. But Eva swept immediately out and Clarisse, who hadn't picked up on Eva's formality and probably thought that she was merely busy, was frowning at her fingernails in a serious way that Delphine knew meant she was thinking of imparting some questionable piece of information.

"Come on," Delphine said to her friend, though she felt guilty now, talking on the job, "business is slow. I've got a minute. Let's hear it."

"In a way, it's nothing that you haven't heard before," said Clarisse, pouting with vexation.

"Give it over," said Delphine firmly.

Clarisse tipped her head down and eyed her friend almost angrily from beneath her brows.

"Hock came to my house last night, late. He stood on the porch, talking of this and that, trying to pretend like we shared some secret until I wanted to scream. I shut the door in his face and stood behind it. He must have stepped up to the door because I heard him whisper like it was right in my ear, *then I'll huff and puff and blow your house down.*"

Clarisse had a talent for looking truly miserable. Her face fell into the slack lines of a much older woman, and she bit the lipstick off her lips, nervously, so that it smeared onto her teeth. She lifted the gloved hand that held the wrapped pork chop, squinted her eyes shut, pressed the pork chop to her forehead.

"Nothing I say or do makes a goddamn bit of difference," she said vehemently. "He turns it around to hear what he wants."

"What are you supposed to be, his tender little pig?"

"Ha!" Clarisse held the pork chop out at arm's length, and spoke to it.

"I suppose you're fed up with me always pitching a moan over Hock. Well, I'm sick of me, too. I'd move away if I could, that's how tired I am of it. But I have a duty here, and more than that. I'm good at my profession. Heech says I know as much as he does about anatomy, and I have been experimenting with a new pump that . . . oh, I'll spare you the details. I've got pride in my work, and he can't ruin things for me."

"I'll tell you what," said Delphine. "We'll get together and knock off the big boy. We'll murther'm."

"Oh," said Clarisse, wistful. "That would be so nice!"

NORTH DAKOTA WILTED in a brutal heat. For Delphine, the summer weather, hot, hotter, unbearably hot the second week of her new job, meant that this was the summer of ongoing terrible odors. The slaughter-house of course began to smell like slaughter. The scrap pile went green and the rank smell of flesh was everywhere. Of course, she couldn't escape the bad smells after work. No sooner was the cellar of her house filled in and the floor scrubbed down, new mattresses, clean blankets and sheets put out, the walls sprayed with vinegar and then vigorously wiped, no sooner was the house fit to live in than the heat crushed the air. She and Cyprian decided to stay in the tent for other reasons, as they attempted to catch some sleep in the night's wet furnace.

A slight breeze flowed off the dwindling water of the river just around three A.M., and Cyprian positioned the tent flaps just so in order to take advantage of it. But that breeze also turned the mud sour and came laden with whining fronds of mosquitoes. The insects batted the canvas of the tent with a tiny insane lust. All night, the whining built and diminished, sometimes so loud it sounded like air raid sirens, some-times low and insistent, but always constant and without letup.

Cyprian bought mosquito netting for the two of them. Draped around their army cots, it allowed them enough rest to see straight the next day. At first they thought they would go mad listening to the bugs clustered an inch deep at the tiny holes through which their warm-blooded scent must have exuded, tantalizing. The next week they bought cotton wax from the pharmacist and pressed it into their ears. No sooner had they solved the problem of the mosquitoes than they were infested with a plague of armyworms. If you looked at just one, it wasn't bad . . . olive brown with an intricate racing band of blue dots. It was their numbers that made them horrible. The worms crept up and down the trees in such thick droves that the bark seemed to be moving. They inched across the tent roof by the thousands and it was impossible to keep them off the ground cloth or even out of their blankets, no matter how tightly Delphine and Cyprian pegged down the tent's bottom. She got used to walking on them, an awful carpet, and leaving footprints of slime when she stepped into the shop. As for Roy, he slept half in the river some nights or on the starry banks, in grass, and all bugs left him alone, perhaps because his blood was eighty proof, said Delphine.

"You'd think the mosquitoes would bite him, at least, I mean, to get drunk themselves. Roy's a walking party bar," she complained one night, irritated that her father could sleep peacefully in that infested heat. She and Cyprian were sweating safely underneath their nets. Lying side by side, before they agreed to lose consciousness, they rolled the cotton wax between their fingers and argued over whether Cyprian should use the DeSoto to run some liquor out of Canada. Avoiding the slap of sales tax was not only a very common thing to do, it was patriotic if you were German, or supplied the liquor to them. No one had hated Prohibition like the Germans, who were convinced it was a law passed as a direct comment on their tradition of Zechkunst, the art of friendly drinking. Since Prohibition was over, heavy taxes on liquor were the new source of resentment and no one took such pleasure as Germans in thwarting the government. On a recent visit up north, even Tante had filled hot water bottles with whiskey and worn them as a bosom in her dress, smiling regally at the customs man as she sailed across the border.

"I'd rather stay legal," said Cyprian, "but the offer's good."

"That means I walk to work one whole week."

"That's not what gets you."

"Damn right."

"I will not, and I mean this," Cyprian said, propping himself up on one arm and staring at her intently, "get caught."

"Scares the hell out of me to think you would," Delphine offered.

"Does?"

"For what it's worth."

Even then, Cyprian just didn't feel like kissing her, but he loved her so much at that moment he nearly overcame his reluctance. It seemed to him that since the end of their traveling show, and since the house was cleaned and fumigated, things were slowing down to normal. He missed balancing, and the travel, but not the insecurity of where to perform and how to set up shows. He wanted things predictable but he also wanted something else. It was a problem with men who had come back from the war, he'd heard, normal wasn't good enough. They had to jack up every situation. Make it dangerous. Maybe he was like that. Or it could be that Delphine's job made him jealous. Not only because she was so tight with Clarisse and then Eva, but because she now bought everything, their food, their clothes, Roy's whiskey. He did feel as though the man should make the money.

"I'm gonna do it."

"Oh God," said Delphine.

"I'm not bad with a engine." Cyprian tried to placate her. "I learned a lot in the war. When I finish this, tell you what, I'll get a job. Maybe set myself up to fix automobiles."

"What do I tell the sheriff?"

"I'll get back here before he even knows. . . ."

His reassurance was cut off by Roy's wild hollering, and the two of them pushed aside their nets and jumped out of bed. Gingerly slipping along a rutted path, they made their way toward Roy's drinking camp down along the river. Delphine carried a small kerosene lamp that cast a pool of light just before them, so she was the first to see, when she reached the source of the panicked howls, why Roy was in hysterics. He had finally been discovered. The armyworms had come across him during a long drunken sleep, and they'd settled in, perhaps to feed on his clothing, or maybe just to rest on their way toward a banquet of leaves. His hair was packed. They dripped from his ears. Not a fraction of an inch of a wormless Roy was visible and he was, indeed, a supremely horrifying sight. So it was a surprise when at Delphine's voice he calmed down pathetically.

"I need a hair of the dog if you please," he said, blinking through a veil of strings of dripping worms. "I got the shakes, little daughter, got the deliriums. Need the whiskey. I know it's not real, but I could swear that worms are covering me."

"You'll be all right, Dad, just stand still," said Delphine, knocking pads of worms from his arms, his shoulders, and then tugging him forward. Cyprian clawed handfuls away, tried to comb the hordes from Roy's head, to shake them off his trousers and gently pluck them from his ears.

"Just stand still and you'll get your whiskey," he echoed Delphine.

"They're in your head," she told him, "stay still. They're all in your mind."

IT WAS TRUE that Cyprian was good with engines. By now, Delphine had totally revised her view of him and touted him to Eva as outstanding for his practical abilities. Repairing cars wasn't as satisfying to him as balancing, but still he had a knack for mechanical work. He babied the DeSoto, and it ran so clean it purred, as he said, like a kitten in a butter dish. Before he left the next day, to reassure Delphine, he did a free once-over on the shiny brown delivery car Eva was so proud of— *Waldvogel's Meats*, it said on the side. *The Freshest. The Finest. Old World Quality.*

Old World Quality. Eva was most proud of that, for it was true that in this country you could simply not get sausages prepared with the simplicity and perfection common in the German street. And she missed that. Other things, too, were impossible to find, she said, and when she said so she sounded a bit like Tante. Marzipan. Herring. Pickles with the right degree of spice. Rolls as soft. Down beds as deep. Fur as lustrous. Cream as thick.

Well, she often admitted, they couldn't do everything. They could only make the sausages. Pity about the bread, she often teased Fidelis. He had come to this country on the evidence of bread, machine bread, a slice of it sent in a package as an example of an everyday American marvel. He'd never tasted that preserved slice, of course. She despised the stuff— it was thin and salty. It crumbled. You could not get it fresh and it turned hard by noon if by chance you did. It wasn't real bread. The crusts were soft and the interior tough. Everything about the bread was backward, said Eva, so she made her bread herself. She sold loaves when she made extra, and sometimes pastries too, from a tall glass case that she rubbed transparent with a sheet of newsprint wetted with vinegar.

Eva prided herself on triumphing over anything that circumstance brought her way, yet she could not keep the butcher shop functioning in the heat with the efficiency she usually demanded. As the heat wave and the drought wore on, the glass collected steam and the counters and floors were slippery with melted grease. Everything was more difficult, for Delphine, too. Nights alone in the tent without Cyprian were unpleasant. It was harder to watch Roy destroy himself down by the river with two buddies who now slept with him in sour comfort. Delphine felt vulnerable in the open, and was afraid to plug her ears for fear one of the drunks might sneak up on her. So she endured the mad whining of the bugs until sleep took her and still, within sleep, she woke restlessly from time to time. It occurred to her that Cyprian had left in order to make her miss him. If so, enough. She did. They were like an old married couple, except that the romance of their youth had lasted about six hours. To get some sleep herself, and help out in the crisis, Delphine started sleeping on Eva's couch every two or three nights. Waking early, Delphine could put in a couple of hours cleaning before the crush of heat.

Now that she was around her friend from early morning on, Delphine could see how Eva suffered. Eva's face was pale with daily effort, and sometimes she declared she had to lie down, just for a minute, and rest. When Delphine checked on her, she found Eva in such a sunken dead shock of slumber that she hadn't the heart to wake her.

After an hour or two, anyway, Eva woke to a frenzy of energy and pushed herself again.

They mopped down the floors of the killing room with bleach every single day. The meat cases were run on full cold, yet they were lukewarm and the meat within had to be checked constantly for rot. A noisy generator was hooked up to power the meat locker and that thick-walled closet was jam-packed with all they were afraid to lose. They bought only the slightest amount of milk to sell because it often soured just from the drive to the store. The cream turned, too, but Eva tried to culture it and use it in her cooking. They stored almost no butter or lard. The heat hardened to a cruel intensity. The boys slept outside on the roof in just their undershorts. Eva dragged a mattress and sheets up there as well and slept with them while Fidelis slept downstairs.

As a gesture, perhaps, of reconciliation, the Kozkas gave Fidelis a dog. She was not a chow, for they'd had too many disappointments with the breed—Hottentot now ran wild, his offspring showed no respect for their masters, and all of his puppies sank their teeth into their buyers. The Kozkas had gone into a steadier line of dogs. They gave Fidelis a white German shepherd of ferocious energy. The dog roamed the down-stairs halls all night and chewed happily all day on great green bones. The dog immediately loved Eva like a sister, and though it was tied out-side the door most of the time, its ears pricked when she passed by in the house. When Eva freed the dog, it wildly bounded about, racing and leaping in astonishing arcs. When it had released its puppy nature, it walked gravely to Eva and stood near her. It didn't beg or gaze at her longing for scraps. The dog was very dignified and treated Eva as its peer. Clearly, the dog considered Eva her colleague, her mate in the task of protecting the dim-witted sheep, the men, from blundering into danger. Eva didn't pat the dog absently, but scratched the dog in places it couldn't reach. Even used an old hairbrush to untangle its fur when it matted. Delphine watched Eva look into the dog's eyes, listened to the way she crooned to it, and thought that her friend's behavior was re-markable. She'd never known anyone who thought that dogs were much. Eva's sensitivity to this animal, as well as the way she treated the outcasts and oddballs who came to the shop, including Step-and-a-Half, convinced Delphine that Eva was a person of rare qualities, and she loved her all the more.

Every day, the sky went dark, the dry heat sucked the leaves brown and nothing happened. Rain hung painfully near in the iron gray sheet stretched across the sky, but nothing moved. No breeze. No air. On the mornings she came from Roy's, Delphine walked through the back door sopping wet, washed her face, and donned the limp apron by the door. The air was already stiff and metallic. The dew burned off in moments. There was the promise of more heat. If it broke, it would break violent, Delphine thought as she filled a bucket. She didn't care how the heat broke—bring on the twister, bring on the volcano, the mighty wind of a hurricane—only make it cease.

She began stripping the wax off the linoleum on the floor in order to reapply a new coat. She had finished with that, and was about to open the shop, when out of the wringing wet-hot air walked Sheriff Hock.

Either it's news of the dead, thought Delphine, squeezing an ammonia-drenched rag out and draping it on the side of the bucket, or he wants to talk about Clarisse.

"Would it be better for me to visit you out at the house?"

For the moment, the place was silent.

"Nobody's here," said Delphine. "Go ahead."

As it happened, she entirely forgot about Eva's son Markus, up early in the heat as well. He was going over the books just on the other side of the counter. He was so quiet, his pencil moving among the columns of debts and credits. Young though he was, Eva had him check her work and he was proud to do it. Delphine was unnerved by the presence of the sheriff, or she might have remembered that Markus could hear all that was said. Maybe the heat, or a low level of panic, dulled her thoughts. She wanted to get the talking over with.

Sheriff Hock nodded sharply; his features pinched inside the frame of firm, thick fat. He removed a sharp pencil from a case in his pocket, and flipped a page over on the hard surface of his notepad. He had the exquisite budded lips of a courtesan, and when he spoke it was hard not to watch them move, just as a rose might if it were to speak. He told Delphine that he had a few questions, and since she was willing to answer them, he went down a predictable list. They were not particularly intrusive questions, having to do mainly with her life with Roy and Cyprian. Apparently, their answers matched up, because he seemed to take no exception to anything she said. Not until he came to a question about the red beads pasted into the floor of the pantry.

"Do you remember them, there in the pantry?"

"Of course I do." The quality of the brittle substance that sealed the cellar door shut was extremely memorable, and Delphine had wondered at that one particular ingredient.

"The stuff was so hard to chip that I wondered if it wasn't some kind of glue."

"I wondered the same," said Sheriff Hock, very solemnly. "I am currently having it tested in the state laboratory."

What state laboratory? thought Delphine, but she tried to humor him.

"Red beads, off a dress? Red beads at a wake?" she said with a dutifully mystified expression.

"Exactly."

"Have you asked my dad?"

"He's vague about it."

"He's . . . not well," said Delphine, coughing discreetly.

Sheriff Hock folded his notebook, tucked it underneath his arm, and took one of Eva's doughnuts from the glass case. The heat weighed on his bulk. He moved with a palpable weariness, and his shirt was darkened with sweat down the spine and below the arms. He ate the doughnut in tiny bites, lost in physical misery and abstract thinking, then he asked. "Where does your father obtain his whiskey?"

"I buy it for him," said Delphine.

"I don't mean the stuff you buy," the sheriff said. "I mean the supply he kept in the cellar."

"I don't know."

"Delphine, you're protecting him now," said Sheriff Hock, shaking his head. "I suspect that the answer to the tragedy lies in the fact that the cellar was littered with empty bottles."

"I suppose," said Delphine, seeing her ruse was useless, "he might have saved the bottles for Step-and-a-Half. She would resell them for home brew."

The sheriff nodded sagely. "Was your father a friend of the Chavers?"

"Well, you know he was, as well as I do," said Delphine.

"For the record," said the sheriff.

"Okay, yes, he was."

"Was he horrified? Shocked?"

Delphine became animated by the question, perhaps because she could rightly answer it. "What do you think? After he learned the Chavers' identities, my father was wild. You should have seen him. He pulled the last pathetic tufts of hair off his head and rolled around on the floor like a baby. Well, you know Roy. He kept howling something about believing the family had gone down to Arizona. I thought, you know, for the winter." Delphine finished in a subdued voice.

"Winter was nearly over when they were locked in."

Fidelis's voice boomed suddenly from down the hallway, and Sheriff Hock turned his attention away from Delphine. Much to her relief. For she was suddenly gripped with an anxiety for her father, and the fear that he had done something to set the deaths in his cellar into motion. Still, having already questioned him about the red beads and in some desperation asked him everything he knew or could think of about the three who died, she was at a loss. Roy Watzka had seemed as bewildered by the dead as anyone, entirely unprepared to provide any useful knowledge.

Fidelis and the sheriff went out back, humming the melody to a song they were complicating with contrasting harmonies, probably over a jar of Fidelis's dark, cold, homemade beer. Delphine's throat ached for a swig of it. Just as she bent over to squeeze out the mop again, Delphine heard a low rustle of paper, the creak of the chair at the desk in the corner, and she straightened up in time to see Markus stepping quietly away from the account books.

"You heard?"

Markus turned to look at Delphine. His thin cheeks had been recently and fiercely burned by the sun, and they still glowed hot red. In the long pause as he looked at her, Delphine gazed clearly back at Markus and saw in his face Eva's steel. He wouldn't speak. For some reason, Delphine was later to think, the boy knew all that was to come. He understood the future, knew why she was there, fathomed the reason that her place in his life would so drastically change. Knowing all of this, he was closed to her, sealed.

"You must be very smart," said Delphine. "You're only eight years old and your mother trusts you to check the accounts."

"I'm nine. She does the math," said Markus, poker-faced.

"But you are smart," Delphine persisted. His indifference was a challenge, and she wanted him at least to admit what he'd just heard, if only so that she could prepare Eva for any questions that he might have. "You're a smart boy, so you know that the sheriff was asking me questions only to figure out the truth."

Markus now looked down at the floor.

"I didn't do anything!" Delphine blurted out, surprising herself. It was only after Markus turned back to her and stared from the perfect mixture of the greens and blues of his mother's and father's eyes that she realized that the boy in the cellar was his age and that of course Markus must have known him.

"Your friend's name," said Delphine, softly now, stepping toward him. "What was it?"

Beneath the raw sunburn, the boy's face went white. What the question did to him astonished Delphine. His face turned to paper and his eyes burned. He blinked. He opened his mouth, passionately miserable.

"Ruthie," he croaked. "Ruthie Chavers."

Then he whirled and ran down the long hall, banged his way out into the white heat of the yard. Delphine stood there a moment, stunned. Ruthie! The girl's name and the new information that she had, so far, avoided hit her. To escape her thoughts, she started using a scraper on the floor, gently scratching away at the places where the old wax had yellowed or clumped. As she worked the white squares whiter, she felt a numb satisfaction. The colored squares unstreaked and became again the original innocent green. As she moved with an increased dedication, the girl's name tapped in and out of her mind. Ruthie. Ruth. Ruth meant mercy, Delphine knew. Yet not one bit of mercy had been shown to her. Delphine might have imagined that to find out that the child in the cellar was a girl would have struck her a blow, increased the unbearable mental picture of that suffering. But it didn't, in the end, and at this Delphine wondered. The floor was drying before she found the explanation in her own heart.

Her inner reasoning surprised her, mystified her, then depressed her. She found that she harbored a belief that girls were stronger and more enduring. Therefore more tough-minded about even such an unexpectedly evil destiny. And needful of less sympathy. A girl child would have a certain fatalism about the event. She would accept the end of her life, and merely sleep as much as possible until she fell asleep forever. Oddly, the closer Delphine identified with the girl's suffering, the more she thought about it, the less sorry she felt for Ruthie Chavers. It was, in fact, as though she herself had sat in that cellar, endured the hunger, then the thirst, then weakened to the point of delirium, and froze, all in a dream.

And died in her mother's arms, she thought, her mother's arms. Then customers began arriving, and Delphine put on a clean apron.

At the end of the day, Delphine turned the cardboard sign in the entry window over from Open to Closed. She went over the floor again to take off the day's footprints. She let the floor dry, and then, in a special bucket, she mixed up floor wax and with a long brush painted the floor, back to front, in perfect swipes. She painted herself right up to the counter, put a box in the entry so that the boys would not ruin the drying surface. She retreated. Hung up her apron, said a quick goodbye, and went home to swelter in the tent, alone. Early next morning, before the store opened she'd return and apply another coat. Let it dry while she drank her morning coffee with Eva. Then between customers she'd polish that linoleum to a mighty finish with a buffing rag and elbow grease. That's what she planned, anyway, and all that she planned did occur, but over weeks of time and under radically different circumstances.

ALREADY THE NEXT MORNING, while Delphine sat in the kitchen with the second coat of wax drying, the heat pushed at the walls. She was pleased because Eva had looked at the floor and declared it brand-new again. The strong black Turkish coffee sent Delphine into a sweat. She drank from a pitcher of water that Eva set on the table and blotted at her throat and temples with a dish towel.

"*Kuchmal hier*," Eva had been awake most of the night, doing her weekly baking in the thread of cool air. "I am not so good."

She said this in such an offhand way that Delphine hardly registered the words, and only answered with a moan of sympathy that somehow included herself, in this heat, waxing floors. But then Eva repeated herself exactly the same way, as though she did not remember what she'd said. "I am not so good," Eva whispered again. She put her elbows on the table and curled her hands around the china cup. Her silence, as though she was listening for some deeper tone or word in the ordinary sounds around them, disquieted Delphine and she watched alertly as Eva stared into the oily depths of the liquid.

"What do you mean, you don't feel so good?"

"It's my stomach. I am all lumped up." Beads of sweat trembled on Eva's upper lip. "Pains come and go."

"Is it cramps?" asked Delphine.

"It's not that, or maybe." Eva drew a deep breath and then held it, let it out. There. She took Delphine's dish towel and pressed it to her face, dragged it off as though to remove her expression. She was breathing hard. "Like a cramp, but I never am quit the monthly . . . comes and goes, too."

"Maybe you're just stopping early?"

"I think yes," said Eva. "My mother . . ." But then she shook her head and smiled wide, spoke in a high, thin abnormal voice. "Crying and whining is all forbidden here with me!"

Eva jumped up. Awkwardly, she banged herself against the counter, but then she bustled to the oven, moved swiftly all through the kitchen as though unending motion would cure whatever gripped her. Within moments, she seemed to have turned back into the unworried, capable Eva. She lifted two great pans of rolls out of the oven. She wielded a spatula and quickly emptied the pans. Then she pushed dough through the round of her thumb and first finger, filled two more pans and popped them back in the oven to bake. Delphine watched her in concern, but then relaxed. There was no trace of weakness in that series of swift and economical motions.

"I'm going out front and start polishing the floor," said Delphine. "By now in this heat it's surely dry."

"Very good," said Eva, but as Delphine passed her to put her coffee cup in the gray soapstone sink, the wife of the butcher touched one of Delphine's hands. Lightly, her voice a shade too careless, she said the words that even in the heat chilled her friend.

"Take me to the doctor."

Then Eva smiled as though this was a great joke, and she lay down on the floor, closed her eyes, and did not move.

FIDELIS HAD ALREADY gone out to look at stock with a farmer, and he could not be found when Delphine returned from Doctor Heech's house. By then, she had Eva drugged with morphine in the backseat of the delivery car, and a sheaf of medical orders in her hands stating whom to seek, what possibly could be done. Furious and sorrowing, Doctor Heech was telephoning down to the clinic and speaking with a surgeon he knew, telling him to prepare for a patient named Eva Waldvogel, who was suffering from a tumor that pressed immediately on her vitals and would cause her death within days if not removed.

Fidelis gone, Franz and the little boys at a ball game, only Markus was home to take the message.

"I will write a note," said Delphine, his mother's suitcase at her feet. "Make sure that your father gets it. I am taking your mother to the doctor."

Markus handed her a piece of paper, dropped it, picked it up, his lithe boy's fingers for once clumsy with fright. He ran straight out to the car and crawled into the backseat, which was where Delphine found him, stroking Eva's hair as she sighed in the fervent relief of the drug. She was so pleasantly composed that Markus was reassured and Delphine was able to lead him carefully away, afraid that Eva would suddenly wake, before the boy, into recognition of her pain. From what Delphine had gathered so far, Eva must have been hiding a substantial suffering for many months now. Her illness was dangerously advanced, and Heech in his alarm as well as his care for Eva, for he was fond of her, scolded her in the despair of a doctor wrathful at his helplessness.

"You should have had the brains to come to me," he said over and over. "You should have come to me."

As she led Eva's son to the house, Delphine tried to stroke Markus's hair. He jerked away in terror at the unfamiliar tenderness. It was, of course, a sign to him that something was truly, desperately, wrong with his mother. Delphine snatched her hand back and spoke offhandedly as she could. Markus, his face and neck flushed brightly, did not look at her, mumbled something she couldn't make out, and was gone.

Delphine finished her note for Fidelis:

> *I have taken Eva to the clinic south of the Cities called the Mayo, where Heech says emergency help will be found. She passed out this morning. It is a cancer. You can talk to Heech and make your own way down when things are arranged in the shop. Find Cyprian Lazarre if you can. Maybe he'll be out in the tent on my dad's land. Lazarre is a good man and can manage things.*

ON THE DRIVE DOWN to the Mayo Clinic, Delphine first heard the butcher sing, only it was in her mind. She replayed it like a comforting record on a phonograph, as she kept her foot evenly on the gas pedal of the truck and calmly caused the speedometer to hover right near one hundred miles per hour. The world blurred. Fields turned like spoked wheels. She caught the flash of houses, cows, horses, barns. Then there was the long stop and go of the city. All through that drive, she replayed the song that she hadn't really listened to Fidelis sing just the morning before in the stained concrete of the slaughtering room. She had been too crushed by the heat to marvel at the buoyant mildness of his tenor. His singing, at the time, hardly registered. Now she heard it. *"Die Gedanken sind Frei,"* he sang, and the walls spun each note higher as beneath the dome of a beautiful church. Who would think a slaughterhouse would have the sacred acoustics of a cathedral? Fidelis was practicing his pieces for the men's chorus, those he'd learned back in Germany, when he'd belonged to the Gesangverein.

The song wheeled in her thoughts, and using what ragtag German she knew, Delphine made out the words, *"Die Gedanken sind frei, wer kann sie erraten, Sie fliehen vorbei wie nächtliche Schatten."* The mind is free . . . thoughts like shadows of the night. . . . The dead crops turned row by row in the fields, the vent blew the hot air hotter, and the wind boomed in the rolled-down windows. Even when it finally started to rain, Delphine did not roll the windows back up. They were moving so fast that the drops stung like BBs on the side of her face. The fierce drops kept her alert. She knew that occasionally, behind her, Eva made sounds. Perhaps the morphine as well as dulling her pain loosened her self-control, for in the wet crackle of the wind Delphine heard a high-pitched icy moan that could have belonged to Eva. A scream like the shriek of tires. A growling as though her pain were an animal that she wrestled to earth.

SIX

The Night Garden

EVERY BUG LAST summer's drought killed or dried up had laid sacs and sacs of eggs destined to hatch this June. Delphine and Eva sat together on broken chairs in Eva's garden, each with a bottle of Fidelis's earth-dark home-brewed beer held tight between their feet. Delphine wore a wash dress and apron, Eva wore a nightgown and a light woolen shawl. The slugs were naked. Tough curls of antlered jelly, with many young, the slugs lived in the thickness of hay and shredded newspapers that Eva had put down for mulch. They had already eaten many of the new seedlings from the tenderest topmost leaves down to the ground, and Eva had vowed to destroy them.

"The last feast," said Eva, gesturing at her bean plants as she dribbled a little beer into the pie plate. "Now they are doomed."

The beer was chill from the glass refrigerator case in the store, newly installed, for Fidelis was one of the first Argus merchants to obtain a liquor license. From time to time, distantly, the doorbell jangled as customers straggled in for an item or two. It was dinnertime and there were no real shoppers. Franz could handle them. Eva poured the top quarter of the next bottle into her mouth before she poured a little more into the pie plate that she had buried level with the ground. It seemed a shame to waste the coldness of the beer on pests.

Slowly, the two women sipped the rich, bitter stuff as the sun slanted through the margins of the stock pens. The tin siding of the cooler gave off heat, and they smelled the scorched brown vines of last year's blue grapes.

"Maybe we should simply have shriveled these creatures with salt," said Delphine. But then she had a thought: We are close to Eva's own death, and can afford to make death easy on the helpless. She said nothing, but did touch Eva's hand. Since Eva's illness had taken this turn, Fidelis had slaughtered twice a week, worked round the clock to make the doctor bills. The loamy soil inside the stock pens, enriched with shit and fear, churned with growing power. The margins already sprouted weeds so thick and vigorous they looked as though they could pull up their roots like skirts and vault the fence. Here, however, thought Delphine, sipping at her bottle, there would not be all that much room for them to live.

Eva's garden, Delphine had decided, reflected the dark underside of her organizational genius. The garden was everything raw and wild that Eva's house was not. It had grown rich on junk. Pot scrapings, tea leaves, and cucumber peelings all went into the dirt, buried haphazardly, sometimes just piled. Everything rotted down beneath the blistering North Dakota sun. And then the seeds in the garbaged cucumbers, the pumpkin rinds, and even the old tomatoes volunteered themselves in scattered flourishes. Her method was to have no method. Give nature its way. She had apple trees that grew from cores here. Rosebushes, bristling near the runnel that collected steers' blood, were covered with blooms so fat and hearty they looked sinister. Eva's favorite flower was the marigold, and she headed them in fall and scattered their seeds everywhere. The high tang of their foliage was in the air. Birds too. She fed them oatmeal.

So far in life, Delphine had never gardened, never bothered to attract birds, never known to care about things that her friend turned into rituals. Since she'd known Eva Waldvogel, and also traveled here and there with Cyprian, she had started to understand how a woman's attention could succeed in making sense of man's blind chaos, and yet women needed their own wildness. It was here. All ran riot. The garden and weedy yard would wax fuller until it turned into a jungle of unhitched vines and rusty birdbaths made of ham tins. Eva's dog, the white shepherd, Schatzie, dug up old bones the former dog had buried and refused to rebury them. It would be awful, Delphine felt, when the leaves withered in the fall, to see the litter of femurs and clavicles, the knobs and knuckles. As if the scattered dead, rising to meet the Judgment, had to change and swap their parts to fit. Until then, the broad leaves would hide the bones the dog had spread through creation.

Delphine's tendency to dwell on fate was triggered constantly by Eva's sickness. Mortality was always before her, and she marveled how anyone lived at all, for any amount of time. Life was a precious feat of daring, she saw, improbable as Cyprian balancing, strange as a feast of slugs.

Eva bent over, flipped out a small pocket of earth with her trowel, and tamped in her quarter-full beer bottle as a trap. "Die happy," she encouraged. Delphine handed her own three-fourths-drunk bottle, too. This one Eva planted by a hill of squash that would overpower all the rest of the garden by fall, though she would not see it. Great, lumpy, hybrid Hubbards would roll out from under the green pads of leaves. Delphine would harvest them, piling the warty, irregular globes beside the back door, then packing them in hay. Eva settled against the crisscrossed canvas webbing of her chair, forked open another bottle. It was a good day, a very good day for her.

The sun's last rays were warm and the breeze was strong enough to keep off the deerflies and mosquitoes. Delphine's head began to feel big and wobbly on her neck. But light. It seemed to balloon above the rest of her. The plants looked fresh. The garden flourished green. Delphine's continual watering had swelled the hollyhocks in bud that gently batted Eva's walls. Her columbines spread full as bushes, trailing complicated spikes. The sharp yellow marigold blossoms spiced the air. Why shouldn't life surge forth, thought Delphine, get better?

"There is no hope," Eva said as though her friend had spoken all she thought out loud, "because there's just too damn many, and they're too dumb to find the bottles anyway."

Unseen, mysterious, the young had moved onto the leaves, almost translucent. They did not seem so much living things as bits of jelled fluid. They were voracious. On some of the leaves, the tough veins alone were left, lacework outlines. It was only the richness of Eva's garden that salvaged it from ruin. There was simply too much for them to devour. And now, from the edges of the grass, from underneath stones and drainpipes and out of the tiles of the gutters, moved snakes. The black ribbon snakes were striped with hot orange, liquid green, and their bellies were pale gold as melted butter. Delphine thought she heard them sliding through the seams of the boiling earth and knew they uncoiled from beneath the hot clumps of straw and hay. Snakes were everywhere, feeding on the tiny slugs; a toad hopped into the waning light blinking its old-woman wrinkled eyes.

"I'm going," said Delphine, but she continued to sit with Eva through sunset and on into the rising dark. It was as though they knew that no peace would be in their lives through the next weeks and that they both would, in fearful nights, remember these hours. How the air turned blue around them and the moths came out, invisible and sightless, flapping against the shuttered lamp at the other end of the yard. They were protected by citronella burning in a bucket, and sprigs of basil, which Eva had snapped off and thrust into their hair. Eva's feet were cool in thin leather sandals. Delphine's gripped the moist, fetid earth.

On a calm night, after work, after she had settled Eva, Delphine would normally have returned to the house she shared with Cyprian and Roy. She would have lost herself in a book, or cooked something to relax, or fixed whatever she could find that needed repair in the house. But tonight she was unfamiliar to herself and did not move. She let the beer wear off gently as the night grew deeper, thicker, black all around them. They were silent. Nothing occurred to them to talk about and at last each beer bottle was planted. They were not waiting for anything particular to happen. Time went by, and yet they did not stir. They had no thoughts, except that Delphine imagined all the bones were hitching in the ground. The dog moaned in its sleep by Eva's foot, and Delphine's eyes shut.

When she shut her eyes, her mind grew alert. Her senses opened. All around her, she felt how quickly things formed and were consumed. How there was so much blind feeling. It was going on beyond the wall of her sight, out of her control. Unheard, unnoticed, the blood dropped into her hands and feet, so that she was anchored. Which she was glad for, because the light was so feeble and the blackness so strong that she felt as though she could drift away like a boat of skin, never to return, leaving only her crumpled dress.

"I wish it is true, what I read, that the mind stays put. The eyes. The brain to read with."

She heard Eva's voice.

Delphine had sometimes thought that her friend didn't care if she became an animal or a plant, if her heart was cycled into the kingdom of nutrients, if all of this thinking and figuring and selling of pork and blood meal was wasted effort. Eva had treated her death with offhand scorn or ridicule, but with that statement she revealed a certain fear she'd never shown before. Or a wishfulness. Her words cut Delphine deeply with an instant sorrow.

"Your mind stays itself," said Delphine, as lightly as she could, "so there you'll be, strumming on your harp, looking down on all the foolish crap people do."

"I could never play the harp," said Eva, "I think they'll give me a damn kazoo."

"Save me a cloud and I'll play a tune with you," said Delphine.

"It's a deal," said Eva, "and you bring your handsome husband. Think you can persuade him?"

They laughed too hard, they laughed until tears started in their eyes, then they gasped and fell utterly silent. For a long time, now, they'd both pretended to believe in a ridiculous heaven, and promised to meet on its grassy slopes.

FOR ALL THAT he was a truly unbearable souse, no one in town disliked Roy Watzka. There were several reasons. First, his gross slide into abandon was caused by loss. That he repeatedly claimed to have loved to the point of self-destruction fed a certain reflex feature in many a female heart, and he got handouts easily when strapped. Women even made him lunches, a sandwich of pork or cold beans, and wrapped it carefully for him to eat coming off a binge. Next reason was that Roy Watzka, during those short, rare times that he was sober, had the capacity for intense bouts of hard labor. He could work phenomenally, doing what he did best, farmwork, and he was happy doing it. He'd milk or pitch out stalls or stack hay out of sheer spiritual guilt, and sometimes he'd take no pay hoping to ensure his next liquor source but also creating the sense that he was, in his own way, generous. And whatever his condition he told a good tale, which drew people. Nor was he a mean drunk or a rampager, and it was well-known that although she certainly put up with more than a daughter ever should have to, he did love Delphine.

Eva liked him, or felt sorry for him anyway, and she was one of those who had always given him a meal when he came around her kitchen. Now that she was in trouble, Roy showed up at the butcher shop for a different purpose. He came almost every afternoon, sometimes stinking of sweat-out schnapps. But once there, he'd do anything. Work dog hard. He'd move the outhouse to the new hole he'd dug for it, shovel guts. Before he left, he'd sit with Eva and tell her crazy stories about the things that had happened to him as a young man in the gold fields or the pet hog he'd trained to read or other things: how to extract the venom from a rattlesnake, an actual wolf man he knew and words in the Lycanthropian language, or the Latin names of flowers and where they came from, recipes for exquisite wines and what the French did with the vinasse. Listening sometimes, Delphine was both glad for Roy's adept distractions and resentful. She knew he was a fountain of odd bits of knowledge. Where had he learned these things? In bars, he said, and out of the battered dictionary that was the only book in the house until Delphine grew old enough to acquire books herself. Yet, she'd cleaned up after him all of her life, and never had he sat and talked to her like this, with such gravity and kindness, such a goodwilled attempt to distract and entertain. Worst of all, his efforts almost convinced Delphine that there was hope for him.

POUTY MANNHEIM HAD developed a fascination with flight, bought a war-surplus Jenny, and spent his spare time fiddling with her engine or practicing rolls and dives and fancy curlicue maneuvers. He liked to buzz low over the shop, waving down at the boys. Fidelis had given him leave to land in the flat field behind the house, and every time he did so Franz threw off his apron and raced out. As soon as Pouty emerged and walked to the house to visit, Franz climbed into the cockpit. He didn't do anything while Mannheim talked to his father, except run his hands over the controls and examine the official-looking log that Mannheim kept of his flights, his fueling, his hours in the air. And when Pouty Mannheim returned, Franz proudly and eagerly acted as what he imagined was a sort of ground crew, turning the prop, uttering the stand-clear. As the plane made its run, gathering speed, the sway of it triggered an excitement Franz didn't understand in himself. He was a reserved boy, but when the plane began to move he always ran, chased it, shouted, threw his cap after the plane when it lifted from the field. There was something about the actual moment that the flimsy-looking wheels left earth, seeing the space between ground and the craft itself enlarge, that dazzled him, filled him with a sense he could never have described, not in the language of his mother and father or in the language of his schoolmates; it was a wordless, wild, tremendous, unbearably physical release of tension that left him almost in tears.

After Pouty had disappeared into the sky, Franz stood very still for a few minutes, quietly gathering himself, before he dared face other people. His mother was the only person, he felt, who even remotely understood what he experienced when the airplane left the ground. In her illness, she had become a grateful listener and he sometimes found himself after Mannheim's visits sitting long with her and talking on and on, as he did with no one else, about the various makes of aircraft and their advantages one over the other, their disparities, all of the quirks and details that he collected from newspapers and magazines. He had a stack of papers, and pictures carefully cut and pasted on the wall around his bed. There was a detailed and graceful Fokker Eindekker, a black cross on its wings and tail, and blurred photos of Immelmann, the Eagle of Lille, of Rickenbacker and "the Ace of Aces," a recent news photo of Charles Lindbergh, and the badges and emblems of the RAF. A homemade banner that read "Beware the Hun in the Sun," and a laboriously copied poem called "The Young Aviator." Franz had drawn a fashionable French Nieuport 11 fighter with its machine gun mounted over the pilot and a screaming Indian chief painted on the hull. His favorite was the Albatros, a German fighter with a big red nose, a heart, a white swastika, and the usual black cross. He had modeled a Sopwith Camel of cardboard and pins, drawn its red, white, and blue bull's-eye carefully with crayons he'd swiped from school. Eva had given him a huge scrapbook and in it he'd pasted news of barnstormers and their photos cut carefully from the newspaper or saved from posted handbills. He read descriptions of their tricks out loud to her when she was restless. On one of these afternoons, while he sat with her, she asked, "What do you think it's like, I mean, over the clouds?"

"Oh, I can tell you that," said Franz. "It looks like you could step right onto them and bounce."

She regarded him skeptically, but with a kind of pride that he could invent such a thing. Which is when it suddenly struck him that he had to go up into the air with his mother.

"We're going to fly," he announced to her right there, and the look of wondering pleasure that crossed her face at the idea convinced him that he had to make it come true.

Pouty had to fly them, he decided, even though Fidelis had forbidden that he ever take Franz with him on his flights. This was different.

This was a ride with a noble purpose. Very quickly the impulse he had to take his mother in the air became an urgent and serious commitment. He thought, staring at Eva, that there were some things that simply had to happen. She had to go into the sky. He had to be there when she did, even though they wouldn't see over the clouds. He went to bed with the conviction, and the next day, working next to his father, all he could think of was how to persuade Pouty Mannheim to take them up in his airplane.

POUTY KEPT HIS PLANE in a barn north of town, a good long walk from the house, and Franz had to make an excuse to go find Pouty right away because he didn't know when he'd happen by. And Franz's sense was this had to happen now, not that he anticipated in his mind how terribly his mother would weaken. He borrowed Mazarine Shimek's bicycle, even though it was a girl's bicycle, and he pedaled the miles quickly. He felt such a stern compulsion about the project that when he talked to Pouty, he couldn't help his voice from rising, his hands from moving, and even from pleading and harassing Pouty once he trundled away to grab a tool he needed from the barn.

"She's sick," Pouty finally said, scrubbing at his round apple-shiny chin.

"That's why," said Franz.

"Fidelis won't let her," said Pouty.

"Which is why you can't tell him," said Franz.

Although Pouty Mannheim wasn't especially thoughtful or even interested in most people other than himself, and although he had very little experience of affection for his own mother, something in the way Franz behaved impressed him. He thought it over while he checked his controls, tightened his equipment, and replaced a bit of paint on the body of his plane, and then he said yes.

EARLY ON THE DAY that Fidelis made his deliveries, Pouty landed his plane in the field behind the shop. It was warm already, and the sky was very blue, but not with that oppressive and metallic blueness that signaled a dust storm. The day was milder than in quite some time, and a fugitive freshness still lingered in the grass, in the leaves, the taste of early dew. Franz ran into his mother's room, quieted himself, and touched her arm. She was awake and already dressed for the ride in a gauzy white housedress with full-blown roses all over it, some pink, some a deeper red in the creases of the petals. Delicate leaves of a subdued green floated everywhere in the folds of the material. Her hair, damaged by the treatments, sprang short and fine off her head in curls of fluff. She'd shakily put on a light coat of lipstick and gargled, he noticed, with a sweet-scented lilac water. Some days her breath smelled of a sad cellar rot, from what was happening inside, she said, and she hated it. She liked to keep very clean. Her eyes were beautiful, Franz thought, slanting green in her thin and paper-white face.

"Mama," he said, shy and proud, "your plane's here."

"Hilf mir," she said, eagerly turning to him, and he helped her straighten her legs and sit on the side of the bed. She smoothed back her hair and then rose, weak, and put one foot and then the next into her lace-up brown leather shoes. She was breathing deeply, to gather strength and also to contain her excitement. The other boys were out in the front of the store with Delphine, who'd been taken into the plan and who had pledged to distract them long enough for the two to get out to Pouty's airplane. Eva tried to step along, not shamble, as she walked beside Franz, but as they made their way into the side yard he stopped her.

With a huge sweep of his arms, he scooped her up and simply carried her out into the field. She laughed with surprise, then put her arm around his neck, thinking to herself, My son, my little son. And when they reached the plane and he carefully set her inside, in the seat behind the pilot, she thought of the boy's father, and realized that when she'd known Johannes he'd not been much older than Franz was now. And the thought pierced her with sorrow for that boy she'd known, and wonder at all that had happened since his death, things that would have so astonished him, and she couldn't help think of heaven and question just how it would be if those assurances of her priest were actually true. Would Johannes really be standing there, on the other side, with all of the dead of her own family, to greet her? How old would he be? And then, what would she say, and what would happen on that day in the future when Fidelis entered heaven as well? Which one would she stay with?

Father Clarence was absolutely stumped on this issue, and Eva enjoyed shaking his confidence. Eva smiled and let the sun hit her face full on as Pouty climbed into the front. Franz spun the propeller mightily and then, when the engine caught, and the body of the plane shook like a wet dog, Franz jumped into the space just behind Eva's seat and grabbed her around the waist.

"Are you holding her in?" yelled Pouty.

"Got her!"

The machine jerked forward. With a bounding rush, an eager gathering of speed and a quickening of power, they hopped into the air. Franz filled his mouth with the wind. He let the moment balloon inside of him. And then he flew, for the first time, holding on to his mother's waist. They rose in what seemed an impossibly steep climb and forgot to breathe, then Pouty calmed down and leveled off and flew due west with the sun behind them. He wanted to fly up along the river, scare up a few herons and maybe some fish hawks for Eva to see. Over the course of the night, as he'd contemplated the ride for Eva, he'd decided it made a sort of hero out of him to give this dying woman the pleasure of a ride. He would explain it to Fidelis later as a duty of some sort— he hadn't worked it out yet, but anyway he was quite sure that when Eva landed with pink cheeks and feeling all that much improved, Fidelis would be glad. In fact, Pouty went even further and imagined that the plane ride might result in a complete medical cure. Such things had happened, and such was his faith in the power of flight.

Perhaps Franz possessed a similar faith, because as he held his mother in the seat he imagined that the wind, whipping the skin flat across their faces, was scouring them smooth and pure as they buzzed down along the gleaming gray snake of the river. They gained altitude and the water became a string of mercury, the dusty green trees puffs beside, the roads black threads in the drought-sick fields. They bounced over the hot drifts of air, turned gently when the river shifted, circled an oxbow, and swooped down low over a farm where Mannheim knew the people. They saw all there was to see and flew until Pouty yelled he was getting low on fuel and must go back to the field. All the while she'd waited for the flight, Eva had the hope that during it, because of the thrill of it, her pain would vanish. That did not exactly happen—in some ways the pain grew more intense, but that was because the joy had, too, not just the physical joy of being up in the sky, she would later tell Delphine, but the mental joy.

AFTER THE TWO had come back to earth and Franz had carried her to bed, Eva had one of her final visions. She was propped up with pillows, drinking sips of water, shuddering with happiness and pain.

"Up in the sky, my brain was gulping new air," she said to Delphine, "I am thinking so fast and furious. I see things."

"What things?"

"*Zum beispiel,*" Eva said, "this Argus was only a spot. We are spots. Spots in the spot. No matter. We specks are flying on our own power. We are not blown up there by wind! What does this inform you?"

She grabbed Delphine's arm, her hand still had a strong grip. Delphine shook her head. "What?"

"There is plan, *eine grosse Idee,* bigger than the whole damn rules. And I always known it. Bigger than the candles in church. Bigger than confessionals, bigger than the Sacred Host." She crossed herself. "I do not know what it is. But big. Much more big."

Then she had Delphine call all of her sons into the room, and she spoke to them, too, and she told them that she had seen something very reassuring and that it didn't have to do with church, even the One True Church. It didn't have to do with taking communion or getting confirmed by the bishop.

"It don't matter if you do these things now," she said impatiently. "If you must need them, do them. But the plan is greater I am telling you. The plan knows the huge thing, and it accounts for the little fingernail." Eva raised her pinkie in the air and held it out between them. Her eyes were just a bit glazed, and glittering with dangerous emerald lights. "If

I die, don't take this too hard," she counseled them, "death is only part of things bigger than we can imagine. Our brains are just starting the greatness, to learn how to do things like flying. What next? You will see, and you will see that your mother is of the design. And I will always be made of things, and things will always be made of me. Nothing can get rid of me because I am already included into the pattern."

Her cheeks now took on just that suffusing rose color that Pouty had imagined his ride would inspire. She took a big gulp of water, coughed a little, and then abruptly her eyes shut. Franz reached forward after a moment, terrified and curious, and touched her face. "She's sleeping," said Franz, his fingers touching her lips. He gently shoved his younger brothers out. If she had died in that moment, it would have been a perfect piece of drama, thought Delphine from the doorway. Maybe Eva even wanted to, but maybe she stopped herself, knowing that to die immediately after that plane ride would get Franz in trouble.

"THE BOYS ARE PLAYING in the orchard. The men are already half lit," Delphine reported to Eva, who smiled faintly and struggled onto her elbows. Delphine helped her sit up and look out the window. She fell back, exhausted, nodding at the sight. The two women could hear the men singing, working their way through a set of patriotic songs, one after the next. Sheriff Hock was particularly good on the high parts of "The Star-Spangled Banner." His voice splintered eerily through the bright, heated air, giving Delphine chills.

"Men are so much fools," Eva whispered. "They think they are so smart hiding the Everclear in the gooseberry bush."

Even though the last few days had been nightmarish, Eva still refused to die in a morbid way and even preferred to suffer in a fashion that was strangely hilarious. She laughed freakishly at pain sometimes and made fun of her condition, more so now when the end was close. Delphine would later believe that the purchase of the chinchillas was a sign of that fast downhill turn. The way Eva got up on one of her last good days, sneaking the delivery truck out to the farm of a strange old biddy, and returning with the creatures. Now, beyond the men, who were drinking underneath the clothesline, the thick-furred things panted, stinking gently in their flimsy network of cages.

Delphine sat beside her friend in the little room off the kitchen, a room filled with jars of canning. That was where Eva had asked Fidelis to set up her bed. A good-size window looked out of that room into the backyard, which was her reason for wanting to die in that tiny place. From there, she could watch the boys complete her chinchilla-money-making scheme. They had constructed the cages out of wire netting salvaged from other people's failed coops, and pounded together nesting boxes out of scrap lumber. It was a diversion, Delphine thought now, with sudden understanding. Watching her friend drift into a short nap, she suddenly realized that the odd, rabbity creatures were a clever way to take the boys' attention off their dying mother.

They'd closed the shop at noon for July 4. Now everyone in town was celebrating. Fidelis had the old chairs and table out there, and on the table he had laid out beer sausage and summer sausage, a watermelon, and bowls of crackers. Beer bottles sweat in a tub of ice underneath the tomato plants, beer to wash down the high-proof alcohol that Eva already knew they were hiding. It was funny, watching them sneak their arms into the gooseberry fronds and snake out the bottle. With a furtive look at the house, they tipped it to their lips. Even Fidelis, so powerful and purposed, acted like a guilty boy.

Delphine watched Cyprian stroll through the rickety back gate. Laughing, he set his own offering beside the sausages. Aged whiskey, probably from a recent border trip. Cyprian was an occasional visitor ever since he'd run the store that first week, when Fidelis and Delphine were down at the Mayo consulting with the doctors. He did all right with the store and nothing disappeared, so Fidelis wanted to hire him, but Cyprian said the meat business wasn't for him. He'd had enough blood and guts in the war. Anyway, he was much better at running liquor and it paid better, he told Delphine, who didn't like it but what was she to do since the car was half his and he was after all a grown man?

He had joined the singing club, though his voice was average. A slightly singed baritone. And he had set himself up to look like a traveling salesman. He even had samples of his supposed wares—hair-brushes, floor brushes, dog fur brushes, horse brushes, long broom brushes, potato brushes—stashed in his car to foil the inspectors at the border and answer the questions of neighbors. Sometimes they bought the brushes, too. Mainly, he was paid by criminals. Dangerous men out of Minneapolis. Delphine not only didn't like that he took the risk, but hated that he dealt in the despised substance. Still, as he didn't drink it much himself for fear of losing his balancing skills, which he still practiced between runs, she let it go. Besides, she was caught up in helping Eva die.

There was no saving her, they were well beyond that now. The first treatment, after her surgery, consisted of inserting into her uterus hollow metal bombs, cast of German silver, containing radium. Over the weeks Eva spent in the hospital the tubes were taken out, refilled, and put back several times. Once she was sent home, she smelled like a blackened pot roast.

"I smell burned," she said, "like bad cooking. Get some lilac at the drug-store." And Delphine had bought a great purple bottle of flower water to wash her with, but it hadn't helped much. For days, she'd passed charcoal and blood, and the roasted smell lingered. Also, the treatment hadn't worked. The cancer spread. Doctor Heech then gave her monthly treat-ments of radium via long twenty-four-carat gold needles, tipped with irid-ium, that he pushed into the new tumor with a forceps so as not to burn his fingers. She took those treatments in his office on Sundays, strapped to a table, dosed with ether for the insertion, then after she woke, a hy-podermic of morphine. Doctor Heech became so angry at himself when he gave her the treatments, which he feared were useless, that he left the room cursing under his breath. Delphine stayed to sit with her, for the needles had to stay in place for six hours. Threaded with black waxed string, they made a spoked wheel poking into her stomach.

"I'm a damn pincushion now," Eva said once, rousing slightly. Then she dropped back into her restless dream. Delphine read, or dozed and knitted, for she couldn't always read. It was the old thing happening, as with the drunks and her childhood neighbors. Again she witnessed great suffering she could not stop. This time her body tried to share the agony: shooting pains in her own stomach as the needles went in, even a sympathetic morphine sweat. A bleak heaviness that accompanied Eva's passages of charcoaled flesh. Dull aches that overcame her sometimes and made her want to lie down forever and be done with things. But she kept on going, never let up, never showed her sorrowing pains. As she approached the house now, each day, she said the prayer to God she used as the most appropriate to the situation.

"Spit in your eye."

Her curse wasn't much, it didn't register the depth of her feeling, but at least she was not a hypocrite. Why should she even pretend to pray? That was Tante's field—she'd mustered a host of pious Lutheran ladies and they come around every few afternoons to try to do their business on a Catholic. When Eva became too weak to chase them off, Delphine tried, but as her position was inferior to Tante's own she had great trouble at it and used other strategies, whatever she could think of, to keep them from crowding around the bed like a flock of turkey vultures and pressing together their bony claws in a gloating, sucking prayer circle. Even now, Delphine thought, she'd bake a sugar cake while Eva was sleeping, in case the mealy-mouths showed up. Feeding them was actually her best strategy, for they filed out quickly when they knew there was grub in the kitchen for the taking. Tante, with crumbs on her mouth, led them away after they'd gorged on Eva's pain and her signature linzertorte, which she'd now given Delphine instructions to prepare, one small step at a time.

Outside, it was a perfect day, sunny and with a slight, cool breeze. Sure to bring Tante out, though Delphine hoped her goody-goody cohort would be dishing out potato salad and slicing watermelon at some civic function. The men's voices rose and fell, rumbling with laughter at the big tales, stern with argument at the outrages committed by the government, and sometimes they even fell silent, or stuporous, and gazed into the tangled foliage of Eva's garden blank with speculation. As always, Fidelis was the center of these gatherings, prodding slightly bolder stories out of the men or challenging them to feats of strength.

In the kitchen, sun calm in the window, Delphine cut cold butter into flour for a pastry. She had decided to make pies for the Fourth of July supper, which the men would need to cut the booze. Potatoes were boiling now. She had a crock of beans laced with hot mustard, brown sugar and black-strap molasses. There were of course more sausages. Delphine added a pinch of salt, rolled her dough in oiled muslin, and set it in the icebox. Then she started on the fruit, slicing thin moons of yellow-green rhubarb, peeling off the toughest bits of rosy skin. It's nearly time, she thought, nearly time. She was thinking of Eva's pain. Her own sense of time passing had to do with the length of a dose of opium wine, a cup of it flavored with cloves and cinnamon, or a stronger dose of morphine that Doctor Heech had taught her to administer, though not too much, lest by the end, he said, even the morphine lose its effect.

He'd taught her to make up Magendie's solution fresh to eliminate the development of any fungus, and now, hearing Eva stir, Delphine straightaway set aside her pie makings. She put some water on to boil, to sterilize the hypodermic needle. The night before she had prepared a vial and set it in the icebox, the one-to-thirty solution, which Heech had told her she was better than any nurse at giving to Eva. Delphine was proud of this. The more so because she hated needles, abhorred them, grew sickly hollow when she filled the syringe and felt the penetration of her own flesh when she gave the dose to Eva. Without being asked, she knew when Eva needed the dose. She did not go by the time elapsed, but by the lucid shock of agony in Eva's stare. Her mouth was half open, her brows clenched. She would need the relief very soon, as soon as the water boiled. Delphine thought to divert her friend by massaging her sore hands.

"Ah," Eva groaned lightly as Delphine worked the dips between her knuckles. Eva's forehead smoothed, her translucent eyelids closed over, she began to breathe more peacefully and said, faintly, "How are the damn fools?"

Delphine glanced out the window and observed that they were in an uproar. Sheriff Hock was holding forth and Fidelis was standing, gesturing, laughing at the big man's belly. "We are potched!" she heard him roar in good humor. Then they were all comparing their bellies. Cyprian's was the flattest one. Delphine knew that his stomach, as her own, was divided into hard and even ridges of muscle that he, anyway, could flex like a keyboard. In the lengthening afternoon light, Cyprian's face was slightly agape with the unaccustomed drink and the fellowship of other men, too, for he was used to being isolated on the farm with Roy or out on the road. There was a sheet pinned on the clothesline and the bellies were pale falls of flesh in its shade.

"They're showing off their big guts to each other," said Delphine.

"At least not the thing below," croaked Eva.

"Oh, for shame!" Delphine laughed. "No, they kept their peckers in. But something's going on. Here, I'm going to prop you up. They're better than burlesque."

She took down extra pillows and quilts from the shelves, shoved the bed up to the window, and propped Eva where she would see the doings in the yard. She went back, put one syringe in the water, finished up the pies and put them in the oven, then brought a little tepid water in a cup for Eva to drink. She did drink, which was good, and her color was up. Her eyes brighter.

"Come on," Eva said, "sit down here." Her hand flopped on the bed. "I think they are up to nothing good!"

Now it looked as if they were making and taking bets. Bills were waved, laughingly. They weren't stumbling drunk, but loud drunk. Roaring with jokes. The boys appeared, clambering up the rails of the stock pens to take in the men's action.

"Eva, do you see?" Delphine pointed to them. Nodding, Eva made a face. What examples! These men! All of a sudden, with a clatter, the men cleared the glasses and bottles, the crackers and the sticks of sausage, the bits of Cheddar and the plates, off the table. And when the table was clear, to a great burst of hilarity, Sheriff Hock lay down upon it. He lay on his back. The table didn't reach down his whole length, so he was a boatlike hulk, balanced there in dry dock, his booted feet absurdly sticking straight up and his head extended off the other side. His stomach made a mound and now on the other side of the table, directly before Eva's window, Fidelis stood. He'd unbuttoned the top buttons of his white shirt and rolled his sleeves up over his thick forearms. His suspenders were unstrapped and his grin was huge, tossing back a jeer.

Suddenly, Fidelis bent over Sheriff Hock in a weight lifter's crouch and threw his arms fiercely straight out to either side with a showman's flair. Delicately, firmly, he grasped in his jaws a loop that the women now saw was specially created for this purpose in the thick belt of Sheriff Hock.

There was a moment in which everything went still. Nothing happened. A huge thing happened. Fidelis gathered his power. It was as if the ground itself flowed up through Fidelis and flexed. His face and neck went thick with a brute, red darkness. His jaws flared bone white on the belt loop, his arms tightened in the air, his neck and shoulders swelled impossibly, and he lifted Sheriff Hock off the table. By the belt loop in his teeth, just a fraction of an inch, he moved the town's Falstaff. Then, the women saw it, Fidelis paused. His whole being surged with a blind, suffusing ease. He jerked the sheriff higher, balancing now, half out of the crouch.

In that moment of tremendous effort, Delphine saw the true face of the butcher—the animal face, the ears flaming with heat, the neck cords popping, and finally the deranged eye straining out of its socket, rolled up to the window, to see if Eva was watching. Delphine felt a thud of awful sympathy. He was doing this for Eva. He was trying to distract her, and from that, Delphine understood Fidelis loved her with a helpless and fierce canine devotion that made him do things that seemed foolish. Lift a grown man by the belt with his teeth. A stupid thing. Showing clearly that all his strength was nothing. Against her sickness, he was weak as a child.

ONCE FIDELIS TOOK two mammoth steps and dropped the sheriff on the ground, to roars of laughter, the men began singing again. Now they sang rougher tunes to go with the rising level of their drunkenness and hilarity. They grew louder, desperately raucous, defiant. Death was watching them, through Eva's eyes, from the pantry window. "Jimmy Crack Corn." "The Wabash Cannonball." "I'm Forever Blowing Bubbles." German drinking songs. A sad, lugubrious ballad about the longing of a sailor's wife. Delphine went back into the kitchen to fetch the solution for Eva. She opened the door of the icebox. Looked once, then rummaged with a searching hand. The morphine, which Fidelis had labored with vicious self-disregard to pay for and which Delphine had guarded jealously, was gone. The vial, the powder, the other syringe. She couldn't believe it. Searched through once again, and then again. It wasn't there, and already Eva restless in the next room.

Delphine rushed out and beckoned Fidelis away from the men. He was wiping his face and neck down, the sweat still pouring off of him.

"Eva's medicine is gone."

"Gone?"

He was not as drunk as she'd imagined, or maybe the effort of lifting the sheriff had sobered him.

"Gone. Nowhere. I've looked. Someone stole it."

"*Heiligeskreuz . . .*" He whirled around. That was just the beginning of what he was going to say, and Delphine left before he went any further. She went back to Eva and gave her the rest of the opium wine that was hard on her stomach. Spoon by spoon it went down, in a flash it came back up. "What a mess," said Eva faintly. "I'm worse than a puking baby." She tried to laugh but it came out a surprised, hushed groan. And then Eva was gasping and taking the shallow panting breaths she used to keep from shrieking.

"*Bitte . . .*" Her eyes rolled back and she arched off the bed. She hoarsely shrieked, gestured for a rolled-up washcloth to set between her teeth. It was coming. It was coming like a mighty storm in her. No one could stop it from breaking. It would take hours for Delphine to get another batch through Doctor Heech, wherever he was celebrating the Fourth, and then find the pharmacist. Delphine shouted out the garden door to Fidelis and yelled at Cyprian to take the pies from the oven. She sped out the other way. As she ran, a thought jogged into her mind. She decided to act on it. Instead of steering straight for Heech she gunned the car and stopped short at Tante's little closet of a house two blocks from the Lutheran church, where she prayed every Sunday that the deplorable Catholic her brother married desist from idolatry and saint worship, and return the boys to Lutheran ways.

"*Was wollen Sie?*"

Tante opened the door. Her face had all the knowledge in it and Delphine knew she had guessed right. Delphine remembered her clucking over the dose of the drug with her prayer friends in whispered consult as they pressed up crumbs of lemon pound cake with their fingers.

"*Wo ist die medicin?*" Delphine asked, at first in a normal tone of voice, only slightly panicked. When Tante gave a cold twist of a smile, she screamed. "Where is Eva's medicine?"

"*Ich weiss nicht.*"

Tante affected ragged High German around Delphine and made great pretense of having trouble understanding her. Delphine stepped in the door, shoved past her, and went straight to the refrigerator. On the way there, an outraged Tante trailing, she passed a table with a long slim object wrapped in a handkerchief. Delphine grabbed on instinct, unrolled it, and nearly dropped the missing hypodermic.

"Where is it?" Delphine's voice was deadly. She turned, jabbing the needle at Tante, and then found herself as in a stage play advancing with an air of threat. It was the feeling of being in a dramatic production that suddenly gave her leave to speak lines she wished were written for the moment.

"Come on, you rough old bitch, you don't fool me. So you're a habitual fiend on the sly!"

Delphine didn't really think that, of course, but she wanted to make Tante so indignant that she would tell her where the morphine was; her aim was just to get the stuff and get it back to Eva. The hollow suffering in Eva's eyes had burned into her. Tante gaped and couldn't rally her wits to answer. Delphine rushed frantically back to Tante's little icebox, rooted through it. With a savage permission, she tossed all of Tante's food out, even breaking the eggs, and then she turned and confronted Tante. Her brain was swimming with desperation.

"Please, you've got to tell me. Where is it?"

Now Tante gained control. She even spoke English.

"You will owe me for those eggs."

"All right," said Delphine. "Just tell me."

But Tante, with the upper hand, enjoyed her moment.

"They are saying that she is addicted. This cannot be. The wife of my brother? It is a shame on us."

Delphine saw that she had been extremely stupid in allowing herself to antagonize the only person who could provide morphine quickly, by merely handing it over. She'd blown her cover, and now she would never get Tante to cooperate. She regretted her self-indulgence, grew meek, and tried to hide her panic and pride. She thought that perhaps if she humiliated herself Tante would be placated and let down her guard.

"I beg you," she let a groan out. "Come, you know the truth. Our Eva is suffering. You only see her when she's comfortable, so of course how can you possibly know how the agony builds? Tante, have mercy on your brother's wife. There is no shame in keeping her comfortable, Tante, the doctor said so."

"I think," said Tante, her black figure precise, "the doctor doesn't really know Eva the way I do. He feels too sorry for her, and she is addicted, that is for sure, my good friend Mrs. Orlen Sorven can tell this."

"Tante, for the love of God . . ." Delphine truly begged from her heart at that moment. She thought of falling on her knees. Tante's cold little mouth twitched and her eyes glowed with rigorous triumph.

"It doesn't matter anyway, I have thrown it down the sinkhole."

Delphine turned and saw that on the edge of Tante's porcelain sink a clean-washed vial and the bottle that held the morphine were drying in the glower of sun. And when she saw this, she lost all control of her power. She was strong, of course, phenomenally strong, and when she grabbed Tante firmly by the bodice and jerked her forward and said, into her face, "Okay, you come and nurse her through this. You'll see," Tante found herself unable to resist, her struggles feeble against Delphine's surging force as the younger woman dragged her to the car and stuffed her inside, then roared off. Dumped her at the house.

"I don't have time to go in there. You help her. You stay with her. You," Delphine shrieked, roaring the engine. Then she was gone and Tante, with the smug grimness of a woman who has at last been allowed to take charge, entered the back door of the house.

It did take hours, and in those hours, Delphine prayed and cursed, implored the devil, made bargains, came to tears at the thwarted junctures where she was directed one place and ended up another. It proved impossible either to track down Heech, or to find Sal Birdy, the drugstore keeper. Fidelis, she knew, was out searching, too, but she didn't come across him. She was returning empty-handed, driving back to the house, slamming a fist on the dashboard, weeping tearlessly, when before her she saw her father stumbling along the road.

His pants sagged, his loose shirt flopped off his hunched, skinny shoulders. As she drew near, an all-seeing rage boiled up in Delphine. She looked around to see if anyone else was watching, for she had the sudden and breathless urge to run him over. She put the gear in low and crept after her father, thinking how simple it could be. There he was, drunk again—he'd hardly even notice! Then her life would be that much easier. But as she drew alongside him, instead of mowing him down, she was surprised to meet his eyes and see that they were clear. She realized he wasn't drunk, yet, or very drunk anyway. He was trying to run in the same direction she was driving, to the butcher shop. As he shuffled anxiously around to the side door, she saw he must have had the usual purpose and despised him with the thought, Out snaking himself some hooch at a time like this . . . Only the bottle in his hand was not the usual schnapps or home brew. Roy held the bottle carefully in both hands, thrust it toward her. It was a brown square-shouldered medicine bottle labeled sulphate of morphia. To get it, he had broken into the drugstore and sawed through the lock of the cabinet where Sal kept the drugs he had to secure by law.

AS DELPHINE SLAMMED the brakes, jumped from the truck, and ran to the house with the bottle, she heard it from outside—the high-pitched whooing keen of advanced agony, a white-silver whine. She rushed in, skidded across a litter of canning smashed down off the shelves, and entered the kitchen. There was Tante, white and sick in shock, slumped useless in the corner of the kitchen, on the floor. Markus and Franz, weeping and holding on to their mother as she rummaged in the drawer for a knife. The whole of her being was concentrated on the necessity. Even the strong Franz couldn't hold her back.

"Yes, yes," said Delphine, entering the scene. She'd entered so many scenes of mayhem that now, as always, a cold flood of competence descended on her. With a swift step she stood before Eva. "My friend," she plucked the knife away, saying, "not now. Soon enough. I've got the medicine. Don't leave your boys like this."

Then Eva, still swooning and grunting as the waves hit and twisted in her, allowed herself to be lowered to the floor.

"Get a blanket and a pillow," said Delphine, kindly, to Franz. His tears dried at the relief of having something to do. "And you," she said to Markus, "hold her hand while I make this up and keep saying to her, *Mama, she's making the medicine now. It will be soon. It will be soon.*"

SEVEN

The Paper Heart

MARKUS REMOVED from a hole in his pillow the tiny rolled notes, the dime flattened by a train into a shining disc, the small red crackling heart of store-bought paper, and the tin clicker painted like a cricket. All of these things were gifts from Ruthie Chavers. He had decided not to think of her as dead. She was somewhere else, safe and just out of reach. Duck feathers swirled out of the pillow with the objects, and he stuffed them back into the hole and then pinched the cloth shut. A piece of solid gold light slanted through the west-facing window onto his bed. He carefully unrolled her first note, which had been fixed around a pencil, and which he had kept in its original shape. The note said, *Hi Markus, I got your letter, signed Ruthie.* After that note, there was another, which told what she was doing after school and was signed *Love*, and a third note, which he felt was the most passionate, in which she said how much she liked the letter he had written her, and then there was the Valentine. He carefully smoothed out the shiny red paper and stared at the gleaming surface.

It was coated with something that made little sparkles come out in the sun, and he'd never noticed that before. This was a new thing, and he tipped the heart side to side to get the full effect. He turned the paper over. There was that one word again, *Love*. After he had gone through everything again, clicking the clicker six times, as he always did, and rubbing the dime, he put Ruthie's things back into his pillow and pinned the opening shut with a safety pin. He plumped the pillow up and put it at the head of his bed, then he left the room.

Sometimes at night, when he turned over a certain way, he clicked the toy and it awakened him. The noise always seemed very loud, but it never seemed to bother his hard-sleeping brothers. It always took him what seemed a long time, though it was at most half an hour, to fall asleep again after the clicker. While he waited for sleep to overcome him, he listened to the dog breathing lightly at the door to his room. Sometimes Schatzie whined a little in her dreams, or snuffed as though something intrigued her. Other times, his brothers talked, sometimes even sat up and argued with or commanded some invisible other. Once, Franz had pointed at Markus and said in a low, hysterical voice, *you forgot to fix the fuel gauge.* Because the noise from the clicker woke him, he came to know something that his brothers did not. He understood that his father sometimes stayed up half into the night and sang to his mother.

The first time he'd noticed the light down the hall and heard the low murmur, he'd been frightened to investigate. The next time, he realized that Schatzie was sound asleep, not even twitching, and he'd reasoned that if there were burglars or murderers about the dog would be at their throats. And anyway, she would protect him if he got up to see what the light was, and the sound. He felt compelled to find out now. Schatzie did exactly as he thought she would, rising as he passed and silently following him, her nails clicking softly on the green linoleum tiles. He shivered a little in his washed-thin striped pajamas and proceeded with infinite slowness. He didn't want to be discovered, didn't want to anger his father, whose voice he now recognized, and who fell silent just as Markus reached the door of the little pantry, where his mother slept.

Markus hardly breathed. Motioned for Schatzie to sit down behind him. Staying in the shadows, just out of the doorway's shaft of quiet radiance, he peered into the room and was stilled by what he saw. There was his father, and he was kneeling at the side of his mother's bed, holding on to her foot. Her foot was slim, waxen white, and almost glowed in the cool lamplight. Fidelis rested his forehead on the place where the foot curved into the ankle. His father's back shook, and after a stunned moment Markus realized that his father was weeping in a soundless and terrible way, a way all the more frightening because it was sobless and tearless. He had never, ever, seen his father cry before. The most upsetting thing was that the movement of his father's shoulders was so close to the movements of convulsive laughter. Then Markus thought that maybe it was laughter. Maybe his mother, who could be very funny, had just told his father a joke. But her face was quiet. He could hear her breathing, for her breaths were deep, rattling sighs. He watched a little longer, but then Fidelis put his head up and seemed to stare straight at him. A scared thrill ran through Markus. He froze. But his father was staring blindly at the shadowy wall and did not see him.

Slowly, his father straightened his back, still kneeling, and then he tenderly tucked the blanket around Eva's feet. When he had done that, Markus wanted to go, frightened he'd be found out, but he still couldn't move. His mother's eyes had opened and she stared deeply at Fidelis, and then she smiled at him. It was a glorious smile, serene and full of joy, a softening thrill of her face that Markus would never forget. Fidelis sat in the chair wedged next to the narrow bed, took her hand. Without her asking, he began to sing to her the song she loved most, a song that Markus knew, the one about the water maidens on the river in Germany. His voice was warm and pure. Markus closed his eyes. His father's voice brought the taste of smooth, brown caramel into his mind. With his father's singing for cover, Markus made his way quickly to his own room. He crept into his bed, thrust his fingers through the rip in the pillow where the pin did not quite shut the gap. Then he fell asleep quickly, safe in the rise and fall of his father's voice, with his fingers touching the paper heart.

*   *   *

DELPHINE BLEACHED the bloody aprons. She scrubbed the grimy socks. Their stained drawers and their one-strap overalls. She took their good suits out of mothballs and aired them and pressed them. She sprinkled Fidelis's thick white cotton shirts with starch, and rolled them up and laid them in the cooler. Every morning, she ironed one for him, just as Eva had done. She took on the sheets, the hopeless sweat, the shit and blood, always blood. The towels and the tablecloths. The laundry itself was a full-time job, and Delphine had no idea how Eva had ever done it, plus so much else. But this laundry was a kind of good-bye gift. For once Eva left, Delphine was leaving, too. She'd already decided that to stay there in her old job, with no Eva, was impossible. It wasn't just that people would talk, for they talked about her already. There was more, things she couldn't say even to her private self. No, she couldn't do it. Besides, there was another person chafing and eager to finally take over. Stepping in to care for the boys and her brother would be a perfect showcase for Tante's pieties.

On the last birthday Eva would ever celebrate, Tante did come around, just in time for the cake. After the blur of useless presents and too cheerful toasts, while the celebrators craned over the large scrolled cake, Tante materialized in her usual black, and said to Delphine in her freezing nasal voice, "This is good cake. How much does my brother pay you extra for taking care of Eva?"

Unknown to Tante, Fidelis stepped behind his sister, so he heard Delphine's reply.

"Not one flat dime, you hypocrite sow."

Tante's cheeks mottled red and white, as though she had been slapped. As for Fidelis, she could have sworn that a surprised smile flickered across his face. Delphine hadn't yet told him that Tante had stolen Eva's morphine. Part of her training in dealing with drunks was to hoard information, never to let go of a valuable nugget until it could be made to pay double its worth. There would come a time, thought Delphine, there would definitely come a time. Tante would pay, somehow, for Eva's pain.

*   *   *

A TINY STREAM that mainly carried spring runoff down behind the house, through the field, had dried into a tough little path the boys used to travel into the woods. They spent most of their time there after their chores were done, looking for arrowheads, for pitted, gray fragments of pots, and little white seashells left from when a great ocean had covered all they saw. Markus sometimes thought about this ocean, which he'd learned about in school. The fact that he was walking on what was once an ocean's bottom intrigued him. Sometimes he imagined the water going straight up, over him, just as the air did now. And all around him water creatures floating and diving. Markus and his two little brothers stopped, pulled from their pockets some of the fuzzed-over horehound drops that Tante always gave them, and spat as they sucked away the lint. They concentrated until they got to the actual candy, a somber, medicinal taste, but sweet. Their faces cleared.

"This used to be an ocean bottom," Markus said, showing Emil a tiny brittle white scallop he'd picked up from the field. The shell was about the size of his little fingernail. His brother looked at the shell without much interest.

"Gimme that," said Erich, and he inspected the little shell, then gave it back to Markus. "Is she dying now?" he asked.

Markus said, "I think so."

All that week, whenever they woke up, Delphine fed them carelessly, old bread or stiff oatmeal, and then forgot to check whether their chores were finished. She allowed them to play wherever they wanted. She was in the other world of the two that existed side by side. One world was of those who would go on living. The other was centered on the one who would die. Usually, the boys stayed outside all day. After dinner, they went in to see their mother before bed, to kiss her goodnight. Her face was gray and sunken, almost like a headhunter's shriveled trophy. Suddenly, her face was full of lines and folds. Wrinkles had appeared around her mouth. Her breathing was so slow it seemed forever between breaths. Her eyes were large and staring, but the boys were not afraid of her. They'd gotten used to her. Markus found that when he kissed her, he felt absolutely nothing except that her taste was a strange taste, earthen and moldy, not human anymore. As soon as he left his mother, crawled between the covers of his bed, and laid his head on his pillow, a numb buzzing noise started in his ears and he fell immediately asleep. He never even woke when Emil crawled into bed beside him on some nights. In the morning, he was groggy and fuzzy, and he had trouble nudging his brother out of his bed.

"My foot's asleep again," said Emil, yawning.

It was happening to them, too, Markus had noticed. Whenever they sat still too long, his little brothers complained, their limbs went odd and prickly. He could see how their eyes drooped. Even now, though it was full daylight and they had precious time to play, they were drowsy. Markus pointed to the riffle of woods just ahead.

"Let's go there," he said. He pictured the soft mat of fallen leaves underneath the scrub birch and maples, how nice it would be to rest there for a while. They each took another horehound drop and spat lint while they walked to the woods. They sat down in a deep pile of crackling, dust-smelling leaves. Then they lay back and looked at the green leaves on the branches turning and flickering. Their eyes grew heavy and Erich began to snore, a light whining sound. The air was dreamy and hot. Ants crawled over Markus's hand and he flicked them off. It was like being underwater just then with the green and changeable light falling through the woods onto them. What if they were lying at the bottom of the ocean? Markus thought of great storms and waves passing over, high above. On the tranquil bed, way down here with nothing to bother them, they lay undisturbed.

Emil was stretched out next to him, half asleep. Markus felt his brother inch a little closer. He pushed him away, once, then he let him draw near again. Soon, with an adult sigh of irritated indulgence, he let Emil hold onto the bottom of his shirt, put his thumb in his mouth, and sleep. Markus stayed awake a little longer and even, once, rubbed his brother's hair in the distracted way he rubbed the dog's head. He missed the dog. But these days she did not come with them on their daily rounds, or out into the fields and woods. Schatzie preferred to stay near his mother, just outside her door. She was guarding Eva and she was waiting patiently to haul her across the deep spaces of the night, the black spaces, to the other side.

THERE WAS NO BEFORE and no after. Days had melted together. Eva's long dying was the ground and the air. For a week now, she'd taken only sips of lukewarm water. Her hair stood up in a peaked cap despite Delphine's attempts to comb it down. Her elbows and knees were knobs and her bones jutted from her flesh. She'd absorbed morphine like water. It made no difference. Her body would not die and would not live. Her eyes were unearthly. She stared through everything, saw nothing. She had taught Delphine to look into her eyes straight on, and when she did the world dropped away. There flowed between them an odd and surprising electricity. Their gaze was a power—comforting, frightening. Delphine was pulled somewhere fast, yanked right out of her skin. With their eyes locked they rushed through the air, ecstatic, hearts lurching.

The night Eva finally died, Delphine woke to the knocking, and knew. She cast off the quilt she'd wrapped herself in at the foot of Eva's bed. Eva's arms were flailing like a backstroker's and her fists rapped the headboard. Delphine grappled with the bedposts and got to her knees, then stumbled blearily to the side of the bed. She hadn't slept more than two hours at a time for days, and now she hardly knew whether she was sleeping or awake as she tried to catch Eva's arms. But Eva was running in place now, her bone-thin legs kicking, her arms pumping up and down at her sides. She was running in her high heels. Again, she was running against Franz and her breath came urgently, gravelly and harsh, as though she was nearing the end of a race. She gritted her teeth and seemed to strain for the invisible finish line. The cords in her neck pulled taut, her face twisted, and then she breathed deeply and a sound like sticks rattling came from inside of her chest. Her arms fell to her sides. Her breath went out and she did not retrieve it.

"Can you hear me?" Delphine said. "Are you there?"

Eva's eyes opened and she took a little air. She said nothing, but looked steadily at Delphine. Her face had become beautiful once again, austere, the flesh pulled across stark bones, the graceful lines of her eye sockets and her skull. After a while, she whispered, for Delphine to light the lamps.

Delphine lighted the lamp and then caught Eva's fist and held it. Delphine's head fell forward and her eyes closed in a swimming heaviness. She jerked awake, took a round, amber bottle of almond oil from a little shelf beside the bed. She poured a small amount into her left palm. Sleepily, she rubbed the oil into Eva's skin until the fist slowly began to relax.

"Franz, he knows nothing about it," gasped Eva suddenly. "His father was not Fidelis. His father's name was Johannes Grunberg, a Jew. Quite a student, and so handsome, so tall and fair. In the war, dead." Her lips worked. At last, she gathered another breath and went on. "Fidelis knows, but he never spoke of it."

Delphine poured out another bit of oil and worked it into the slack, dry skin of Eva's forearm. This was the fourth time Eva had labored to tell her this. Usually, from this revelation she went on to give Delphine directions on when to marry Fidelis and how to care for the boys. But this time, she said something different, something she'd never said before. She said it with a clear simplicity.

"I want you, only you, to handle my body. And please write to my *Mutti*. Tell her that you took care of me. Tell her this: I loved you."

Delphine looked into Eva's eyes expecting to become hypnotized, but this time something gave way, she could feel it. Their thoughts had pushed through an invisible barrier, a magnetic field, and there was suddenly a lightness that lifted them giddily into a storm of calm. Later, Delphine was to think that she should have called Fidelis or the boys. But at the time it did not occur to her. Delphine didn't look away from Eva's face, even for a moment, because she knew that Eva was afraid. She did not let go of Eva's hand, because she knew that Eva wanted her to hold her hand, just as a child would when it must enter a new and foreign place. Delphine did not move to adjust her friend when the sticks in her chest rattled again, even louder, three times. She did not pound Eva's chest when the breathing stopped. Eva was still looking into Delphine's

138

eyes, and so, during the time when she might have taken another breath, Delphine saw the light go out behind that silver streak, like a crack behind the door.

"STRUB'S FUNERARY, how may I be of service?"

Benta's voice was sleepy, but Delphine knew that they had kept track of the progress of Eva's disease and had been waiting for a call.

"I should have got hold of Clarisse, but I know if I did I'd break down," said Delphine.

"You think it's hard, at first, that she's your friend," said Benta. Her voice now stronger, down-to-earth. "You'll find Clarisse can be a great comfort to you. Can we come over together?"

"Yes," said Delphine, and then she sat in Eva's kitchen listening to the boys and Fidelis, together in the other room, the murmur of their sorrow. One comforted the other, gained control, and another broke down. Delphine needed to hear them, for she felt very much alone. She couldn't be with them, it wouldn't be proper for her to enter that room now. She had washed Eva with her lilac soap, pinned a towel between her legs, smoothed her face into a calmer expression and closed her eyes before she called Fidelis. She thought that perhaps she should accompany the body back to Strub's, too, as Eva had made that final request. But now everything seemed too much for her, out of her control, and somehow strange, as though with Eva gone it was no longer right for her to be there. It seemed a long time before the Strubs arrived, pulling up to the back door in their long, pearl gray hearse. Delphine answered at their knock and Clarisse entered, took hold of her with an embrace that radiated a practical kindness. The Strubs brought her effortlessly into the room where Fidelis and his sons sat with Eva. When the others entered, Fidelis bent down and picked up Eva in his arms. He looked so bewildered, then, holding his wife in the air with no place to take her, that no one could move until Aurelius put his hand on his shoulder.

"Put her down, Fidelis, we'll take good care of her."

Gently, Fidelis lowered Eva to the mattress. With a wild, rough cry,

Markus broke away and stumbled to his mother's side. He bent over and with a passionate gesture he kissed his mother's ankle, just as his father had. He cradled her foot, closed his eyes, and touched his forehead to the place he had kissed. Franz stepped behind him, embarrassed, and was about to pull Markus away when Delphine stopped him. Just as she touched Franz, a sound emerged. It was a roar of grief, a loud, keening bellow, and it filled the room. It seemed to come from all of them, or no single one of them, or from the walls of the room itself. Delphine never was to know. The sound released everyone, as though from a spell, and they stepped away from Eva and left her.

NOW ROY WATZKA passed into an unprecedented period of sobriety. Dry days passed into weeks. He was able to accomplish this because of the starkness of Eva's death. And then, too, what had happened in the cellar came back to haunt him. At last something had unnerved him. In his periodic bouts of delirium, the dead had appeared. The Chavers came for him, snapping with beetles and sprouting grave moss. Their hands reached with insane stroking motions, dragging him to their cozy wormhole in the earth. This vision had plagued him since the discovery of the Chavers, and finally, when Eva died, the experience became unbearable. He found within his thoughts, for the first time, a horror to which even the terrors of withdrawal were preferable.

For once, too, he didn't farm out his wasted muscles to other people, but concentrated on his own house. Cyprian was astonished to return from a run up north to find not a Roy tooted happily down by the river, but an old, faded, quiet Roy calmly brushing the sides of the house with sunny yellow paint. The house was cheerful, the blue of the doors and windows restored. He even sanded down and varnished the floors. Filled the cellar in more thoroughly, and blacked the stove. Delphine had her hands full with the Waldvogel boys just after Eva's death, and it came as a shock to her that Roy was capable of taking care of her in any way. In the mornings sometimes, he handily made breakfast. She would emerge from the room she shared with Cyprian, and there it would be, close to a miracle as home life had ever come. A bowl of oatmeal steaming hot, butter melting in a pool with a lump or two of dark brown sugar. Cream. Sometimes eggs or toast he made by holding the bread on a fork and passing it evenly before the gas—for with her money Delphine had bought a stove on timed payments. Cyprian got a delivery set up for a small icebox. Breakfast seemed a surprise compensation for all they had been through. The food laid out on a shined-up table, jelly quivering in her mother's tiny cut-glass bowl Delphine thought for sure had long since been pawned or broken. Breakfast had helped her get through the storm of Eva's dying and now through its aftermath. She expected Roy to relapse once she finally quit the shop, but instead his good behavior continued. He turned on the charm that he'd brought to Eva's sickroom. He sang songs he learned in the hobo jungle by the river. "Blue Tail Fly." "Joe Hill." "Big Rock Candy Mountain." Soon there were actually chickens in the coop out back, big orange Rhode Islanders, and the back porch steps were nailed onto the back porch, not scattered all over the yard.

"The dead have more power than we know," said Delphine to Cyprian, sitting on those very back steps one evening in the last of summer.

Cyprian shook his head. Did her statement refer to Eva or to the change affected in Roy by his waking dreams? Whatever it was, Cyprian was glad of the change as well and had even considered quitting his own shady line of work in order to pursue something on the up and up. Roy was setting weasel traps around the outside fence of the chicken run. The previous day, he'd tacked a light wire drapery on the top of the fence to foil the Cooper's hawks. Roy was not the only one who'd improved the place, either. In the past two weeks, Delphine had turned the inside of the house into a golden haven. She set an eggshell pale yellow on all of the walls, and stuck the old furniture back together with horse-hoof glue, twine, and C-clamps. She'd restuffed a couple of chairs and accepted a fancy, tasseled lamp from Step-and-a-Half, who gave it to her in a seeming fit of bewilderment after Eva's death. In their room she'd oiled the lacquer dresser and they bought a brand-new mattress, not that they took advantage of its spring. She told herself that life had been too sad for anything but comfort, but that was not true. There would have been plenty of comfort if Cyprian had thrown himself to her in thick desire. But they usually fell asleep touching hands. That was good enough. He held her like a sister and often, long into the night, they talked.

Now, as Roy turned from setting his traps and walked toward them, Delphine had the idea that she would make a Hungarian-style goulash that Eva had taught her, a thick stew of braised meat in paprika sauce, ladled over spaetzle. Sour cream topping it. As she turned to walk into the kitchen, a sense of the fugitive sweetness of the scene assailed her. It was like a gift from Eva when she died—all good things to follow. Her dad acting like one, Cyprian so attentive, playing checkers or cards with the old man and helping him stay off the sauce. As terribly as she missed Eva, there was also the relief of having done with the grand horror and the mess of death, the organized tedium, the vigilance and dragging heartbreak. She didn't have to put up with men drinking underneath the clothesline or with the sharp wing of Tante's scorn. She could smell the maples, the pine, the ooze of the river instead of the raw primitive cavernous smell of cows when they are split. And now, it was good to turn toward her cooking in the cool day's remaining light, and to have in her new icebox both meat and butter. In her apple bin, apples. In the onion box, onions. So why, when she felt this goodness, did a wave of fear and sorrow pass through her? Why the sudden memory of looking down into the cellar, and the dead moving their mouths, their words rising toward her in flashes of green fire?

It was because she must have known even then that more was coming. She must have known that there would never be an end of it. No peace. For even now, as she made her way dreamily toward the cooking, the boy, bruised and aching, slipped out his back door. He had decided to run to her. She stirred more flour and an extra egg into the spaetzle, cut two more onions into the goulash. Used all the meat. For some reason she made extra. It was as though she knew that by the time he figured out the back roads and cut through the corn, the sand pickers, the ditches and the pastures, he would be tired. He would be ready to drop. He would be hungry, that Markus.

*   *   *

LOOKING CLOSELY at Tante's face as she complained about Markus the next morning, Delphine picked out each one of Fidelis's features. On his face they were precisely placed with a level and a ruler. On her face the angels had been less attentive to their work. Every feature was off—the frozen blue eyes too far apart on the skull, the nose thicker and too short, the upper lip much thinner than the lower, and the whole mouth so small that Delphine wondered how so many words came out of it, or how she ate more than one pea at a time. Delphine had to examine the talking face to remove herself from the words it said. If I listen to the meaning, I'll paste Tante right in the chops, she thought. So she calmly watched the odd concoction of flesh and bone, then she shrugged and said, "I haven't seen him."

"Lie!" said Tante, but she didn't leave the little front porch. Delphine, in the doorway, folded her arms. Tante understood with disappointment that she wouldn't be asked in for a piece of that astounding cinnamon cake she smelled, and she swallowed hard as Delphine dusted flour off her blouse. Or maybe it was powdered sugar. Tante clamped her teeth together and bit back her hunger.

Delphine had been successful in not listening to all of the specific details of the diatribe, but she did know that it was a self-serving lecture that might explain his bruises. A calculated effort to undermine his innocence, for Tante repeatedly made reference to the contrast between his frail looks and devilish wiry ways. She'd had to switch him, then beat him, and then for some reason he ran off. Delphine said again, yawning, "Haven't seen him."

"If Fidelis was here . . ." Tante muttered. But Fidelis had the truck, packed with sausage, out on a wide sweep of deliveries to various grocery stores.

"The kid's no dummy," said Delphine. "He'll find a place to hole up for a while. At least until his dad gets back. Don't worry about him."

"Oh, I'm not worried about *him*," said Tante. "But what does his dad do when he comes home and finds the boy is gone?"

"What," said Delphine, "are you scared Fidelis'll take down the bull's pizzle and give you a good whacking?"

Tante reared back, not certain whether she should be severely offended or laugh at Delphine's joke. She did try to laugh, but as always the chuckle came out thin from her tiny mouth. The bull's pizzle was a homemade switch, a dried bull's penis that hung on the backside of the door to the shop. Used with disciplinary intent, it was painful but it left no marks. Eva had once told Delphine that Fidelis almost never used it on the boys—twice on Franz for dipping into the till, and he had used it on the little boys for setting the outhouse on fire, never on Markus. The existence of the pizzle, its customary threat, was enough.

"I'll be going then," said Tante. "Got to feed Erich and Emil. Those two eat like little pigs." She swirled off in her rusty black. As though her leaving were an insult and not a blessing, thought Delphine. Satisfied, she retreated into the house and watched the car jounce around the road's bend.

"Come on out," she said to the bedroom door.

Markus slipped out and ran to the window.

"Is she coming back?"

"I doubt it."

For some reason, he'd put his best clothes on to come to her last night. This morning, they were all he had to wear. They were the same clothes he'd worn at the funeral, the store-bought shirt with the front pockets and the notched collar. Short itchy brown pants, which he hated, good wool socks with no holes in them and Franz's formal hand-me-down, lace-up shoes, still too big but shined up nicely.

"We should put you in some overalls," said Delphine, and she directed Cyprian to go buy a pair in town.

"Now," she pointed to the kitchen, "let's get you some breakfast." And she made him what she'd made the others, a stack of pancakes studded with the last of the sweet wild blue saskatoons. Dabbed butter on the top. Drizzled on a little maple syrup that Cyprian had traded for with a Chippewa up north on his last run. She carefully put the tin jug back in the icebox. Then she poured herself a cup of hot coffee and sat down while Markus ate. She talked while his mouth was full, not expecting him to answer her. Last night, he'd simply appeared, eaten, his eyes drooping while he chewed. He'd gone limp and let them tuck him into bed. She hadn't had the heart to ask him a single thing.

"You're going to stay with us, here, until your dad gets back," she said now. His eyes went round and he nodded quickly, relieved. Delphine kept talking.

"I don't need to know how come you left, though you can tell me if you want. Or you can tell Cyprian. Don't tell my dad, Roy, though. He blabs. What I do want to know is this: Why did you come to me?"

The boy stopped chewing, suddenly, swallowed and looked at her with his fork and his knife poised. The roan freckles stood out on his pale face. He bit his lip, uncertain, and his eyes . . . there was all the sadness in the world in his eyes, thought Delphine. All the sadness there could possibly be. And as they were Eva's eyes, for a moment she swam into them and then he spoke, and his words were clear, though very low.

"You took care of her."

He started eating again, his face darkening, going hot and red while Delphine blinked and stirred the coffee round in her cup. So what the boy said—that meant Delphine could take care of Markus, too? Or was it his way of saying that since Delphine loved the mother, she would love and defend the son? She watched him eat with some satisfaction. He shoveled the food into his mouth as though he'd seen no food for over a week, and soon Delphine got up and made him more pancakes.

SO MARKUS STAYED and helped Roy mow the yard and grub young trees and pull wild morning glories from a patch they wanted clean for a pasture. Roy was now ambitious to have a cow. Little by little, as Markus joined the checker games or made a quick study of Roy's cribbage strategies, things came out. First, Markus would start to worry about the chinchillas. He'd wonder if Franz was changing their water or just adding to the old stuff in the dish, as Eva had directed them not to do. Then he'd fear the twins would torture the creatures by shoving sticks into the cages and chasing them here and there, which would damage their coats. After a while he'd shake his head and worry that Tante didn't know the first thing about mixing their food. She couldn't make food at all.

"What did you eat?" asked Delphine casually, hiding the speculative glee in her voice.

"She could make crackers," said Markus.

"Oh, right from the barrel?"

He nodded solemnly, eyes sparking.

"Could she make cheese, too?"

"Right from the wax!" he crowed. "She mostly cleans." He sobered down. "She cleans a lot, and then she yells, and then she cleans up some more. We got hungry so we ate a lot of green apples."

"Did Emil and Erich get the shits?"

"Oh, did they!"

"So then she had to do more laundry."

"I made her do more laundry, too."

Delphine just nodded. She knew exactly what had been going on, ever since Markus had insisted on sleeping on the floor with just a blanket over him. And then, every morning, he got up before they did and she'd see the rag he'd used to clean up under himself drying on the line, already rinsed in the river, and his shorts put back on rinsed, too, still clammy and cleanly washed. There had been none of this before the death of Eva, so Delphine knew the cause, and she knew the cause for the beatings, and more than ever she had the fantasy of wringing Tante's neck just like a chicken's, or sending her flying with a kick. But what could she do except keep Markus here? And if the sheriff heard, there might be charges. But again, what could she do?

"By the way," she said, "lay low if the sheriff drives up. Better yet, if you're out in the field fade into the brush, then sneak down to the river. And meantime, if it will make you feel better," she brushed his strawberry blond forelock of hair, the second time she'd ever touched him, "I'll go check up on your live fur coat."

She didn't want him to forget they were supposed to kill the things. He was ahead of her, though. He brightened.

"There's going to be about six babies, and the does need bone powder mixed in their food. I figure we have over three hundred dollars worth when we sell them this fall. Then we'll keep the babies in the heated shed over winter, and make two thousand next year!"

"Who's buying these things?" said Delphine.

"There's a dealer. He's a fur maker."

"Well," joked Delphine absently, "now I've heard of everything."

But of course she hadn't, and of course the creatures had no water when she got there, so she had to feed one or two with eye droppers to revive them. And then Tante wondered why she was not minding her own business.

"They were Eva's rabbits," said Tante, "not yours."

"They're not rabbits," said Delphine. "They're rodents, and where is Franz?"

"Where he always is these days," said Tante. "With the airplanes."

Ever since Tante started cooking for them, Franz had decided to eat with the aviators at the new airfield. Once he was done working in the shop, he now spent all of his time there, glued to his local heroes. He'd gone even more airplane crazy and he adored Lindbergh so much that he tried to dress like him. He followed every move "Slim" made and held forth on every last detail about the *Spirit of St. Louis*. The gas storage tanks' placements in the nose, wing, rear. The wicker pilot's chair. The touchy steering equipment that had helped keep Lindbergh wakeful. One of his scrapbooks was now devoted to Lindbergh alone, and it was filled with pasted clippings and pictures. Franz's fanaticism was of a practical nature as well. He'd do anything to put an airplane together. He tinkered with the engines the way he'd worked on the stripped hulk of an old Model T out back by the stock pens.

"You've got to have the little boys mix the food up like this," said Delphine to Tante, who puffed back into the house and sent Emil and Erich out to learn the routine. They appeared, strong as little bull calves in their short pants and ripped shirts, barefooted for the last weeks before school. Delphine smoothed their ragged hair into wings and crouched to their level.

"You can make some money from these animals," she told them.

The boys nodded, bored with the idea.

"What are you going to do with your money?" Delphine asked.

They gave each other quizzical and amused looks, as though she had said something secretly hilarious.

"It could be a hundred dollars each, Markus thinks, maybe more. How much do your soldiers cost, each?"

This they knew, to the penny, and they knew how much each piece of equipment for their battlefields would cost, too, if they could get them, each horse and each cannon. Every rank of every officer was a different price, and these they recited to Delphine. Their armies were fighting wars of the last century. The officers they'd bought still reared heroically on caparisoned horses, instead of creeping belly down through mud. By the time Delphine finally made them understand that the chinchillas equaled money equaled soldiers, or lemon drops, licorice whips, and ice cream downtown at Birdy's Drugstore, and that they would have shares in the profits equally with Markus provided they did not let Tante take over the cleaning and the feeding of these creatures, they were serious, determined, alight with calculating greed.

IN THE MIDDLE of the night Delphine shook Cyprian awake because the wild dogs were howling again. A pack of strays and leftovers, skimmed out of the town's rich backyards, poor shacks, and middling main street shops, had banded together. Delphine had often seen them around the far edges of the butcher's yard. Eva had pointed them out, gray shadows of every dog shape, some big and rangy and others small as whippets, a classless and breedless roaming menace led by that rogue stud Hottentot. They came around the butcher shop often, and had furtively lived off the occasional ball of guts that Fidelis flung out for them, or the forgotten mess of chicken heads nobody bothered to clean up in the tall weeds. They had never howled around the butcher's shop. Because there was good pickings, they'd never give away their presence.

Out of town, on wild nights they rode the moon, howling themselves back to the shapes of wolves. Their song was gurgling and eerie, but without the coherence of urgent joy and sensible thought she'd heard in the voices of the real wolves, up north, where she and Cyprian had listened while camped outside a small two-bit town with no money, right before a show. She shook him awake anyway because the sound made her lonesome, and a little romantic, as it referred to their past in which there had been that single deep sexual interlude. Now he woke up, as he always did, completely alert and ready to talk if she wanted, or eat, or play cards. This was one of the nice and comfortable things about Cyprian. He liked waking up and was always obliging even in the first minutes, though not obliging in every way. Still, because she needed him and the dogs were out, howling, she said, her voice ragged, "Make love to me."

Cyprian took his breath in sharply. He'd worried about this for a long time, wondering when she would get tired of him lying like the butcher's dog, that's what he'd heard it called, to sleep alongside your woman without taking advantage of her tenderness, her sex. Just the way the butcher's dog never touches what it loves, but parks itself with trained indifference next to a juicy haunch. Knowing this time would come, he'd made his mind up to do something that he felt an ethical repugnance for—picture men. He'd even lined up the ones he'd use most effectively. Now, he mustered his collection. He summoned them. He got the picture of a pulsing throat, a chest, the whole works, and he kept the picture going, shifting, even though a breast got in the way, or her sighing voice, or whatever else. He did the act with desperation and no skill and he did it too fast, just to make sure he finished it, but then afterward he tried his best to make it up to her, to not fall asleep, but keep his hands moving, his mouth moving, until she arched under him and cried out and was dead silent.

"Delphine," he whispered, after some time had passed, "are you hungry?"

She did not answer, and he felt sure she was pretending to sleep. But he couldn't sleep. The whole thing made him conscious of his mess— what he called the thing that was the truest desire in his life. But it was a mess, because what was he going to do with it and where would it all end up? For sure, there was no future in living with a man. In setting up

a house. He'd never heard of that, except for in the cities, and he imag-
ined they were different than he was. They didn't get along with regu-
lar men, he thought. All that aside, there was Delphine herself. He never
talked to men the way he did to Delphine, or had such good times, or
felt this sweet impulse to protect. Yet his hands in dreams fit themselves
around men's hard shoulders, and their faces, and God, the way they
smelled and the way they sounded. And so much else in the deep-red
world he had just summoned. Now he couldn't help think of those things
once more, and guilty at his hardness and his excitement, he turned Del-
phine over and began with a blind abandon to make her shudder, to make
her swear in a whisper next to his ear, to make her feel the damage in
his heart, to shut her up, to kill some little man inside himself angry that
she was a woman, and then, when she battled him back, biting his lips
and in a silent struggle pinned him, Cyprian lay back in careless luxury.

The dogs came close to the house. They seemed to howl right un-
derneath the window. He forgot just what she was, man or woman, and
felt the simple dark of lust for a moment, the ease and pleasure of being
drawn out to his length in her mouth. He stroked her hair and touched
her lips, tight around him, and then he lost himself, and when she was
finished he put his hands on her face, smoothing her cheekbones,
wiping her mouth, for some reason murmuring, "You poor thing, you
poor thing," until she began to laugh at him.

SO THERE THEY WERE, in the middle of the night, frying up a single
pork cutlet, arguing how to split it, when Markus stumbled out in his
little-boy shorts.

"Now we have to split the damn thing three ways," laughed Cyprian.
What had happened in the bedroom made him light-headed, he felt
drunk and a stranger to himself. How had she done that, made him for-
get, for a second, what she was? She could have been a wolf. Now the
little boy looked embarrassed at himself until Cyprian said, "Just sit down
and let the table cover it." Markus sat down grinning.

Delphine was wearing a Chinese robe, a floating brilliant red with
apple blossoms on a long stem embroidered on the back, and her feet

were bare. First, she held it shut, then she pinned it so she could use both hands chopping potatoes.

"We might as well just eat," she said, and fried an onion. Put some water on to boil for chamomile tea. "After this, I'm drinking this sleep tea. It's an herb, I'm looking for work tomorrow and I'm getting my beauty rest."

The dogs were gone, their howling had stopped as soon as the lights went on. Roy had made a bed for himself in a small summer shack right beside the chicken coop. He'd fixed it up for himself with a little pallet set in the wall, even stuffed a mattress and dragged out an old bedspread and a pillow that Eva had given to Delphine when she told her, long ago, how they'd had to burn every single thing in the house. He had slept out there since so as not to disturb the two of them, he said. They had let him.

"Listen," said Markus, now, his eyes very wide. "There's something out there."

Over the sizzle in the pan they heard it—the rhythmical growls and the sudden snorts and the high-pitched whimpers.

"That's Roy snoring."

The old man was perfectly clear, even from across the yard and locked up in his tiny house. Delphine shook the skillet. What would they do when it got cold out, come winter? Having grown up with it, she was used to the sound the way people get used to living next to train yards. But poor Cyprian would be kept awake tossing all night. The thought, coming to her as she turned over the brown, crusted potatoes, was the first for a long time she'd had in which she imagined a future with Cyprian. And all because they'd had this one night. Well, that was stupid! She knew what was going on, him with his eyes closed tight. What was he seeing in his head? She turned the potatoes back and then used the spatula to set a heap on each plate. She set the plate before him, touched the side of his face with the back of her hand, wishing to know the answers, but already protecting herself. It might not happen, after all, for another eight months or a year, and what the hell did she really think, anyway, was going on during his trips up north?

*   *   *

DELPHINE WAS OUT BACK setting new straw down on her potato beds when Fidelis drove up in the meat-market truck. She straightened, brushed her sweaty brown curls back from her forehead, narrowed her eyes although she didn't think they'd have a run-in. She'd expected that he would come out looking for Markus when he returned. School was starting soon. He walked toward her, his arms motionless as hooks at his sides, his face quiet. He wore a rumpled plaid shirt—she'd never seen such a thing on him. And his pants were stained on the thighs where he'd wiped blood off his hands. Fidelis was usually immaculate, but of course that had been Eva's doing and then her own. As she walked toward him, she added another secret piece of gloating to her store. Tante couldn't keep up with the laundry. They stopped with about three feet of space between them and stood without speaking. Delphine cocked her head to the side. The sun was behind her and full in his face, a ravaging white sun that blotted out his features.

"Where've you been?" she asked.

"Running around like a fart on a lantern," he said, "I come for Markus. Where is he?"

"Like a fart on a lantern, huh," said Delphine. "That's no excuse!" Her temper flared, her heart caught. She suddenly missed Eva and that lonely pang turned to anger. "Of course he's here. Do you think I'd let that bitch of a sister of yours beat him black and blue?"

Fidelis grew very serious, though he didn't look surprised. He looked down at his feet in the tough steel-toed slaughterhouse boots, and he frowned so hard at them that Delphine looked down, too. There was nothing to see but that cracked leather planted in the soil.

"I come to get him," said Fidelis in a low voice. Delphine waited for him to say something more. Thank you wouldn't be out of the question, she thought. But he held his silence, which annoyed her enough so that she asked an abrupt question.

"Are you going to give him a whipping?"

"Why should I?" said Fidelis, then raised his eyes and looked full on at Delphine. Even through the blast of sun she could feel the power of his pale gaze. As on the first day she met him, she felt a jolt of strangeness. Not fear, just an instinct that there was more, much more, happening in that moment than she could grasp. He was withholding an energy composed of menace and promise. Tons of power were behind his slightest gesture and she thought of a great smooth-faced dam.

"Come in, take a load off, and I'll pour you some iced tea. Roy and Markus are down at the river, but I think it's too hot for the fish to bite. They'll be back any minute."

She was stalling, trying to find a diplomatic way not to send Markus back. Fidelis came into the house, still darkly cool as she'd kept the windows shut against the growing heat. She now opened the windows, sensing that undertone of cellar rot that crept in elusively and smelled to her of despair. There were six green ash trees outside that changed the air around in the late afternoon. The rooms would cool. The place was clean, scrubbed to a finish. Earlier, she'd cut a lemon into a jug of clear brown tea and stirred in the sugar, then set it right next to the ice block. Now she poured the tea into the glass beer mugs. The sides of the glasses filmed over and sweat. Fidelis looked at the tea a little sadly.

"I don't have beer," said Delphine.

Fidelis took a long drink, and Delphine refilled. Then he put his mug down and asked, "When are you coming back?"

Delphine mulled that one over, and then thought, Here's my bargaining point. "That's a hell of a question," she said.

Fidelis leaned forward and hunched his shoulders as though he was going to say something very difficult, but all he said was, "Tante can't run things alone."

Delphine realized that it was a form of betrayal for him to make even the mildest critical statement regarding his sister. That was the way of those old German families. Tante was the only family he had over here. She wrote descriptions of whatever he did in endless script letters. Tante was always mailing off a stack, foreign postage. It was said that Tante wanted to go back to their pretty town in Germany, Ludwigsruhe, if only it weren't for Fidelis. She couldn't just leave him in this country, especially now, with those boys. Still, his troubled frown, and obvious discomfort, annoyed Delphine.

"I suppose I could think about coming back to help out—that is, if you'd tell her to pack her bags and get."

Fidelis looked like he'd been knocked on the head with a sheep mallet. Such a thing must not have occurred to him, and Delphine had to laugh.

"She can't cook. You're losing business because she's snotty to the customers. Your clothes look like hell. Your boys are running wild. And I won't come back if she's there, you can bet!"

Fidelis gave a cool nod and closed up. He wasn't going any further with that, Delphine could tell. Maybe she should have been amazed that for such a big man he was such a coward before his sister, but she understood a lot more about him now.

"Look," she said, pretending to soften. "I guess it's tough. I like your boys, so I'll think about it. Just leave Markus with us another couple weeks. He can start school from here. Cyprian can drive him in. He's too much trouble for Tante, and he's good help to us."

Fidelis agreed to that, and when Markus came back Delphine watched very closely to see how he acted with his father, whether he was eager to return. But Markus was wary when he saw his father's truck in the yard, and he seemed relieved to stay on with Delphine. She brought a lemon pound cake to the table, and tension eased up quickly. Fidelis ate the cake with great attention. Eva's recipe, he knew. He experienced a wave of feeling when he gathered the last crumbs, and he made a ceremony of putting down his fork, slowly lowering it to the table. Delphine felt his sorrow, then, as a current of energy. Leaving, Fidelis nodded in approval at the good-size fish his boy had caught despite the heat, and took the fish as a gift. Markus put his shoulders back and strutted a little, which made Delphine laugh because he was such a skinny, unassuming boy. Yes, he had to stay. There was no doubt about it. She had to teach him a few things before she let him face Tante, and she had plans how to do it.

*   *   *

DELPHINE STILL OCCASIONALLY dreamed of getting a show to-
gether, a large-scale drama production, or of putting the balancing act
somewhere in the plot of the thing. To do that, they'd have to take it on
the road because the town could not support a cast of professional play-
ers. But Delphine no longer wanted to leave. Not with Roy behaving
and with Markus near. Losing Eva had taken something out of her, too,
and she began to spend more time with Clarisse. Another reason to stay
in Argus. Still, the question lingered whether she and Cyprian were still
essential to the investigation. Nothing had come of the sheriff's plan to
solve the Chavers' deaths, nothing that she had heard, anyway. Del-
phine thought that she would like to know where things stood. She was
curious. It struck her that she should pay a visit to the sheriff. So she
left Roy napping in the shade one afternoon, and as Cyprian had driven
the car up north, she walked to town.

By the time she got there, she was wringing in the unseasonable heat.
Usually by now they had a break in the weather. Not this year. Sweat
darkened her armpits and her neck was damp, her hair springing out of
the pins she'd fastened in wet tendrils. In town, with the wide reflect-
ing streets and the puny trees, the sun shone hotter. The sheriff's dim
office offered some relief. He had a ceiling fan going, and on his desk
a little, black, official-looking fan whirred as well. The brick walls were
insulating and the inside of his office was cool and peaceful. Sheriff
Hock was doing paperwork when she entered, and he looked glad for
a diversion.

"So," said Delphine, after they'd complained to each other about the
heat, "what have you found out about the Chavers? Roy and I are won-
dering." She didn't mention Cyprian, for it struck her that Sheriff Hock
might ask where Cyprian traveled off to from time to time, and she
wanted to avoid the story about his being a brush salesman. But Hock
didn't seem at all interested in Cyprian's excursions; he was, he said, in-
terested in talking to her. Just lately, he said, he'd been wanting to ask
about costumes.

"Costumes?"

"What you and Cyprian wore when doing your shows, your balancing acts. What did you have on?"

"We wore regular clothes. Cyprian said that part of the surprise of what we did was that we looked so normal, then our act was all the more unusual. Besides, at first we couldn't afford anything fancy, no sequins."

"Or red beads?" said Hock.

Delphine understood, thinking of the pantry floor. "Oh, now I see what you're getting at. Are you saying that we could be suspects?"

"Well," said Hock, "you know the beads. They're still the odd component. Your dad says that nobody at the wake wore anything like a sequin or a bead or anything fancy that he remembers."

"Not that he would have noticed, stewed as he got."

"Likely," said Sheriff Hock. "So I've also gone through the props department of our local company. You probably don't think I remember!" He wagged a finger at her, twinkling his eyes in a way she didn't like to see on a sheriff's face. "I know you and Clarisse had a good time with that witch scene. I have a feeling either one of you'd have made an excellent Lady Macbeth."

"We just understudied the part," said Delphine carefully. She didn't know if Hock was veiling an accusation. She attempted to lighten the moment. "Why don't we revive"—she was careful not to tempt bad luck by saying the actual title—"the Scottish play!"

"Sadly, I am bound to my profession. I haven't the time anymore, and anyway, do you think that the people of this town want to see their sheriff as, say, the eponymous murderer? I would lose their confidence."

"People wouldn't think . . . or you could always play Banquo."

"No, no, no, to many, art is life. I am the sheriff, so I must play the sheriff round the clock. To accept any other role while wearing the badge would only confuse people." Sheriff Hock squeezed his chin in his fist now, frowning. In a low voice he asked, "How *is* Clarisse?"

"She's busy." Delphine said this quickly to disguise her jolt of unease.

"Is she really?" Hock said in a light, menacing voice. "Busy? Or is she just avoiding her destiny? I like to think of myself as inevitable."

His sly self-assurance tripped a wire in Delphine. "Inevitable!" she cried. "You're a mental wreck. She hates you. I don't care if you are the sheriff, you should leave her alone."

"Caramel?" Hock extended a dish that had lain beneath some papers. He unwrapped one from its waxed paper and slowly fitted it between his lips.

Delphine shook her head and turned to leave. Already she regretted having lost her temper. Insulting Hock was a bad idea.

She stopped by the drugstore and bought a phosphate, drank it quickly to calm herself. Then she walked straight to the funeral home.

EVERYTHING ABOUT THE Strubs' establishment was tasteful—painted gray and trimmed in dark maroon; even the awnings on the windows were made of matching, striped canvas. The porch was railed with turned cast iron. The lawn was a perfect swatch of muted green and the flowers in the summer garden were hushed lilac and mauve hollyhocks, white petunias, delicate blue bachelor's buttons, nothing too colorful. The back door, also painted a calm gray, was fitted with a modern electric bell. Delphine pushed it, heard a pleasant stroke of music from inside. She looked nervously around to see whether she had been followed. When Clarisse came to the door, Delphine gestured at her to quickly let her in.

"Is it Roy?" said Clarisse, in an anxious, knowing way that temporarily unnerved Delphine.

"No!" she cried out.

"I'm sorry," said Clarisse. "What was I thinking? Come in, come in. How stupid of me." She put her arms around Delphine and led her into a soothing little back entry room.

"We have to talk now. Where can we talk?" asked Delphine.

"I can take you downstairs," said Clarisse. "I'm working with Mr. Pletherton."

Delphine nodded. The basement was a carefully planned space, cool in summer, heated minimally in winter, always just the right temperature for work. There, Clarisse and her uncle and Benta concentrated their attentions on the town's dead. Delphine knew that she was privileged to be permitted to enter—no one else, except Doctor Heech and, in a case of suspected foul play, the sheriff, was allowed downstairs. Delphine had never been particularly bothered, and now she found the Strubs' preparation room much less upsetting than the back cooler of the slaughterhouse. And for sure, anything they said there would go no further. So she went down the back stairs, following her friend, who wore a crisp white coat and now peeled off her gloves with a snap.

"I thought I had a date with a guy from South Dakota, but he stood me up," Clarisse's voice floated back. It seemed that her profession was still as unsettling to potential boyfriends as it had been in high school. The boy had quickly made it clear that if she wanted to date him, she'd have to quit. For a while she and Delphine talked the way they used to, exchanging news of the states of their emotions. Clarisse said she wondered how she could respect a man who was afraid of her job.

"He called me an *undertaker*, Delphine. You know how I hate that! He's like the others. None of them would probably come down here, even if I asked them. They're chicken." Her expression shifted to a startling mask, and she hunched and croaked, "They fear I'll drain them dry as hay."

Delphine laughed, although Clarisse's sudden transformation, in the basement surroundings, slightly unsettled her. In one corner, a phonograph record played lovely, swelling opera music. Clarisse played the music not only for herself, but also, she claimed, the notes had a soothing effect upon the flesh of the bodies she was working on, causing them somehow to absorb the fluids she pumped into them more evenly. She swore it was true, but perhaps her current client did not appreciate opera music. The place was brilliantly lit and Mr. Pletherton, whom Clarisse paused to regard critically before she wheeled him back into the cooler, looked gray and actually dead. Perhaps Clarisse was still trying to get the quality of dye right. She was constantly experimenting, trying to choose the exact right mixture of arterial solution for the peculiarities of each body. "They're all so different." Clarisse gave his arm a clinical stroke as she put him away and there was a small crackling sound. She frowned and muttered, "Postmortem emphysema.

"I'm having a lot of trouble with him, Delphine. He died of food poisoning. Fargo restaurant." There was a whisper of distress in her voice. "Tissue gas."

The north wall was outfitted with glass-fronted cabinets, the top shelves neatly decked with small tubs of lip pins, mouth and eye cement, bandages, and glue. There was a small box of leftover calling cards from visitations. Benta kept the cards to dip in paraffin and she used them instead of cotton to make a durable barrier between the gums and lips. There was Bon Ami, used as a tooth polish, massage cream and lemon juice, vinegar and soap. Piles of clean towels. Hand brushes, hairbrushes, nail files, and clear lacquer. The broad lower shelves were stocked with serviceable gallon bottles of methanol or wood alcohol, ethanol, arsenic solution, formalin, and smaller bottles of oil of cloves, sassafras, wintergreen, benzaldehyde, oil of orange flower, lavender, and rosemary. Aurelius Strub's original embalmer's diploma, the first awarded west of Minneapolis and east of Spokane, hung from the wall in an elaborate frame. Although the basement was always cool, the general heat was wreaking havoc with the burials. Amid all of this Clarisse maintained her cheerful curved smile and her graceful prettiness. She suddenly put Delphine in mind of Malcolm's line, *Though all things foul would wear the brows of grace, yet grace must still look so.* She pushed the quote from her head.

There were two nice plush chairs in the corner, and even a tiny electric stove and a pot for brewing coffee.

"All right," said Clarisse. "I'm all ears. Now, what is it, really?"

Of course, an afternoon visit signaled some emergency, inner or outer, and Delphine got immediately to the point.

"What costume did you wear when you played the lady in *The Lady and the Tiger*?" asked Delphine.

"It was a cute little number, all—"

"Red, pink, peach flapper beads, those tube iridescent kind."

"I sewed a million on that dress, remember? It was practically a work of art."

Clarisse was, in fact, a clever seamstress and used a variation of her stitching to create perfect hidden sutures in her clients, even using two crisscrossing needles sometimes and hiding the knots. Even underneath the clothing, where no one would ever see, her work was perfect and she scorned lock stitch or bridge sutures—*That's just sewing*, she'd say.

"Where is it?"

"I think it's in my closet somewhere," said Clarisse, easily. "Why?"

"Get rid of it," said Delphine.

"After all that work I put into it?" Clarisse dropped her jaw in false outrage.

"Listen, I got wind of the way Sheriff Hock is thinking. You know the cellar door at my house was pasted shut with this awful solid goop and in it there were beads just like your beads."

Clarisse opened her mouth, but then a look of pain and panic suffused her face, and she put her hands to her pretty cheeks. Her little oval nails whitened with the pressure of her fingers, "Oh God, Delphine! I told you that Sheriff Hock practically ripped the dress off me that night . . ."

"I have this feeling that Hock's cooking something up in his fat, fevered head."

"Hock is baiting me," said Clarisse. "He's . . . impossible. I can't reason with him. He'll use this coincidence—the dress, poor Ruthie and Doris . . . how can he? There was a little girl down there!" She burst into quick, frustrated tears, but after a few moments, she took down her hands and said, "No, no, I'll not let him get the better of me. He should lay off. I'm a professional and I have to finish Mr. Pletherton by five, and he's a really difficult case." She suddenly drooped, very tired, frowned at Delphine, and then shook her curls. "Hey, would you be a real girl pal and grab that dress from my closet? Just go home and throw the damn dress in the fire."

Delphine said yes in the conspiratorial intensity of the moment and walked out the door in a blur. When she reached her friend's house and opened the back door, she realized that she was doing something stupid. It would look terrible if Sheriff Hock caught Delphine removing the dress from her friend's closet or in fact found her anywhere near the dress at all. And anyway, what was she supposed to do with it? The beads might melt but it looked as though they wouldn't burn up and disappear. Swiftly, worried, she walked up the stairs to the room in which she'd stayed over often with her friend. She had treasured those nights, normal family dinners, an easygoing family life, all she didn't have. No wonder the Strubs liked their jobs so much—no emotional surprises from the dead, though Delphine knew very well they often presented difficulties. The only joke Aurelius Strub had ever permitted himself, and it might have been simply an exhausted mistake, was to refer to the boy who went through the corn picker as a grave challenge.

Delphine entered Clarisse's room—childishly messy—her friend needed some place to let her hair down, after all. What to do with the dress, the dress that she knew, already, from a hollow feeling in her chest, would be composed of the same color of apricot and sweet pink and red beads she remembered pasted into the pantry floor? Delphine argued with herself, but eventually she walked smoothly out the door with the dress in a sack and ducked around the back of the house. She couldn't fulfill her promise to Clarisse to the letter, she decided. If she brought the dress home the piece of evidence, realistically she had to call it that, was in her hands. There would be no explaining it away. She could just see the beads glittering in the ashes of the outdoor fireplace. Delphine got a shovel from the shed beside the house and began gardening instead. She worked for about half an hour. In case anyone should see her, she thought it best that she just be thinning her friend's iris bed, taking some extra perennials home for herself. In the process, she dug a deep hole and then very quickly stuffed the dress down into it. She shook the bag out, making certain every single bead was in the ground. She put some iris roots into the bag, a few crowded daylilies, and then returned the shovel to its place and walked home.

AS SOON AS she got back to the farm, Delphine made a quick outdoor cooking fire in the fireplace, let it burn down to a perfect bed of coals. She rolled some potatoes into the glowing embers, next, put the grill over the coals, and built a bit of a fire over the ashes to pan-fry some fish in bacon grease. She took a second picking of beans from the icebox, where she had left them to marinate all day. They were cold and sweet and vinegary. Outside in the cool of the evening, the mosquitoes quelled by the smoke, Roy, Markus, and she ate. Delphine took out the cream she'd bought in town and the raspberries Markus picked. That cream was a luxury. She had to admit she liked the money that Cyprian brought back—he gave her most of what he made—because it gave them leave to eat like kings and she had fixed up the house. Still, she was hit with a wave of irritated relief when he drove up as they were finishing, for although she kept him in the back of her thoughts, his absence had been a nagging worry. She hated to admit how glad she was to see him safe, and she grabbed him, hugged him, and shook him, all at the same time.

"You're staying," she said.

He kissed her hand and slowly lifted his hot black eyes to hers. He could flirt, even worn out, with great conviction—had he learned it as a kind of protection for his secret, or was it just in his blood?

There was plenty of fried fish left, and she heated up the string beans in more bacon grease. She prodded a baked potato from the edge of the coals, juggled it from hand to hand before she forked it open on his plate. A jet of steam rose from the potato, and she spooned bacon drippings into the soft meal. He made a grateful sound.

"Tomorrow," she told him, "I am going to try getting a job as a telephone operator. Do you think I have a good voice?"

"Everything is good about you," said Cyprian, sighing over his full stomach and the good feeling of lounging around a fire in the gathering dusk. He really meant what he said. He was glad to be back. Outside the crackle of the flames, the mourning doves uttered their delicate, cool, evening chant. A catbird went through its repertory, song after complicated song, and brush-stroke clouds scattered across the green sky. After a short time, Roy, who had the stamina and routine of a mere mortal now that he was sober, dragged himself off to his little sleeping shack. Markus sagged and then toppled over, dead asleep, and Cyprian carried him into the house. When he returned, Delphine asked a question.

"The way you like men," she said, "do you like boys too?"

Cyprian gaped at her in the firelight, and made a grotesque face. "No!"

"Don't act so shocked," said Delphine, "I had to ask. You sprang that other on me. How was I to know? Anyway, I have this idea I need your help with. Markus. You have to teach him to piss."

Cyprian had just driven twelve hours straight, and he thought that maybe he was hearing things.

"I mean it," said Delphine, "he doesn't know how."

"He sure does know!" said Cyprian.

"Not good enough." Delphine was adamant. "You have to teach him self-control, then the fancy stuff to do with his pecker, like write his name in the sand. You have to teach him to turn the faucet off without touching the spigot. That kind of thing. Otherwise I can't send him back to the aunt."

Now Cyprian got the picture. He knew about the floor and the boy's routine on rising every morning. He nodded slowly as Delphine's intent came clear and then he looked at her with some respect. How many women would think of this? Not a one in all creation, which was why he loved her. It might work. So he agreed to it, and then, the very next morning Delphine made two pitchers of lemonade. One for each. She sent them out behind the henhouse with the lemonade, and every morning after that she did the same. They practiced, and by the end of the week, Markus was dry in the morning. But that was only the beginning of what she felt she had to teach him about survival.

DELPHINE DIDN'T HAVE the chance to go on to the next phase of her teaching plan—how to deal with a raging Tante Maria Theresa. Her idea was to teach Markus to throw a convincing and horrifying epileptic fit. He could learn to roll his eyes back to the whites and bubble spit between his lips. That would fix Tante. Before she could start his lessons, the meat-market truck pulled into the yard, and once again Fidelis stepped out in his rumpled shirt. This time, his pants were oddly shrunken and he wore no socks. There was a tired gloom about him; the skin underneath his eyes was soft and bruised looking, and he was very quiet. Some of his power was sucked away. That was exactly it. He looked as though he'd been deflated, and then Delphine realized that he'd grown almost thin. His raw bones came to the surface, knobs of wrists and knuckles, and his cheeks had slightly hollowed. This time he stood outside the door and refused to come inside even for a glass of water. It was plain that he needed to say something.

"Please."

He wasn't one to say this word, to anyone, not a woman or a man, and he especially wasn't one to say it with the aching quality she heard in his voice. Delphine wondered right then if she'd ever hear the word again, from Fidelis, and she let it sit between them like a small monument.

"I told my sister to leave the place."

Delphine cupped her hand to the curve of her neck and gazed at him, and then took her hand away and stuck it on her hip. She looked out over the field, past the chicken coop. This was something very big. Fidelis had chosen her over his own sister. She took a deep breath and acknowledged that she now had an even more implacable enemy in Tante. Where she had been simply hostile, rigid in her convictions, mouthy, now Tante would need revenge. Getting rid of his own sister was a sacrifice Fidelis had made to get Delphine back into his life. And for it, Tante would surely turn his family against him. Plus now he might act as though she owed him, Delphine thought suspiciously. But his look was only weary.

"She's not coming back," Delphine said, making certain.

Fidelis slightly inclined his head, his eyes dull blue, a little blood-shot.

"Look here, Fidelis," she said, hesitant, for indeed she didn't know that she wanted to return, "I won't do much better than your sister."

Fidelis looked as though he very much doubted that was true. Delphine turned away from him, considered. Her world right now was orderly and peaceful, the first time in her life it had ever been so. As a telephone operator she would be able to make connections, tell time, give numbers, and come home at the same time every night. More peace and routine. Probably more money, too. But then she thought of the boys, how Eva had taught her to handle things, and how she could make the household run smoothly while managing the store. Eva had showed her the tricks, the shortcuts, the patience with details, all of the skills she had gathered through painstaking trials and mistakes. Eva had given her a whole life's worth of knowledge, had trained her, and she'd accepted, because she loved her—very simply, she had loved Eva. She remembered very well all of the times Eva had instructed her about Fidelis and the boys. Near the end, she had been wildly determined that Delphine would take her place. It had helped her to concentrate on lists and habits and little eccentricities of diet for Delphine to note. What had Eva told Fidelis? What had he promised? What did he think? Delphine opened her mouth to ask, but the words stuck.

So she just said, "All right, but here's how it goes. I'll be there eight each morning. I'll work the busy hours and make lunch, then dinner. I'll stay through six each night." She made the terms. She set the rules in a firm, indifferent voice. Waited for his nod of agreement and when she got it, like a man would, she stuck out her hand to shake.

EIGHT

The Burning of the Mutts

A FAMILY IN GRIEF has accidents and stumbles a lot. There are scabbed toes and the terror of eyes nearly put out. Falls off the roof, falls from bicycles, falls slipping in the sawdust of the meat-market floor. And too, the sorrow makes a path for every illness. Mysterious high fevers. Any local pox. Even the sturdy can catch diphtheria, pertussis, not to mention gross stomach flu and run-of-the-mill runs, plagues of snot or crusted eyes and infected ears, lice. Once it grew cold, it seemed that every possible small malady came the way of the boys and Delphine was hard-pressed to keep the hours she'd insisted on with Fidelis. Sometimes she just had to nurse them through a night. Sometimes she had to sleep at the foot of their beds. She became an expert at rendering a chicken into hot soup. She made a routine of daily checks behind their ears for eggs and nits. And even when they all were healthy and breathing hard in boys' dead sleep, she stood in the doorway and worried. They had done this to her. Activated some primitive switch in her brain. She couldn't turn it off. Sometimes before she left, with superstitious intensity, she counted their breaths and made sure they were breathing regularly. She counted exactly ten breaths each, then forced herself to turn and leave at that exact number, not one more or less.

Worry made more worry, made her restless. Sometimes at night she woke, beside Cyprian, and found that against her will her brain restored old scenes of shame or betrayal by girlfriends, boyfriends, long in the past. Or calamities her father's drinking brought on the house. She relived them. Often, she woke Cyprian and made him talk to her, but she never told him that she'd waited with curiosity and daring all the next month after they'd made love, hoping and not hoping, imagining a child. And he never told her that he'd done the same, for with Markus around he couldn't help thinking of it, and he'd always thought that he'd have children. He pictured himself with a son, a daughter, teaching them to add numbers, teaching them to balance, telling them where he was from, and all he knew. So when he talked to Delphine in the night, he thought he might ask whether she was pregnant, but did not, because it would raise the issue of sex, and he didn't want the emotional complexity of that. He had to prepare himself, it required an effort. It was so much simpler to be neutral, and loving, and to stroke her face and hold her hand, to put her back to sleep with stories about his brothers and the stubborn old horse they shared. It was easier to be her brother, but he wanted children all the same, and he wanted to stay with Delphine. As the months passed, he knew she was not pregnant with his child, and so one night, in the moonless dark, staring up into a blackness that seemed a shaft into outer space, he asked her to marry him, for real, with a solid gold wedding band.

The darkness was so dense that night it swirled green around them, and for a long time she didn't answer. But she wasn't thinking it over, she was thinking how to tell him no. There was only one way.

"No."

The long vowel floated over them.

*　　　*　　　*

THERE WERE GOOD THINGS. Delphine ran the shop with an almost joyous dispatch. She hadn't known she'd like the work so much now that she was partly in charge. She didn't mind the hard grind of cleaning, and she had the boys to sweep up and spread new sawdust, to scrub down the display cases and the floors, and Franz to wait trade when things were busy, after school. She began to take an almost embarrassing delight in selling things—a loop of the best liverwurst on this side of the Atlantic, or a piece of the Colby you couldn't get just anywhere, or dried herring from a case recently cracked open, exuding brine and smoke. Eva had given Delphine the magical belief that everything that Fidelis made was unbested and every morsel the shop sold was of a superior quality only their own customers deserved.

This conviction was good for business, and Delphine had, as well, a shrewd eye for what would sell and when to knock down a price. She instituted a weekly drawing for one dollar worth of groceries, and that drew in customers. Except for the banker and the few other rich, who lived in green-lawned flamboyantly painted mansions on a bluff over which their unpredictable river had never yet risen, everyone was broke half the time. Many were worse off—so ravaged and destitute that they couldn't afford any meat at all. Delphine was good at extracting money from the wealthy, and also good at trading carefully with the poor. She stocked barrels of dried beans, peas, made shrewd deals with farms and traded like a horse dealer for the items she was certain that she could sell. She began to deal with an ambitious wholesaler working out of the Cities, and stocked all sorts of new items that made people curious enough to stop in for a peek. Soaps she tried herself and could recommend, powdered health remedies, boxes of steel-cut oats, cider vinegar, walnut oil, pots of mustard. She had a dairy case set into the wall—before, they'd drawn milk from a can back in the cooler. Now she stocked cream, daily milk, butters of three grades, and fresh eggs from Roy's chickens.

Roy was still not drinking. Perversely, this had begun to concern Delphine. Still, how could she quibble with the quiet work he did all around the house? He kept busy, even drove up north with Cyprian from time to time, and didn't snitch from the stash they smuggled across the border and then sold. Sometimes Roy lied to her with a clear and listening expression—told the same sort of stories he'd once told Eva. How once he'd had a part in an Italian opera, or killed a bear, that he had learned to weave from a Navajo and could recite long prayers in Hebrew. Delphine thought she didn't know him. Who was he, sober, anyway? Her father was a stranger, a man of whom she had no knowledge and did not know exactly how to approach. It used to be so easy. Their relationship consisted of times he'd crawl to her and beg for money, and she'd refuse. At least he still socialized with the other men in the singing club. Roy came to the shop after hours to sit around the table with the men and slice rounds of Fidelis's sausage onto square crackers. Cyprian came too. They drove Delphine home after she finished in the kitchen. It was a routine, she later thought, she didn't treasure enough. An even life, without any jumps or starts. No stalls either. It was the kind of life you didn't know at the time you were living it was a happy life.

Every day now, Markus checked the chinchillas, for the fur buyer was due any time, and he wanted their coats in top condition. Delphine didn't understand how Markus could name the creatures, how he could be so careful with them, not to startle them, how he even seemed to love them, and yet didn't express the slightest compunction about their imminent deaths. Delphine guessed she was learning about the nature of a butcher's kid—to see the animals come and go. The only creature exempted from this fatalism was Schatzie, who had lain at the foot of Eva's bed and now slept on guard in the doorway to the boys' room every night. The white German shepherd was serene and intelligent, but bristled with protective inquiry at a sudden noise. Delphine had seen the dog go rigid, growling with authority, at the intrusion of a strange deliveryman. Sometimes the dog looked at her with eyes of clear amber so alert and watchful that she experienced a shiver of recognition. There was no question, this dog was not to be considered on the same level as the other animals whose fates were concluded swiftly once they left the stock pen, or the ones raised for fur.

Markus gloated over figures that his chinchillas would bring, and figured and refigured profits with his younger brothers, pencils in their

small, thick fingers, biting their lips. Franz had declared from the first
that he was too old for such schemes, so among the three younger, they
were to realize all of the money, and they concentrated on the splitting
of it in myriad ways, making this and that argument over whether to
pool their money for some grand object, or divide it, or if there would
be enough to get a new bicycle for each of them. Meanwhile, the valu-
able gray little animals skittered here and there, unknowing, in their
baskets of frail hardware cloth, in and out of their clumsily shaped nest-
ing boxes, softly growing fur, until one Friday night.

After a short appetizer of sheep's offal, the wild dogs leaped and
squeezed through the back fence. Schatzie barked in the front of the
store. While Fidelis searched for burglars and tried the locks, the wild
dogs feasted. They overturned the long line of cages, and plucked out
the chinchillas one by one. They gulped them down or tore them to
shreds, and then were gone, silently as always around the butcher's
house, but leaving their scrambled tracks.

"DELPHINE!" It was Markus, and she thought later with slight shame
that it was a compliment he came to her first thing on the next morning,
just as she entered the shop. His face was broken, sobs were tamped in
his chest, a scrap of fur hung limp in his fist. "They got them, they
killed them!"

She ran out back with the other two boys and saw it was true. The
cages whirled all over the ground, ripped open like shopping bags, and
there was not a chinchilla to be seen. Markus's tattered scrap was the
only remaining piece of evidence the dogs had left, and he held it now
with an attitude of disbelief. He walked forward a little, staggered with
the loss. There was the pie in the sky of big money, but also, Delphine
now saw, these were in a way Eva's odd legacy to the boys, the project
she'd started, and whether they knew it and acknowledged it or not
these creatures were of her own making. Wild dogs should not have had
them. And Delphine could see, when Fidelis surveyed the ruin, that a
similar feeling was building in him, an obscure anger that started low

and crept over him like a heavy cape until he bowed his head a little, looked up from under his brows, and made a decision.

"*Sei ruhig,*" he said to his sons, and in a manner rare to him, he set a hand on each of their shoulders. Then he turned without a word to Delphine, and he stalked back to the slaughterhouse. He gathered old freezer-burned meat, some that had turned in the cooler, molded scraps from a side of beef he was curing for the banker, and he then carried the pans of this out to the edge of the field, dumped it. The boys watched him, Delphine too now, and next they followed to see him enter the little room on the side of the slaughterhouse where he kept his rifles. He loaded both guns, then filled a pocket with extra bullets. He put a chair on his shoulder and he brought this chair outside and set it underneath a tree. He remembered something and went back to the cooler. From its sighing interior he took three beers. He took a loaf of bread, baloney, some cheese and apples. Then he returned to the shade of the tree, in sight of the meat scraps at the edge of the field. From the yard, the boys and Delphine saw him set both rifles across his knees. At last, he opened a dark bottle.

Delphine went back into the house. The bell on the door rang, and it was Step-and-a-Half looking for the usual pan of scraps. Fidelis had just dumped the pan out back to lure the dogs. Delphine looked carefully through the glass at the thickly marbled and perfect cuts of expensive meat, and chose a nice piece of beefsteak. She wrapped it in white paper and twine, and she handed the package over with no explanation.

Step-and-a-Half gave Delphine a strange, barren look and inspected the package, weighed it in her hand.

"Take it," said Delphine, a little roughly.

Across the older woman's elegantly cut features there passed a look of raw suspicion, and she asked, "How much?"

"Just take it!" Impatient with the odd scruples of the other woman, Delphine was perhaps too sharp.

"I don't think so," decided Step-and-a-Half. This was, Delphine understood, a little too close to charity for her stomach, a bit too rich.

Step-and-a-Half rummaged brutally through layers of clothes and pockets, then set down a nickel on the counter. It was the first time she'd paid money in Delphine's experience. Delphine scooped up the nickel, made change of three cents, and tried then to give the pennies to Step-and-a-Half.

"Keep the damn change!" she growled in an insulted huff, then turned to stride out the door, muttering about the terrible price of things.

OUTSIDE, THE BOYS were crouched in the sun on the topmost timbers of the stock pen. Delphine watched them from the kitchen window as they chewed the ends of grass and quietly watched their father. She was surprised to feel a stirring of excitement around her heart, and then guilty as she looked at Schatzie sitting alertly in the shade. In her agitation she prowled to the window repeatedly to see if the other dogs had appeared. As the fall sun rose higher, overhead, the boys came in to eat and she spread the rolls with sweet butter, then wedged in slices of chicken from the old hen she'd stewed yesterday. They took sandwiches to their father, and their own lunches back outside, and sat waiting. More hours passed than anyone would have thought. It seemed when you weren't looking for them, the dogs were always skulking around the field's edge. And then when you waited, they did not appear. Maybe part of the rage Fidelis felt was that in the past he pitied the scraggly pack and fed the mutts. They'd taken advantage of him—a thing he could not allow.

It was late afternoon, and the boys were nodding off in the shadows of the grapevines, when Delphine heard the first crack of a shot. Fidelis had waited, had watched the dogs gather, and now he was shooting steadily. Delphine ran out the back door, climbed the stock-pen sides along with the boys, and saw the dogs go down. First the big solid brown caught a bullet that spun him like a top. The gray took one neatly in the head, skidded to a puzzled halt and slowly toppled. Two medium-size with long, matted fur were hit and ran off howling, to die before they reached the woods. A red dog growled and bit the air before a bullet clipped its jugular. There was a dingy white that crept belly down in the grass. A bullet creased its spine. It stopped. Six more were felled. The last, a speedy gray, loped desperately off and Fidelis sighted carefully along its sinuous back and bore it to earth. The last shot echoed across the field. Fidelis turned and gestured to the boys.

"Pile 'em up," was all he said, and the boys did as they were told, hunted down and carried back each dog and laid them together like a heap of rugs. One of them, Delphine noticed uneasily, was the big brown chow dog that had run wild on the Kozkas. Best, thought Delphine, to get rid of the evidence, and she said nothing. Fidelis came out of the shop with two tins of kerosene. He dribbled one can over the dogs and then he added pieces of wood, downed branches, refuse. When the bonfire was as tall as his shoulders, he poured the kerosene on the top of that. He made a torch of a long roll of paper and carefully tossed it onto the soaked wood.

There was a hollow pop, and the whole thing went up. The fire burned and burned, long into the dusk, and the boys kept adding junk. It smelled for a while like a regular fire and then smelled of roasting meat, then smelled of nothing. The hot fire consumed everything, and into the dark the boys, and Delphine, watched it dreamily, with an intensity they did not understand. For they didn't want to take their eyes away; it was a mesmerizing thing. The timbers collapsed into coals so hot they consumed green wood. Even the bones of the dogs would be ash. There would be nothing left. The fire went on burning, they kept feeding it, and at last it grew so late that Delphine had to send the boys to bed.

Fidelis slept in a room across from the boys, but he slept hard and never woke. So every night, she gave the watch over to the dog, not Fidelis. She never said good-bye to Fidelis, or indeed, made it her business ever to be alone with him at any time. He was working late, now, to make up for his day under the box elder tree with the rifles. As she turned from the doorway to the boys' room, after counting their sleeping breaths, she touched Schatzie and the dog looked up at her as always in agreement. Tired, she gazed a bit too long into the dog's eyes and suddenly she couldn't look away. She stood rooted, tears filling her own eyes, for it was Eva who stared back at her with an expression of extraordinary sympathy and calm.

Delphine's back chilled. "I'm losing my damn mind," she muttered out loud to break the spell. It seemed to work, although she didn't dare look at the dog again. She turned her back on Schatzie and walked out into the yard, past the tangled garden where she'd harvested lumpy squash that day, down to the edge of the field. She stood there alone. All around her, the dark seethed with fall insect noise, with a humming life that rose and sank, surrounding her with inchoate music. She breathed deeply of the spice of weeds under the harsh smoke. "Oh hell, Eva," she heard herself say. Then she was simply talking to her friend, nothing special. Laughing at the boys, the men, the customers. Speculating about the reasons people did things. Since the end, Delphine hadn't wept, she had put all thoughts of Eva firmly from her mind, preferring to let the loss settle wordlessly into her. Tonight, as she stood talking in blackness, an alien sorrow that held some despairing comfort, too, bubbled into her, and she let herself cry with a lost, croaking, ugly sound, until the last coals collapsed into a dull, red foundation and the dark crept close to cover everything.

THAT'S THE WAY it will be, she thought, driving home, her thoughts gloomy and exalted, when I, too, experience the end of things. Those last coals of light going out, extinguished, and then the dark creeping to the corners of her vision. As she turned, a shape on the road, red eyes reflecting her head lamps, leaped away in a ghost arc. A dog. Abruptly, Delphine laughed. Well, maybe even Fidelis could not rid the world of feral dogs, and maybe they would still howl in the dark around her house. And maybe they would even come for Roy's chickens. For no good reason, the thought of one dog escaping Fidelis's seamlessly accurate shooting cheered her and she found her mood oddly buoyant as she entered the yard of the house. Getting out of the car, she heard the rocking rumble of her father's snore. There was a light on in the kitchen, probably Cyprian playing solitaire or reading the cheap drugstore crime and mystery pulps he favored, or even practicing, as he did every day, some small feat for the show he was concocting.

Delphine walked in the door. None of these things. Cyprian was slumped on the table, waiting for her, sleeping in one lamp's dull light. He was in his undershirt and she could see the lightning bolts of war scars, the tough shocks of muscles, the soft gold of his skin. Sleeping there, his face half in the dim glow, he was extraordinary. His face was of such a perfected geometry that he seemed a creature from a fabulous painting, a fallen hero in an ancient scene. Delphine put her hand on his back to wake him, and as he woke, he took her hand in his and held it to the side of his face. For a long while, he held it there, and then he spoke to her, telling her that if she married him she would never have another worry. He would never go with men, he would be faithful to her in the deepest way. The feelings, the things that drove him, that made him seek men, he would give those up. He would stop his thoughts. He would be different. And he could do it because he loved her, he said, and if she loved him back they would be happy.

Delphine sat down next to him, not across from him where she'd have to look into his eyes, but right next to him where she could put her arms around his shoulders. There was nothing she could really say in the face of his trust—if she hadn't seen him with the other man, maybe she could have believed what he said. But she had seen him, and what he did was—she couldn't name it exactly, she couldn't put it into words except clumsily—what she saw was *him*. Truly Cyprian. If someone had an essence, his was in that quick stirring between the two men, their energy and pleasure, his happiness, even, which she had sensed from her hiding place in the leaves and which was still there, changing swiftly as she stepped out into the open.

Instead of answering his question, she told him what had happened that day, all about the morning's discovery, the trap Fidelis had set. She felt him grow interested when she talked about the rifles lying calm across Fidelis's lap, and she was encouraged and went on, distracting him. She told him about the long wait, and then about the shooting, how of a piece it was. Not one shot went astray and none was wasted. It was a great surprise to her, afterward, that Fidelis killed every dog with an ease and precision that she couldn't register in the moment of it for the heat of the simple killing. Only afterward, she told Cyprian, she heard the shots as so regular and seamless they almost seemed one noise.

Cyprian nodded, took in everything she said with a silent and compelled interest, heard about the bonfire and how it was made and the silence of the surprised dogs, and understood the fury of calm that was the killing. All the time that he was listening to Delphine she couldn't know it, but he was thinking something very different from what she might have imagined.

So Fidelis was a sniper. That was his thought. A German sniper. I wonder if he ever had me in his sights, without a helmet, my back turned. I wonder if he was the one who blew the brains out of Syszinski, or the hand off Malaterre, or the heart from the chest of the one I loved?

FIDELIS WALDVOGEL and Cyprian Lazarre never spoke of the war that they shared, yet it lay between them very like the Belgium mud once terrible and now grassed and green. The trenches covered, the tunnels collapsed, the armies of men desperate to live sowed instead through the layers of the earth. Sometimes when they drank together, one of them would have a thought about the war, for neither of them ever passed a day or even several hours of the day without remembering the war. A picture, a sound, a word. Something would enter, and either one of them would pause, wage a small interior struggle, and go on. And the other would have felt the impact, like the aftershock of far distant shelling, and be content or relieved to make a joke or take a long draft of beer.

Only once, when things were quiet of an evening, and Cyprian was waiting for Delphine to finish with some piece of her work, when he and Fidelis were sitting at the kitchen table, did any piece of their subterranean knowledge pass into the open.

"You took fire," said Fidelis, with a critical gaze at the scars radiating lightly upward from Cyprian's throat, one line scored back of the ear to vanish in his shining, crow-black hair.

"And you, clipped here." Cyprian indicated on his own chin the shattered area, a pit of little more than an inch, where the bullet had glanced downward through Fidelis's jaw. They both stopped there, already weary. They could have gone on. Fidelis could have showed him the very bullet, dug from his shoulder, which he wore on his watch chain. Or the saber cuts on his back and across his arm. The astounded flesh of his hip where the caisson went over him the time he was taken for dead. Both men had sustained injuries graver than the obvious ones, hidden by their clothes and hidden, also, by the men they now were. But neither of their experiences had been the kind men built into stories and repeated at drinking tables with other veterans. Those stories were of times behind the lines, usually, of women and of other men, and if there was action or killing involved it was short and glorious. Neither Fidelis nor Cyprian had known glory, and though both had known the grandeur of horror, there was nothing to say about it.

TANTE WAS STEWING. Delphine could feel it like a waft of town sewer gas just down the street. Her standing in the town and among her Lutheran church group had diminished when her own brother asked her to leave his house and brought in this Delphine, a woman who— Tante was easily gathering up the information—was the daughter of the town drunk, under suspicion for murder, a Catholic, and even worse, a Pole, a woman married (if she was, and it was whispered she was not) to a too handsome foreign-looking man who shared her house, a former stage actress and need she say it, all but a blankety-blank. In addition to all of that, this Delphine had moved in on Eva's sickness and befriended her because she knew a good chance when she saw one coming—an eligible widower with his own business and four bright sons—she knew what she wanted, said Tante with dark nods, oh yes, she knew what she wanted, that Delphine.

Tante wrote and sent off a flurry of letters to Germany, full of dark summons, and right away there came back answers that she propped on the cash register and dared Fidelis to ignore. He did read them, tightened his face, but said nothing. He was distracted. In his clothing drawer there was a cigar box containing a jumble of medals, including an Iron Cross. He had arrived in the country with only a suitcase full of sausages he sold and knives he kept, and he had worked fanatically. Only to see everything around him, here, falling into a collapse as devastating as German inflation, which caused his mother, so she had once said in a letter, to cart wheelbarrows of *reichsmarks* to the baker for her loaves. He'd left one Depression to encounter another. And then, after all, his parents had had a great stroke of luck. They managed in the worst year of all to recover a piece of property that was theirs before the war, a store building, and from the share that would have been his, they sent money.

With that money, he had bought the farmstead in North Dakota and opened the shop. He had worked skinning steers and butchering hogs eighteen hours a day to bring Eva, Franz, and then Tante to abide with him. His forbearing, kind mother, and his father, strict and distant, he missed. And his brother, who now shared the family business. But there was work and more work, always more of it, always he was behind what should be done. There was no question, now, of leaving even to visit his family. He read their letters and set them aside before they penetrated to the still center of his person, where he could feel such a thing as loneliness.

Tante took the letters back and slipped them into her purse with a grimace of dissatisfaction. She concentrated even harder on making him aware of her list of shocking true facts about Delphine. He waved her off. She bit her lip at his defense of the Polish woman. Fumed with frustration. To other people, she couldn't go too far in her criticisms, she could not include her brother, lest his business be spoiled and his customers frequent the butcher on the other side of town. Some of her resentful angers had to simmer; then, as stews do, they thickened. She brooded on the grave injustice dealt her by her brother and fantasized returning to Ludwigsruhe. These imaginings, also, grew thick with detail and brimmed with improbable incidents. For instance, into her mind there came the picture of her return complete with boys—well, maybe not Markus, but the other three. Or the twins alone. That could be done.

The way she saw it, she could not return to Germany alone, having failed to find a husband in this new land of men unwinnowed by war. She had to return with something. Motherless children would do. As the heroic guardian of her brother's children, she could reenter town life as their aunt, not an old maid aunt but an aunt with dependents. She would have some status. Otherwise, what was there?

Sometimes, in her spare little house, her sitting room dominated by the cheap teacher's desk she'd bought secondhand at that, her mind jumped like a rat in a cage. She couldn't keep doing bookwork like this, drying up a little more every day, becoming brittle as the pages she wrote on and stiff as the figures she added and subtracted. And yet, if the truth be known, what was all that attractive and important about having a husband? Her friends each had one, and all they did was complain about their men's dingy remarks, their gross habits, their absences, or boast about the types of foods and quantities they ate. There wasn't any real use that she could see in a husband, unless he was rich. And without a rich husband, she had only the books of three struggling concerns to balance—Krohn Hardware, Olson's Café, and the butcher shop—and they could hardly pay her the pittance she asked. So it seemed to her that the only way out of her stark room was to find a rich husband, or to get rid of Delphine and somehow wangle Emil and Erich away from their father while they were still young enough to charm others and not so old as to give her any trouble.

Of course, there was another way. She could, herself, make money. She thought about it. Make money. Nothing occurred to her. She thought about it some more and came to believe it was her only hope. The wish for money began to turn in her brain with a frantic compulsion. She dreamed dollars, dreamed oceans, dreamed of walking off a steamer back to Germany wearing a fur coat. Money danced behind steel bars at night, just out of her reach. One afternoon, over her pale meal of bread and one white veal sausage, a thought struck her that seemed so crazy and outlandish she put it aside. But it came back. She found herself unable to think of anything else.

By the time she got up the next morning, Tante had decided to sell the last remaining piece of her grandmother's jewelry, a cameo that her grandmother had left her, a large and spectacularly carved profile of a woman both demure and sensual. The carving was very fine, and the face sensitive and yet a little wild, the cream hair flowing into the pink of the shell. Tante had admired the cameo as a child, and when she took it from its hiding place, a tiny aperture in the wall behind her dresser, she remembered how she had touched it, softly, pinned to lace at her grandmother's throat on a sunny day at a garden picnic. Times long past. For her it represented all that was secure and comfortable, all that was irreproachable and solid about her life in Germany before the war. She wore it often, too often, to remind herself. To give it up was no small thing. But she was determined. She put the cameo inside a sock and put the sock in her purse. She would sell it, and with the money she would buy a new and fashionable suit. Wearing that suit, she would go to the bank and not leave until she had a job that would eventually, somehow, because it was situated near a large amount of cash, all the money in the town, make her rich.

DELPHINE NEARLY FELL over when she saw Tante, later that week, wearing not the black dress she had inhabited like a second skin, but a skirted suit welded from some fabric of an unusual metallic sheen and stiffness. The thing looked to have been cut and soldered together much like an armor. Tante looked invincible, which was her intention. As she walked to the bank owned and run by the only man in town she knew could afford steaks every night of the week, she felt that things were going to change for her. The suit would do it, she was positive. As she sat outside his office, waiting, and even as she looked at all the bank tellers and clerks, younger, all young men, she still had faith in the material of the suit she wore. The suit's glazed weave sustained her. And even when she was refused a position of any type at the bank, the suit helped her not to lose her belief. She decided to walk down the street, up the street, all over town, and not to quit until she had a position that would bring her money—whatever it might be. Whoever might hire her. The suit would find the place. The suit would bring her there.

So maybe, said Delphine to Cyprian later, the thing was magnetic. It looked it. How else should it happen that Tante should be struck by a car that looked to have been made of the same substance as what she wore? Dragging her feet, worrying the one dime in her purse, Tante crossed the street without looking and was hit by the car of Gus Newhall, the former bootlegger who now sold patent medicines, just coming from the bank, where he'd made a substantial deposit. The car upended Tante in the dust and rolled her sideways into a tree trunk, but didn't do actual, serious damage to her person that could be seen from the outside anyway. The suit wasn't even dusty, but when smoothed gave off the same luster as before. Tante righted herself, pushed away the arms of alarmed witnesses, and would have told Gus Newhall that he was a reckless fool, a swine, a dog's blood cur, only he was a good customer to Fidelis. So she shut her mouth and staggered off, already aching. She made her way to her house. In her front room, on a thick oval of braided rag rug, she lay down. Steadily and with a German effectiveness and efficiency that surprised even herself, she cursed everyone she'd met that day starting with the jeweler who had bought her beloved cameo and who would not, she was certain, trade it back for the suit that had betrayed her.

FRANZ WAS RIDING Mazarine Shimek's bicycle and Mazarine was balancing. Her rear end fit into the U of the curved handlebars, and Franz held tight to the rubber grips on either end. He tried to peer over her shoulder, under her lightly sweatered arm, onto the road before them. He tried not to look at the way the lilac-flowered material of her dress stretched over what rested on the handlebars. Her feet, knees together, white anklets and heavy boy's tie shoes, were carefully placed on the front fender. Her light brown hair was long and curled out of the dull, frayed ribbon she used to hold it back. Strands of it brushed the end of Franz's nose, or touched the top of his lip, or grazed his cheek, as they rode into a light breezy wind on their way to the airfield.

Mazarine liked airplanes, too, or said she did, and collected pictures of pilots and race flights for Franz's scrapbook. She also came along with him to watch the airplanes and sat in the shade of the barn when one of the pilots who kept their machines either in the barn, or who had landed there for the day, allowed Franz to work on his engine. While Franz worked with the men, she got a book from the strap on the rear of her bicycle and did her sums or geography lessons. Sometimes, when she got bored, she did Franz's homework, too. When it was done, she got up and walked around and around the barn peering critically at the airplanes until finally Franz was ready to go home. But they didn't go home right away. They had been going together as sweethearts for months now. They stopped just before the turnoff to the shop. Franz slipped Mazarine's bicycle behind some weeds. Holding hands, they walked to a little spot underneath a pine tree where the branches came down all around them.

"It's gonna get cold here pretty soon," Mazarine said, settling herself on the soft, rust brown needles, "then what?" She pushed Franz's hand away from her knee. He sat back a little and waited. Once, she had taken hold of his hand very carefully, and set it on her breast, the left one, and then said, "Go in circles." He tried that, but soon she frowned and flung his hand off, and said, "That doesn't even feel half good." He kept his hand still, just in case she should want him to try again. Her upper lip was thin, but curved provocatively. He liked the way one curve, the left again, was a little higher than the other and rode up a fraction over her teeth. And her lower lip was full, a deep berry color. Franz knew her lips very well, and her ears, too. She always let him kiss her ears and then go down her throat to just below the delicate ridge of her collarbone. Her eyelashes were so long they made shadows, and she said the other girls envied her. They were lush brown, like her eyes, and much darker than her heavy sun-streaked hair, springing out over her shoulders.

He touched her hair, even dared tug it gently, and moved closer. She moved right next to him and sat in the curve of his arm. They were resting against the base of the pine, and had to be careful always to leave before it got dark, so that they could pick sap and pine needles off each other's back. He turned his face to hers. She closed her eyes like an obedient child, opened them when he finally drew his mouth away from hers. She licked her lips, looked at him mockingly, then thrust her hand right between the buttons of his shirt and up the side of his chest, scratching her nails lightly along each rib. Mazarine had simple rules. Franz was allowed only to do the precise things she permitted. She, on the other hand, could do anything she wanted to him, provided he stayed still and didn't grab for her. And that, Franz found, was very difficult when what she did became unbearable.

SHERIFF HOCK WORKED late into the evening, by the intense light of a green-shaded banker's lamp, putting his files in order. Most all of the crimes he dealt with were petty, small thefts or disorderly conduct, saloon troubles or domestic fights, or so large as to fall beyond his influence. Of the latter category, which included acts of God and automobile accidents, he dreaded most presiding at farm auctions and foreclosures. Even though Governor Langer had ordered the banks to cease, Zumbrugge managed one or two every year, and it was the sheriff's job to keep the peace at the event. Sheriff Hock had been approached several times in regard to auctions that would have stripped Roy Watzka of his farmstead. Yet each time the bank came near to foreclosing, Roy would at the last minute come up with the money on his loan—no one had any idea where the money came from. But he would pay the money and then drink until the next payment was due, at which time the entire process would repeat itself.

For the first time in many years, Roy had paid the bank on time. Sheriff Hock stared at the brown cardboard file in the pool of light. Surely, he thought, Roy's prompt fiscal responsibility had to do with Delphine's return. He wanted very much to close the case, to name the incident a terrible mistake—after all, the wake had been disorganized and people did get locked in cellars. But then there was the strangeness of it, the horror of the death. The weird glue of peach juice and ornamental beads and dog crap. The damn beads. Clarisse! He passed his hands across his face, recalling the old humiliation and Delphine's contempt for his pain. Helpless before the memory, he cringed in his chair and diverted his thoughts. But they all led back to Clarisse. He thought of her all the time, even when he wasn't thinking of her. She was the background to his every minute, everything he did. His best method of evading her was to imagine himself locking her in a closet. Stuffing her in. Tenderly kissing her. Turning the key. It always took her hours to get out and while she was struggling he could focus on other concerns.

There was the odd fact of Roy's deafness to the noises underneath his house. Sheriff Hock wished that he could feel the certainty that some in town, anyway, felt about the guilt of Roy Watzka. But he had the sense that Roy was honest, if soused half the time, and basically as harmless as his daughter insisted. Sheriff Hock was, he liked to say, a man of instinct, and his gut feeling was that something was missing, some information. He wasn't at all certain that this information had to do with Roy, and yet he saw before him, in another unclosed file, a chance to set a certain event into motion that might shake loose a fact or two. From that file, he smoothed a document which he read over slowly, nodding at the words. Deciding, he slapped his hand on the paper. Then he folded it neatly and lifted it to his front pocket. The paper crackled as he turned off the lamp.

IT WAS A BRISK gold afternoon and leaves were swirling through the air when Sheriff Hock arrested Roy Watzka for the theft of the morphine. Although the theft was way back when and Fidelis had immediately gone to the sheriff, just afterward, and explained the entire situation, Hock behaved as though he'd just begun the investigation. Fidelis had been paying Sal Birdy a little each month for the medicine, and Sal had easily accepted that. Nevertheless, Sheriff Hock made the arrest. Roy went along peacefully and seemed resigned to his jailing. He went to the cell he'd often inhabited before, only then he'd been immune to his surroundings, drunk and snoring, and hadn't cared about the tattered blanket or the stained walls or the faintly reeking piss bucket. He walked in, as usual, closed the door behind him. This time, things were different. As a sober man, Roy had become surprisingly finicky. The first thing he did, to the amazement of Sheriff Hock, was request a certain pine-scented ammonia he'd used to make the chicken house habitable, along with a mop and bucket, water, a brush and rags. He stuffed the old blanket through the bars and tried to pound the bugs out of the mattress. And all without even asking whether his plight was yet known to his daughter. Sheriff Hock took it upon himself to go to Waldvogel's and inform her, but first he made certain preparations to ensure that he could spy on her actions following his news.

The moment Sheriff Hock walked into the shop, Delphine knew with a sick clarity that Roy was in trouble. She knew all of the good and calm times she'd feared too good to last had been indeed too good to last. They were over. The news would be humiliating, because of course Tante was in the shop, too, talking to Fidelis just around the corner. Delphine prayed their conversation would turn into a long involved argument, that they wouldn't step into the shop. Of course, if they shut up, they could hear everything from right where they were.

What Sheriff Hock had to say would not be good because he wore his stage manner. He couldn't help play the part, Deliverer of Bad Tidings. The drama on his face was heavy as stage makeup. Delphine had that disengaged feeling, the same she'd had when confronting Tante with the needle, that she was playing a part, too, and that she knew all he would say and all that she would say, that this moment had been rehearsed since the beginning of time.

Just as the sheriff opened his mouth, the voices on the other side of the door ceased, so of course Tante heard what the sheriff said. It would be repeated all through the town in minutes.

"I've arrested your father."

"I want to see him." Delphine's voice was very calm. Wearily, she blocked herself from imagining the gloating shock that had just appeared on Tante's face. She asked the amount of bail and Sheriff Hock told her that would be determined by the town judge, Roland Zumbrugge, brother of Chester, and that she was free to pay it and get him out, although, he also said, Roy was settling in very well.

"Oh, I'm sure he's perfectly at home there," said Delphine, her voice twisting with as much sarcasm as she could muster. Then her part called for sincerity, and she gazed into the cushion-cheeked but sharp-nosed face of the sheriff. "You know he didn't do it," she suddenly blurted. "He's a harmless person."

At once, the sheriff's face became slightly more watchful. As he'd hoped, Delphine had just assumed the charge was related to the three dead in her father's cellar, and now Sheriff Hock cautiously hedged, in case she should make some slip in her state of false assumption, some small mistake that would afford him more information. "Nobody, in my experience," said the sheriff, "is completely harmless when drunk. It would probably be best to find a good lawyer."

"And where," asked Delphine, now bitter, "am I to find the money to pay a good lawyer?"

Sheriff Hock's girlish smile pursed, then twitched, and again his eyes got that twinkle in them that Delphine thought very menacing in an officer of the law.

"Our friend Cyprian could probably raise a little extra money on his trips up north," the sheriff suggested.

Delphine wished an immediate stroke of deafness on Tante's flaring ears and maintained a blank expression with great difficulty. Inside, her heart surged; she turned her face aside as though mystified by Hock's reference. "I have no idea what you're referring to," she coldly said. After that, there were no lines to follow, no script at all. So she quickly returned to familiar ground.

"When can I visit my father?"

"Any time."

She kept herself from automatically saying thank you, turned on her heel, and slapped her apron on the counter in order to alert Tante and Fidelis, the eavesdroppers.

"You heard it," she said to Tante as she passed, "shut your damn mouth."

Tante remade her delighted indignation into a pout of false distress. Fidelis had already removed himself and followed Sheriff Hock. Maybe he can find something out, thought Delphine. Out the back door, in the cold and brilliant sun, Delphine breathed hard and went over the exchange. Her mind kept sticking on the part about the evidence. What evidence? Where did it come from? Whom? If they had enough to haul Roy in, there had to be a witness, or at least a set of circumstantial facts that would be set out before a judge. Panicked, she went to find Clarisse.

DELPHINE ENTERED the basement mortuary and Clarisse, at the sink, turned with a perfectly glowing look and said, "I'm so glad you're here!"

When her work was successful, Clarisse was vivid with satisfaction, sparklingly fresh and alive. Her skin was satiny, pure white, not a freckle on it. Her lips were a deep unlipsticked red and her eyes transparent with delight at her friend's visit.

"I've got to talk to you again," said Delphine.

With a dancer's flourish, Clarisse indicated her work area.

"I've got to show you someone!"

"Not now, Clarisse. Sometimes you get carried away," said Delphine.

"This is the last view these parents will have of their child," Clarisse answered, her face serious. "Is that carried away? Perhaps, well, I'll tone down my manner, of course. I was just—"

"It's okay, it's okay. I'm overwrought, Clarisse. Roy's in the jailhouse."

"It's that damn Hock," said Clarisse. She shook her curls a little and handed Delphine a cup of freshly brewed coffee. "Although, come to think, you must admit, it *was* his cellar. And he *was* very drunk that night, well . . ." She fluffed the hair out around her ears and shook her head, conveying sympathy without implicating herself. "I didn't see a thing. I wish I had. Oh, look at you. You must get more rest! You've got dark circles under your eyes." She took Delphine's hand in her own, just the way they used to when they were girls together talking earnestly down by the river. "Don't worry," she said, "we'll think of a way to get Roy out."

Delphine nearly shook her hand away.

"You *do* think he did it! He's a souse, but he wouldn't deliberately do anything that cruel. You know he's been strictly on the wagon—"

"But when has he ever not fallen off and disappointed you?" asked Clarisse gently.

"Never," Delphine said.

Clarisse looked at her solemnly, put her fingers up, and pinched her lips shut.

"I know what you're trying not to say," said Delphine.

Clarisse nodded. Then she unpinched her lips.

"I will say this, Delphine, you should get out of here. Just leave him be and go to secretary school. Be an actress. Anything. Take a train to the Cities."

Delphine laughed. "With what money? And by the way," she lowered her voice, "I buried your dress in the iris patch."

Clarisse now looked very grave and thanked her for hiding it. "You're on my side," she said. "You've always been on my side."

"Of course I am," Delphine said. "I just wish I knew."

"What?"

"Who locked them down there."

"You just have to believe it wasn't Roy, don't you?" said Clarisse.

Delphine nodded.

"Then it wasn't him," Clarisse said. Reaching over, she put her arms around Delphine and held her head to her shoulder. Delphine's breath ballooned up in her until she sighed. She let herself sag against her friend. Clarisse smelled of formalin and bath powder. There was coffee on her breath and blood on her shoe. From time to time, Delphine thought, life fooled her into thinking there was someone on earth she would be as close to as Clarisse. Then the person was hauled away, or died, or retreated, and it was just the two of them again. Odd women out. Unique girls. Strange.

HIDING A MAN of his bulk was extremely difficult, but Sheriff Hock was used to assuming the disguises of the stage. His automobile would have been too conspicuous in the empty town streets, so he had borrowed a shabby buggy from a deputy's barn and commandeered a tired old horse to draw it. Shortly after leaving the shop, he put on a farm hat and a torn canvas coat. He then drove the buggy to a safe distance for surveillance, pulled to the side of the road to let the horse crop grass, and put his head down on his chest. From there, it was an easy matter. Following Delphine was simple—in the strictly platted town he could easily project her destination, and with no trouble keep her in sight down the wide dusty avenues and streets. The funeral home was no surprise to him. He thought of Clarisse in the tight, red, fabulously shiny stage dress. Was there some way to bring her back into the picture? Closer, so she would see what kind of man he really was? He put his hand to his cheek as if he could still feel the lump she had raised when she slugged him at her father's rowdy wake. She was much too fierce for anyone else in this town, he thought. He was the only man who wasn't afraid of her. He deserved her. And he was getting tired of the way she evaded him and put him off. Her excuses and protestations. If she would only, only, surrender her hard little nut of a heart! Let the shell crack! Reveal the love! He was positive it was there. It made him so angry with her. She was stubborn, wasting precious time. Youth was fleeting. They should be walking along the weedy riverbank and planning their future. Sheriff Hock set his teeth and felt his face harden. When this wave of frustration engulfed him, he wanted to shake her until she woke up, to yell into her face until he broke her composure, to crush her until she cried out his name in a pain that sounded like passion.

DELPHINE WAS ALLOWED to sit upon a small rickety caned chair just outside the bars of her father's cell. He was morose, "but at least it's clean, now," he said, nicking his frowzy head at the newly scrubbed floors, walls, and the bed, which was now outfitted in sheets that Delphine brought. Apple Newhall fixed the prisoners' meals, and the contents varied according to her feeling for the prisoner. Roy was a favorite of hers, and for dinner he was given a plate of beans baked in tomato sauce, a large beer sausage, and half a sweet onion. Delphine watched him eat. Roy's rough claw dipped the dark syrup from the beans. He chewed tentatively because of his frail old teeth. From time to time he stopped and sighed in the drama of his entrapment. He missed the picture of Minnie, his small personal shrine, and he dearly wished for the afghan he said that she had knitted, which Delphine had rescued from the grand stink and soaked clean in the river. It had become something of a security blanket to him ever since he'd sobered up. Why now, thought Delphine. Why now that he's sober and thoughtful, and living as a good man, does he get in the worst trouble of his life? Perhaps she forgave too easily, or perhaps she wasn't really able to recall, out of self-protection, what a failure of a father he really had been all along. She hated this pity that overwhelmed her and covered him. His failing physical state twisted her heart—she didn't want to see how his hands shook, how he shuffled instead of stepped, how thoroughly the booze had unstrung him over the years.

She held one of his beat-up paws, "Dad, you didn't do it, I know. You'll soon be out. I'll get a lawyer."

"What lawyer?" Roy peered at her with an incredulous frown. "Of course I did it . . . everybody knows, they saw me. I had to."

For a panicked moment Delphine hushed him. Sheriff Hock was standing near and now, having heard every word, he had stepped up behind her with a lightness surprising in a man so large. He was listening, Delphine suddenly knew it, to see if his trap would spring, listening to hear her next words, which she drew cautiously from a neutral store. "So Fidelis has offered to pay your bail, if there is—"

"Fidelis told Albert here what happened right off! Eva had to have the stuff and you can bet I was going to get it for her. I cared for that woman, she was a good and a kind person," said Roy with great emotion. "Made a thick sandwich for a man and understood my thirst."

At the mention of Eva's name, Delphine's picture radically shifted, and with some difficulty she responded to the changed scenario. She stumbled a bit, though, her brain connecting with the stolen morphine, before she turned to Sheriff Hock. "How come now?" she said, masking her relief with indignation. "If you were going to charge him, why didn't you pick him up right after?"

Sheriff Hock, subtly disappointed, rocked back on his heels and lied that before he could get word to Sal Birdy, the drugstore owner had reported the theft to the state commission. Mr. Birdy very much regretted having done so, but now, to everyone's annoyance, the commission had demanded a full investigation of the occurrence. Roy's arrest was carried out to satisfy the record, and he'd be free as soon as all of the paperwork was finished.

"This is only a formality," Sheriff Hock concluded, and walked off in an air of slight embarrassment.

"A formality!" Delphine's voice let go—she tried not to sound too relieved, attempted the appropriate indignation. But she wanted to sink her face in her hands and breathe very deeply. Wanted to shed the low hysteria she'd felt at the prospects and plans that had whirled in her head—the lawyer, the trial, the jury, the judge . . . all of the implications of a murder charge. Now, she had only to sit still. So Delphine stayed with Roy for a while longer, listened to instructions regarding the various personalities and proclivities of his chickens. "I've got a Romeo and Juliet in the bunch," he said. "Star-crossed banties. Don't disturb the two black rosecombs that perch together. As for that loud dominicker, you can stew him for all I care. Let the little guy take over with the big reds. He can do the job." Roy kept talking, clearly did not want to quit, didn't want to face the moment when Delphine had to get up and leave him alone in the place where so often he'd slept unconscious but that he now, fully aware, occupied in a virgin state of shame.

DURING THOSE persistently dry years, the stock was less and less worth butchering, the cows were so bony and lean, fed on green thistle alone or the poorest scrapings of slough grass and even young cottonwood bark. But for the last week, Fidelis had sudden business. He worked late into the night, worked until his knee gave out on him and he had to put on the leather brace Heech had sketched and then ordered from a harness maker. Though his knee creaked and ached, Fidelis believed this brace and Heech's sewing abilities had kept him from becoming entirely lame. For sure, it helped him work strange hours. Farmers sometimes didn't get their animals in until just before dark. They had to kill by the light of torches, wrestling steers into the killing chute, then skinning and butchering until almost dawn. This morning, Fidelis had slept two hours, then jolted awake to get the boys out of bed for school. For a moment, he stared into the gray air, entranced by an unfinished dream in which he followed Eva down a certain street they both knew in Ludwigsruhe, and entered behind her into an unfamiliar shop.

The place was tiny, studded with merchandise of every type from pins and fabrics to pots of jam. It went on and on, back into the side of a hill, a catacomb of gray wooden corridors lit dimly by bare lightbulbs. She was wearing a dress of light plum cotton and it floated behind her as she swiftly turned corners. Suddenly, at the end of one cramped hallway, Eva turned around at his call and came toward him with a smile of surprise, as if to say, "What are you doing here?" And then he woke, of course, and although each cell of him wanted to lie still, to sleep on and on, through weeks, he must rise and wake his sons.

He stumbled out of his room and into theirs, shook Franz awake wordlessly, and then touched Markus. All he had to do was touch Markus, or even his bedpost. Emil and Erich must be awakened with more care. They'd doze off instantly if left a moment. He walked to the bathroom and drew a mug of water from the tap, rinsed his mouth out, pissed, took his pants off a hook on the door. Then he walked into the kitchen and set a kettle of water on the gas range for the watery morning chocolate he added to their milk. He warmed the milk in a pan. Into another pan of water he dumped some oats, then turned down the heat so they wouldn't boil over. His eyelids kept flickering, shut. He filled the coffeepot with water, a handful of grounds, eggshells from a bowl of them he'd saved. Then he sat at the table with his hands cradling his head, and fell asleep. Wakened when Emil entered the kitchen wearing only one boot.

"Where's your other boot?"

"Schatzie must have hid it in the night."

The dog's one awful habit.

"Find it," ordered Fidelis, rising to tend the stove. Next, it was Markus, who said that pulling on his jacket he'd torn the sleeve half off. How could that happen? Fidelis examined the jacket. Impossible. "You were fighting yesterday?" Markus hung his head and couldn't look at him. Fidelis flung the jacket back at him. "Tonight, you work. A liar works twice as hard in his life as an honest man." Fidelis was certain that this wasn't true, from what he had seen, but the phrase came out and sounded right. He pushed Markus toward the bathroom. "Get clean."

Next Franz, no problems, but just being Franz there was always an intensity about his grooming—nobody must disturb his routine. "I found Emil's boot," he said, but it was clear he wanted to punch his little brother, and couldn't, because he was a young man after all and had his dignity, so he brooded over his hair.

"*Essen.*"

Fidelis brought the pan of oatmeal, bowls, brown sugar, milk, his precious coffee, to the table. Now it was Erich's turn. He wandered into the kitchen in his pajamas. "Where's everybody?" He had crept into the bathtub and managed to fall asleep without anybody catching him.

"Get back in there, get dressed!"

Of course, he didn't know where his clothes were, where anything was, and Fidelis felt his blood surge with irritation, and also sympathy. He ached for sleep, too, just the same. If only they two could crawl back into bed and curl in the blankets and snore like bears until Eva rocked the headboard and sang out for the lazybones to come and get their breakfast. Fidelis trudged back down the hall to the room. The clothing was still crumpled in a ball from last night, and faintly sour, but he made Erich put it all on. And his boots weren't missing. By the time he got back to the kitchen, the coffee was beginning to stir his brain cells.

The numbness of sleep left his face. He stretched and groaned as the boys secured their books with bookstraps, and grabbed their lard pails of the lunch that Delphine had made the previous afternoon. A cold potato, a piece of meat. An apple or a carrot. Sometimes she fried great rings of doughnuts or made a thick gingerbread. They piled on their coats and then pitched out the door. By the time they left, Fidelis was on his second cup of coffee. He'd learned to make that right. He brought the coffee into the bathroom and set it on the windowsill, added a good long dribble of Fornie's Alpenkrauter. Then he mixed a lather in his shaving mug, and soaped his face with the silver-handled boar's-hair brush that Eva had given him, along with a matching hair-brush and razor, as a wedding gift. After shaving, he patted his face with a towel, then rubbed his chin and cheeks with bay rum, and at last walked out into the shop.

The sun streamed through the heavy windows onto the wood-block tables and counters. The wood was hacked, scored, blackened in the marks and seams, but the tables' surfaces were scoured white. The blaze lighted his block of knives. He examined his knives, blearily clung to his careful selection for the sharpening. Next, he brought from the cooled back room halves of pig, scalded and gutted and hung yesterday. As he worked, diminishing the pork with economical clarity and swiftness of motion into perfect cutlets and medallions, he felt the leaden numbness that ran up his fingers diminish. The muscles in his arms grew limber, and he used the knife to cunning effect. All the while that his body moved, of its own will, his mind grew heavier with the need for oblivion until about eleven, having worked and cut steadily with only a short break, he had to stop. The sleep pressed behind his eyes with such an intensity that only a brisk turn outside in the yard would help. Again, he shook the sleep off, and then returned to his work until late in the afternoon, when Delphine told him to go back and lie down. She said that his eyes were bloodshot. She said it rudely.

"Get out of here," she ordered. "I will handle things."

For the first part of his life, Fidelis had been taught to read only crude signs from women, but Eva had instructed him in looking for subtler clues from her sex. So he knew that Delphine was careful to show no hint of sympathy, allowed not even a personal word of kindness to pass her lips, because she did not want to begin something between them that she considered impossible. And he, too, was immaculately impersonal in his behavior toward her. Every word referred to the business, or to the children. He and she were strangers living parallel lives, working alongside each other every day. Between them, they had put up an invisible wall. Fidelis knew it had to stay intact or something would crash down around him, around them all. He sensed the power of what their strict rules held back and kept himself from wondering at the nature of the force, its shape, its name. It was just a thing that must be left alone. He went back into his bedroom, shut the door, and took off his shoes. He lay down on the bed, and when he did, he felt his bones through his flesh and his muscles, unstringing, and he stretched immediately into a sleep so black it was like being dead.

He slept for hours, then started awake the way he had that morning, staring at the ceiling. Only this time, his body half lifting in the bed with that buzzing sensation of pleasure in having truly rested, he lingered in the warm sheets because of the unfamiliar sensuousness of that relief. These were the times he would, in the past, turn to Eva and begin the slow lovemaking that they'd learned from each other. Over the years, they had added to their private love—unlike others, he suspected, who did what they did to get the need over with. Other men joked or complained about the length of time their wives gave them—a little longer, maybe, if they behaved well that day. Fidelis never said a word when men got into those sorts of conversations. He knew things were different between himself and Eva, that there was something greater than the thing the other men discussed. That something had its own grandeur mixed inevitably with loss. When she died and was truly gone, the day he, and then each of the boys, threw the first clods of earth upon her casket after it was lowered into the ground, he'd had the sense of some beautiful immensity passing overhead in the heavens, away from him forever, and he'd gone very still. He'd tried not to move. The other mourners had seen a man rooted to the earth, standing like a block, dumb as a turnip. He'd become embarrassed at the picture he made and forced himself to step away. But some part of himself never did leave, he thought now; he was still standing at the edge of her grave. He was still feeling the blood squeeze through his heart, the hum of his brain, the clutch of his fingers, the earth drying in the cracks of his palms. He was helplessly alive, wholly divided into life, powerfully different from Eva. Sometimes he still felt the wonder of it.

DELPHINE DID EVERYTHING she could to distract herself from the fact that she had to thank Fidelis, had to talk to him about having freed her father on bail. She transferred all the meat from one case to the next, and scrubbed out the first air-cooled case with a sharp mixture of vinegar and water. Then she arranged all of the meats in the case again, placing between each tray the careful decorations, cut of green waxed paper, that set off the pork chops and sausages and steaks. While she was finishing, she thought of all of the other jobs she could do, but even as she added them up she grew irritated with herself. Why not talk to him this very minute? In the middle of dunking a rag to make another swipe at the glass and enamel, she wrung it out instead and laid it on the steel counter. Closed the sliding doors.

"Fidelis"—she stood behind him and he turned from his task— "you paid the bail for my father."

He nodded, wiping his hands on his apron.

"Yes." He acknowledged Delphine, then tried to turn back to the meat he was grinding and spicing, but there was more.

"You'll get it back."

"Sure," said Fidelis.

"I will pay you back," said Delphine. "If he . . ."

"But he won't leave."

This was going to force him to say more, and he knew it, and all that morning he had thought it out. But it was still hard for him to say what he had to say to this woman. He took a huge breath, and made the attempt. "What you did for Eva, and then what Roy did . . ." But that was as far as he could go.

"She was my friend, and good to my dad. I didn't do it for you." Delphine had decided to speak plainly.

Fidelis shrugged to say that didn't matter, but she preempted this.

"Look," she said, "I don't want people to start saying things. And Tante, her especially."

"She doesn't know I paid."

"But she will. She does your books. And then so will everybody else in town."

Fidelis frowned, considering this, but remained stubborn.

"So if they do," he said, "they'll think of what you and Roy did for Eva."

"I don't want people thinking about that." Delphine tried to keep her voice low, but it rose beyond her, sharp. "I know what they think already, I've heard it, and I know that your sister feeds those rumors with her gossip. I want an end to it. But I'm glad . . ." Here she stumbled a little, for it was hard for her to say this, and her voice dropped, low and shamed. "Thank you for getting him out. I never knew my father sober before this. It was hard on him, getting locked up, and in real trouble, after he'd finally taken the pledge."

This was more than she'd ever said to Fidelis here, or revealed to him in this shop and in Eva's house. It had been easier to speak her mind to him on her ground back at the farm. They turned away, both relieved and exhausted. Delphine wanted to go home and sleep. Fidelis felt a heaviness pressing on his chest. For a while that day, everything they did seemed twice as difficult, but gradually, as they ignored each other or spoke only in the most necessary monosyllables, things returned to normal. Any stranger walking into the shop would think the two disliked one another, but the truth was, neither of them could bear the danger of displaying any hint of the weight of tension each lived with regarding the other. So their rude, clipped interactions were safe ground where they could calmly coexist.

There were times bound to arise after that unprecedented exchange of words, even whole sentences, where the same might easily happen again. Not long after they spoke, Delphine became convinced that Eva's boys were going to kill themselves. She told Fidelis, but he shrugged and said, "They are boys." She had dealt, already, with their summer shake-ups, the near drownings, and the damned swing that, if they failed to jump off in time, smashed them headfirst into the tree trunk. Now that the leaves were off the trees and the snow had not yet fallen for them to slide on and, doubtless, to devise cunning ways to kill themselves rushing downhill, she didn't think they'd have much else to do but hammer their thumbs or crash the homemade car they raced downhill. Thank God that Fidelis hadn't the money to buy them guns. She could not have anticipated what they did come up with, what obsessed them, what began to run their lives after school in the late afternoons. She only had a sense of it, some tension and excitement in their doings. There were arguments and conspiratorial noises that stopped abruptly when she entered rooms. Tools were mysteriously missing. She found a great deal of dirt in the creases and the pockets of their clothing.

NINE

The Room
in the Earth

$\mathcal{A}$ YEAR HAD PASSED since his mother's death when Markus found himself fascinated by the idea of excavation. Raw or abandoned construction sites are magnets to children of a certain age. There was a place just on the other side of the pine and oak woods a mile or two behind the butcher shop where a grand house had been planned, the basement dug out, the dirt piled in a huge heap behind a mass of trees. The prospective owner of the place had run out of money early on. Not so much as one board had been set in place, nor had a rotting shed in the yard been pulled down and hauled away. Markus stumbled on this place one day when out hunting, which is what he called aimlessly wandering with a slingshot and a pocket of stones. He, of course, jumped down into the basement first, walked the gumbo bottom, then had trouble clawing his way out. Next he admired the scavenging possibilities of the broken-roofed shed. He ducked inside, kicked the mice berms, and poked the swallow nests to see if he could scare the birds out, but they had already flown south. He found rusted cans on the floor and, thrillingly, the head of an ax with a broken shank, which he hefted and carried out with him. Following a short, rutted trail, he then discovered the mound of earth removed from the basement. It was so high and new that it wasn't even yet grassed over, just sprouting the coarsest weeds like a balding head. He clambered up the sides of the hill. At the top, he put down the precious ax head alongside his slingshot, lay down, and stared up at the sky.

While he was watching the pale streaks of clouds, it seemed to him that something moved beneath him, as though the earth shrugged a little. Perhaps it was the dirt pile rearranging itself, perhaps nothing, but the sensation of the earth's living quality was very pleasant and he waited to feel it again. Nothing happened except, as often occurred during that first year, he found that he was crying without reason and without even being aware that it was starting. This weeping plagued him, it was very annoying, and he had to watch himself closely when at school, for fear that some of the other boys might see the tears. Several times he'd been forced to run to the outhouse as though he had the shits, just to gather himself. So it was a relief to be alone, with no witnesses, and just let the tears run down naturally, out of his eyes and down the sides of his temples, until they stopped, which they eventually did. When they quit flowing out, he sat up, grabbed his ax head and slingshot, and tried to slide down the hill over the slick weeds. That didn't work so well, though he ripped up a lot of plants and made a crude tear in the earth.

At the bottom, sitting against the side of the hill, he again had the feeling that it moved, twisted against his back as though within it a giant had turned in its sleep. He wondered suddenly if it was hollow, like the hills he'd heard of in wonder tales. He turned, pressed his ear to the ground where it rose up behind him, and heard his own heartbeat bouncing off the solid, packed hillside. But it seemed there was something more the hill required of him. So he sat there a good while longer before, almost out of boredom, with no real outcome in mind, he began to dig against the side of it with the head of the ax.

The deeper he dug, the more earth he pulled away, the more exquisite the vision that developed in his mind. At first, he didn't know what he was even imagining, or what he was starting, but as the hole got large enough to admit a shoulder, then his head, and as he chopped downward and finally effected a shallow, bowl-shaped groove, he understood that he was digging something into which he might fit. The ground was heavy, a crumbling black containing tiny white fragile snail shells and clamshells the size of fingernails; it was packed to a tight wall but sometimes he hit a space where it was softer, easier to dig. Sometimes clods of it fell from the upper side of the hole, and he pushed them out impatiently with his feet. When he had dug farther and scooped out a deep pocket in the earth, he backed himself underneath the overhang of ground and sat there. The dirt under him was soft, and he was very comfortable—he found he didn't want to move although his stomach hurt, he knew that he was hungry. Which made him think that next time he came out, he'd bring some food, which made him realize there'd be a next time. He had only started on this thing.

That day, he sat there for a very long time. Surrounded by the smell of earth, those uncontrollable tears that plagued him with no warning came again. And when they came, he let them drip down indifferently, in fact he welcomed them. Into his mind there came the picture of his hand. In his hand was the clump of dirt he'd taken, just like his father, to throw down onto the lid of his mother's coffin. He'd looked at his hand and the dirt in his hand, and then he had frozen over the lip of the grave. He regarded the white sprays of flowers as in a trance. Instead of opening, his fist shut tight. Franz had turned back to him. Franz had held his fist over the hole, pried his fingers apart, and shook out the dirt. Franz had dusted his palm. Grabbed his arm so he came away, stumbling, from that mysterious sight. And when he was well away, Franz had dropped his arm, and said nothing.

Nobody had said a thing all the way back from the graveyard and after that, it seemed to Markus, the silence had grown deeper, surrounding everything that had to do with his mother. His father never spoke of her, referred to things she did, or even mentioned objects that might remind anyone of her. All she owned seemed to vanish—her flowered wash dresses, her shoes, her fur-trimmed cloth coat. Only Delphine said her name. It was not as though his mother vanished, for then her things would be left to hold. It was more as though she'd never existed at all.

Not for Markus. In his thoughts, she was more powerful than ever, and stubbornly, he nursed words and pictures and spoke of her to himself. Others might let her go, but he didn't have to, that was his choice.

The dirt sighed a little, sifted down his back. The hill was still shifting and rearranging itself, still settling mote by mote into its most compact shape. Markus closed his eyes and drifted. He actually fell asleep. When he woke in the shallow den, and came to consciousness without opening his eyes, he realized, before he knew where he was, that he felt wonderful, that he had the good feeling that he'd used to have in summers or looking forward to Christmas or his birthday, before his mother got ill. He had no idea what it was, this good thing that he anticipated, but as he gradually swam toward the surface of his thoughts, he knew that he would find it if he dug.

ONCE HE GOT HOME he couldn't help telling Emil and Erich, the excitement of the find was too much. He thought as he talked, invented as he waxed eloquent—this fort, this tunnel, this stronghold, this cave they would dig could be reinforced just like a real miner's mine with boards from the abandoned shack, and branches cut from the woods. It was Markus who thought of swearing people in, too, not allowing just anyone to tag along and join the construction. Having taken an oath of secrecy, made solemn by hot wax dripped on the inside of their wrists, the boys stole shovels, snatched sheets off clotheslines to haul the dirt out of the tunnels, cached away loaves of bread and hard apples, nuts, potatoes to roast, the ends of sausages for the ravenous gang to eat. After school, they gathered at the unfinished house site, worked at their task until dark and beyond dark, by the light of lanterns sneaked out of barns, the flames of candles snitched off their mothers' bureaus and even, thanks to Roman Shimek, the worst boy in town, candles from the altar of the Catholic church, a disappearance that sent Father Clarence Marek into a fit of outraged sermonizing.

The Waldvogel boys, because they didn't go to church anymore—not the Catholic church since their mother died and not the Lutheran church, even though Tante waged a campaign with Fidelis—never heard the sermons on the missing candles. They did hear about the sermons from the other boys. In the past they might have been worried, even felt the need for confession. Now they puffed with pride. Felt badness swell in them. Swaggered. For without their mother they felt entirely forsaken and therefore godless. Why should they believe in a God who could so easily and with total indifference to their prayers take her away? They scoffed at God, then, made wax signs on their wrists, took oaths of blood, and licked the rusty ax head. Fidelis knew none of this, and Delphine had only a suspicion.

ONE SATURDAY, Franz brought Mazarine home on her bike. She sprang off the handlebars as the bicycle slowed and then walked beside him, waited as he leaned it against the side of the house. She gazed up at him with a steady smile, trying to hide her nervousness. Franz's father was a forbidding person and she was sure that he didn't like her. When she'd visited before, Fidelis hadn't said a word, hadn't teased her, hadn't even given her the kind of neutral but appreciative glance that grown men gave her now. Sometimes their looks were much more obvious, and she wasn't asking for that. The fact that Mr. Waldvogel didn't acknowledge her at all was unnerving. She hesitated a little, then followed Franz into the shop and watched him put on his apron. She heard Fidelis out in the farthest corner of the slaughtering room but his voice was muffled and she was glad he didn't come into the shop to greet them.

"This is Mazarine," said Franz, when Delphine appeared, wiping her hands on a towel.

"Both of you have z's in your names," said Delphine.

Mazarine looked at Franz with a startled little bolt of delight. For all her fooling with their names on the back pages of her notebooks at school, she'd never made anything of the z that they had in common. And now this woman had given her a brand-new piece of old information. Z. Delphine laughed a bit, noticing the pleasure in the girl's eyes. She turned away, but she had already softened because she could see that this Mazarine, who wore boys' shoes and had one dress to her name, whose family was dirt-poor with that one bicycle their only wealth and with a bill run up they'd never pay, and whose brother Roman was a little hell-raiser, loved Franz. Why not? Any girl would, it was true. Franz was the type for whom girls developed easy crushes. He had the rich girls after him, doing errands at the shop for their mothers and craning their heads to see if he was working out in back. Delphine knew that Franz didn't have the capacity for similarly shallow feelings. As he'd carried his mother to her room from the plane ride, she'd seen how much he loved Eva. From that, she had also seen that his attachment to his first love would be deep, maybe even dangerous.

Delphine thought that she'd have to strangle any girl who ever hurt one of the boys. It was seeing them so helpless and lost after Eva died. Even then, she had the thought that anything a woman did would echo back into the sorrow and love they felt for Eva. After she had given this Mazarine the once-over, she asked for a hand with some chores, just to ascertain if she was steady. There was an order to be wrapped for the freezer. Delphine showed the girl how to tear off just the right amount of paper, how to make the crisp folds, then draw down the string from the spool that hung from a hook on the ceiling and secure the package with a flourish. Mazarine did everything carefully and efficiently, and then asked whether there was more that she could do. So Delphine had her wipe down the shelves out front and clean off the canned goods. She did that. And came back again for more work.

"Mazarine, are you hungry?" said Delphine.

"Oh no," she waved her hand, but gulped. There was hesitation, and Delphine realized that she shouldn't have asked. It was probably a matter of pride with her to have eaten.

"Come back here with me," said Delphine. She led the girl back to the kitchen, and heard a little intake of breath as Mazarine paused at the doorway. The afternoon light was slanting through the windows, falling richly on the blue bread bowls and picking out the luster of the polished copper trim on the bins of flour. The tablecloth with the fruits in the squares was on the table, just washed, the colors quiet and cheerful. There were apples in a wicker basket. Delphine remembered how she had felt the first time she had entered Eva's kitchen, and a wave of feeling for Mazarine flooded through her. She made a meat sandwich, put a doughnut on the plate, an apple beside, poured the girl a tall glass of milk.

"Eat anyway," she said.

Ten minutes later, when Mazarine returned to the shop, she asked if she could do something else.

"You don't quit, do you." Delphine grinned.

"No," said Mazarine. Her voice was shy, but firm. Delphine remembered things she'd heard about the girl's father, a roamer with something of a name for his bad temper. And the mother, pendulously fat in spite of the lack of food and laid up with sick headaches people said was lazy nervousness. The girl probably knew that the mother had run up a bill here, and this could be her way of doing what she could about it. Or maybe she was just trying to impress Franz. Or be close to him on the days he had to work. Maybe, thought Delphine, there would be some of Eva's clothes from the trunks upstairs that could fit Mazarine. But then again, that might bother Franz. At the end of the afternoon, she gave the girl a package of smoked turkey drumsticks and some bacon, all wrapped together, and also told her casually, privately, that she'd taken money off her family's bill. Mazarine flushed, but then raised her head and nodded sharply.

Maybe the girl could use some of her things, too. She had a pair of shoes that didn't fit right, but they might look good on Mazarine. As the girl walked out the door with Franz, Delphine realized that she was starting to rescue Mazarine. Maybe she saw in the girl a capacity for self-sacrifice similar to her own and wanted to call out a warning. I should stop myself, thought Delphine. The girl really hadn't asked for it. Plus she had a mother, however half-baked.

ON THE WAY HOME to the Shimeks, they stopped and hid Mazarine's bicycle, walked through the high brush and into the trees, then up a slight rise to their pine tree. "We should bring a blanket here," said Franz.

"I can just see us, a blanket on the back fender of the bicycle—try to explain that!"

Franz began to kiss her. He could smell the apple on her breath. Some grains of sugar clung to the dip in her throat just above the lavender collar of her dress. When he licked the sugar from her throat, Mazarine looked up into the branches and tried to hold herself together. She didn't want to be the first to tell him how she loved him, so she bit her lip. When she felt as though she'd burst, she pushed Franz fiercely over and stared into his eyes a moment. Slowly, she brought her lips down far enough just to graze his. Then she pinched him, let him grab for her. When she fell in a sprawl, she let him lie on top of her, but only until his breath came quick and hoarse. While he still had his eyes closed she rolled away and ran, mocking him, hair flying, toward the road.

IN THE YEAR after her father was released from jail, it seemed to Delphine as though he was being slowly erased. He thinned all over. His skin softened to a ripe peachiness, his eyes blurred. His hair was a candy pale floss sticking straight up on his head. Roy diminished, became almost gamine in his appearance like a small, ancient boy. Those strange unfocused eyes regarded the world with too mutely affable a gaze. Before, the drink made him bold and loquacious. Now, he was dreamy, slow, forgetful and often disturbingly at peace.

Still, he was industrious enough. He spent his mornings at the shop, doing whatever came his way to be done. And then, taking as his pay ten cents and a slice of sausage, he went on to his afternoon position. He began helping Step-and-a-Half with her sortings and haulings, assisted her in picking through town leavings. Together, they ranged across the town plucking scraps from back porches. Step-and-a-Half and he had occasionally worked together between his binges. Now they saw each other every day. They made a strikingly odd pair—she tall and heron-proud, fierce-beaked, fabulous in her collection of skins and rags and he stooped and pale with the roses of shot veins, old whiskey in his cheeks, his skin ever more translucent and fine except for the purple onion of his nose. He began to improve her equipment. Roy constructed a clever light cart out of broken crates, bent hardware, and bicycle tires. One would push and the other holler as they passed up and down the streets collecting all there was to collect, which in those times was dire stuff unless you knew, as Step-and-a-Half did, the banker's cook, and were accepted at the back doors of the greater and the lesser rich—the former bonanza farms swallowed into the town limits and the shop owners, who stayed in business by only the slimmest margins. By reason of her long-standing fidelity to her trade, she was welcome in these places, and so, now, was Roy Watzka.

Step-and-a-Half's collaboration with Roy was an irritation to Delphine. She knew that she should have been glad that her father had joined in the pursuit of an honest trade. But to align himself with such a strange character, and thus make himself the subject of more talk, was hard to bear cheerfully, though she made a good show. And, as well, Delphine was sure that Step-and-a-Half disliked her for the mere fact that she had to all appearances taken Eva's place behind the counter.

Yet there came a day when Step-and-a-Half spoke to her. She came into the shop for her pickings one morning, and didn't leave after the small ceremony in which Delphine handed her the sausage ends and trimmings. She picked through them with her usual discernment, then Delphine took her choices and wrapped them neatly. There was a kind of snobbishness about her, Delphine thought, an insistence on choosing the best of the worst. And why was she still standing there with the package in her hand, glaring, clearing her throat with a rusty scrape? Step-and-a-Half had a sharp, camphor-ridden, wolfish but not exactly unpleasant smell. This day she wore a fabulous scarf, a broad band of turquoise velvet, in a sort of turban around her head.

"Found a cat," said Step-and-a-Half.

"Roy told me."

Apparently, now, she kept a kitten in her stuffed cabin, a little gray thing with tiny fierce teeth. Maybe she wanted milk, thought Delphine. She asked Step-and-a-Half to wait, went to the cooler, and dipped a bit of milk into a cream bottle.

Returning, she handed the bottle across the counter. But Step-and-a-Half only took it with a small nod of incredulous thanks, as though offended by Delphine's extravagance. She did not turn to leave. For a few moments, she squinted at Fidelis's ornate diploma from Germany, as though she was reading it. The diploma hung in a heavy, carved wood frame on the wall behind the counter, but the words were German script and too small to make out. Finally, Step-and-a-Half dipped her regal head, crowned with the velvet wrap, and stated directly to Delphine, "They're making a tunnel down to China."

Delphine, startled, understood now that Step-and-a-Half was making crazy small talk.

"They're digging their own graves. You better stop them."

"All right," said Delphine carefully, "I'll stop them. I don't want any trouble."

Step-and-a-Half agreed with a sage look. Suddenly she lunged halfway across the counter and peered into Delphine's face.

"I know his family, the Lazarres. Bunch of no-goods. You watch yourself around that Cyprian and hang on to your money."

"Who asked you?" said Delphine, mystified. "And I'm the one taking his money, for your information." She added the last just to stump the other woman, but it didn't work.

"So you think," said Step-and-a-Half, turning on her heel. With a swish of robes and a clatter of her man's boots, she strode banging out the door.

AS THE DAYS grew short, Cyprian appeared at the shop every night and most often had a beer with Fidelis around dinnertime before Delphine finished with her work. Sometimes the three of them ate together after the boys came home—their faces flushed and ruddy with cold, wringing their chapped hands, sweaty from running, dirt sifting from their shoes. While the boys took their baths, Delphine would clear their plates and replace them with new. Then the three grownups would eat whatever Delphine had the time that day to make—riced potatoes, goulash, maybe a cake if she had the eggs. Unsold meat that wouldn't last, on the verge, she cooked up, too. Often, Tante joined them, and sometimes Clarisse came around, or Roy or any number of Fidelis's friends and members of the singing club. Delphine and Cyprian usually left Fidelis and some assortment of people at the table, unless they were practicing, which meant they all stayed late. One ordinary night, as she was in the middle of a shop inventory and had a hundred small items to reorder swirling in her head, Delphine left just the two men, Fidelis and Cyprian, sitting together over the remnants of kidney gravy and mashed potato pie with nothing to distract them from each other but the bottles in their hands.

When Delphine left the room for the office, both of the men felt a sudden itch of a tension. After a silence, Fidelis said he wanted to try flying in an airplane, like Franz, and Cyprian answered that the automobile was good enough for him. Then they each took a drink and didn't say anything for a while.

"But I wouldn't want to be in a tornado again," said Cyprian.

Fidelis nodded, but pointedly didn't ask when Cyprian had been in a tornado before. The tornado suddenly seemed too loaded a topic to discuss, as did the merits of various makes of automobiles, Roosevelt's visit to Grand Forks, the CWA, milk prices, whether there'd be anything to butcher if the drought continued or the liquor tax or the burning of a neighboring town's opera house. The only topic that seemed safe was the food, what was left of it, so Fidelis said the kidneys weren't too bad.

"'Not too bad,'" said Cyprian. "What do you mean by that?"

"I mean, she fixed them good."

"Damn right," said Cyprian, as though he'd won some challenge from Fidelis, put him under, or at least his remark. Fidelis couldn't help it, a shiver of anger twitched up his back. He took a long drink, and so did Cyprian, and then the two laughed uncomfortably to try to right the disagreeable feeling that had suddenly grown between them.

"Did you read about the damn eclipse?" said Cyprian, hopeful, feeling that the heavens were the only subject that could save them.

"No," said Fidelis, trying to keep his voice neutral.

"Supposed to be a dark one," muttered Cyprian, who knew nothing of it himself. Then he came up with what seemed like an inspired path to follow, one that wouldn't give out. "So the leaves are off the trees," he said, "you getting much game in to butcher here?"

Fidelis readily took that up. "A deer or so, then Gus Newhall shot a bear up in the Minnesota northwoods. 'Course he nearly brought down a goddamn Indian doing it, the guide was just ahead, as I hear it, Gus got overexcited and fired, nearly took the guide's head off and—"

Cyprian froze with the beer half to his lips and slowly lowered the bottle, and then his black eyes looked into Fidelis's light eyes, which was a dangerous thing, for now they couldn't unstick their gaze from each other. Nor could they blink, for the first one who did would be obscurely beaten. Fidelis didn't know what he'd done to land in the frozen deadlock, but there he was. He had learned not to blink during the war, looking through the sights of a rifle, so he wouldn't miss the flicker of a careless instant of exposure, or ruin the steady press of his finger. And Cyprian had learned not to blink when he trained as a boxer, for that's how two boxers sized each other up to start with. Stared into each other's eyes. The best could move a deadly punch to the throat as fast as the eyelid dropped. So their stares held, and held, and as they did not move they breathed the harder. Their eyes dried out and burned and their noses stung. The tension grew immense, ridiculous, then unbearable. Delphine walked in just as, with a ringing report, Fidelis's hand shattered the beer bottle he was holding. All three gazed down in astonishment at the spurt of bright blood. Fidelis said, "So Cyprian, what tornado were you in?"

And smooth as silk pie, Cyprian answered him, "Belleau Wood, where they burned the wheat and still we came on, blasted Germans from the trees. We kept coming, they couldn't stop us. When those snipers hit the ground we finally got to use our bayonets."

Delphine wanted to back out of the room, but instead she got a bottle of rubbing alcohol and dabbed the stuff on Fidelis's hand while she talked to Cyprian. Lightly, she put things to rights. "I thought they declared an armistice way back when, so what's all this about?"

Cyprian shrugged, and Fidelis, though he struggled with a sudden surge of anger, laughed and made a face at the sting of the alcohol.

"Sure," he said easily, suddenly feeling foolish at the degree of inexplicable hatred he'd felt for Cyprian, whom he had always liked fine up until this evening. "I wasn't there at Belleau Wood. The war, that's done with, finished."

"Oh yeah," said Cyprian, recovering his usual mildness. "All done with but for the beauty marks." He tapped his throat, the roped white flesh.

LATER ON, when the two had returned to the farmhouse and settled into the bed, Delphine wearily unfolded herself, stretched her feet long underneath the quilt that Eva had sewed for her on her good days, tiny postage stamps of color. She was troubled by and wondered at the palpable strain in the kitchen—she'd felt it between the two men even before she entered, from the silence, and then there was the sharp explosion of the bottle, Fidelis's hand slashed. And Cyprian had been poised on his chair as though he was cocked to explode. Now, he was breathing quietly beside her, quite sleepless.

"What were you two arguing about?" she asked.

"You," he said, no hesitation in his voice.

"Well, that's sure stupid," said Delphine, feeling stupid herself.

"Maybe."

Delphine laughed unpleasantly, surprised that he should be jealous when he treated her like his sister, and then obscurely angered that he thought he had any right over her at all. She simmered for a few minutes, her thoughts prickling.

"I think," she finally said, though she had not actually thought this out herself, "we should stop sleeping together if you're not going to love me like a woman. What do you think of that?"

As soon as he got up and left the bed, she missed the weight of him next to her, wanted to curve around his back and throw her arm over him. She always fell asleep in seconds if she took her breaths in unison with his. Restless, she lay for a time in the quiet darkness, and then she sighed and rose, wrapped her red robe around herself. She found him sitting at the kitchen table. "Oh hell. Please," she said. "Come on back." So Cyprian followed her back into the room and they lay together in the peace of the house, and in the blackness, Roy snoring beside the stove. But there was between them, even while they curled close as children, a sorrowing knowledge. Cyprian knew he had no right to his anger, and he knew as well that Delphine pitied him for it. What was he to do? And next to him, instead of falling asleep directly as she'd anticipated, Delphine was again restless. The inside polish of the fake wedding band on her finger was flaking away, and the base metal itched her finger. She couldn't quite get comfortable. She turned and twisted, resented it when Cyprian's breathing evened into a gentle rhythm, stayed awake a long time after he slept and listened to the quiet knocking of his breath.

FIDELIS WAS AWAKE overlong that night also. He had to shout from the kitchen three times for the boys to calm down and sleep—they were extra-excited about something. In the past, Eva would have found out what it was and told it to him. Fidelis wasn't one to ask. They had their own lives and he didn't pry into their business, nor did they come and tell him about the things they did. There was a wall of reserve between Fidelis and his sons, a formality that was part exhaustion and also the way things had always been in his own family. He had never spoken to his own father about personal things, not even when he was a grown man.

Late as it was, Fidelis had to rifle through the stacks of bills from his suppliers, figuring out which to fend off, which to string along, which needed immediate payment. He was dividing up the tiny amount of cash he had available to see whether he could figure or refigure a sum that would satisfy the lot. After he figured, he'd go back and reduce the amount on each bill, resign another to the bottom of the pile. Every so often, he put his fists on either temple, stared blindly at the mass of paper. Then he'd make some inner calculation, and adjust the bills into yet another mysterious order. As for the money that was owed to him, he'd given the job of collecting it to Tante. She was better at squeezing blood from rock, that's what bill collecting and bill paying was all about during those desperate years.

The animosity he'd felt for the man who had turned out to be a sturdy, respectable baritone, and whom he thought of as Delphine's husband, was still disturbing to him, too. At one point, weary of his piddling calculations, he stood up and paced around the kitchen. Four steps took him across the floor, and four back. Frustrated by the smallness of the room, he thought of walking the hallway outside, but he didn't want to wake the boys now that they had finally settled themselves. So he continued his striding back and forth along the short course of kitchen tiles. Then in the center of the room Fidelis stopped, abruptly. He put his hand on his head and laughed.

So that was it! That was the thing about Cyprian! There was something. He had always known there was *something* about the man. And he hadn't caught it. Not until they sat across from one another and stared their unblinking challenges into each other's eyes. Thinking of that now tipped off Fidelis. Plus the way he had described Gus Newhall's bear hunting. Fidelis recalled the staring match. The man's eyes, that pitch black, the pupil melted into the iris, the flint-black stare. The deafened guide. It came to him. An Indian. Cyprian was an Indian. That's all it was, all along, that uneasy feeling. Somehow he'd known and not known, the man was different. Thinking of Cyprian as an Indian now made things all right. Or almost so, for Fidelis also understood that the sudden antipathy between them was also and most strangely based on Delphine's absence, or presence, or maybe sheer existence.

THE ENTRANCE to the boys' dirt fort had become a grand thing, shored up out of the bed of an old wagon box, a horseshoe even nailed to a lintel constructed of a short piece of beam found underneath the sagging shack. The first part of the tunnel was reinforced, too, with boards knocked from the walls of the place and dragged through the short riffle of woods. There was a die-hard bunch who had remained with the construction—Markus, the twins, Emil and Erich, Grizzy Morris, and Roman Shimek. The others had fallen away, but that was fine with the core crew. They were at the best part. They had achieved the center of the hill and now were engaged in the satisfying toil of hollowing out their den, their clubhouse, their mighty chamber, their secret room.

The tunnel was a belly-wiggler for about twenty feet before the entrance to the room. The secret interior of the fort was at first extremely small. Markus used their tool of first attack, the blade of a hoe, and scraped out a slightly larger round than the tunnel. Roman Shimek had stolen a big square piece of canvas, and the boys used it to shovel the dirt into and then drag it out. Markus worked the hardest, digging away and hauling the dirt out himself even when the others sat in the grass resting or trying to figure out how to smoke the rust brown fake tobacco plants, rolling the stuff up in newspaper. He didn't admonish them, reproach them, or care if they sat around outside the hill. What he was doing so absorbed him that it didn't matter if they were in on it or not. To crouch and enter the impressive doorway, then crawl into the black heart of the earth, and to enter a chamber so quiet that he heard his blood sigh in his lungs, his heart's rush and clench, his ears fizz with a humming and electric silence, this gave Markus a deep and almost violent satisfaction. When they left for home he was calm, and a little silly, and he slept the nights through for the first time since he had lost his mother.

No one discovered exactly what they were doing. It was, for sure, a wonder that the boys were not filthier when they came home, but it was a dry early November and most of the visible dust that filtered into their clothes and hair could be brushed away or smacked out or somehow disguised. And then, first thing they did upon returning was sneak past their parents, or, in Markus and his brothers' case, Delphine. Sometimes she wasn't even there, as she often left at her regular time each night. She drove home with Cyprian and left the boys' dinners warming in the oven. Their father, working in the shop or at his cluttered desk, or drinking a beer or two with other men in the kitchen, didn't notice them until they were cleaned up for the night. And then he noticed them in a way other than to really *notice* them. They were upright, breathing, not in any visible distress. In his exhaustion, this was enough.

Though the sky went dark sooner and the earth was colder every day, the boys went out to the hill and burrowed into it with the eagerness of gophers anxious to hibernate. Slowly, incrementally, they enlarged the inner room so one boy could kneel, then stand inside it. Two could squeeze into it, soon. Then three. And then it rained.

IT WAS A COLD, gray, pounding November rain and it lasted three days, wore the skies out, flooded the ditches and then the town's sewers, topped the river, filled the sloughs, made running streams of the streets and a great square pool of the unfinished, clay-bottomed basement of the abandoned house where the boys had their fort in the hill behind. Then suddenly as it had poured the sky cleared, the sun blazed weakly and a cool wind dried the surface of the fields from black to gray. After school, the boys met as they'd agreed, and ran out to the hill anxious to see whether their work was damaged, which of course it was, and yet not so badly as they'd feared. A few boards sagged down, the hill itself was eroded where they'd liked to climb for the lookout, but as the tunnel had been dug at a slight upward angle the inside itself, even the secret interior room far inside the hill, was surprisingly, deceptively, dry. For the earth above was saturated with water and many times heavier than when they'd first begun.

Eagerly, the boys began working on repairs.

"Drag the boards over here," Markus commanded, "we're gonna reinforce." He liked the grown-up sound of that last word and said it several times; it was a word that sounded right for the job, a word that smacked of the professional. He'd lifted a crowbar from his father's tools—no one had noticed yet, and with it the boys pried several more boards from the old shed. Sun fell through the sides of the shack in brilliant slats now. The air smelled clean from the rain, washed, and the boys worked efficiently, knowing that they had only an hour or more of sunlight left in the late fall day. The earth that had fallen in where the boards collapsed was wet and clumped, which should have told them something, for it was much harder to drag the wet stuff out than it had been the dry. But the day itself was so windy, the air sucked moisture into it. They cleared the entry out all the way back to the room, which was only partly supported by a flimsy board framework.

"It's gonna get dark," said Roman nervously, as Markus dragged a board in behind him, "I gotta go."

"Just wait a minute. Help me push this board in."

Roman pushed the board along the tunnel as far as he could, but only one boy at a time could fit through the narrow aperture. Markus forced his way in through the half-collapsed part of the tunnel, pushed his head through the space, wiggled one shoulder into the opening, and then the other. If his shoulders got through, the rest of him was easy. In the blackness he felt his way forward, reaching back with his feet, gripping the board. He knew that Roman had fallen back now, and he breathed a sudden dampness of air inside the middle of the hill. He shouted for the others to follow along, bring the hoe and the piece of canvas, but he didn't really care. In his pocket, he had a candle stub, and matches, for he meant to give himself a bit of light to see by in order to place the board he'd dragged along just so. Yet, he didn't light the candle right away. The blackness seemed friendly, welcoming. The silence soaked up around him, comforting and pure. He felt the walls of the room, reassuringly dry. Deciding that he needed no light to put the board where he wanted it to go, he wedged it by feel up on top of two other boards that he'd stuck upright along the sides of the wall. He'd buried the ends of those boards a foot deep in the ground to stabilize them, and so he was able to fasten the first board up pretty well, and the next, too. He crawled back for one more and took it from Roman's fingertips halfway down the tunnel.

"I'm going home," gasped Roman. "It's almost dark out there. C'mon!"

"Yeah," Markus said, "soon's I get this last part reinforced." There, he'd said it again, and with the board in one hand he now wiggled backward through the damaged part of the passageway into the room. He had just succeeded in forcing that board up into the ceiling as well, when the boys outside the hill witnessed a strange thing. They had all left the entrance and were trudging back to the broken shed to grapple out one more board before they left for home, when something soundless but palpable, some earthen energy, made them turn and look, curious, at the hill. At which point, with a sound like nothing else, a dull interior *whomph*, the hill relaxed. One moment it was a high domed shape. The next, its top sagged. It took the boys in their astonishment several minutes to remember Markus was still in it.

THE PINE NEEDLE BED was dry on top but still wet underneath, and for a while Mazarine and Franz didn't do anything at all but talk together, sitting on a low shelf of stone near their tree. Lately, because of his football playing, Franz was getting an increased amount of attention from Betty Zumbrugge, and it upset Mazarine in a way she could hardly admit to herself. Betty drove her father's car to school, wore a different dress for every day of the week, and silk stockings. Her hair was very blond, maybe too blond said some girls, and she wore a brilliant scarlet lipstick they said she'd bought in Minneapolis. Betty stopped Franz in the hallways and offered him rides after school. She tried anything, to the point of looking foolish, said Mazarine's friends. So far, Franz had not responded, and Mazarine was too proud to say a word to him about it. For his part, he was unaware that anything that Betty did could possibly bother Mazarine. He looked at her in the dappled piney light.

"Come here," he said, easing down onto the soft needles.

"They're damp," she shook her head.

"We'll dry off before we get home," said Franz. "Don't worry about it." So she slid down the side of the rock and curled beside him, looking up the spiked tower of the pine, from along the powerful trunk, into the sky. Franz leaned over and smoothed her hair away from her forehead. The line of her hair could have been drawn with a fine pen, it sprang so evenly away around her face. He kissed her eyebrows—brown and straight, very much like his own—and then he cupped her face in his hands and kissed her mouth, deeply, his heart pounding thick in his chest. The rain had brought out the scent of pine and the feral earthen odor of mold from the dead leaves. She smelled of harsh school soap, of paper, of the salt of her own body. He leaned back and held her hand carefully, desperately hoping that she'd place his hand on her breast again. This time he would not touch in a rough circle. But she did not.

With an electric movement, swift as an eel, a rustle of purposeful motion that stilled him, she twisted from his arms and knelt beside him. She reached forward and then slowly, with a firm calm, she slid the end of his belt out of the first loop, smiled at him and drew it from the hook, tugging it toward herself. He lay back in a state of wonder. She pushed away the two sides of the belt and rubbed the button on the top of his pants. He bit his lips and his whole brain begged *Please*. And she undid the button. Then with a mocking motherly care she slid the next button from its buttonhole, and the next, all the way down. She opened his pants and then she lay down next to him. She put her cheek on the thin cotton of his undershorts and he surged up toward her, aching. She put her arms around his hips. He fit alongside the curve of her throat. Reaching down, he held her shoulders, put his hands underneath her hair on the back of her neck, and murmured their private words to her. Her face was hot against him, heavy, her hair seemed molten trailing up his arms. A light wind came into the pines and made a rushing sound.

THE RAIN HAD BEEN extremely good for business—farmers used the rain as reason for a town visit, and during their dealings with Fidelis more than a few had decided to butcher a dozen old laying hens, say, a milked-out cow, even a fat enough pig or a steer so as not to feed it through the winter. He had a few busy and profitable weeks lined up and, in his mind, the pile of bills on his desk would happily shrink. He would be able to see the grain of the wood beneath, maybe, and even afford some new boots for the boys this winter. Things looked that much better. He had sold a bit more than usual on his rounds to the neighboring town grocery and general stores, and Zumbrugge had paid his outstanding account. So the constant nagging undertow of worry about money, a current that pulled on his strength, was weakened and he felt an unusual ease with the whole of life. When he greeted Cyprian, who was lounging in the yard on the hood of the DeSoto, waiting for Delphine, he offered him a beer and invited him in to take a load off, just as though nothing odd had occurred in their last meeting. Cyprian thanked him, politely enough, his tones neutral, and said he'd just wait with the car. That was when Fidelis should have left well enough alone.

It was his nature, however, to bring out everything within a situation. Usually, he got what he wanted by poking fun. This time, Fidelis didn't want to joke around at all, his motivations were very different—he was simply feeling good. Also, without ever acknowledging it, he wanted to make up for the Gus Newhall story and the deafened Indian he'd laughed at in the telling. He wanted Cyprian to know he didn't hold his being Indian against him and that even, if he were to tell the truth, that aspect interested Fidelis. He was curious about the whole way of life—he'd heard about that back in Germany and hadn't seen much of it here. So instead of leaving Cyprian to himself, and letting the unsaid tension in their last meeting gradually release over a few days or weeks, Fidelis took two beers from the store's cooler. He unlatched the beer caps from the tall dark amber bottles and a plume of cool smoke escaped each as he walked back outside.

"Here," he said, offering the beer to Cyprian. "It won't kill you."

Cyprian took the beer, tipped it back, took one drink but said nothing. He found himself staring down, dumbly, at the churned muck of the delivery yard, examining with fake interest how the dirt had cemented itself in channels. He wondered at himself, why he couldn't just say thanks and be easy with Fidelis. It would not happen. There was a huge rock in his chest. He couldn't seem to breathe past it. Even the beer going down didn't help, but tasted sour to him. Then he surprised himself, watched his hand upend the bottle and pour the beer in a stream onto the hardened mud. The bloom of hops drenched the air between the two men for a few seconds, then faded. Fidelis went still, and put his own bottle down on the hood of the car. Now it was too late. Now a wave of affronted rage gripped him and he moved to stand within Cyprian's line of vision. As he did so, he stepped back, out of reach of a sudden punch, and carefully untied his apron. He dropped the stained white cloth, rolled his sleeves up his arms.

Cyprian was still watching the ground, the delicate tracery of the beer finding its way into the crust of earth. He frowned as though something in what he saw gripped his thoughts. He knew when he looked up that it would begin, and he was, now, in no hurry. He was lazy. He was filled with a glad black sense of this moment's inevitability, so much so that he mumbled, in satisfaction, "It had to happen."

"So you want this, you get it," said Fidelis, his voice flat.

And at those words Cyprian walked sideways, away from the vehicle, and then slowly raised his head to stare again into the white-blue eyes. He removed his hat in the lock of their gaze, shrugged off his jacket, rolled his own sleeves up, too. And there the men stood now, arms loose and ready by their sides, the one dark and tense, his body lean with eager strength, the other solid with power. Their strengths were very different, and they planned accordingly, each thinking how to maneuver the other in order to use his own talents to the best effect, but that all came to nothing. Fidelis, for the second time that day, broke his pact with discipline. An unexpected blind fury took him at the thought of the wasted beer, and he lunged forward in a low crouch intending to simply grab Cyprian and smash him against the side of the car. But Cyprian had already decided that he wouldn't let the butcher get that close. He crouched too, and with a sudden hook cracked Fidelis from under the jaw, giving the punch a spin to torque his neck, and then Cyprian danced backward to assess the damage.

Not much. But the punch snapped Fidelis from his loose rage, restored his grip on his temper, and caused him to step back and gauge his next move with narrowed eyes. The two men circled with a fixed intensity now, not fury so much as a cold meditative watchfulness—for everything, for all the nothing, for something they would not admit to until it was over, for the shame of it, the foolishness of fighting over a woman neither of them had any claim on, or would admit to fighting over in the first place. And then right there, between that one punch and the next move that Fidelis made, between the intention and their half-realized urge, the boys' thin yells of panic came to the men clear as birds' cries across the dead grass of the fields. Seeing the men in the yard, the boys' cries grew more desperate and shrill.

Fidelis put his fists down with a sideways look of warning at Cyprian, and the two, their attention now completely riveted to the obvious sounds of some catastrophe, strode toward the children. Roman was hoarse and gasping, Emil bawled out something about the hill. Erich, white and stiff as a cutout of a boy, plunged along behind on his short, little sausage-fat legs. When the men neared, Fidelis suddenly experienced a wave of sick intuition and broke into a run. So he was kneeling with Emil as the boys tried to tell him everything—the fort, the hill, how the hill sagged, the room inside of it, Markus—and he didn't at first understand. It was Cyprian who grasped it all and said, "Shovels—we've got to bring shovels." And it was Cyprian who instructed Delphine, who came running after, to gather up as many men as could be found. It was Cyprian, also, who said to her, out of Fidelis's hearing, to be quick about it, and bring the doctor, too, that he thought Markus was buried alive.

ONLY IT DIDN'T feel like that from inside the earth. When the thunder of the hill's collapse did not kill him, but wedged him in a fragment of space beneath two buckled boards, Markus felt very sleepy. The dirt had closed him in its fist. He wasn't hurt, though he couldn't move, and he wasn't dying. Air seeped into his lungs but it was a sleeping gas, he thought, wearily passing into a dreamless fuzz of childish exhaustion. It was like when he was very small, the time his fever broke, and his mother curled around him in the cool blankets. She held her hand on his forehead and rocked him. He thought her hand was there now. And behind him the comfort of her great dark body. He was falling asleep. They were in the hull of a boat of silence, and blackness, and they were rocking to the end of the world.

*   *   *

THERE WAS JUST ENOUGH light for the men to see the shape of the hill, and to make out the doorway in the earth and see that it was shut. Fidelis threw himself forward at once and began to shovel with a maddened strength, but then Cyprian put his hands on his arms and stopped him. It took all of his strength to stop the butcher, to hold his arms. The men looked at each other in the shadow, Fidelis's eye rolled white, and Cyprian said, clearly, urgently, "Don't—you'll bring down the rest of the hill. We must go very carefully."

He showed him the tools that the boys used, and put the broken hoe into Fidelis's hands. Then he and Fidelis knelt and began to enlarge the tunnel by scratching at the earth with light, furious movements. As fast as Fidelis bit the earth away, Cyprian gathered and pulled it onto the canvas and hauled it out. And the boys in their silent terror dumped it somewhere and brought back the canvas. The dirt that had fallen in was easy to remove, but the men had to enlarge the opening to accommodate their larger selves and so, by the time Delphine and the lanterns and the rescue party got there, the two men had barely disappeared into the opening of the hill, and they were drenched in the sweat of effort. As Fidelis inched into the hill, working from his stomach, his great arms straining forward at the shut seams of ground, he called to Markus.

Fidelis's cries bounced off the dirt and struck Cyprian, but the other man did not take them in. He'd heard the sounds of the dying on the battlefield, the huge collective hell shrieks the mud gave after bloody encounters, and he did not react. From the past, he knew it was best not to let despair near, so he did not. Those outside the hill were not so disciplined. The whole singing club had gathered, and it was a terrible and useless meeting. The men could do nothing but mutter logistics and touch the hill on all sides and wonder whether there was another, better way to rescue the boy. They were unnerved and then worn down by the butcher's constant hoarse cries to the point where some openly wept or turned away and put their foreheads against the trunks of the trees and waited—for that was all there was to do: just wait, and keep the lanterns going, and despair and speculate. The men inside the hill now would not quit or accept any relief.

The boards that the boys had used were guides, and as they made their tortuous way along, Cyprian righted the boards and set them up to bear, he hoped, the weight of the ground again. The top of the tunnel scraped along their backs, and if it should go they would not die instantly, he knew, but slowly feel the life and air crushed out of them. Still, he continued on behind the butcher into the center of the earth, until they entered a small passageway that had survived the collapse. They forced their bodies through it, now thoroughly inside the center of the hill, and Fidelis said, *Gott Verdienst*, and stretched his arm, strained his entire being forward, and touched the sole of Markus's shoe.

Cyprian felt the shock ripple through the butcher's body, and he grabbed the man's ankle. *Wait*, he said, *wait*, for the earth was coming down in tiny clumps around them, threatening to give, and if the butcher pulled hard the boy, who was probably dead after all, and whose body might be entirely buried, could dislodge the entire frail board system. Or say the boy was alive. Then they'd all be buried together. *Wait*, said Cyprian. *Just feel for his position*. And so the butcher edged forward, pushed more dirt aside, made a narrow slot for him to straighten his shaking arm. He stretched to feel along the boy's side, groped gingerly until he ascertained, with a wild gasp, that Markus had breath. But also that the boy was halfway buried and that the margin of space in which he survived was held up by only the flimsiest means, board on board, an accident of the collapse. And when the butcher understood how perilously close the boards were to giving, Cyprian felt the shock and fear communicate itself through Fidelis's body.

Trembling and sweating, soaking wet at the earth's heart, the top of the passage pressing down already on his spine, Cyprian breathed away the panic that communicated from the butcher's body with a quick electric buzz. *Slow*, Cyprian said. His voice surprised him with its gentle firmness. *Slow and easy*. Fidelis was using all his strength to move his hands, just his hands. *Ich weiss nicht*, Cyprian heard the butcher say.

And then he heard himself tell the butcher in that same calm and compelling voice that he could do it, that Fidelis must back out of the hole with him, that he must let Cyprian go back in alone.

"I have done this before," said Cyprian. His voice told a calm, kind, reasonable lie. As though it were an everyday thing to fetch a boy from a crack deep in a mound of earth. He didn't know how he caused his voice to sound so persuasive, except that he knew Fidelis would listen to nothing less than an utterly convincing argument. He must be given no way to argue back. "You're too big—you could kill him if you try to drag him out. I'm trained for this. I can get the boy out. For your boy's sake, come out with me now. Come out."

And like one tranced and obedient, Fidelis did as he was told at that moment. Their antagonism had abruptly turned to a magnetic loyalty. The two men inched backward, crawled slowly back out the passageway into the blaze of lanterns. When Cyprian's boots appeared, men rushed forward to help and he screamed them back again.

At his terrible yell, they did fall back and crouched in a circle around the entrance that looked impossibly small for two grown men to have gone into it, disappeared as though the hill had swallowed and then in some act of peristalsis conducted them to its center. Cyprian edged out and then gently, bit by bit, the butcher emerged. Kneeling in the white light, both men entirely blackened by the wet dirt, gasped their lungs full. Cyprian called for rope.

"I must go back," the butcher said, lunging toward the hill. It was unbearable to have left the boy. Cyprian tackled Fidelis and held him around the waist, wrestled him backward, called out, "Delphine, Delphine, tell him." The light blazed around them in a slick radiance. The air was cold and wet with the first drops of a blowing rain.

"Cyprian can do it," Delphine said evenly, seeing the shape of things. She held the butcher's eyes in her gaze. "Let him go."

Those who watched said, later, how Cyprian seemed to dive into the earth, plow himself in as though he'd suddenly grown into a boneless earth swallower, a great human night crawler. He disappeared. And Fidelis, stunned and shaking his great head, his eyes wide and white in his mud-crusted face, stayed behind. He slumped in the dirt, waved the other men off with a violence they understood at once. They fell back, away from him, took the lanterns aside and left him in darkness as he wished. Only Delphine had no fear of him and did not leave his side. He seemed of the earth itself, waiting there, his breath ragged. Although she was too lost in her own suspense of terror to dwell on Fidelis, she did wonder whether he was praying. She never had known him to pray before, and although she released what she felt were foolish, beseeching, desperate words from her mind, she knew even as she thought these words that her prayers were not prayers. She should have listened to Step-and-a-Half. Now her pleas were no more effective with the powers that made the earth than the protesting bellows of cows prodded into killing chutes. Still, she begged despairingly for the rain to hold off, for the earth to mesh, for the flimsy tunnel to hold. Perhaps she muttered something out loud, for the butcher reached over and grasped her hand as though to quiet her, or perhaps himself, or maybe he didn't know what he was doing at all with Delphine's hand, or that he even had hold of it as the two of them knelt like petitioners at the entrance.

IT REALLY WAS a matter of finding his balance, only not in air, but inside the earth. When Cyprian went back in, he eased himself into the ever narrower tunnel with a swift intention he hoped would carry him past the point, halfway through, where panic came up, shutting down his brain, racing his heart. It was natural, this fear, like the stillness he encountered nearing the top of a flagpole where he'd actually stood. He saw a yellow screen of lights, breathed in an even whistle to control what he knew, from the war and from his more dangerous tricks. His first limit. He had a benchmark where he encountered the first level of his fear, and he knew he could get beyond that initial sick drop of his guts by thinking only of one breath, the next, then the next. By balancing along his own interior wire. And so he breathed himself through the tightest center of the passageway, and he crawled deeper. At last, he came to the place where Fidelis had reached up into the tiny hatch of space.

The boy was there all right. At first he thought with a wave of terrified disappointment that the boy was dead. But then he felt along Markus's body and with his fingertips touched the boy's lips and was certain he felt a small burst of warmth. And further, at a right angle to the boy, he discovered a small space into which he could pass the earth he removed in small handfuls, for that was all he took away. One handful, another judicious handful, a scraping of dirt here, some brushed away and some plucked, as though he were an archaeologist uncovering an ancient and fragile treasure. Even so, twice, the earth seemed to shudder around them. He didn't know that it was thunder from an approaching storm, a storm that would drench the watchers and cause ten of them to wrestle Fidelis to the ground when he dropped Delphine's hand and tried to reenter the earth.

Cyprian concentrated only on each bit of dirt he pulled away, only that, until he was able to expose the boy sufficiently to unwedge him just by inches, to bend him slightly at the waist. As he'd worked incrementally, Cyprian had understood that he'd have to fold the boy out of the place where he was caught. So he continued, in complete blackness, to draw the earth methodically first from one limb, then the next, then to turn the boy, then to fold him at the waist. He wrapped Markus's arms across his chest and then with the tenderest of little pulls, slowly, through the tiny aperture, he delivered Markus onto the passageway floor.

There was a flop of dirt as the boy came free; one of the boards gave way just where Markus had lain, and Cyprian put his hands around the boy's face to shield it, but the tunnel did not give way entirely and the earth held around them once again.

It was good that the boy was unconscious, for Cyprian could feel that a bone was broken in one arm, and who knows what else, and he was afraid the boy might thrash around in pain if he came out of shock. So he roped the boy's limbs, tied him up like a package, and he left a loop he could pull. He took that piece of rope in his teeth and edged backward, feet first, down the tunnel and out into the rain. And when the lights blazed over him, and the men roared at the sight of him, Markus came quietly and momentarily awake. Emerging from the narrow opening, blinking away the dark, the first face he saw was Delphine's, in a circle of radiance, as she unlashed the ropes and drew him into her arms.

FRANZ AND MAZARINE had lain so long beneath the pine that on rising they felt half drunk, dizzy with a peaceful happiness. He could still feel the print of her face there, her breath cooling in the fabric of his clothes. Her hair was still smooth and alive underneath his hands when he finally arrived at home. Immediately, he saw that something was wrong. He knew that this was the night the men met to sing back of the shop, but the place was silent except for the steady drumming of the rain. The door to the shop was unlocked, the lights were on, and there was no one anywhere. Franz stood in the kitchen, saw the food set out on the table, the glasses of milk. He flexed his hands, sat at the kitchen chair, lifted a piece of cold meat off a plate as though there'd be a message written underneath. The first shock of finding no one at the shop and house wore off, and he knew for sure now that some disaster had occurred. But he didn't know where to go, and he didn't know what to do, and even the dog was gone. The storm moved in. The rain came bursting down.

Helpless, Franz prowled the inside of the place, then got drenched and cold outside, walked in again, lights blazing. And slowly, as he paced, as he thought of what he'd been doing while all the while something at home went wrong, he rubbed his hands on his shirt to erase the feeling of Mazarine's hair. He felt a terrible fear for his father, for them all, mixed with a deep embarrassment that he had lost all sense of duty and of time and fallen half asleep with her against him. Whatever happened, he grew convinced, was his fault. He stood outside shifting nervously, made another desperate round of the place. And then, as he made out small wavering lights approaching over the fields, he began to run toward them, shouting.

TEN

Earth Sickness

$\mathcal{M}$ARKUS FELL into an illness after he came out of the hill. It wasn't just the broken arm, though that was an interestingly complicated break, said Heech, but some other nameless invader dragged him down, made him feverish and sleepy. Delphine called it earth sickness. In her mind, the ground had chilled him and its influence still drew him toward the sullen coldness where his mother slept. When he looked at Delphine sometimes, his stare was so calm and unflinching that she couldn't meet his eyes. Then one day she understood that his stare was only the mysterious regard of a newborn baby, and she let him be. She stopped trying to distract him with poems or amuse him with games. It occurred to her that he needed to think. To grow back into his life. The pupils of his green-blue eyes remained dilated. Yet, if he was filled with an interior blackness, it wasn't after all the deathly effect of his burial, but that he was emerging from a strange gestation.

One day she noticed that he'd begun to look more like Fidelis. It was the quality of penetrating silence, a place where he was comfortable. Though he seemed at once brand-new and older, she thought it best to treat him in some ways like a younger boy. She nursed him carefully along during the day, running back from the customers to make him eat the heavy dumpling soup that Eva had taught her to make for the boys when they were sick. She made him sit in the sun when there was sun. And when a dust of early snow fell over the bottom rails of the holding pens, and the back garden was a blue arrangement of frost, she made him stay near the window to get the reflection. She thought he needed light, constant light, bright light. She thought that he'd swallowed darkness in that hill.

MAZARINE WAS RIDING her bicycle when Betty Zumbrugge passed her, as she had many times before, driving her father's fancy car. Only this time when Mazarine narrowed her eyes to gaze into the windows of the car as it passed, she saw Franz, and he saw her. He looked at her right across Betty's back as she bent forward to steer. Their eyes met for that one second, and then he was gone. There was no message in his look that Mazarine could read. The neutral and almost foolish expression on his face shocked her—she'd never seen him look stupid before.

He turned back, upset, to gaze out the window. Seeing his distraction, Betty said, as if she didn't know he had gone with Mazarine, "That's Mazarine Shimek. She has one dress to her name."

"That's not true," said Franz, his voice awkward and despairing.

He had not spoken to Mazarine since that last day beneath the pine, the time that made him obscurely responsible and her by extension, for the collapse of the hill. His thoughts veered off Mazarine and the wrongness of such happiness, which seemed to have been reckoned and judged by his brother's near death. He looked over at Betty. Her face was tilted up to peer over the steering wheel, which gave her little pointed chin a charming shape. Her round cheeks were powdered and rouged, her red lips were drawn in a slick curve. Franz wondered what happened when you kissed a girl who was wearing lipstick. Would it get all over his own face? It was so shiny, like wet paint, dark as blood. The thought of his face smeared with red gave him a low thrill, and he shook his head suddenly to clear his thoughts.

"What's with you," said Betty.

"There's a bee in the car," said Franz, cranking open the window.

"Scared of getting stung?" Betty's voice was amused and coy.

Franz shrugged uncomfortably, said nothing. He felt like grabbing Betty's hands off the steering wheel, telling her to pull right over. Kissing her. At the same time, he thought that if she did pull over he'd jump right out the passenger's side door and run like hell. Her hair was arranged so carefully he wondered how she ever slept—sitting up? There was a sharp smell of sweat when she lifted her arms. She couldn't hide that. The feral scent made him shiver, as though he'd walked by the den of a fox.

"Come home with me," she said. "I need help with mathematics."

She smiled at the road, flying rough across a pothole. Franz wet his lips and told her he couldn't go to her house, stumbled on explaining that he had to work. And right away. He was late in fact, his father would be waiting. The thought of all he had to do made him suddenly grateful. Betty shrugged and turned the car down his road. When she stopped before the shop, he jumped out. Safe, he rounded the hood and leaned down into her open window. From outside, he was able to laugh and apologize all at once in a natural way that he congratulated himself, later, for sustaining even while he ached to be alone.

AFTER THE CAR PASSED, Mazarine got back on her bicycle and rode the rest of the way home over frozen dirt, her head buzzing, but calm, not weeping. She cleaned up after her mother, who was resting, and looked around for something to make for dinner. There were a few cups of flour left at the bottom of a sagging sack, a little lard in an old brown jar, three fat golden turnips with purple smears where the sun had hit them. She boiled the turnips with their peels on, scraped them and salted them. She made biscuits with the flour and the lard. She left a biscuit beside her mother's bed, and then she sat on the steps of the rough little house, waiting for Roman. She ate her share of the dinner, slowly, and saved the rest in a clean towel for her brother. As she sat there it suddenly occurred to her that Betty Zumbrugge had a z in her name too. When Mazarine thought of this she froze, staring at the bare tangle of young trees at the side of the yard. And then, with no warning, tears spurted up in her eyes, tipped over her cheeks, and ran straight down, hitting the tops of her hands.

A COUSIN OF Gus Newhall's was married to a Braucher, a healing woman. This woman had some powerful healing secrets passed down from her family, he said, persuading Fidelis to let the woman visit Markus. In her own illness, Eva had been urged to see such a person, but as she had no time for Russian-Germans, she would not. "They wear out their women," Eva had said, and recited a saying she'd heard from those western settlements.

Weiberschterba, koi Verderba
Pferdeverrecka, des brengt Shrecke.

"In other words," she said, "when women die it is not a tragedy. But when horses die, it is a disaster!"

No one could deny now that the most renowned clinic in the Middle West had failed to do a thing for Eva. Besides that, it was well-known that the practice of Brauche was especially effective in dealing with children. Another customer's family had allowed this Braucher woman to tie an egg to the stomach of their child, transfer an illness into the egg, and then burn the raw egg in the fire as she said the precise words to bind the illness in the burning yolk. She was also an accomplished Messerin, a measurer, who read tendencies to certain diseases in people's measurements and knew the appropriate Brauche verse to repel harm from each part of the body. So the woman was sent for, and one day she showed herself at the door of the shop. She was not wearing a black head shawl/scarf of the Russian-Germans, as Delphine had expected, or a gathered apron-type skirt, nor was she even fat. She was a small, neat, sturdy little woman with short dark brown hair and ruddy, freckled skin.

"Wo ist das Kind?" she asked, all business.

Delphine brought her into the boys' bedroom, where Markus lay sleeping underneath a pile of quilts, and called Fidelis, who came and stood in the doorway. From her handbag, the woman drew a length of blue string, which she wound on her hand as she drew the blankets away from Markus and gently awakened him. She spoke some quiet words to him in German, then asked him in English to please lie still on his back while she measured him. Still caught up in his dreams, Markus obediently stretched his arms out while she put the string to them. As she worked, his eyes widened, his face took on an expression of disbelief. The Braucher measured all of him—torso, thighs, neck, hands, feet, and head—and then she stared at him assessingly, put the string back upon him, measuring in the same sequence, only this time reciting German words in a calm firm voice every time she moved the string. By now Markus had gone rigid with an outraged fear, but neither Delphine nor Fidelis really noticed him. They were caught up in the drama of the measuring. When she was finished, the Braucher pulled the covers up around Markus's neck, patted him gently, and turned away. On her way out, Fidelis paid the woman a shoulder picnic ham. Delphine was distracted by customers, and so she did not check back in on Markus. Meanwhile, he lay in his darkened room, thinking.

"Hello." He suddenly appeared in the doorway that led into the shop. "I'm hungry," he said for the first time in many weeks.

His voice was flat, suspicious, and he looked sideways at Delphine in a way she didn't understand. "You feel better?" she asked, amazed at the Braucher's success. She brought him back and sat him down at the kitchen table. Markus nodded, sullen and watchful. Slowly, he swallowed spoon after spoon of potato soup, sopped it up doggedly with bread. "I'm going to school," he announced, and picked up his books with his good arm.

Delphine stopped him, put a hand on his forehead. He glowered up at her from underneath her fingers.

"You still have a bit of fever."

"I don't care." He knocked her hand away and moved past her with stiff dignity. It was clear that he was terribly offended, but Delphine had no idea in what way until Franz asked, a few days later, "What's this about Markus getting measured for a coffin?"

Delphine looked at him, speechless at first. "What are you talking about?"

"He's telling all the kids in school, bragging sort of, that he was almost dead. That the undertaker's wife came and measured him for a coffin."

Delphine had meant to tell him the truth, but then, she feared suddenly, what if he were to simply crawl back into bed? And refuse to be roused this time at all? Whatever else, the Braucher's visit had infused him with an indignant horror necessary to his sudden improvement. Markus did seem recovered, though he moved with an air of self-righteous injury and babied his arm. She waited for several weeks before she told Markus what had truly happened. By then, his nameless sickness had entirely passed, and he was firmly among the living.

ELEVEN

The Christmas Sun

THE SNOW FELL as a bitter powder all December, light dustings that did not soften the earth's iron. The sky was clear. Day after day the sun rose, attended by two fierce sun dogs, glittering with collars of rainbows, cold fire. Where the snow was blown aside, the old plow marks and grooves in the earth sprouted a miserable stubble of wheat and cornstalks. In some places, where the crops had entirely failed, the dirt had drifted up against some lone tree or the occasional fence line. The dirt went so deep it would not be lost, it would always be there, but already it was clear that a great deal of the life was sucked from it. In higher places, the soil had leached an anemic whitish gray, like an old man's pallor. The stuff mixed with the snow to make a gritty and punishing substance that polished the paint from the houses in Argus, and painfully scoured the cheeks of schoolchildren, who walked to school backward with their arms tucked up in their sleeves, in little groups, taking turns as lookouts. Snow is a blessing when it softens the edges of the world, when it falls like a blanket trapping warm pockets of air. This snow was the opposite—it outlined the edges of things and made the town look meaner, bereft, merely tedious, like a mistake set down upon the earth and only half erased.

TANTE DID NOT GIVE UP when the suit betrayed her, she couldn't, not even when that first day she was nearly run over in it. Not even when she was sneered at and glared through in the county offices. She made the rounds. She went back to the bank so often that the tellers rolled their eyes at her approach. She even considered for a brief, mad moment approaching the owner of the pool hall and asking if he needed someone to clean. She got as close as the back entrance. But the smell of stale beer, sweat, piss, and worse, as well as the knowledge of what she'd find there for trash, was too revolting. What awful something might be hers to scrub and wash, she didn't know, but she couldn't over-come even the phantom of her disgust. So she went on searching. And to its credit, the suit held up. The fibers of the weave did not wilt or fray. The suit carried itself around her like a shield. Even when she'd failed for the day and dragged herself toward home, and some scrap of a meal, the suit rallied her and stiffened her resolve. Instead of starv-ing that night, she went to her brother's and straightened her back before she entered, swept in as she always had, snatched the food as though it was her due, grandly, because she had to claim it without hu-mility, or she could not claim it at all, not in front of Delphine, whom she both depended upon and hated.

Ever since the hill, Tante had found that Fidelis was more sympathetic to her ideas about bringing the boys back to be raised in Germany. She couldn't help pointing out that Fidelis's sons had gotten themselves into tremendous danger. What might happen next? It could be worse! And they were boys, hell-bent, saint-worshiping, furiously happy, danger-loving boys, no doubt about that. They would get into trouble if they could. Tante felt it her duty to tell Fidelis that she doubted that, even with Delphine there for part of the day, he could keep a close enough eye on his sons. They were not safe. They were running wild and swat-ting themselves with the sign of the cross. And with the wages he had to pay in the shop he could barely keep shoes on their feet. You could see the newspaper linings inside of their old boots. She went on in this way until Fidelis left the room, but she could see that she'd made an impression of some sort. She played on his guilt over what might have happened, what came so close. Markus buried in the hill.

In the suit, the sun glancing off it in the afternoons, a heavy set of woolen underwear beneath keeping her snug, Tante made her way through the town, thickening her skin for the inevitable refusals. She went out. She asked for work. And then one day she actually got hired.

The place had just opened, whatever it was. At first it was hard to tell what exactly was sold there. A jumble of baskets and tobacco cans spilled out onto the sidewalk. A wide front window held bolts of new fabric and neatly cut piles of old, a large tin sieve with half-moon handles carved of horn, some handmade lace, rickrack, ribbons, and a brand-new sewing machine. A placard on the door said merely Notions. Tante stepped close, entered. On the other side of the half-painted, half-scraped door, there was a battered dressmaker's dummy, more bolts of fabric—all sorts, from wools to calico—and a display of brilliant hat trims. There were also baskets of dyed feathers, ten kinds of machine lace, a fur collar that would have looked very fine sewed to her old black coat. There were used mason jars, odd pieces of silverware, rolls of chicken wire in a corner, a perfectly good rake hanging on the wall. Squash, cucumber and pumpkin vine seeds. Scrap paper. The variety of things for sale was bewildering, cheerful, a bold mishmash. Tante walked around the small shop once and then addressed a stern and orderly-looking woman behind the counter, asked her usual question. Whether there was work to be had. The woman walked out from behind the counter, hugely pregnant, and said, "I got to stop for a while. Can you sell?"

"I can sell!" said Tante, her voice stout and grim.

"Then just a minute," said the woman. "I'll get my boss."

She went behind a muslin curtain, spoke to someone, and then out walked Step-and-a-Half.

At first, Tante didn't register the situation, and she gave Step-and-a-Half the irritated once-over, the condescending twitch of her mouth, that, at best, she gave her at Waldvogel's when Step-and-a-Half claimed her scraps. And she waited, staring past the saleswoman, for the boss to appear. Then she looked back at the woman behind the counter, and at Step-and-a-Half, who was regarding her with a tigerish amusement.

"Well?" said Step-and-a-Half.

"I'm here to see the boss," said Tante, her eyes flicking all around the little room.

"You're looking at the boss," said Step-and-a-Half.

Tante heard that. Her head swiveled, and the complicated knots of her hair fairly writhed at her sharp movement. She thought that she couldn't have heard right, and gave a short, barking laugh.

"What do you mean?"

"This here is my place."

The woman behind the counter blew the air out her cheeks impatiently. "Well you *said* you was looking for work, didn't you?"

Tante still couldn't take it in, but she nodded dumbly in the affirmative. Then cleared her throat and said in meek puzzlement, "Yes."

"Can you sell?" Step-and-a-Half asked the question now.

Somehow an affirmative answer emerged from Tante.

"And do you know a damn thing about all this stuff?" Step-and-a-Half swept her arm around the festooned store walls. The supercilious grandeur that had always seemed absurd when she was a scrap hauler now seemed more appropriate for the owner of sumptuous bolts of fabric, the huge variety of extraordinary pickings and leavings stacked in piles and lovingly displayed on nails or set off in a celebratory way on shelves.

Though she still had not emerged from her shock, Tante took up the challenge. "I know much!"

"And do you have to wear that thing?"

Step-and-a-Half nodded at the metal-buttoned suit, but Tante reared back and folded her arms and shut her astonished mouth. Her need for work smacked up against her pride and drove hard against the impossible image of this tattered and flamboyant scrap hauler now mysteriously turned respectable business owner. And potential boss. Things were turned right over in her mind. Her social pride was upset. And yet she could have stood that. It was the slight of her clothing, the specific suit, which she yet wore with honor and offended loyalty, that she couldn't bear.

"This is a good suit, and most costly," she informed her. Step-and-a-Half waved away her stiff words and kicked her foot at a graceful, womanly, black enamel electric Singer with delicate gold flower trim and an optional wood cabinet that fit beautifully beneath.

"If you can work the thing, you can sell the thing."

"I'll learn to work it," was Tante's promise. She couldn't take her eyes off the gleaming instrument, the very latest model, streamlined and yet familiar. The whole room seemed to narrow to that machine, as though a spotlight were turned upon it. All else fell into blackness and insignificance, even the idea of working under Step-and-a-Half, a surprise so grave that the potential humiliation hadn't even sunk in or truly registered with Tante. The lustrous, compact little businesslike machine with its sparkling needle and shining chrome flywheel was enough, for the moment, to still the larger picture. For it made sense of her dilemma. Tante touched the cool curve where the arm accommodated the cloth, ran her hand curiously over the carved oak of the cabinet.

"Sit down at it," said Step-and-a-Half. "Mrs. Knutson can give you the rundown."

Charmed and fascinated, Tante sat down at the machine and accepted instructions. Even when the person she despised most in the town, Roy Watzka, stepped past her bearing in his arms a bolt of purple felt to place in the window, she hardly acknowledged him. She was learning to thread the needle.

THE COLD DEEPENED but the snow remained sparse, disheartening the sledders and the snow fort builders, though the skating was fine. The ice was dark and clear. You could see straight through the quartz gray surface into a frigid depth where leaves and air bubbles swirled, trapped in silver cracks. Franz had agreed to meet Betty Zumbrugge for a date once the school let out for Christmas holiday. On that first evening of vacation, she drove up to the shop in the big black car, parked it outside and kept the motor running, but did not come in. Franz took off his apron and hung it up. He'd told his father when he was leaving, but not with whom. Fidelis, peering out the window while he absently sharpened a knife, said, "That's Zumbrugge."

"It's Betty," said Franz.

"Why don't she come in?"

"She's picking me up."

Fidelis looked hard at Franz, and his son flushed, but shrugged on his father's worn old jacket. "Don't get polluted," Fidelis warned. Franz waved him off. He wasn't much of a drinker. He went outside. There were swirls of snow in the air, bright flakes biting his cheeks. He jumped into the car and leaned his elbow on the window, held the hand strap on the passenger's side. Betty turned the car around with a screech of the wheels and they barreled out to a little roadhouse that had once been a Prohibition blind pig. Betty jolted to a halt, laughing, and lighted a cigarette. For a while they sat together in the car just looking at the place.

"You ever been to one?"

Franz just shrugged. He never had been. The roadhouse was a low clapboard building with a thin porch tacked on all around. Betty told him about her family, her plans for nursing school, her sisters and their boyfriends, her father and his problems. Franz tried to listen with careful attention, but his mind kept drifting. At last, they got out of the car and walked up to the door of the roadhouse. They could hear someone playing a slow Canadian waltz on the accordion. Inside, the place was lit and warm, the walls full of advertisements. The chairs and tables were made out of thick, worn, battered wood. They chose a table toward the back of the room where they could see whomever came through the door, but not be spotted at once. They were served two neat whiskeys with chasers of beer.

The beer wasn't much, but the whiskey, that was different. The taste was harsh and golden, the burn sweet. The stuff hit Franz's stomach, bloomed through him with an amber warmth. He looked into Betty's bright blue eyes and smiled at her with an indulgent pleasantness. In spite of her grown-up clothing and makeup and car, she seemed younger than Mazarine. He waited for a while as Betty told him something she obviously considered serious—her look was urgent and, once, she passed her hand through her careful yellow curls, messing them a little, so their smoothness divided into rings. They had another whiskey and the rings blurred into an icy halo. He refused a third whiskey, but Betty drank it, and then they walked out to the car.

The cold had deepened, and the skin of their hands and faces numbed in the wind, but the car was very modern and the inside heated up a little as they drove. Betty turned down a road where they would not be bothered—it dead-ended at a farm foreclosed last spring. Her father had foreclosed it, Franz remembered. She stopped the car and turned off the lights. Gradually, their eyes adjusted to the snow light outside the car and the world turned a distinct blue with black shadows pooling in the ditches. They could see the faltering sprinkle of town lights through a haze of windbreak, but all around them it was very calm. Betty pulled some blankets from the backseat, and said, "Let's talk."

"What about?" said Franz, reaching toward her. He held her face in his hands, kindly, as though he really meant to ask this question, but he was teasing her. Betty was serious.

"About us," she said.

"Well, what about us?"

"Aren't you going to kiss me?" asked Betty. "I'm starting to wonder what's wrong with you."

"All right," said Franz. With his finger, he smoothed her lips, then he used his thumb to rub the lipstick off. He didn't mean to keep her in suspense, but what he did seemed to mesmerize her and she tipped back her head. He put his mouth on hers and then he knew, right away, that he had made some sort of terrible mistake. He expected her to kiss like Mazarine, but it was all different. Her lips were plump, fruity, then wet. She opened her mouth so wide he had to creak his open, too, and when he touched her tongue it was a stiff, little, fast-talking tongue. He didn't like her tongue, her teeth, the smoky way she tasted, the way she smelled, even though it was probably expensive perfume. There was too much of it, too much of her, and he fell away from her side of the car, dizzy. But she fell with him across the seat and then his hands were inside her coat. He was surprised to find that suddenly her dress was open, and without any warning at all his hands were on her breasts. Her brassiere was made of something warm and tight, a smooth fabric. He put his hands underneath and lifted it off and when her breasts filled his palms he drew a ragged breath. His hands stopped moving. He pulled her brassiere down and closed her coat, sat up and turned away.

"I've got to get out," he said, opening the car door. "I've got to walk."

Because of the scarcity of snow that year, he knew that he could get to Mazarine's across the fields.

HE WAS HALF FROZEN by the time he reached the Shimek house, hardly more than a shack, really, with a boot-shaped tin chimney and an outhouse near the back alley. That part of the town was divided into blocks, cut with dirt roads, now frozen but usually all dust or mud. There were scraggly sweeps of woods all around Mazarine's house, and her mother kept chickens and an old cow that gave a bit of milk. All the way there, outdoor dogs, mostly chained to their houses, took turns barking at Franz as he passed, so he was sure she'd have heard him approach and come to the door. But that was just the lingering effect of the whiskey, perhaps, a lapse in perspective. Franz was so filled with the mission of his walk, and the drama of leaving Betty, that he became convinced that Mazarine would know and understand that he was due to arrive, even though he hadn't talked to her for weeks. She would be waiting. She would know all that had happened. Instantly, things would be as they were before. When he stepped up to the unpainted door, which was almost level with the ground, knocked, and waited for her to answer, he was slowly bubbling up inside with the excitement of a man about to be rescued.

Her mother opened the door and filled the doorway. She squinted at him, touched strings of gray-brown hair away from her face and groaned a little in recognition but said nothing. Shut the door and left him standing outside. After a while, he knocked again. This time, Mazarine opened the door. The dim light inside outlined her, slim in her summer dress, her hair as always alive and curving around her shoulders and trailing down upon her breasts. Her face was completely in shadow, but he could see that her features were calm, and, he thought, sad.

"What do you want?" she asked.

"To come in," he answered, now understanding this would not be the way he'd imagined it, but very different, "just for a minute."

Mazarine glanced behind, and Franz saw the great, naked white pillars of her mother's legs in the gloom. Mrs. Shimek had hiked up her dress to sit on a wooden kitchen chair and watch the door.

"Please don't come in," said Mazarine.

"I'm half froze," said Franz. "I walked here across the fields. It was maybe six miles."

"Why were you out there?" Mazarine asked. A light wind came up, terribly cold, and swirled the hair around her shoulders. Oblivious to the biting air, she stared at him, waiting. She could smell the alcohol he breathed, and the thought of him drinking faintly shocked her, then wounded her. She'd never known him to drink, although some of the boys did. Mrs. Shimek cried out for her daughter to shut the damn door. Mazarine began to shut it once again on Franz, but in his desperation he stepped forward and she had to fall back a little and let him in. It wasn't the first time that he'd ever been in her house, but somehow things looked worse. Maybe her father had really gone off on the boxcars the way he'd threatened. Or maybe her mother had gotten sick for real. Mrs. Shimek sat there, strangely monumental on the small chair, staring at him with a solemn, owlish opacity. There wasn't another chair, he realized, so he just stood there as Mazarine walked over to the woodstove and stirred it up and put in two pieces of wood.

"Don't use it up," said her mother.

Mazarine ignored her and spoke to Franz. "Come stand over here." She beckoned him to the stove, and he understood that he was cold, now, deep down and not just surface, because he began to shake so hard his bones knocked inside as his body warmed. The whiskey had provided a false warmth and energy during the long walk across the fields. He'd tramped the iron clods, even run across the wavelets of windblown snow so fine and hard it resembled a fine plaster on the ground. Now his blood was cold and thin; his bravado sank away and he felt lost, foolish. The fire blazed up in the iron stove and the heat finally began to penetrate his clothing, then his skin. It radiated into him so that he almost controlled the shakes. From time to time, his body still shuddered. He stood there, silently waiting for what came next. Mazarine stood next to him. And her mother sat watching them from her chair.

Mazarine didn't move once she found a still place inside of herself. What should she feel, she wondered, knowing it was odd that Franz's presence in this house should leave her so indifferent. She couldn't muster the correct gratitude for his return, if that's what it was. He hadn't said so. She couldn't feel gladness, nor could she feel the proper anger. Her friends had said, "Don't you just hate him now?" But she hadn't. She'd felt patient, even when her first grief turned to the lassitude of despair, and she had shrugged off their avid sympathy. After she'd lain with her cheek against him on that November afternoon, and turned once, twice, and kissed him there long and smooth and slow, she had to erase him from her mind. She had bricked up all thoughts of Franz in a cold little room. He was nothing. Because the next thing she knew, he was with Betty. If she thought of those afternoons underneath the pine, she'd die of the shame of his abandoning her. So even though he stood right here, right now, she couldn't really see him. Things were utterly changed, weren't they? Shouldn't they be? She poked up the fire and stood there, watching him for signs that would tell her what she should do.

There was no word spoken. Nothing but the fire's simple crackle. As he warmed, Franz became increasingly unnerved by the dead silence, and once he felt capable of leaving he said, "Thanks," in a subdued voice. Mazarine walked with him, the few steps to the door. As he reached out to open it, he asked in a low voice, "Do you want me to come back?"

The no came out automatically, her voice a white scratch on the tiny syllable.

*   *   *

JUST IN TIME, everyone agreed, the snow began to fall. It came in pic-
ture-postcard flakes that sifted down straight through a windless day.
Everyone came out of doors, exclaiming with pleasure. The children
caught flakes on their tongues and planned great doings, dug tunnels
in the drifts, fought snowball wars. At last the sleds could be used. The
Christmas trees had a backdrop. The carols and the church nativity
scenes made sense. The wind so rarely stills on the plains that the sin-
gular piling of light flakes was a marvel. Fence posts grew caps. Tree
branches were outlined and pine trees were dressed in puffy shawls.
The people of Argus went out walking just to marvel at the odd shapes
that the new snow gave everyday objects as it landed gently and stuck
atop automobiles, doghouses, trash bins, bleak grape arbors, the statue
in front of the courthouse, steps, and ornate railings. Argus suddenly
looked sweet and amusing, like a village in an old fairy tale.

Clarisse, emerging from the back of the funeral parlor, had this very
thought as she buried her hands in a knitted fleece muff and walked
home. She thought of the house made of gingerbread, deep in the
forest, the roof made of iced ladyfingers trimmed with sugar gum drops.
She thought of the quaint Swiss hut pictured on the tin of chocolate
she'd bought for herself. When she got home, she decided, she would
treat herself to a great pot of cocoa. She would scald the milk and driz-
zle sugar into it, then shave the chocolate into the pan and stir until it
melted. There might even be enough cream left in the bottle she'd
bought at Waldvogel's, from Delphine, to whip for a fancy topping. The
question she now confronted was whether she should ask Delphine to
join her, and maybe bring along some extra cream. She reached her
house. Suddenly, there was more to think of. In the new snow leading
up to her front door, there were tracks, great and solid tracks, a man's
tracks. And there he was, waiting on her porch.

AT LAST, on the strength of his associations, and after dogged appli-
cation and reapplication to Judge Zumbrugge, Sheriff Hock had ob-
tained a warrant permitting him to search the home of Clarisse Strub.
He was a very neat man, meticulous and fussy about his surroundings.

His house was immaculate; everything he owned was stored and filed, his clothing was neatly folded in his dresser or hung in his dusted closet. He kept his badge, well polished, in a small wooden bowl just beside his bed. He could have told anyone whether such a thing as a red tubular gleaming glass bead was wedged into the crack of the floor of his closet. He would have noticed. In contrast, Clarisse saved her precision for her calling and let her house go, kept her rooms in a state of feminine disarray. After Delphine had removed the dress from her closet, some time ago, she had swept the floor. But she hadn't examined the cracks between the boards with a powerful lamp and a shrewd, scanning eye, the way Sheriff Hock did now.

"This won't take long," he said to Clarisse with a firm and even kind formality. "I apologize for discommoding you and impinging on your privacy."

"With all due respect to your office," said Clarisse, in despair, "go to hell."

"I've been there," Sheriff Hock said, looking up at her with deadening simplicity. "You put me there, Clarisse."

"I didn't mean to." Tears started into her eyes. She held them back, then let go. Maybe, if he felt sorry for her, he'd leave. "I don't want you to feel badly—"

"Then," said Hock, setting down his lamp with a surge of unruly hope, turning toward her, "you must feel something."

Clarisse stared at him, paralyzed, hearing fuzzy noises as though wires in her brain had just crossed.

"For me," he pursued.

"I've always felt that we could be friends." Clarisse felt her voice rising, higher, higher, toward a shriek. She tried to take a deep breath. She got some air, but a red tide was choking her. Sheriff Hock shook his head with sorrowing gravity and aimed his beam back at the floor. Clarisse watched him, thoughts swirling. Of course, he'd find a bead, a thread, a bit of cloth, something to implicate her. Then he'd have her cornered and she'd have to decide between him and a murder charge, wouldn't she?

"Leave," said Clarisse. "This is my room. Get out of here."

Hock rose and though he didn't move toward her she felt his energy, a menacing and self-righteous energy, surge at her in a wave. She stepped back. With a small, pursed smile and a low, disarming whistle, Hock turned away. Arms folded, lips set, Clarisse leaned in the doorway of her bedroom and watched the awful, strained, cheap, twill material that stretched across the buttocks of the kneeling sheriff. His belt cut into his belly. Above that, his torso filled his shirt in a way that made it look like it was wadded with heavy quilting, not flesh. But there was flesh beneath, a body, make no mistake about that! A body that had decided it owned her. Clarisse let her thoughts go. *Why not just murther 'm. . . .* It would be so simple to slip a knife beneath those padded ribs. Her fingers shook slightly on the door frame.

"Please go away," she whispered, and when he didn't respond she said something that her mother used to say. "Don't make me lose my temper."

Hock glanced up at her. "Oh? What will happen then?" His voice was pleasant and indulgent.

"I don't know," she turned aside. "I have never lost my temper before."

What would she do with him? Stuff him in her closet? Run away? Let him rot? She would have to disappear. Here it was the holiday season, her favorite time of the year, and really not a good time for her to leave Argus. She'd always enjoyed the bitter blue air of Midnight Mass, walking to the church, and it seemed unfair that she should be forced to miss out on a ritual that had been hers since childhood. Her fingers were still shaking so she flexed and rubbed her hands to still them. She watched the sheriff root through her underthings with a delicate hand that made her feel more perused and invaded than if he'd flung her panties due north.

She had to contain herself, had to control the jolting of her heart, but the awful sense of outrage was too rich a soil. Instant, snaky, quick-growing weeds were bolting up inside her. She wrung her hands together, suddenly giving way. Catching hold of herself again, she calmly left the sight of the sheriff in her bedroom, and she walked down the stairs. She kept her hand on the railing, so as not to trip. Why should she be the one to trip and fall? Perhaps he would trip, Sheriff Hock. She imagined his huge bulk slipping and windmilling down the first flight, breaking in two pieces at the landing, and then in quarters at the bottom like a china pig. She almost laughed at the sight. The picture lightened her frame of mind. Maybe she'd step outdoors, have a rare smoke to calm herself. After all, what was there to find? The dress was gone—dug up and disposed of in a clever way. She congratulated herself, and then she thought of how, once ripped by Hock, the damn thing dripped beads. She remembered the broken threads, the thousands of broken threads, and there was suddenly an icy little whirl in her chest.

Clarisse walked rigidly down the steps to where she kept her cigarettes—in the kitchen, on a shelf, in a little airtight can right above the knives. And the knives, she stored them safely in a drawer where knives should always be kept—safe from little hands. Hers were the only little hands in the house. Suddenly she found that instead of removing a cigarette from the can, she was opening the drawer. Then she was examining her favorite knife, a long, slender carving knife. It was a beautiful, tempered blade with a slight curve to it. Clarisse tested the blade with her thumb, then removed a small whetstone from the drawer. Sharpening the blade was routine—she kept her knives very keen. She tested the edge again and it still drew no blood. She paused a moment, then leaned into the work and made the blade edgier yet. As she was sharpening the knife to a whisper, she thought how it was a shame that so many people—even her best friend, Delphine, and Sheriff Hock, for certain—underestimated her. She wouldn't kill him, of course, but she could scare him off. He'd have to leave and once he was gone she'd bolt the doors. She'd get a lawyer, not one in Zumbrugge's pocket. A real lawyer. Maybe one from Minneapolis. She'd tell all to her uncle, though she was ashamed. Together they'd make certain that a Strub was not threatened and chased around and made to endure invasions of personal underwear drawers. She would have to burn every slip, bra, and panty he had touched, Sheriff Hock, and they were nice things. She spent a lot of money on slips, especially, real silk.

She wished she had the red dress. She'd felt invincible that time she put it on and wore it to the wake underneath a somber black coat. That dress had given her the courage to accept that her father was gone. The rustle of blood-red beads had assisted her in saying good-bye to him. The knife wavered. The unholy nerve of Hock to corner her at her own father's wake! Maybe, if only he hadn't put his mouth on her, she wouldn't have slugged him so hard. He had tried to take away the purity of her own grief, and no one knew better than she what a sacred and precious thing true grief was. He pretended he was comforting her. Well, maybe he actually believed that! Carefully, she straightened the blade and made certain she hadn't put a small nick in the edge. But it was persnickety sharp now. She thought of Delphine, then of the Scottish play, *a black primer for my quailing heart*. She'd lost fear. She gave the knife an extra razor's edge, imagining that it was by now so sharp the sheriff might not feel it, at first.

When she entered her own bedroom, and told him to leave again, she gave him fair warning. She kept the knife behind her back, but said, with only the slightest tremor in her voice, "I'm warning you, Sheriff Hock. If you don't leave, I'll have to hurt you."

He stood. He had the nerve to smile at her, and then to try to engage her in a long look, to penetrate her defenses.

"I'll huff and I'll puff and I'll blow your house down," he said gently. "I warned you, too."

He gave a small laugh, his lips budding modestly. "Why not me, Clarisse? There's nothing unacceptable about me, I have a good job, prestigious even. I do not drink. *I* do not sleep with other women and I never will. Take a look at yourself. You're pretty as an angel, but you're an undertaker. Men are scared off by your line of work. Not me."

Hock held his arms out, and his smile was feral, his eyes filled with an ignorant and innocent greed. When Clarisse did not step toward him, he dropped his arms slowly. He reached into his pocket and plucked out a piece of paper with one red glass bead folded into it.

"I found it here," he said. "State's evidence."

"State's evidence? Oh, for God sake's, don't be ridiculous. Let me see that." Clarisse snatched at the paper with her free hand.

"Uh, uh, uh," he gave an awful, playful croon. Then he tucked the bead back into the paper, folded the paper into the breast pocket of his shirt, opened his arms, and lunged.

Her arm thrust forward on its own.

He didn't know what had happened, not at first. He turned away in shock, and in turning he even did some of the work for her. He wrenched around so that she could see in her mind's eye the keen blade slide along inside of him, lopping apart viscera. The stuff that spilled out inside of him would kill him, but much too slowly. Quick is better, she thought, and she reacted only to her thoughts, which remained steady and rational. She had to use the knife as a saw. Fast as she could, she cut right across his midsection as he threw up his hand and tried to struggle away. She bobbed side to side without letting go the wooden handle. She had to use both hands and avoid his flailing clutch. He was tougher than she'd thought, but through her work she had developed a shocking strength in her grip. How very surprised he was to see the knife move along his belly with such speed, parting the threads of his shirt. Absurd phrases formed in her head. Her thoughts were strange and far away. He is distinctly not pleased! He was, she saw, extremely troubled at this unexpected development. His brows knit and he seemed unable to say a word. Just stared at her, mystified. He did not expect this, after all, and she had some sympathy—surprises were not for her, either, and this was a very big one.

"Sit down," she said, her voice neutral and informative. "It won't take long."

He thumped backward, rattling her closet door on its hinges, soaking her silken slips and puddling blood in her shoes. Quickly, she snatched her favorites from beneath him. With a grim satisfaction she saw, too, that he had used his pocketknife to pry another red glass bead from a crack in the floor. So much for that! She plucked the bead up, showed it to him, opened her mouth and swallowed it. He looked very dull now, even stupid. After a while, checking his pulse, she felt it slow to a terminal pump and then with clinical care she watched the pupils of his eyes become stuck and unresponsive. Nobody home, she finally said. She realized she'd hardly breathed. Standing, she put one hand on her chest and the other on her abdomen, drew in new air from the lowest point of her midsection, just like in voice class. Thought of hiding him. But what was the point, anyway, of standing him up in her closet? That would hardly do the trick for long. She threw a tantrum—tears and wild, sobbing groans that she could hear from a place outside herself. The noises she made filled the room, alarming her. Shut up now, she counseled, or you'll never stop. She crossed the hall to draw herself a bath.

While the water was running she removed the knife from the sheriff, washed it clean. She covered him with an old bedspread, reached past him into the closet. From under her bed she drew a large brown suitcase. After she was clean, she would pack.

The next day was Christmas Eve and as Clarisse soaked she made her plans. The thing now was to act, not to feel anything. She'd have to visit the bank during the day, of course, and then she thought with sudden approval that it was a very good time to take out her money. People spent so much at Christmas on unexpected or extravagant gifts. The problem was that people also often died around Christmas, and there might be emergencies at work. After Christmas, though, people usually waited until after New Year's to die. "Except for you," she called to the sheriff across the hall. "You couldn't wait." After the bank, she thought, she'd get herself organized, pack some more, lightly but sensibly, and plan her route. With some satisfaction she realized that, if she was very efficient and if all worked out properly, she'd be able to go to Midnight Mass just as she always had, and then she could snatch a few hours of sleep, before she left on the morning train.

CYPRIAN KNEW, but the knowing did not help him. Nothing was going to happen with Delphine. Christmas brought it all out in the open, which was not surprising. As both of them had long agreed anyway, that holiday was a booby trap. What made it worse was that Cyprian was trying to make it the first good Christmas ever. He had wanted to make up for the lack of Christmas in Delphine's childhood. Maybe his, too. Their Christmases had never been anything more than occasions for their parents to get spectacularly drunk. There were no special dinners, no little gifts, no garlands, no paper stars or candles in the window. Only the cold iron stove the children tried to stoke all by themselves. There was no school to divert them and no teacher to feed them from her own lunch pail, just bumbling adults reeling in at all hours and falling full length on the kitchen floor.

Remembering this, Cyprian went out and bought a goose from a Bohemian farmer who'd fattened it on corn and grain. And Delphine made strings of popcorn and paper chains with the boys and got Franz to take a hatchet out to the woods and cut two young pines. She'd decorated one for Fidelis and the boys, and tied the other to the hood of the car and brought it home. She had candles, too, in little tin holders with small reflecting shields behind the flames. Each of the boys had gifts, and there was one for Cyprian and one for Roy. Although Cyprian tried not to wonder if Delphine had bought or made a gift for Fidelis, too, he couldn't help it. He did wonder. A few days ago, he had even dug into her dresser to see if he could find a wrapped suspicious object, but he found nothing except her clothes indifferently folded, and then his own gift, which looked like a scarf. What he did embarrassed him. He'd thought he wasn't the sort of person who would rummage through a woman's things, but now it looked like he was. He'd gone out and bought her an extravagant ruby ring.

When he picked her up from work on Christmas Eve, she was brooding over something and said little on the way home.

"Are you all right?" he asked.

"Tired." She told him that everybody had come in at the last minute for their goose or turkey or pork roasts or whatever they were having on the holiday, plus they'd wanted special cuts or trimmings of all kinds, and there were last-minute requests and then, too, she'd tried to make a stollen cake and that failed. After that she burned a batch of cookies for the boys. He tried not to think of Fidelis. Were those cookies really for him? Anyway, her tiredness was understandable, and he thought, trying to put it optimistically, it would make his surprise dinner for her all the better. He had just dropped Roy off at the back door of Step-and-a-Half's shop. She had a room over the store, which she had leased with the stashes of money that, it was rumored, she had kept buried in tin snuff-boxes under rocks, trees, signs, fence posts all along the roads she traveled, far onto the plains. She was hardly ever at the shop, so Roy often kept the fire going when the temperature dropped. Cyprian and Delphine would be alone.

"You're going to like what I cooked," said Cyprian.

"You cooked?"

Her voice was polite, but listless. Cyprian looked at her, folded in the seat next to him. She seemed small that night, almost delicate, although he knew she was sturdy and her fragility was only a trick of the light, moving across the planes of her face, and the reflected blueness of the winter sky and earth. She seemed lonely, but he really couldn't figure it, for he was there, ready to cook for her and sing if she wanted and give her the ring over which the jeweler had sighed, upon selling at that price, saying it was his favorite piece, and he really shouldn't, but he needed Christmas money, too.

"Come on," said Cyprian coaxingly, "I bought us a special bottle of brandy, real old. We'll toast the holidays to come."

"Oh," said Delphine—unpleasantly, thought Cyprian. "Our future." There was a note of contempt or derision in her voice that stabbed at his cheer, but he willed himself to ignore it and went on with his mental planning. Instead of talking, he whistled an old tune he thought, vaguely, might be a Christmas tune.

"Why are you whistling that?" said Delphine after a while.

"What?"

"'Mine Eyes Have Seen the Glory.'"

He said nothing, hurt.

"Oh," she said after a while. Her dark mood surprised her. She couldn't figure it. All day she'd struggled out of her low feelings only to sink back in. Now, she made a new effort, spoke kindly. "I get it . . . of the coming of the Lord. 'Mine eyes have seen the glory of the coming of the Lord.' The birth of Jesus. Sure."

"Right," he said shortly, pulling up the road he'd shoveled that morning. He got out of the car, slammed the door a bit too hard, and breathed deeply of the cold, still, blue air. The purity of it hurt his lungs. He breathed until he'd recovered his equilibrium and then he thought of his attempt at baking gingerbread. Surely that would, at least, make her laugh. But when she walked in the door, she only said, "God, burnt gingerbread!" She dumped her things on the floor, kicked off her boots, and groaned as she eased herself into the chair across from the Christmas tree.

"I feel old," she said, really to herself. "I feel a thousand years old tonight."

"You're just used to a lousy Christmas," said Cyprian. "Here." He handed her a piece of the stone-dry gingerbread, with the burnt part scraped off, wrapped in a clean dish towel, then he blew up the fire in the stove and stoked it with two logs. He shut the door tight and opened the flue all the way so that the fire would roar up inside and make a cozy crackling noise. He took out his box of matches and lighted the candles on the window, the candles on the tree. She was quiet when he did this, and although he didn't turn to look at her he was sure it was because she was finally appreciating his efforts, feeling the peacefulness of the night, maybe tasting her gingerbread, getting used to the fact that he was taking care of her. But when he turned around, he saw that she'd fallen asleep with the gingerbread, still wrapped, on her knees.

"Oh, the hell with it," he said, loud enough to wake her, but she didn't wake. He blew out all the candles and went into the kitchen and fixed what he hoped was a passable oyster soup. When it was nice and hot, he poured the milky soup into a shallow bowl, stuck crackers all the way around it, and then peppered it and laid a lump of butter on top to melt. He brought the bowl in to her and set it on the floor. Kneeling beside the chair, he kissed her cheek, waked her gently. When she opened her eyes, he saw that she'd really not been asleep, she'd been crying, which he didn't need. Not that night. He gave her the bowl of soup.

"Thanks, that's nice," she had the grace to say. "Where's yours?"

"I'm getting it." He went back to the kitchen, ladled his own soup out, and carried it before him while he dragged along a chair so he could sit down next to her.

"Hey," he said, even though he knew he was in dangerous territory, "you know what they say about oysters."

He was relieved when she didn't come up with anything sarcastic, and hopeful when she said, "This tastes good."

Before he ate, he put his soup down and quickly relighted all the candles. They flickered and glowed, shadowing the walls, and made the room into, he thought, a very beautiful and secret-looking place. He sat down with her and sipped at the hot, briny soup, and said nothing. Perhaps the peace of the room itself would get her into the mood he was trying to inspire.

"Say," he said, "how about that tree? You see I got tinsel?"

She didn't say anything. He was getting angry now. He could feel that cold trickle up the center of him, that shiver.

"I'm trying to make you happy." His voice was tense, ready to rise out of control, but she didn't seem to care if she pushed him over his limit. She shrugged and looked away from him.

He got up, snatched away her soup, spilling some on her dress, and brought the bowls into the kitchen. "Steady," he said aloud, to himself, in a low voice, but there was pressure behind his eyes. His skull seemed to press on his brain, like a too tight hat, and he thought for a moment he should just step outside again into the black cold, but he didn't, and he made the mistake of walking straight back into the room and glaring down at Delphine.

"Why the hell don't you just go back to them, then?" he asked.

"What are you talking about?"

"You know. Him. Them." He was so choking mad that if he said the man's name he knew he'd explode. And yet he was helpless because had no right to explode. He took the little green-and-red-wrapped box from his pants pocket and, just exactly the way he didn't want to do it, he flung it at Delphine with a light movement of scorn. "Here," he said, "I bought you a present."

The tiny box landed in her lap. She didn't pick it up. But she looked at it for a while. He breathed hard, standing in the doorway, and bit his lip so that he wouldn't shout at her to open it. Finally she nudged it, though gently, with a finger.

"It's pretty," she said, "what is it, a ring?"

"Yes," he said, his voice cracking a little, his anger changing all of a sudden to a longing so precise and painful he felt his heart squeezing, hot, in his chest, as though her initials were branded on it. The skin on his face prickled and he wanted to throw himself at her feet. She looked up at him from where she sat in the chair, the little box in her lap, and her foxlike face blazed in the light of candles. The flames jumped in her eyes and her hair sprang out in a dim aureole from her warm, flushed cheeks—she smiled at him but it wasn't the smile he wanted, it was a weary sort of smile. He sagged a bit against the entrance and looked down at his feet.

As for Delphine, sitting there in the flare of Cyprian's hopeful candles with the ring box in her lap, she thought back to their balancing act. The secretive light sent her into a strange, reflective, obstinate mood. Again, she saw herself walk out before the crowd in her long red skirt. There was the tea tray, set on her torso. She became the human table. Only in her mind, instead of chairs one by one men came out and balanced on her flint hard stomach. A stack of boys and men. Cyprian and Fidelis. The twins, Emil and Erich. Then Franz, and Markus, at last her father. All were precariously balanced on her phenomenally tough midsection. And she was down there, thinking what thoughts, feeling what feelings? What could she say? One word and they all might topple. One word could throw them off. So she didn't say anything, but her arms and legs started to shake.

"Delphine," said Cyprian, quietly now, his voice neutral and impassive, "why don't you just go to bed?"

But she was still looking down at the little box. She was staring at it as though she could see through the wrappings into the velvet case. So he picked it up out of her lap, put it back in his pocket, and left her.

*   *   *

CYPRIAN GOT INTO THE CAR, sat for a moment gathering his thoughts and then he started the car up violently and roared down the road into town. He felt slightly better as he entered the pool hall, and much better as he made himself exquisitely drunk. He left the pool hall in the blackness before dawn, already feeling the whiskey fade. Immediately, he drove to the house of Delphine's friend, Clarisse. He knocked too loudly, pounded really, with a drunken indignation.

Clarisse jumped off the couch where she was sleeping, ran to the door to shut up the racket. She opened the door suspiciously, blinking sleep from her eyes. She was wearing a flimsy gown in which she seemed quite bitterly cold. Her usually rosy face was pale, her lips almost blue. Shivering, she let him in. There was a large, packed suitcase on a mat next to the door, and a smart red hatbox sitting on a chair. While he stomped his feet and rubbed his hands, she took her time, walked away from him, as if she didn't know he could see her ass and legs through the thin pink material. She picked up a fluffy blue blanket from her sofa, but didn't wrap it around herself until she'd passed from his sight.

"Come on in," she said, beckoning him toward the kitchen. He sat down at her table. Suddenly, she seemed all recovered—toasty looking. Her cheeks glowed and her curls gleamed. She spun around holding the blanket on with one hand. She said she'd make him some coffee. Once she prepared the coffeepot and left it to boil, she sat across from him, rubbed her eyes with soft little kitten fists. Yawning pertly, shaking her head as if to clear it, but really making her curls bounce charmingly, she said, her voice a dreamy pout, "So, what is it?"

"Merry Christmas," he said as he slowly pushed, across her kitchen table, the tiny green box.

THE CRATE FROM GERMANY, which the boys had waited until Christmas to open, contained extraordinary things. For Franz, there was a coat made of top-grade wool, beautifully sewn and lined with the heavy sort of satin Fidelis remembered from his youth. The boys each had a pair of leather boots, and the boots fit, thanks to Tante, who had kept her mother updated as to the boys' sizes in her letters. There were small things—carved and brilliantly painted tops, the books *Max und Moritz* and *Der Struwwelpeter*, and small horses with legs that moved. For the twins, vast regiments of soldiers in every pose and their equipment, too. For Markus, a thick hat and knitted sweater. Tante received an embroidered shawl, which she pretended was a scarf. A shawl was an old person's gift. Fidelis, a meerschaum pipe and Turkish tobacco. Everything was packed in great wads of worthless old *reichsmarks*—a trillion to the dollar. On the top, there were a few precious newspapers which Fidelis and Tante fought over good-naturedly as they ate their burnt cookies and sweet stollen and drank cups of strong coffee.

After everything was opened and the songs were sung, after the candles were put out and the boys were immersed in playing with their gifts, Tante and Fidelis continued to sit together. They talked about how well their family was doing, at last, back in the old town. Pictures bloomed in their minds, and they looked silently into the air, half smiling. They remembered the brick shop building that their father's father had built, with the stone rosettes placed under the eaves. Three stories, it was.

Here in North Dakota, the *Deutsche Freie Presse* or *Die Rundschau* very cautiously reflected general news from Germany. So it was good to get the local doings and goings on from an actual German paper in which people were named whom they both knew. Births, deaths, weddings. They started reading aloud to each other. Fidelis drew on the pipe, filled his mouth with the rich dark sweetness of the tobacco. He wondered if they could get together enough money, soon, to go back there to visit. Tante hid her sudden alertness and only mentioned, casually, that she thought it would be good for the boys to see their grandparents, see the way real Germans did things, stay for a few months, even, so they'd be able to speak the language later on.

Fidelis turned his massive head toward her, looked right through her with his hollow blue gaze. He knew what she was doing, all right, but he also knew that there was something in what she said. The boys were not being raised as he had been—no discipline, very little learning, and a wild sense of entitlement to freedoms that he never thought existed. And even now, they could not always understand him when he spoke at length in his language, and he could not match the fluency of their English. When he overcame his reticence to talk to them at all, and tried to speak, nothing he said came out right. Nothing they answered made much sense. He couldn't keep track of their doings, nor buy for them the things they needed, nor keep them from getting into trouble and falling sick. It would be better if he had a wife, he knew that. But there was nobody for him. At least no one available. Sometimes when Delphine turned to look at him, boldly, her golden eyes held a meaning he didn't dare read. Nor could he bring himself to examine the cipher of his own attraction to her. After all, she was taken. She belonged to Cyprian, the man who had saved his son.

"WHAT THE HELL is wrong with me?" Delphine asked herself on Christmas morning, ashamed to remember how she'd treated Cyprian the night before. "Maybe," she amended, eating an oatmeal cookie as she sat before the tree, "nothing's so very wrong. I'm just fed up."

It was partly the fault of the Christmas tree—strung with long loops of popcorn and cranberries, tiny stars cut from tin and painted green and gold, paper angels with cottony down wings, frosted milkweed pods, twigs dipped in silver paint. The tree was very beautiful, loaded with these tiny decorations, and even without the candles flaring and although the morning light was stark and reflected a white sky, the charms of the decorated tree were so calming and reassuring that she found herself falling before it into a serene meditation. She had watched it last night, too, and had offended Cyprian.

She ate the corner of another cookie, her breakfast. The irritation that had flooded her the night before shamed her now that she could see what painstaking preparations Cyprian had made. She gestured at the tree with a piece of the cookie. "I should love him, right? That's the message of the tree. But last night I was tired. Just tired of trying so hard. I guess this is what happens when you just don't love somebody. Is it my fault?" The rest of the cookie went into her mouth. She chewed it up.

"You end up talking to a damn tree, that's what."

Delphine jumped up in gathered energy and dressed herself quickly, warmly. She bundled on her coat and boots and made ready to walk into town with her gift for Clarisse—a pair of expensive silk stockings. Delphine knew how much Clarisse liked having fancy stockings and showing off her pretty legs. She thought herself clever, too, for wrapping the stockings in a flowered head scarf and using a hair ribbon to tie the package, not that Clarisse often wore a childish hair ribbon. Maybe she could trim something with it, though. Damping down the fire, Delphine prepared to leave. She left the key over the door lintel, for Cyprian and Roy. One or another of them would probably beat her back home, she thought, ready to eat a late Christmas dinner.

CLARISSE WASN'T HOME and her door was locked, but Delphine knew her friend kept an extra house key underneath an iron boot scraper. Sure enough, Delphine rocked the heavy thing aside and drew the key from beneath it. She let herself into Clarisse's house through the rattly glass-paned back door, into a tiny mud porch. The porch, littered with boots and newspapers, led into the kitchen, always much tidier than Clarisse's other rooms. That her friend might be sleeping late occurred to Delphine as she entered, and so she called out from the kitchen. Then she walked over to the stairway that led up to her friend's bedroom, and called from the bottom step. No answer. She thought of walking upstairs, but that seemed presumptuous, even though at one time she'd had the casual run of Clarisse's house. I'll just leave the gift on the table, thought Delphine, maybe write a note to go with it.

She put the package on the white painted surface of the kitchen table, and was rummaging in her pocketbook for a pencil and a bit of paper, when she saw something that arrested her attention. A small box lay opened on the kitchen table, its candy-striped ribbon flung aside. A small wad of cotton batting lay tumbled from it next to the sugar bowl. Something about the box was immediately upsetting. She stared at it until she realized that it was the same green-and-red box that Cyprian had tried to give her. Just the same, down to the candy-striped ribbon. Whatever it had held—a ring, she'd guessed—was gone of course. There was just the box lying on the tabletop, spilled open. Delphine eyed it for a moment, and then thoughtfully hefted the gift she'd brought Clarisse, as though all of a sudden it weighed a great deal.

Walking out, Delphine locked the flimsy door and replaced the key underneath the boot scraper. Making her way through the back lot into the alley, she saw the car that she shared with Cyprian—the DeSoto. The car was parked to one side of the alley and covered with a new, frail dusting of snow. All was white, all was still. Up and down the block, nothing moved. A holiday inwardness, a sweet pause had gripped the houses. Plumes of smoke poured from the chimneys, and the windows were icily blank. Delphine drew from a corner of her pocketbook her few keys, which she kept on a little brass ring. She unlocked the car door, got into the cold car, pumped the starter button with her foot. Then she drove out of town, back up the farm road, and parked the car where it could be seen by anyone who passed.

Inside the house again, she shook snow off her coat and draped it across an armchair, set her boots neatly beside the door. She tossed the gift for Clarisse back underneath the tree. In the kitchen, she built up the fire in the stove and warmed her hands while she waited for her tea to boil. As she turned her hands back and forth in the heat, she puzzled things out. There was only one thing to make of it, at last. Failing with her, Cyprian had driven to her best friend's house last night and given her the ring. She nodded as she concluded this. Delphine poured herself a cup of tea, stirred in a dollop of honey, added a bit of thin cream, and went back to sit in the chair before the Christmas tree. What might it mean, she wondered, that the car had still been parked in the alley? A moment later, her face stained red with heat, embarrassment. It occurred to her that the car was still there because the two of them, Cyprian and Clarisse, had been, at the very moment Delphine had entered the house, upstairs in her best friend's messy bedroom. Half asleep in Clarisse's musty sheets. Waking to hear Delphine's voice at the bottom of the stairs. She could practically see the expressions on their faces! And she could picture the relief when they heard her walk away. Her lip trembled. More than anything, Delphine hated feeling stupid. And then, quite suddenly, she laughed at herself.

Wasn't this the perfect solution, if she looked at it objectively? Wasn't this exactly what she'd have wanted if she could have solved the impasse she and Cyprian had found themselves in the night before? She did not love Cyprian, and even though his sudden defection stunned her, it was definitely better that he found someone else. A burden had been lifted. She already felt lighter. The scene with the man in the park, he and Cyprian twining almost invisibly in the dark, flashed before her. If that happened, she thought, so be it. Certainly not her problem anymore. The situation even contained an element of its own revenge. Delphine knew herself well enough to understand that, contradictory though it was, she'd need to comfort herself occasionally with the thought of the difficulty that Clarisse faced in loving Cyprian Lazarre. And vice versa, she thought, too, recalling the red bead dress.

CLARISSE ALWAYS LEFT out things that had more use in them. Carelessly packed in boxes, sacks, or tied in old skirts, they made a tumbled pile on her back porch. Step-and-a-Half was prompt and regular in her visits to gather what was left. Sometimes the castoffs were of a quality that she could sell, like the glitter dress all hung with red beads. She'd found the dress some time ago, wrapped with newspaper, tied with string. The dress had some dirt on it, as though it had been in the ground and dug up, of all things, but the garment was perfectly fine once Step-and-a-Half aired it out, picked away the grains of dirt, sponged down the fabric with a fine soap. Step-and-a-Half had got three dollars for the dress from a lady who came traveling through with her husband, a man who dealt in scrap metals. No, Clarisse had been a lucrative source, a discarder of valuable rubbish, although sometimes Step-and-a-Half wondered whether some of the things—the hats, the shoes, even items that Step-and-a-Half ended up using herself—might have belonged to the dead people Clarisse fixed up in Strub's basement.

Just after dawn, on the back porch, Step-and-a-Half found a trove. Pots, pans, a whole set of kitchenware, a very good carving knife. Step-and-a-Half gathered up her finds and brought them back to the little room behind her shop that she used for sorting her pickings. She

scoured the knife clean and placed it among her own cooking imple-
ments. Then she went through the rest of the objects, frowning with
critical attention and testing the strength of handles and weighing the
heaviness of the pots in her hands. After she had decided what to do
with all she'd found, Step-and-a-Half treated herself to a breakfast of
chicken wings, a pile of hardtack, and a wrinkled carrot. As she chewed,
she assessed the bolts of fabric that surrounded her—the calicos and
broadcloth, the light and heavy woolens. She wanted to give a present
to a person she thought deserved it.

Once she'd finished her meal, Step-and-a-Half pulled forth a length
of heavy cotton printed with stripes, but then shook her head and re-
placed it. She turned aside from the flowered prints altogether after a
few moments of thoughtful attention. No, they weren't at all right. The
wools were better, warmer, for skirts. The linen would do for a blouse.
That way the top could easily be washed, and the linens wore very well,
she was told. She tested a heavy butter-colored fabric with the tips of
her fingers, and then smiled at the texture of a very pale blue. This blue
was the color of the palest sky on a cloudless November day, a watered
blue just a shadow brighter than gray. And the subtle plaid in the brown
woolen, just the slightest hint of gold and yellow in the blue and green
weaving, would be perfect for Mazarine's hair. She nodded, putting the
fabrics on the broad table fitted with a yardstick tacked tightly to the
near edge.

The Christmas sun came bitter through the window, just a ray or two
played across the frozen fronds of ice. The little potbellied stove cast out
a steady heat from the tiny room just in back where Step-and-a-Half did
her account books and wrote out new orders. For a collector of scraps
and town remnants and discards, Step-and-a-Half had extremely fas-
tidious personal habits. She was, in fact, the influence on Roy that had
caused him to clean his jail cell the year before and effected such a sur-
prising alteration in his standards. Around Step-and-a-Half, Roy had to
blow his nose on a real handkerchief, wipe his lips on a real napkin, and
excuse himself when he made rude noises. Fortunately, she herself was
a snorer and used to vast sounds occurring in her sleep—the windows

rattled in the store when they slept there, he on the floor and she in the little cot bed, but they dreamed in black unawareness.

Step-and-a-Half lowered her eagle's face to glare at the fine expanse of the cloth now. She adjusted the angle of the fabric just so, then hefted an extremely sharp pair of shears with painted black handles and made the first cut, which she followed with a steady concentration until she'd lopped off the perfect length. She folded the soft plaid wool, then measured and cut the two pastel linens. Last, in a kind of reckless gesture, she swore hard and swiped down, from a side shelf that featured her most luxurious materials, a figured midnight blue satin that she herself found irresistible. Every woman who spent any time at all in the shop, poring thoughtfully over fabrics, stopped before this fabulous satin and fantasized, she could see, herself in a gown made out of it. An evening gown—though where could it be worn, here, in this town? A nightgown, then. Something so warm and cool at once, so understated, so exquisite that fingers couldn't help extending and stroking and figuring and then, with a regretful sigh, rejecting.

Step-and-a-Half cut a dress length off quickly, before she could argue herself out of it. She laid it on the counter along with some colored threads, pursed her lips, set examples of buttons against the plaid and the linens, and added those along with the rest in a little bag. Lastly, she put some ribbons in. Hair ribbons for a girl. She wrapped the package up in plain brown kraft paper and thin string, then bundled on her coat. Pulled on a man's fur-lined leather hat, mitts, slipped her feet into rough boots, and banged out the door with the package underneath one arm. She was muttering, irritated with herself for thinking of this much too late. If she'd only thought of it yesterday, she could have dropped it off in the cover and comfort of her favorite time of the night.

DECEMBER'S FUGITIVE thaw turned into implacable cold; the wind brought on a headache as a person walked outside. In her room, far from the stove, Delphine slept under every quilt in the house and when she got out of bed she immediately put on a set of wool long johns underneath her skirt. She wore her coat in the house. Now, she was standing near the stove, bundled up, peeling potatoes for a potato pie. Thinking of browning a lump of uncased sausage she'd brought home from the shop. Maybe an onion, if they weren't all sprouted. Suddenly the door banged open and then shut on an icy blast of air. Roy rolled into the house shedding his padded woolen coat and unwrapping two knitted scarves from his head.

"Murder and mayhem," Roy announced in an aghast voice. "Terrible doings. Clarisse under suspicion!" He nodded to Delphine, as though, since she was Clarisse's friend, she should know all the details. Then he continued to speak in newspaper headlines. "Whole town in shock. Sheriff found stabbed!"

Roy sat down at the kitchen table, his mouth agape. He shook his head in bewildered protest. "Hock," he stated, as though trying to persuade himself. Then wonderingly, he said again, "Hock. Of all people!"

Delphine held up the peeler, riveted in shock. She stared at her father as though he'd suddenly spoken fluent French or grown a hoof.

"Of course, upon reflection," Roy said, "when we say 'of all people,' so often the person is the logical person to become a victim after all. He *was* the sheriff. He *was* in love with Clarisse Strub. He *was* found with his pants down around his ankles, obviously planning to violate more than the privacy of her bedroom."

Delphine waved the peeler in distress, still unable to speak.

"Hock." Roy returned to his shocked attempt at self-persuasion. "Hock. Yes, *Hock*. Died in the Strub girl's boudoir. They're saying that the necessities of her profession drove her around the bend." Roy's face turned grim. "I concur, poor duck. Her uncle shouldn't ever have let her take on clients. Sawing up the dead. Replacing their blood with vinegar! And she's just a sweet young thing. You ever hear of a girl undertaker?" Roy's hands twisted together, clasped as though in prayer. He bit his knuckle, and softly marveled. "A slip of a thing, yet she gutted him neat as a pig."

"She didn't use vinegar, and she was tough as an old rooster," Delphine muttered, turning from her father, wildly revising the narrative she'd concocted after leaving Clarisse's house on Christmas morning.

Roy glanced up at his daughter, then shook his head as if she had it all wrong. "She was a little duck," he insisted, "and Hock entered the sanctity of her nest. I never saw it coming, never took it all that serious. Oh, Hock wrote songs for her that he'd even try on the rest of us, but it was all a romantic fairy tale. And then, under the pretext of an investigation he conducted 'a search,' had a warrant, everything. Now they think she"—Roy nicked his head in the direction of the pantry, the boarded-over cellar door—"killed them, too."

There was something unsettling in the way her father gestured, Delphine thought, an awkwardness. As though he was suddenly struck with inspiration and acting a part, and poorly. But she attributed his clumsy insincerity to the strangeness of things in general, for the compound mystery was linked—the three who'd died in Roy's cellar, Hock who was investigating their deaths, and then Clarisse.

"She didn't hide, why should she," said Roy, stoutly slapping his hands on his knees. "She had to protect her innocence, after all. The world is hard. Men are capable of the unthinkable. People saw her. She boarded the morning train with her big brown valise and a little round hatbox. Red. Ticket to Minneapolis."

"I expect they'll catch up with her there," said Delphine, sitting down now across from her father, feeling tranced and dizzy. "They'll arrest her. What then?"

"Don't count on them finding her," said Roy with a keen and prophetic glare over the top of his bulb nose. "I knew her grandfather and two great uncles. Slippery buggers. Once in the city, she is likely to go to ground, change her identity. She's an agile survivor."

"I thought you said she was a little duck," said Delphine, but with small appetite for arguing.

"A tender female of a venomous species then," said Roy. "How delicate, how winsome, the eight slender legs of the black widow spider. How fragile the lady scorpion's barbed tail! And the mosquito, who stands on her head to bite. She's hardly a wisp of air, barely a living thing at all, weighing zero, yet she can kill you with malaria."

Roy continued in his meditation on the contradictions of the female sex, but Delphine had already stopped listening and gone to her room, where she piled all the quilts upon her bed and slipped underneath, to get away from Roy and yet stay warm enough to think.

AFTER A FEW DAYS of shock and strangeness, days in which people in Argus could talk of nothing else and strained after each detail, explanations stalled. Just as Roy predicted, Clarisse had disappeared. Sheriff Hock's body was removed from the house, wrapped in a tarp, sealed, and driven to the coroner in Fargo. The house was locked tight. A deputy was appointed and the town's life began to flow around the jagged events like water. The horror of what happened would be worn down by daily ordinariness. By talk. More talk. Years of talk and speculation. Eventually, the bloody mess in Clarisse's closet would become a colorful piece of town history. She vanished, but with flair, she and her red hatbox and brown suitcase. She vanished right out in the open, just rode away on the train, apparently got off in Minneapolis, changed trains, changed names, changed her whole self perhaps. Because there was no sighting of her. No capture.

As for Cyprian, no one had seen him leave town. When questioned about her friend, Delphine did not volunteer the details of her Christmas morning visit, and no one asked. The presence of Cyprian's car near Clarisse's house had gone unremarked. That morning's new snowfall had hidden Delphine's tracks. No one had seen Delphine drive the car to her house. As she kept it parked where the corner of it could be seen from the road, no one even realized for months that Cyprian was not living in the house with her. Even Roy thought that Cyprian was consumed by some clandestine smuggling activity, and he noticed only how the winter dragged without the younger man's presence. Once, Fidelis asked Delphine, with studied casualness, whether Cyprian had quit the singing club. When Delphine shrugged and told him, "Not as far as I know," he shut up. Only Delphine was aware of the connection between Cyprian and Clarisse. For a while it ached in her thoughts, a sore place, a strange place right beside the black sinkhole of the murder of the sheriff. She examined and revised, reexamined and analyzed, submerged herself in all that she knew of her friend Clarisse, and still came up gasping for air. She missed Clarisse the way she would miss a leg or an arm—always and in all she did. Work was harder. Loneliness distracted her. She visited Aurelius and Benta. They sat and drank coffee together, but it was no good.

Delphine began to read with a mad attention when she wanted to talk to Clarisse. She saw that in her life there was a woman-shaped hole, a cutout that led to a mysterious place. Through it, her mother, then Eva, and now Clarisse had walked. If only she could plunge her arms through and drag them back.

TWELVE

Traumfeuer

THERE WAS IN the butcher's
kitchen a large crockery preserving jar into which Delphine cut up the
last bits of fruit as they went in and out of season—cherries, tough
peaches, raspberries, raisins, bananas, apples, and grapes. Over each
addition she dumped sugar and a measure of brandy. The stuff, spooned
over pound cake or ice cream if they ever had it, was a dessert reserved
for weekends, when it didn't matter if the boys went to bed slightly tipsy
and woke up late. Perhaps that was the origin of its name, *Traumfeuer*,
dreamfire, and the reason they loved to eat it just before they went to
sleep. Delphine, who never stayed that late, didn't know where the stuff
went and had no idea that Fidelis let the boys get into it. On the day
before they were to leave for Chicago, she was eating a large bowl of it
in the middle of the afternoon. She'd poured *Traumfeuer* on a hard
piece of sweet bread and added a bit of cream, treating herself because
she'd packed the boys' clothing into a suitcase that would be roped on
the top of the car. It was more, she knew, as she spooned herself an-

268

other powerful helping, a way of blotting out the next day's plan.

Tante had finally persuaded Fidelis to let her take the boys, excepting Franz, since he was nearly finished with school, back to Germany. Tante would raise them with the help of the grandmother, who was lonely. With the sewing machine, which she had purchased instead of acquiring a husband, Tante felt confident of returning. And now she was bringing the boys along, although, she pointed out, it would not be forever! It would be a year, at most two, before Fidelis came over and brought them back himself. Without the exhaustion of taking care of them, the store would flourish. They would be more responsible by then. Old enough to help.

Maybe it was the pile of bills that had finally persuaded Fidelis, or that he could not pay Delphine for the hours she was working. Perhaps what had happened to Markus in the hill was the reason. Or the forehead of Emil, peppered with still healing dents made by a neighbor boy's BB gun. Maybe it was Erich's last fall off the roof, which laid him out cold for half an hour. Or the raft they had constructed of trash lumber, which had whirled them miles down last year's spring river. Maybe it was all the clothing they needed and Fidelis could not afford. Their wristbones had grown past their sleeves. They were still in short pants, which galled Markus.

The plan for tomorrow was for everyone to drive down to Chicago in the DeSoto. Fidelis, Tante, and Delphine would ride in front. The boys in back. For three days, Franz would take care of the shop. They would leave in the middle of the night, get there in the morning and handle all of the passport proceedings and red tape with the consulate on that first and second day. On the third day, Tante and the boys and their luggage would board a train to New York City. The day after that, their ship embarked. They had reserved one cabin with an added floor pallet and a tiny window, luxurious according to the agent they had telephoned, and yet a bargain.

Delphine spooned more fruit onto the sopping bread. The brandy loosened her shoulders, but her face burned and a ringing started in her temples. She sealed the top of the crockery jar and decided that she would go home and get some rest. It felt as though she were dragging herself through an underwater atmosphere. As though she were suddenly twice as heavy. Added gravity. As she was washing her bowl and the rest of the dishes in the sink, she felt Markus enter the kitchen. She did not turn. He walked up behind her, as the boys often did when she was working at the stove. As always she pretended not to hear him, allowing him to draw very close to her.

"What're you doing?" he asked.

"Just washing dishes."

He stood with her, watching her hands move in and out of the water and the suds. Delphine had noticed that there was something about a woman doing kitchen chores or standing at a stove that seemed to make boys feel safe. With her back turned, they would be apt to confide in her. They would stand right next to her while she was stirring or frying food and they would tell her things they'd never reveal if they were, say, sitting at a table across from her. Markus, especially, was apt to do this after his school day was ended. Delphine stirred soups endlessly and drew out her chores just to keep him talking—over potato soup he'd told her, for instance, that he'd got a Valentine once from the Ruthie who died in the cellar. And he'd also told her what it was like to sleep inside the hill. He told her some of his dreams, and he also, with a lonely eagerness, talked about his mother. And when he talked about Eva it was good for Delphine as well. Once she'd said, ladling out a bowl of dumpling soup, "Your mother taught me this recipe, but I'll never make it like she did."

"Yeah," said Markus, "but yours is good, too."

And when he'd said that, a rough emotion grabbed her throat, and she'd put her hand on his head, actually stroked his hair.

Now she was supposed to say good-bye.

"I'm going to send that soup recipe to your grandma. That soup you like so much," she told him.

"Oh," said Markus. "That's good. Do they make good dumplings in Germany?"

"That's where the dumpling was probably invented," said Delphine.

"Noodles, too, spaetzle, and they bake bread like nobody's business. Your mother told me. She said they have a chocolate so dark it is almost black, that tastes of oranges. And they have this light cheese they spread on toasted rolls in the morning, and jams of all kinds. Marmalade. You ever have marmalade?"

"It's on the store shelf."

"I don't like it, but she just swore by it. She said the marmalade they have over there comes from oranges in Spain. Not like the pitiful oranges here, she said, all rindy and full of seeds and too sweet. These Spanish oranges taste like bitter sunshine even preserved in sugar."

"That sounds good," said Markus, his voice clogged as if he was about to cry.

"I know it sounds like I'm hard-hearted, talking about marmalade when you're leaving all the way to Germany," said Delphine, turning to him. "I'm all broken up inside. I don't want you to see it."

She turned away and as she did so Markus put his head against the back of her arm, and leaned there. She did not move. There was a long sigh of quiet in the kitchen. He had chosen her, once again. At that moment, Delphine decided. He was hers. That was that. She would not let him go. It was just a matter of finding the right way to keep him, but she would do it. Tante hadn't a chance.

Eventually, Markus grew embarrassed and moved off, wishing that he could speak, but unable to choose the right words. He started eating a cheese sandwich she put into his hand. Hypnotized by despair at the familiarity that he was soon going to lose, he chewed too quickly. He wanted to tell her that he could not go. Maybe even to beg her to hide him, or bring him home with her, or do something to persuade his father that this was a mistake. But his tongue was fat in his mouth, numb and stupid. The sandwich was dry and sticky all at once, and very difficult to eat. I'm just luggage getting moved from here to there, he thought. A thing that doesn't matter. A stuffed pants and jacket. He couldn't find the words to tell this to Delphine.

*   *   *

IN THE DEEP BLACKNESS, they loaded the car and the boys crawled sleepily into the backseat, collapsing immediately back into their slumber. Fidelis would take the first shift, driving, and so he got behind the wheel. Tante made certain she slipped into the middle seat, jostling Delphine aside in her haste to set herself next to her brother. Her sewing machine was latched in the trunk, nestled in its traveling case, crated besides so it would not suffer on the voyage. A small valise of her clothing was also set in the trunk, and her large black leather purse was secure in her lap. Tante was prepared. She had freshly aired and pressed her tough and shiny suit. She'd brought five boiled eggs in a sack—it hadn't occurred to her to bring one for Delphine. But no one would notice the eggs, anyhow. Delphine had made sugar cookies in the shapes of animals, special for the boys, and she brought fried doughnuts, sausages, bread, hard cheese, apples, and a small insulated box that contained bottles of beer.

Delphine was wearing an ordinary suit and coat, but in a round green case she had brought along two changes of underclothing and her one smart wool suit with a pinched-in waist. The suit matched a hat with a curved green feather stuck in the band, a hat she could tilt rakishly over one eye. There was a short dotted veil inside the hat that she could put down if she wanted to look more coquettish yet. But she didn't. She just wanted to get through the whole mess. While Tante and Fidelis wrangled papers and got passports cleared, her job would be to take the boys out to see the monumental sights of Chicago. After lunch, she switched places with Fidelis. Driving, she could concentrate silently on the road. The car's atmosphere was gloomy. There was some cheer from Tante, but Delphine thought it morbid. The boys drowsed and drifted in sleep. The closer they got, the more Delphine felt that her appointed task—walking around with them looking at parks and historical markers and art museums—seemed about the grimmest, most upsetting thing she could think of to do. Once they were settled, she decided, they'd find a circus.

WE SPENT TWO DAYS *feeding peanuts to the goddamn elephants*, she would remember with Markus, later on. Because while Tante and Fidelis made their complicated arrangements, that's where they were. At the beginning of the stay, Delphine went into a bookstore, consulted a guidebook, and marked out in her mind which educational sights they should supposedly be seeing. After she made the boys memorize facts about the sights, they went straight to the circus and spent the morning at the sideshow feeding the monkeys and elephants and talking to all of the attractions, who were on duty in their carts and behind their cages or on their little podiums, their placement depending on their oddity. Because it was a raw late winter day and there weren't many gawkers, and because the boys were so obviously smitten with wonder, but mainly because Delphine liked to talk to people, they made friends.

There was a woman called the needle, so thin that when she turned sideways she was supposed to disappear (she didn't). There was the usual fat lady—hers spread in pools beside her where she lay on a bearskin rug, as though she'd half melted. Seal-O was a young man with flippers for hands and completely turned-out feet. He had a mean personality and made fun of the boys' worn and shrunken clothing. Seeing they were stung with shame, Delphine said to Seal-O, "You're a fine one to talk. You should be balancing a red rubber ball on your damn nose." He laughed at her in a nasty way, and she grabbed the boys before he said anything worse. They talked to Mr. Tiger, whose skin was really striped. He let them try to rub the stripes off, and they couldn't. Girl Wonder Calculator made their heads spin. "How come you're here," asked Delphine, "not in the university?" There were a very bored strong man and a frightful person of no determinate gender who had another frightful half-a-person growing out of its belly. There was an exotic four-breasted mermaid, whom the boys were not allowed to see, but Delphine did see. She told them later that the top was real but the bottom was definitely made of rubber. And at last there was the Delver of Minds, a little off from things, in a solemnly draped tent.

The boys, as could be expected, had no interest in having their minds delved. Delphine bought them some cotton candy swirled on a paper cone, told them not to get lost, and paid a quarter to enter.

Of course, thought Delphine, the Delver of Minds was a woman.

She looked up rather grumpily from where she sat next to a little charcoal burner that she stirred with a slim iron poker. Without a word, gesturing abruptly for Delphine to sit in the wooden chair across from her, the Delver busied herself with unwrapping and then sprinkling onto the charcoal some powdery substance, maybe a kind of incense, that gave off a penetrating spicy aroma. The smell was extremely pleasant, and Delphine breathed it in and looked curiously at the woman.

She had white hair but her face was young. Perhaps she was not much older than Delphine. Although she was quite delicate, and seemed a bit chilled even swathed in misty blue folds of material, she also had a broad-lipped mouth and powerful hands. Her wrists, as she laid out a pack of cards in some peculiar order, were bony and slender. But those fingers, thought Delphine, could crack walnuts.

"You're watching me pretty close, miss," said the Delver.

"I was just noticing your fingers—strong enough to crack walnuts open—that's what I was thinking." Delphine laughed.

"Crack walnuts. The man in question does that with his fingers. You can look at me all you want," the woman said, putting away her cards, "but you paid to get your own mind read."

"Well," said Delphine, unnerved by the walnut reference, "go ahead then."

"You're in town on some desperate errand," said the Delver.

"Pretty good," said Delphine. "I'm here to send off the man's boys, the man I work for."

"They're going to Germany."

"What?"

"You're in the meat business," said the woman. "I looked at your hands, too."

Nicked and gouged, already missing a tiny corner of a fingertip, scarred with small white nicks, roughed with lye and toughened from mixing hot spices for Italian sausages, Delphine's hands had changed. She looked at them, lying there on the little copper table, as though they were the hands of an alien being. "I never noticed," she murmured.

"No," agreed the woman, "you never even tried to hide them when you walked in. Women around here wear gloves. That says something, too."

"What does it say?"

"You're not going to hide anything," said the woman. "There are people who pretend to themselves they are honest, and there are people who actually tell the truth. You're still between the two. But you're heading toward the latter. I hear music. This man, you love him."

"No," said Delphine. Then she added, "He sings."

"Oh, all right," said the Delver. She closed her eyes and then pinched her fingers to her temples, as though she was suffering from a sudden headache. "There's some kind of animal in your way. Oh, I can't be right." She began to laugh to herself. "I am seeing in your mind the picture of a large black bug . . . skinny at the middle like an ant."

"Well, you are right," said Delphine, too amused to be totally surprised. "It's the boys' aunt."

"You hate her guts with good reason."

"You could put it that way."

"But she's going."

"She's . . ." and now Delphine's breath stuck, painfully. "She is taking the boys."

"And you love them."

"Yes," said Delphine promptly.

"The man is too bright to look at, too dark inside to read. He is a widower. Marry him."

"I can't," said Delphine, now obscurely irritated.

"You're no coward, either," said the Delver, "so the reason lies elsewhere." She turned over the glowing coals and sprinkled a different powder onto them. A bitter and soothing scent rose between them. "You're tired of holding them all up, aren't you?"

"Yes," said Delphine.

"Then let go of the ones you can do without. She won't let you take them all, anyway. You will not prevail over her, or divide the sister from the brother, not if they're blood."

*   *   *

DELPHINE GATHERED the boys and walked away from the Delver's tent—she'd said other things, statements Delphine needed to sort out. And her head now ached mildly from the smoke of the powder she had breathed. That afternoon, the boys were getting their passport pictures taken, anyway, and they were to meet at the hotel just before.

"Let's get those strings of candy off you," said Delphine, brushing Emil's suit jacket, which she'd let out as much as it would go. She plucked away some spiderwebby bits of pink floss. Markus brushed Erich off and unstuck some pieces of straw from the elephants' bedding from his wool socks. Erich grinned, his two front teeth looked huge and comical. His other teeth were still missing or only half grown in.

"Now you all look good," said Delphine, but her voice stuck in her chest and came out half strangled.

As they walked back to the hotel, there entered into her mind the unwilling but compelled conviction that she had to talk to Fidelis alone. And she would do it. Never mind what blocks Tante threw, she'd make sure that she and Fidelis had the chance to talk this over before the four of them took off on that train—who knows, it could be forever, the way things were going. She'd kept track of what was happening over there ever since the purge of 1934. Details of that terror were still coming out and she collected them in her mind, would not forget the slaughter as Fidelis and Tante conveniently did when the Saarland was returned and then the Rhineland militarized. All they could talk about was the strength, the prosperity, their family's increased holdings. The strange, compelling genius of the leader. At the bottom of a Minneapolis newspaper's foreign section, a tiny blurb on a rampage of hate against Jews and glass breaking made Fidelis shake his head, but then say, after a few moments, that things had always been so. There was always this poison, a few who would express it. *Johannes, er war Judn,* he said, but didn't translate or explain. Now, even though Delphine was convinced she could argue him down, even though she believed she'd thought more about the situation that the boys faced than Fidelis, she was afraid to talk to him. Even the thought made her heart beat uncomfortably fast, made her tough hands sweat.

It wasn't the argument about the politics—it was the other, the un-expressed. All that she feared about the lay of her heart and did not ex-amine. Nothing is by accident, nothing is by chance, she told herself. I went in to see that delver of minds for a very good reason: whether or not she could see the whole thing, I wanted to get my own mind clear. I had to hear myself say those things, had to hear out loud what I don't even know I am thinking inside. I had to sit there with that white-haired lady and put it all out where I can see the shape of it.

THEY ALL WALKED together into the great stone building set inside with tiny corridors of offices where papers were processed. The office ran in balconies around a central shaft open to the ground floor. Dusty light poured down from a vaulted skylight ornamented with obscure struggling figures. The boys craned upward, and Delphine held their hands, walk-ing them up the broad stone stairway. Outside the room where passport photographs were taken, people waited in a line along the corridor, some on the floor, some slumped against the wall. It was a very long line. Tante was tired, but she didn't slump. Her stiff suit seemed to hold her up. She made a face of severe annoyance, and said that the boys needed to eat.

Delphine seized her chance. "Let's go and get them some sand-wiches," she said to Fidelis.

Tante said immediately, "Don't bother. No. We're not that hungry."

"The boys ate nothing," Delphine said, with a composed firmness.

"They'll live," said Tante, curt and loud. She produced, with an air of triumph, a clutch of lemon drops from her purse. Their sugary coat-ing had gathered the usual purse dust, and they were stuck together in one lump. Tante cracked it lightly against the wall and gave a piece of the candy to each of the twins, a tiny sliver to Markus.

"There," she concluded, "that will hold them."

"That stuff'll rot their teeth," said Delphine. "Let's get them some nourishment," she said to Fidelis. Then she looked straight into his face, opened her eyes, let the dull radiance from the great central sky-light cascade down upon her, and she smiled.

"You could use the air, too," she said. "Come along." And he followed.

Outside, in the street, walking toward a delicatessen they'd both spotted, Delphine began to speak with a simple urgency. "I've got nothing to lose," she said to Fidelis, "so I'm going to talk. Listen. You can't let Maria Theresa take them back to Germany, Fidelis, it is all wrong. Impossible. You can see that she doesn't know crap about taking care of boys."

"My mother will care for them once they are settled," said Fidelis.

They reached the doors to the shop, and almost entered, but Delphine's mind spun furiously. She didn't want to divert Fidelis from the problem with the mundane selection of cheap sandwiches. "Let's keep walking around this block. I've got more to say."

"It is done," said Fidelis.

"No, it's not, and you owe me to listen."

That got him—he never liked to owe anyone. And he knew she was right, knew that she'd cared for his sons to the full extent of her powers and beyond the limits of her job ever since Eva died. So they didn't go into the deli but kept walking.

"In Germany," explained Fidelis, "they learn the proper way to do things."

"Maybe so." Delphine breathed deep, tried to stay calm so she could argue reasonably. "But then what? Do you think they'll want to come back here and help you in the shop? Do you think Tante will even let them come back?"

Fidelis looked down at her, his face distinctly tightening. It was clear that he'd thought of this deep down, but stuffed away his apprehensions, or argued himself out of them. He paused, but then he spoke in a light, determined voice.

"Then I go over there and get them myself!"

"I read in the newspaper that new government is keeping any Germans who visit," said Delphine. It was purely a rumor at the time, though it would indeed prove true, but Delphine decided to use it. "And the boys . . . what if the borders shut? You know what the war was like."

But that was going too far. Fidelis became serious and spoke with an earnest fervor. "I have seen war—there could never be another war! *Es ist unmöglich!* I believe this Hitler is strengthening the country for peace. That is why the family does good—and they buy things for the boys. They have money."

"Money!" said Delphine, fighting a surge of anger. "All well enough, but these are the sons you had with Eva!"

Her name dropped between them like an anvil.

Now Delphine used the fact that she had been saving for a moment like this, when the stakes were huge.

"Tante stole the morphine—you must know that. How can you send your sons with the woman who made Eva suffer? At least leave Markus here! I'll take care of him!"

They both stopped walking at the same time. There, in that windy street, they looked at each other. Fidelis's face was grim and ashen. Her face turned up toward his, a challenge, her eyes narrowed and watchful. When she stared at him, her eyes a magnetic ore, Fidelis felt himself moving toward her, nodding, allowing her to take control. As though the wind had pushed him, just a little, off his feet, he took a step to right his balance. He couldn't think of anything else to say, because of course she was right. Tante wasn't good with Markus. And yet, he looked away from her. Tante was right about some things. The younger boys would be better off back in Ludwigsruhe, surrounded by family, not digging their way into hills and floating down the river and nearly drowning themselves.

"I can't watch them enough," he said to Delphine, and he put his hands in his pockets and looked down at the mottled concrete sidewalk between them. He had something more to say, and he didn't want to say it. "I don't have the money to pay you anymore."

"I know," said Delphine, impatient. "That doesn't matter. I want . . ." Then she was staring at the sidewalk, too. They stood there so long, both with the next words on their lips, that it seemed as though they might sink right through the stonework. The words had too much weight. Fidelis put his hand to his chin, looked down at her standing there, the smart taupe hat cocked over one side of her face, the little veil, the green feather. Without any warning, surprising him, his hand reached out. He touched the tip of the green feather. Her lips were naturally dark, not pink at all, but a deeper brownish crimson. He took a ragged breath.

"Cyprian," he said.

She looked at him and then her smile flashed, and her comma-shaped dimples, her strong white teeth. He was dazzled by the freshness of her expression even before she spoke, shaking her head.

"Cyprian and I were never married."

He took that in. That was something, and it was nothing. The two started walking again, side by side. They had nearly circled the block again before Fidelis found the words he wanted to say. It was difficult finding them at all, because he was ashamed of what he'd thought right after Cyprian had rescued Markus. Along with the relief and gratitude, Fidelis had suddenly been struck by an understanding: he could never, ever, in any way, make a claim upon Delphine. He owed the man she was with, the man he'd fought. He owed Cyprian. Even as he wished it were otherwise now, too, the marriage vow or lack of it did not figure into the picture. Delphine and Cyprian's union was perhaps a shocking thing, but in fact it often happened that two people pretended to be married to thwart small-town gossip. He had noticed for some time she wasn't wearing her wedding band. They had come full circle, around the block, and returned to their starting point.

"You have slept with him?" he bluntly asked.

"No," said Delphine. "Yes and no. He couldn't . . ."

Fidelis stopped and looked at her with a rising sense of comprehension. All of a sudden he thought he understood. When he grasped it, he shook his head to clear it of all thoughts of Delphine. So *that* was the nature of Cyprian's wound. As well, the reason for his touchy and protective rage regarding Delphine. Fidelis shielded his eyes with his hand, to blot her away from his sight. The only thing left to ask, Fidelis decided, was whether Cyprian was coming back.

"Is he ever—" he began.

Just then, Tante, furious, her jacket gleaming off her chest like a scratched glass mirror, emerged from the great doors of the stone building and yelled across to them. She charged toward Fidelis, the boys tailing her as she crossed the street. Fidelis saw her, turned back to Delphine, gave her a strangled, almost desperately pleading look, as though he wanted her to finish the sentence for him.

"Is he ever what?" said Delphine. But without waiting for an answer, she lunged toward the boys, afraid of the traffic. Fidelis grabbed his sister's arm at the curb, propelling her alongside him.

"Come, Tante, we found a good place." He waved at the delicatessen that stood open and gleaming just down the street. "Let's go in. Let's sit down."

Tante began to berate him for leaving them all and where, she wanted to know, were the sandwiches anyway, and she was missing her lunch, and that always made her light-headed. Fidelis calmly marched her into the delicatessen, which had small tables placed before a slide of great modern plate-glass windows, and he sat her down. Delphine took charge of the boys, settled them at their own table just behind Tante and Fidelis, and told them what they could have, what they could choose from the things that were cheapest on the menu. At one point, after their order was taken, as she sat with them, she looked up at the table where Fidelis was facing into the little storm of complaints his sister was making. He was nodding at all Tante said, but he was watching Delphine with thoughtful gravity.

THEIR HOTEL WAS what they could afford, one bathroom down the hall and a dreary gray feeling to the whole edifice. At least it was clean, the other people weren't threatening, and there didn't seem to be any bugs. The boys slept with Fidelis, and Tante and Delphine were together in a room. Delphine had dreaded this, and she hadn't even thought about sharing the bed.

The first night, the two had been so exhausted that they merely rolled in side by side, turned their backs to each other, and managed sleep even though Delphine was awakened several times by Tante's tossing out one hand, the fingers flicking dreamily just under her nose. She nudged the hand away and slept on. This evening, after they had eaten the remnants of the food they'd brought, they were going to bed early, as the train was scheduled to leave the next morning.

Tante sniffed as she entered the dim room.

"Someone has been here."

She went immediately to her bags and began methodically to check through them, ticking off her possessions beneath her breath. Delphine sat on the bed, and watched her. Tante knelt before the brown cowhide valise and removed each piece of clothing as though it would explode. Then examined it suspiciously. What is she thinking, Delphine wondered, that someone entered our room, tried on her clothing, and folded it back into her suitcase? There was really nothing, besides the sewing machine, of any value in Tante's luggage anyway, and she had left the sewing machine with the manager, safely under lock and key. She'd checked to see that it was still there before she'd retired.

"I think I'll wash up," Delphine said.

"Well, all appears in order," said Tante, with a grim look. With infinite care, she began repacking her shabby slips and tissue-thin bloomers, her newly sewn skirts and crisp blouses, all put together on her machine. Delphine walked down the hall to the bathroom. It wasn't a dreadful place, but the plumbing stank, and the water that came into the little tin sink was only a cold gray trickle. Still, she took her time, soaping herself, combing, rubbing almond-smelling cream into her face and hands. She wanted to give Tante a chance to put everything away and then get into her sleeping gown—the night before had been a big production, but she'd been too tired to care then. She found that her frustrations were brimming. She didn't want to blow up. She wanted to think of a way to get one more chance to talk to Fidelis. She combed her hair back, smoothed her eyebrows, rubbed sweet oil into her lips, until at last there was no other choice than to walk back to the room.

Tante was a frightening picture with her hair down. She had released it from the complex of interlocked braids and whorls, and was brushing it. The hair lay in see-through scraggles and bumps, spread across her shoulders, a gray-brown horsy color. She had changed into her sleeping costume—a thick column of scratchy wool nearly as stiff as a blanket. And she was rubbing, into her skin, a concoction of lard and petroleum jelly. The stuff was scented with camphor and orange water, but that did not hide the rancid undertone. The air in the tiny room was penetrating, thick, intense. The first thing Delphine had to do was open the window. When she did open it, asking at the same time if Tante minded, there came from the older woman a horrified shriek muffled by a woolen scarf.

"If cold air should drop upon my skin," said Tante, panicked, "I could be sick by morning!"

The stuff she laid upon her skin was apparently a kind of salve or preventative. She feared, in the city, an infection coming upon her, and she was making preparations to sleep that involved a soldierly defense of her health. There was the muffler, wrapped around her head, a towel covering her throat. Upon her feet, felt slippers laced like baby booties. Her chest bore the weight of most of the stinking grease, and a square of flannel besides, laid upon it, would contain the heat that her body would generate. She tottered to bed with a Frankensteinish stiffness, lay on her back with her hands crossed on her belly. She closed her eyes and uttered a long prayer underneath her breath, in German, and dropped off as Delphine lay down next to her in the dim space of clogged air.

AN HOUR, perhaps two, after falling asleep, Delphine snapped awake. Her brain was flooded with thoughts. The small room, a rectangle of dark city noises, seemed to rise up and up in the nothingness above the earth. She had the sense of how alone they were, meaningless as individuals, stacked in the hotel like herrings in a crate, one over the other, side to side. All of the confusions of the day swept over her, and she remembered first of all the white-haired woman in the layered blue gown, fold upon fold of material, obviously meant to make her seem mysterious. Yet, she truly was. Men are strange, flawed artifacts, she'd said to Delphine, and whether we struggle to love them, or not to love them, it is all the same. And then Delphine thought of Fidelis walking around and around the windy streets, his face heavy in the stony light with all that he could not speak. She thought she knew what he wanted to say, and what he tried to ask just as Tante emerged hysterical from the office building. She thought she knew, but then again how could she?

Delphine knew that she was no delver of minds, and the deep look that Fidelis had given her as they ate their food might have been a look of warning: Don't come any closer. Or perhaps a look informing her that he was still in grief and could not even think of such a thing as she thought, sometimes. Yet, her father's drinking had made her immune to the love of grown men, she decided, because the reason she gave any consideration to Fidelis was the feelings she had for his sons—she was helpless before those.

Delphine ached with the one sleeping position she had to hold so that she would not bump against Tante. Carefully, she shifted. Tried to rearrange her limbs slightly. Tante's hand flopped over and Delphine carefully folded it back onto Tante's stomach.

"Nein," said Tante, *"gib' mir deinen Finger."*

She was talking in her sleep and her voice came out of the muffler, but what Tante said was what the witch in the fairy tale said to Hansel, which seemed an alarming omen to Delphine. She made herself breathe deeply, let her limbs go soft, shut down her mind, and waited for sleep.

THE BOY HIMSELF took care of the whole problem of telling Tante, by becoming extraordinarily ill in the night. It was to Markus himself a great and secret triumph, one he'd not even willed, not that he knew, although in the years that followed he wondered if his hidden self had predicted what would have happened to him if he had boarded that train to New York, then the ship to Germany. On waking that morning they were to leave, his cheeks were brilliant, his eyes glazed. He tossed in a fever so high that Fidelis tapped on the door before sunrise, and asked Delphine to stay in the room with the boy while he went out looking for a pharmacy. She entered, sat down next to Markus on the tiny cot. The twins were sleepily dressing, pulling on socks between yawns, and she could feel their gathering excitement. But Markus was dry with the heat of his fever, and his lips were a vivid bruised plum. His temples were white and his breath was short. She felt for the pulse in his wrist—it raced unsteadily. His face contorted.

Delphine swiped the wash basin smoothly from the boys and held his head over it. After he felt better, she took the wash basin down the hall. She cleaned it out scrupulously, and put a little cold water in the bottom, wet her handkerchief in the water when she brought it back and began to wipe his forehead, his thin high delicately freckled cheekbones, his throat, his ears, his slender wrists, his forearms. And all the while she looked carefully and pityingly down at him, she inwardly marveled and also feared that his illness would pass as suddenly as it had begun. But it did not.

When the aspirin only made Markus rave, Delphine said firmly that he could not leave, and no one challenged her. There was no use for it but Tante thought it terrible to waste a ticket and determined to find a way to sell it. She barely concealed her own relief that Markus wouldn't be joining them. She held her hand before her face and said good-bye to him from the doorway. Delphine leaned into the embrace of the twins, held their scratchy coats for a moment, breathed their dusty boy hair. She held their rough hands as they kissed her, smoothed their foreheads. They tugged away from her, their eyes bright with excitement at their adventure. Then they were gone, the two of them, out of her life.

EARLY IN THE AFTERNOON, Fidelis drove the car to the hotel entrance and then carried Markus, limp and burning, down to the lobby. Delphine followed with the luggage, such as it was, and they packed the bags into the trunk. Put the boy into the backseat, and laid the car blankets over him. He threw them off restlessly, and anxiously asked, as he had over and over, where they were going.

"We're going back to Argus. Going home," said Delphine, as she tucked the light wool robes around Markus again. He looked up into her face with such a luminous joy that she was startled, then worried about delirium, that perhaps his fever had taken a dangerous turn. While Fidelis paid a tip to the manager for letting them stay longer in the room, she checked Markus carefully and thought that the worst might have passed. Maybe he just felt the way she did, light with hunger and the surprise of reprieve.

Fidelis drove and Delphine directed him out of the city. Soon they were on the highway north. They said nothing for several hours, except to murmur about the way the fields reminded them of the Dakotas, then farther on how it looked more like Minnesota. How big the barns were, how well-kept. Like they were through with the Depression down this way. Some threatening clouds came up over the horizon and they mentioned those, speculated about a possible storm. When it didn't come to pass they switched their attention to Markus, stopped several times to check his fever and to make certain that he drank a little ginger beer from a bottle Fidelis bought. He slept as though drugged. All that day, while the sun was out, they managed to stay on safe and neutral topics of conversation. Or they fell silent, took turns driving, slept in the passenger's seat. Once the afternoon light waned and the shadows grew long and then smudged into the general darkness, their efforts failed. Silence collected, became uncomfortable. Their quiet became waiting, then suspense.

During the day, an interior restlessness had plagued Delphine, an itch to say what must be said. It wasn't like her not to blurt out the truth as she saw it, and she had realized that the avoidance and the careful maneuvering was wearing on her. She didn't like the thin invisible path she had to tread around Fidelis. She drew a deep, stubborn breath and then held it so long she almost burst. When she let it out, her heart beat slower and she was calm. She had decided to provide an explanation whether or not Fidelis wanted one.

"Listen here," she burst out. "Cyprian is like a brother to me. We're not married and we don't do anything together. He doesn't want to."

"Want to?" Fidelis swerved a bit. His brain had fixed on a war wound that robbed Cyprian of manhood. It was hard to turn his thinking from that. He didn't want to? Cyprian didn't want to? She could think what she liked, but he was sure that Cyprian did want to. What else could Cyprian say, and keep his dignity? Fidelis shook his head, but to enter into an argument or obtain more details was beyond both his English and his emotional reach. He stared straight forward. There was no other car on the road. They were going fifty. He tried to think of some way to advance the conversation, but nothing occurred.

Delphine crossed her legs, then folded her arms, sank her head down so that she lounged in her seat like a sulky boy. She was embarrassed at having volunteered so much, and maintained a stubborn silence. After a time, Fidelis spoke.

"What does it matter?" he said, low. "Cyprian saved Markus. He risked his life, dragged him out of the earth."

Delphine considered that for a while, and tried to see the structure of Fidelis's thoughts. For if he'd held himself back because of Cyprian, it must mean that he had feelings for her by the very definition of his resolve. And yet, too, the possibility of Cyprian could be the excuse Fidelis had for not acting toward her as in fact he did *not* want to. He may have sensed that she was possibly open—even she did not know if she truly was—and neatly banished the issue by conceiving of this species of honor that would divide them from each other and keep them excused from facing what shivered between them.

"I doubt he's coming back," she said. "If he does, it won't be to live with me."

He took that in for several miles, the headlamps cutting through falling darkness now. Her answer left him without assurance, left the whole weight of the situation upon him. Did that mean she was open to him, or that she was simply through with Cyprian? Would loving her, if Cyprian chose not to, betray the man who had saved his son? His thoughts turned this way and that. When he'd come to Eva just after the war, things had been so clear. Carnage and sorrow had made all questions of the heart too simple, maybe, but the way was strictly laid out. No ambiguities, no doubts. He had delivered his death message, she had fallen into his arms. He had visited her to help her get over her shock, comforted her, and in that storm of open emotion, it had been easy to move forward, straight into each other. Here, however, the situation was a maze. It seemed to Fidelis that there were too many people involved, but then it struck him, suddenly, that it was only repetition. Here was Delphine—the best friend of Eva as he'd been the best friend of Johannes, both dead—and now the whole entire set of events was repeating itself because Delphine could rescue him, his boys, the same way he had rescued Eva and Franz.

This, at any rate, he could tell Delphine by way of a story. He could say it to her now. Maybe if he told it all, there would be a way out, an answer in the telling.

A light fog had risen and the smoke of it swirled in the high beams. As the car cut through the evening, Fidelis told all that had happened beginning, as he thought he must, with Johannes.

THE FIRST TIME Johannes saved his life, he had dragged Fidelis out of a pile of dead when the bullet that had slammed through his jaw knocked him senseless. The next time, he had shot an onrushing French soldier when his friend's rifle jammed. Johannes had saved Fidelis twice only to die himself in the trembling of continual music. This happened in the war's final days. Through two days and nights in the elegant ruin of an aristocratic house, Fidelis had stayed with Johannes. The place was a stop on the mad retreat, the place where all the wounded and the dying were dumped. All day and all night the walls trembled with the continual shelling, not far off. In the small eternities between each impact, the glass in the windows, smashed all over the sills, shook with a gentle brilliance like chimes in the wind.

They stayed upstairs because below in the cellars the wounded were being smothered when the fit sought shelter, and the reek was even worse, and the screaming and the cursing, the groans, the insane shouts. Fidelis thought it better for his friend to die in the rain and wind, in the random music. His guts blown, his throat filling, it was hard to say what killed him. Dysentery or the shallow, filthy wound or the murderous exhaustion of all of the retreating and despairing men. Johannes whispered, "Sing to me, old friend." In a freezing room, in one corner of his shattered country, accompanied by the fractured ringing of glass, Fidelis sang. Afterward he'd laid Johannes out and wrapped a silk scarf his mother had given him for luck around Johannes's face, but he hadn't had the courage to stay behind and bury him. Fidelis walked on. And where he walked there was more chaos and dying, and he'd walked past that in hobnailed boots and past all he possibly could until he got back to his childhood bed, his mother, his eiderdown cover, his books, his father and sister and Eva. He told her about the death of her baby's father, and then . . . He said to Delphine, *"Es war einfach. Wir haben verheiraten."*

"You married," said Delphine, her voice hushed, "so that the baby, Franz, would have a father."

"Yes," said Fidelis, because that was the simple answer. And because he thought it was the answer that Delphine had to hear, but it was not the only answer. His body and Eva's had told them the answer before they'd known it, in that first meeting, when he saw her more naked than he ever would again. In the darkness now, his face became very hard. When he remembered these things, the sad weight of them closed upon him and he had to breathe in and out deliberately to loosen it, like tight bands around his chest. He certainly couldn't explain this to the woman sitting next to him. Delphine did not seem to notice, anyway. She had removed her pumps and drawn her feet up on the seat, curved there in thought. She sat there neatly, the way an animal might crouch. He could feel Delphine's awareness drift deep along some current he couldn't fathom, and it was a long time before she came to her conclusion and spoke.

"So if we married it would be the same thing all over again."

"Yes!" He was surprised she put it all together. But she hadn't, not the way he thought, not the way it was a box of four people that strangely dovetailed. Delphine had reasoned that, since he'd married Eva not out of love but rather out of duty to the unborn child, this was not a thing that Fidelis wanted to repeat. And that was understandable, she thought, in a calm relief. Because who knew, after the child was grown, if the two would ever get along? And she herself did not know. Couldn't read her own heart. Whether it was the sons or the combination of the father and the sons she loved. But at least, in that hour as they cut through the blackness, she admitted the possibility that he was included. And then, from behind them, Markus woke and the blankets rustled down around him as he leaned toward the front seat.

"Papa," he asked, his voice thick with sleep, still miserable, "sing to me?"

Delphine didn't know that there were times when Fidelis showed a certain tenderness to his sons, times he sang to them. When they had trouble sleeping, when they were very small, when Eva asked him to, and when they were ill, he sang the old German lieder to them in a restrained voice that filled the room with a comforting resonance in which they felt protected. He sang the one he knew was a favorite of Markus's, and he sang it over and over just as Markus always asked. *"Ich weiss nicht was soll es bedeuten, dass ich so traurig bin. Ein Märchen aus alten Zeiten, das kommt mir nicht aus dem Sinn."*

It was the song about the Lorelei, full of pictures. The women sat on the great rocks, combing their golden hair with combs of gold. Hearing their song, men sailed closer, their hearts were pierced and fascinated by the beauty of the Lorelei, and then they were drawn onto the killing reefs. It wasn't a song that Delphine knew and only gradually did she piece the meaning together, and when she did she wondered at him, this Fidelis, who casually stuck chickens and stunned sheep, who brought down a dozen mutts in one noise and burned them up like trash, who mourned his wife with a gravity that added to the stillness he possessed already, but said nothing, who made of the complications already between them an indecipherable maze, and who sang to calm his sons. Gradually, she fell under the spell of his singing, too, with Markus, and at last she was lulled into the blackness.

Fidelis let the song drift, heard their honest drawn breaths, nodded slowly at the road, and hummed a new and simpler song, to keep himself awake. It was a song he'd sung with Johannes, drunk, in forgetfulness which he could not now forget, as the wheels turned them forward and forward, far from Germany, onto the wideness of the plains of America where the wars were not between the same old enemies he was used to, but were over before he'd got there, the great dying finished, and the blood already soaked into the ground.

THIRTEEN

The Snake People

When Delphine had asked him the obvious question, Roy's answer often was, "I drink to fill the emptiness." Delphine hated that line. Once, she pushed him backward into a chair and yelled, "Hey, I've got news for you. *Everyone* does *everything* to fill the emptiness." While it may or may not have been true, Roy was comforted to think that his personal emptiness was universal. He felt less special, especially when it came to the dark, fixed hole that his lost love had left in him, but he felt a kinship, too, with other empty souls. From then on, one of his favorite bottoms-up slogans was a toast to the great void. During the long sobriety that he enjoyed after Eva's death, he'd taken Delphine's remark as an earnest directive. Everything he'd done, he did to fill the emptiness. Unfortunately, nothing worked like alcohol.

"Nothing can fill the ache of the abyss," he said one night to his singing cronies. The men were sitting on old crates and creaking chairs in the ruins of an arbor that grapevines had half pulled down with their quick-growing weight. Fidelis always kept them organized, singing song after song, practicing. When he was occupied elsewhere, as now, the men often drifted into gossip or even self-pitying monologues.

"Nothing can fill the nothing," Roy went on lecturing, "except love or booze or a great religious impulse. And I ain't got Minnie's love anymore, or the lack of an imagination to believe in the God of the Lutherans or the Catholics! Nor do I got the depth to invent my own rattletrap version of the Lord Almighty."

Everyone nodded, but no one answered for fear of setting him off on some other open-ended, infinite topic. "Nothing," he said, pulling his nose. "God made schnapps for a reason and one reason only. He left a hole in us. Yes, He left a hole when He molded us from the clay. A cup. And then He felt sorry for us and He gave us fermented spirits to pour in the cup. Why do you think they're called *spirits*?" He looked around fiercely. "Think about it." They all should have known that Roy was heading for a relapse.

Gradually, first with small trickles of beer and then in an increasingly fabulous wash, Roy proceeded to fill the emptiness again with his favorite substance. He often lied to his daughter about working with Step-and-a-Half, when he was really swigging away down at the bum's jungle or sitting on the back steps of the pool hall (he was not allowed inside anymore), or he was somewhere else, anywhere that would have him, getting juiced to the gills.

Hoping to keep Delphine unaware, as well as avoid another series of visits from the unruly dead, the drunk Roy stayed away from his house. The spirits of the piteous Chavers family left him alone as long as he avoided the scene of their undoing. He was still able to sober himself up for two or three days each week, and on those days he stayed with Delphine and was, perhaps, overly solicitous. He cooked heavy breakfasts and washed his own clothing. He scrubbed floors. It was his absence and his homely industry then, an exact pattern she'd never known in him, that kept Delphine in the dark for such a long time. She only discovered the truth once she returned from Chicago and started to look for work.

Delphine hurried over to Step-and-a-Half's shop the next morning. Outside, on the skim of concrete and the beaten dirt of the entry, an arrangement of butter churns, their paddles worn by female hands, listed slightly one to the next. She stepped around washtubs, an old iron mangle, chipped jars, and dented or bunged pots. Eyed an array of gap-toothed rakes, dulled hoes, brooms worn to the binding of the straw. The spill of junk into the street, which Step-and-a-Half didn't always bother to bring inside at night, was meant to entice customers. Instead, the stuff made a barrier that either tripped people or sent them off the walk into the street to skirt the mess. Delphine entered with the hope that she could have Tante's old position, but she took a small step backward when the junk picker leaned across the scarred wood of the counter.

"Tante's old job? I gave her a job because I felt sorry for that bag of bones. Why is it you high and mighties from the butcher shop always come to me?"

Delphine folded her arms. "Forget it, then! You could sure use me around this place, but I'm not going to beg to sell your ratty old crap."

"That's more like it!"

Step-and-a-Half smiled to herself and put a toothpick in her mouth. Cigarettes were becoming scarcer, expensive. The roll-your-own bags of Bull Durham made harsh smokes and she'd started chewing toothpicks instead of lighting up around the precious fabrics because the wools, especially, absorbed the stink. She began to shred the toothpick with her teeth. From time to time her eye opened wide to fix Delphine in a light of intrigue. At last she spoke.

"You don't need the work. You should just get away from that damn old drunk. Leave him to pickle. You could go anywhere and get away from him. The whole damn town feels sorry for you."

"What do you know about it?" Delphine was furious now.

"I know plenty," said Step-and-a-Half. "I kicked him out of here just yesterday, soaked."

"He's not drinking!"

"Your head's in the dirt. He's an old wino, Delphine. They do not change."

"They do so," said Delphine. "He finally *has* changed. The pledge took this time. You should see him."

"I did see him and I smelled him, too."

"Bullshit," said Delphine, although she knew she was hearing the truth. An immense, dispirited darkness of mood caved down on her as she took in the fact that she'd ignored the signs in Roy. Why was she such a realist in every other way except when it came to her father? She left the store without saying another word, walked home, and crawled into bed to catch up on the sleep she'd missed out on in Chicago. When she woke, the cloud descended again. Heavy-brained and still groggy, she stumbled to the kitchen to cook herself a pair of sunny-side up eggs.

"So the old man fell off again," she mumbled to the spatula. Worry over her father quickly changed to the exhausting old fury. "What the hell do I even care for," she fumed, forking the eggs up straight from the pan into her mouth. Her lonely greed and nervousness embarrassed her. She put the fork down and vowed, "I won't go looking for him! I'll check on Markus instead!" With resolute haste, she made up a quick pot of the same dumpling soup Markus had survived on after his near burial. She wrapped the pot of soup in a towel and drove to Waldvogel's. On the way there, she realized that she had only ten dollars left to her name and, now that she couldn't count on Roy for a contribution, no prospect of paying end-of-the-month bills. If she didn't find another job within the week, she'd sell the car, she decided. The prospect steadied her panic.

THERE WAS A RICH SMELL of garlic in the air of the shop. Fidelis must be mixing up a batch of Italian sausage, Delphine thought, and then she began to notice things. The cream was not put away. *Watch that*, she pointed as Franz came out of the side cooler, *it'll spoil*. Nobody had cleaned the fingerprint smudges off the case's glass front. Delphine grabbed a rag and did it herself, then threw the rag down.

"Where's Markus?" she asked.

Franz gestured her to the back rooms and she left all that was distressingly undone in the shop and went back there, concerned to find that Markus was still in bed, but glad at least he wasn't any worse. Of course, he hadn't changed out of the clothes he'd worn to Chicago, even down to the same socks.

"God, those stink!"

Delphine coaxed the socks off his feet.

"I feel good. I just can't stand up! I fall over!" Markus laughed. He was a giddily cheerful patient, glad to be home. Delphine was drawn to stay with him. His face was eager, his pale, peach-bright hair stuck every which way in bent curls. Delphine rummaged through the meager supply of clean clothing, found an unmatched, ragged, clean pair of pajamas. He clutched them to his chest and walked, weaving, light-headed, to the bathroom to put them on. Delphine tightened his sheets and remade his bed. Fluffing his pillow, she felt a sharp object in the cheap feathers, reached in and drew out the bundle of mementos from Ruthie, the notes, the clicker. Delphine began to examine these things, then realized they were private and stuffed them back. Markus came in, slipped into the bed, shut his eyes against vertigo.

"Drink this soup," said Delphine. The name signed on the bottom of the notes stuck in her heart. He must have loved Ruthie Chavers, as only children love, to keep her notes hidden in his pillow. Delphine helped Markus sit up and then tried to feed him a spoonful of soup from the pottery bowl she held. "I'm not a baby," said Markus. He took the spoon from her hand, swallowed the soup in it, and held out his other hand for the bowl. He fed himself, slowly and carefully, sipping broth and holding each dumpling for a moment in his mouth, as though he was grateful for it, absorbing its taste. Watching him, Delphine breathed deeply and then felt a quietness descend between them. The air was still, the sounds from the shop hushed and far away. The dog on the floor whined lightly in her dream. The spoon clinked against the side of the bowl. The boy carefully swallowed. Delphine felt as if this eating of the healing soup by the ill and hungry boy, and her watching of it, could go on and on and she would not mind in the least. It was as though she were witnessing some sacrament. She was sorry when he put the bowl to his lips, drank the last drops, and handed back the spoon. She waved it in the air.

"More?"

With a sleepy, refusing nod, he gave her the bowl, too, and then slid down beneath the burst quilt. He closed his eyes with a great sigh of release. In moments, he was breathing deeply. His fair skin flushed a delicate rose from ear to ear. His lashes were thick and faintly red and his hair bristled pale against the tattered pillowcase. Delphine continued to sit in the chair, watching him, holding the empty bowl in her lap. She smoothed his hair back, but didn't dare kiss him or tuck the covers up tight around him until he was asleep.

Walking out past some customers, Delphine overheard someone say that a bookkeeper's job had opened at the lumberyard. It would be pleasant to work in the scent of fresh sawdust rather than raw blood, she thought as she left. Roy was still not home when she returned—that was perhaps a good thing. She locked the door, doused the lights, and went to sleep. The next morning, she put on her work dress, a somewhat worn hat, and her old coat. She did not want to appear in her very best—those things Cyprian had bought for her—since it wouldn't look right. No matter what they might have heard at the lumberyard, she wanted to give the impression of an extremely respectable woman, but not one who could not afford, say, a hat with a little green feather. A plain person. Trustworthy. Not a person who had a murderer for a best friend or who'd lived with a vaudeville acrobat or who had a gabby old souse for a father. Delphine, she wanted people to say of her, she's awfully quick, but she's solid and reliable.

The spring wind was a quiet and sustained moan, fluttering bits of paper and driving down needles of sleet. The skies were pale purple, the trees soft gray, leafless. There was a watery freshness to the morning light. Delphine's mood lifted as she walked, for she had always loved this time of year, before the leaves came out, when the wind was wild. Clarisse, in her dramatic way, had had the opposite reaction. She had always fallen into a perverse and severe mystery and worn black to school. Traced her eyes with the soot from a burnt match, and rouged her cheeks, sometimes with circles so she looked clownishly tubercular. To Delphine, the hesitation of March was cheering. March was all expectation, a gathering of power. Still cold but marginally warmer every day—a hopeful time of the year. Walking down the nearly empty street, Delphine's thoughts turned calmly optimistic. And that was good because when the creature stumbled toward her from the opposite direction, she was somehow prepared to deal with what she saw.

Gray, naked, hairless, more ghostly animal than human, the wild shape flitted around the corner of the drugstore. Then it jumped from the alley, howling, and threw itself down, clutching at the frozen mud. In the hoarse call it made, she recognized her father. He clambered toward her on his knees and then hopped up as if pulled by strings. He was blown against a storefront like a ball of Russian thistle. He twirled off a front stoop to sprawl in the runnel of a rain gutter. Delphine ran for him, but he saw her and with a start of horror stumbled backward, then turned and ran, streaking crazily back and forth across the street. His legs and arms were skinny and wasted, but his belly was round and frog white. His genitalia were small purple decorations underneath. He didn't bother to hide them, or seem aware at all that he wasn't wearing a stitch. He just wanted to run. It didn't matter where. And he was quick and clever in delirium, Delphine knew. He was always very hard to catch.

Delphine chased her father up the main street, then he cut behind the Lutheran church. She chased him all the way around the building, hoping to trap him in the pastor's yard. Cutting through a patch of blazing forsythia, he nearly ran down Mrs. Orlen Sorven, who threw her round arms up and hollered for help. They left her bellowing cries behind. Roy leaped a primrose gate and sprinted over to the little town park by the river. There, he vaulted picnic tables, sped around the swings. Luckily there were no children of an impressionable age, though a woman with a toddler hid its eyes and dropped her jaw wide. "He's harmless," called Delphine. Panting now, she chased Roy up the winding hill. Roy darted from there toward the fire station, then veered north probably to climb the water tower. Delphine closed in. She had the youth, the stamina, but was hampered by her respectable, job-seeking heels. When he eluded her, swinging around the gas pumps again on main street, weeping in terror at what his brain showed him, she reluctantly took off the shoes. She set them near the pump and then gave chase in stockinged feet, chagrined that her last pair would be ruined. Delphine tackled her father as he ran toward the town grade school. She bore him to earth and then the gym teacher ran outside with a towel around his neck and sat on Roy, putting the towel down first. Roy's legs were streaked with filth and shit. Once caught, he was meek. Delphine took off her coat. She and the gym teacher threaded his arms into the coat's arms and buttoned it down the front. Children and teachers gaped at the scene from the windows as Roy swayed to his feet and let himself be led along, step by step, toward home.

Once there, Delphine gave her father some water with sugar and salt sprinkled into it, put him to bed. She rolled him up in a sheet, and, although he hated to be confined, she safety pinned the sheet together in back and laid him on his side. She called Doctor Heech, who agreed to come and see him when he'd finished with his appointments. When she was sure that Roy was deeply asleep, she walked back to the lumberyard only to find that the job was *filled just this morning, very sorry. And could you make sure your father doesn't sleep again in the lumber piles? We're afraid he'll take a match to the pallets, build a fire. That's a hazard, you understand.*

"IF WE WERE to take a nice, sharp, carving knife and slice you open," said Doctor Heech, drawing a line with his finger up Roy's stomach to the breastbone from the groin, "and if we were to push aside your stomach and your guts and take hold of your liver . . . say we ripped it out and showed you the poor, abused, pulsating organ, we would surely find you've done tremendous violence to it."

Doctor Heech shook his lank silver curls, touched his eyebrows, almost whispered in his reverence for the liver. He went on talking to Roy in a gloomy, dreamy, tone. "This piteous, innocent, earnest helpmeet. What you've done is quite unforgivable. Liquefied in places, surely reeking, here petrified, there pickled. Just by gently palpating . . ." With a faraway frown Heech jammed his fingers into Roy's side and closed them on something deep in his midsection, causing Roy to yelp, then sob. "I can tell this noble liver of yours is kaput."

"Leave it alone," groaned Roy, pushing the doctor's hands away. "God knows I tried."

Doctor Heech huffed in disdain and turned to regard Delphine. "I heard you ran a fast fifty-yard dash this morning."

"It was more like ten miles," said Delphine. "Will he live?"

"He defies all physical laws," said Heech, "so I would be foolish to make a prediction. But I don't know how it is he keeps the flame burning in the wreckage as it is." Heech looked down at Roy. Suddenly his assessing forbearance turned to rage and he roared out, "By God, you *will* live! I've put too much effort into your damn old carcass for you to die before you show consistent goodness to Delphine." He jabbed a finger at Roy's wasted face. "You will not die now! It would be disrespectful! I won't allow it."

"Taper him off," he said to Delphine. "I don't have to tell you how to do it. And give him this for the cough." He handed her a bottle of strong cherry bright syrup. Then he put his hand on her shoulder for a moment and said to her, making sure Roy paid attention, "When he does croak, bury him in a packing crate. Don't give him much of a funeral. Use the money on yourself."

NOT THAT PEOPLE aren't kind, thought Delphine, but when they say no, do they mean because they really don't have work, or because I'm me? She didn't know, just kept looking, and eventually to her great relief, for she was down to the last two dollars in her purse, she got a temporary job. Tensid Bien, the precise old man who sampled Sunshine cookies, who must have known she'd often given him an extra slice of baloney for his nickel, put in a good word for her. She was hired to file papers for the county offices in the courthouse. So her days became as dry as the wind outside. She worked in a back file room on an accumulation of boxes filled with old land settlements and myriad complaints. Nobody else really broke the tedium—one secretary took calls and worked up current papers on her smart black typewriter. Since she considered herself too important to be bothered by conversation with a file clerk, Delphine hardly ever addressed her and after a while she could not remember the woman's name. Delphine rarely saw a county official in the flesh—they seemed busy doing county business somewhere else. It was a sleepy job. When she got home, she dosed Roy from the bottles of syrup and schnapps she carried with her and never left alone with him. Once he slept, his cough quieted, his breathing was so calm he didn't even snore. Delphine made herself dinner and went to sleep, too.

Sleep fell over everything, monotonous and soft. Snowy fluff burst off the cottonwood trees and collected in the grass. Delphine moved slowly through the mild wind and hush of spring green, drugged with sleep like her father. She felt herself sinking away from the grind of life as she crept from her warm bed, through the astonishing light, to the dim rooms of dry papers where she worked. It was a kind of hibernation that she thought might last for the rest of her life. She grew fond of the boredom, the routine, and she wouldn't have given it up for just anyone at all—but there was Markus. And behind him, or before him, she didn't know which, massive in the new wheat, stuffed with the strength of many, there was also Fidelis.

IT WAS USUALLY Markus's task to shred cabbage across the big wooden shredder, a thick paddle-shaped board inset with a sharp blade, easy to set over the wooden washtub that Fidelis used for mixing and fermenting his sauerkraut. He'd had Markus shred the stuff for hours after school already, but after seeing how white his face was and how slowly he moved, even a month after Chicago, Fidelis had taken pity on the boy. He sent Markus to bed. After supper, Fidelis finished the job. He took a cabbage head out of the crate and began to saw it lightly against the blade. Using just the right amount of pressure, he reduced it swiftly underneath his hand until there was only the thickness of a leaf between his palm and the metal. He tossed aside the leaf and took up a new, tightly packed whitish green head, began on that, stopped halfway down arrested by the sudden sensation of having recalled a tremendous task that he had left undone. That was his conviction of what oppressed him, anyway. The problem was, he couldn't think what this task was at all. He picked up the cabbage again, but the impression in his mind only grew stronger. At length, he was so severely haunted by it that he threw down his apron and went outdoors.

There, in the spring-frosted meadow of the front yard, under a quarter moon that blazed in a fresh black sky, he remembered—it was not a task, but very definitely it was something he hadn't finished. The question was, he thought now, was whether it ever could be finished. If he took it up again, would it go on forever? Also, did he have the courage? Did he dare go and see her?

DELPHINE WAS READING and dozing over a thick Book-of-the-Month Club novel she'd got from the little lending library run by some schoolteachers out of the courthouse basement. The plot was intimate, British, and safely romantic, one of those in which she had confidence she'd not be left for days with heartache. She had always been a reader, especially since she lost Clarisse. But now she was obsessed. Since her discovery of the book hoard downstairs from her job, she'd been caught up in one such collection of people and their doings after the next. She read Edith Wharton, Hemingway, Dos Passos, George Eliot, and for comfort Jane Austen. The pleasure of this sort of life—bookish, she supposed it might be called, a reading life—had made her isolation into a rich and even subversive thing. She inhabited one consoling or horrifying persona after another. She read E. M. Forster, the Brontë sisters, John Steinbeck. That she kept her father drugged on his bed next to the kitchen stove, that she was childless and husbandless and poor meant less once she picked up a book. Her mistakes disappeared into it. She lived with an invented force.

When she came to the end of a novel, and put it down and with reluctance left its world, sometimes she thought of herself as a character in the book of her own life. She regarded the ins and outs, the possibilities and strangeness of her narrative. What would she do next? Leave town? Her father would die without her, a failed thread of plot.

The lives of the Waldvogels would simply proceed on in the absence of her observation, without the question mark of her presence. A new story would develop. Delphine's story. Could she bear it? Maybe after all she'd live her story out right here. Something in her was changing as she read the books. Life after life flashed before her eyes, yet she stayed safe from misery. And the urge to act things out onstage could be satisfied cheaply, and at home, and without the annoyance of other members of an acting company. Her ambition to leave faded and a kind of contentment set in. She hadn't exactly feared the word *contentment*, but had always associated it with a vague sense of failure. To be discontented had always seemed much richer a thing. To be restless, striving. That view was romantic. In truth, she was finding out, life was better lived in a tranquil pattern. As long as she could read, she never tired of the design of her days. She did not mind living with poor decrepit Roy on the forsaken edge of a forgotten town beneath a sky that punished or blessed at whim. Contentment. The word itself seemed square and solid in her mind as the little house—Roy's—that she thought of as her own house. Her house at the end of the world. Horizon to all sides. You could see the soft, ancient line of it by stepping out the door. From the west, later and later every night, flame reflected up into the bursting clouds. Skeins of fire and the vast black fields.

After she watched the sun go down, she lighted the lamps, picked up her latest book. Before she dove into the words, she sat and looked at the walls of her quiet room. This was her nightly ritual: she read, she dozed, she roused herself, refreshed and a little dizzy, she made herself a cup of strong tea and began again. Sometimes she read until three or four A.M., knowing that she could take a nap behind the file cabinet the next day. Several times a night she carefully looked around her, pleased at the details of her surroundings. The pinkish light from the expensive lamp that Step-and-a-Half had inexplicably given to her glowed on the pale gold walls. Delphine had hung forest pictures cut from calendars and framed with scraps of birch wood. Gazing into those leafy prints, she entered a peaceful and now familiar state of suspension. A radio that Roy had acquired from Step-and-a-Half and fixed played soothing, tinny orchestra music. There was no heater, but she had the quilt that Eva made for her draped up to her waist. Sometimes she traced the pinched little stitches that her friend had taken, and thought strangely that the stitches might as well have been taken in her own skin, and Eva pulling them. She was reminded of Eva many times a day. She still retained the imprint of her friend's personality, and in that way, another comfort, she liked to think she kept her alive.

Eva would like this room, she thought. There was a small, ornate, feminine, wooden desk where Delphine paid the bills. A huge padlocked sea-trunk of bent blond pine, secured with iron bands, held two more quilts used on very cold nights. A small oval rag rug gave warmth, she believed, to the center of the plain board floor. She hadn't decided whether the figurine of a dog, set on a rickety table pushed up underneath a window, was ugly or elegant. It didn't matter. All of these shabby objects were bathed in the kind light of the rose-shaded lamp. In that light, Delphine gazed upon them with a warm satisfaction and shut her ears to the cold, subterranean creaking of the earth.

Yes, they were still down there, the Chavers. Not their bones but some vestige of their desperation. Half asleep, sometimes, Delphine talked to them, tried to explain. *I didn't know. I wouldn't have. I am so sorry. Go away.*

When she heard someone knock on the door, she started and thought first of Ruthie. Then contained herself. It was just that they never had visitors. Though the town was growing, few came out that way, certainly no one ever at night. Delphine looked through the window before she opened the door and saw that Fidelis stood hunched into his woolen greatcoat. He was heavily scarved against the sharp spring wind and booted against the mud. For some reason he had walked. Delphine's heart leaped suddenly in worry for Markus, and she lunged to open the door. Fidelis stepped in with a swirl of night air, and she swiftly shut the door behind him.

"Markus?" she asked.

"Sleeping," said Fidelis, untying his heavy work boots. "He's not sick, *er ist sehr müde.*"

He left the boots behind him on some newspapers set near the door.

"Dad's asleep in the kitchen," she explained, "so come, let's sit in here."

Obediently, he walked in his wool-stockinged feet to the chair. The socks were gray, the heels and the toes bright red, childish looking in a way that might have endeared Fidelis to Delphine, if she didn't pinch off such a thought before it formed. Without asking if he'd like some, she put the water on the stove, for mint tea, and came back in to sit with him while she waited for it to boil. Fidelis told her there had been a letter from Germany. The boys had started school and were involved in a government youth group that Tante said was extremely hard to get selected for. She implied that she had had to use money that Fidelis sent with her to bribe government officials to admit the boys, though they had passed some rigorous tests. As for Tante, she had at first conducted sewing demonstrations with her American model machine. Then she'd realized it was inferior to the German model.

"That's enough," said Delphine. "I'm not interested in your sister." She began to quiz him about the boys at home. Were they eating well? Washing? And the business. Were the people he had credited paying their bills? Some. Not enough. Were the suppliers giving him good prices? Obviously, from his answers, he did not have the time to spend with them in wangling better profit margins. Delphine frowned. "One or two percent here and there will make or break us," she said, "you'll find out!" She slapped the arm of her chair to hide her slip. Us? What was she saying?

"Just tea again." She mocked his disappointed look, and said, "You drink too much beer anyway." She rose and went into the kitchen, stepped around the sleeping Roy, and swirled mint leaves into the boiling water in her heavy brown teapot. She took out cups and put a lump of sugar in the bottom of each one. She brought the pot and the two cups, balanced, back into the living room and set them by the china figurine of the dog.

"Have you ever seen a dog like this?" she asked Fidelis.

It had long floppy black ears, white and black markings, a pointed muzzle, and sat alertly upon a green porcelain cushion.

Fidelis picked the dog up and turned it this way and that, almost playfully. "I don't think another like this dog exists on earth," he finally said, putting it back.

Delphine said nothing. She was startled by the frivolous tone in his voice. There was an awkward, flirtatious quality about him. It was upsetting for her to hear him say anything that was not tied to the store. She addressed him on safer topics, and for a while they managed to skate a comfortable surface. Then Fidelis asked with no warning whether she knew, yet, if Cyprian was coming back.

"No!" said Delphine, her voice caught in reluctance to be thrown, so suddenly, into the personal.

Fidelis leaned back now and looked directly at her. The rose light polished his features, lent to the whole of him an incongruous sweetness. He'd hung his jacket on the chair behind him and was now in his shirt sleeves. The light picked up the bronze of the hair on his forearms and she gazed down a bit dizzily at his heavy-boned wrists. He glanced at the darkened door of the kitchen, hitched his chair a little closer to hers.

"I gave Cyprian enough time," he said. His voice thudded. The statement seemed ridiculous. But when he leaned forward, Delphine smelled the spice of him—white pepper and red, a little ginger and caraway. And the male scent of him, the wool and the linen of his shirt. The tart shaving tonic. She knew he rubbed cigar ashes on his teeth to whiten them and then brushed with baking soda. Knew he lathered his whiskers with Eva's old bars of hand-milled French lilac soap. All of these little things about him were hers to know because she'd kept his house while his wife died. Then she'd cared for his sons. She'd told herself all along that these things had nothing to do with him, Fidelis himself, but now here he was, removed from the intimacy of his family. And yet she knew his habits while he'd hardly seen the inside of her house. He knew little of her. Nothing so personal as the type of soap she used. And what was she to make of this giving Cyprian time?

"Gave him? What do you mean, 'gave' him?"

"Time," said Fidelis, "to come back."

"Well, yes," said Delphine. His meaning dawned on her. A contrary ticklish energy seized her. She wanted to make things difficult for Fidelis. Why not? Why should he come here so easily and overfill the small pale gold room, her private nest? So she began to laugh, as though he'd said something very funny, and then she calmed herself and took a drink of her tea.

"Did you think he had deserted me?" She would never give away the reason they had parted. She would never tell that he'd left much earlier than people thought. "So like a man, to think that." Perhaps she was a little under the influence of one of her drawing-room novels, in which people sparred over such topics as love, for it delighted her suddenly to be in the position she was in, to have Fidelis here trying to explain himself and her believing that she finally read his heart. So he had waited for her!

"Fidelis." She shook her head, the curls of her brown hair lashed her shoulders, and she raised her eyes to his with a lazy knowledge. But when she looked into his face his expression was of such helpless ardor that she forgot her small artifice.

IT WOULD SEEM for months afterward that there had been a great collision, that two glaciers had through slow force smashed together, at last, and buckled. The two were dazed, a bit slow with other people, forgetful. Delphine kept her job at the courthouse, but cut the hours back and came into the shop to wait on customers each afternoon. She came to be near Fidelis. As before, she tended the kitchen and, if she had time, did laundry for the boys—not Fidelis. Since she'd left, he'd begun to iron his own shirts with a soldierly precision.

One afternoon, she found him at it when she arrived. That day, for some reason the whole place was quiet. She walked into the cold concrete-floored utility room, where the water was piped out of the wall into a double soapstone tub. There he stood, chilled in the loop of his undershirt, arms moving above the wooden board covered with a padded cloth. He had bought a modern plug-in iron, and was putting a crease in the starched, sizzling shoulder of a sleeve.

To watch him in his power doing work women did so often filled

Delphine with a low electricity, and she brushed the side of his arm, above his elbow. Her hand was still in its glove. He put the iron down. Took her hand in his hand and then pulled off each finger of her glove while looking into her eyes with a steady gravity. When the glove was off, he lifted her hand in both of his and regarded it intently. He stroked her knuckles, scored with white scars, and at last, tentatively, brought her hand to his lips. He fit his mouth over the crease where her fingers came together at the palm.

Then he moved too quickly, in a way she didn't like, with an arrogant sweep, and tried to pull her to him. She sidestepped his rough gesture and walked out of the room, still breathing the heady scorched scent of clean ironing. That was the first time they'd ever touched, or kissed, though it was more than a kiss and not yet a kiss. Walking home later on, she thought of his eyes as he pulled her glove off, and then she was suddenly home. She realized that she'd walked, tranced, down the long road, without seeing a thing around her. She had no memory of how she got to her door. And yet, though she couldn't stop thinking of him in this new way, she avoided him. For when they were around each other now the stage was bare, all the scenery pulled away, and there was only the full burden of their attraction. It was too much, to let it happen all at once. They came together by the smallest incremental movements.

Weeks later, they still hadn't kissed, hadn't let their mouths touch. And yet one day in the dusty office filled with paperwork, Fidelis knelt before Delphine and with his hands smoothed the insides of her legs up to the tops of her heavy silk stockings, felt where they were hooked with metal garters, traced the slices of material up underneath her skirt. He spread her legs apart so wide she was embarrassed, there in the leather chair, and then he kissed the insides of her knees. She caught his hair back in both fists, pulled so hard it must have stung, but only stared down at him, his face immobile between her legs. She shoved him away with all of her strength, and pressed down her skirt.

"Jesus Christ," she said. "What are you thinking?"

"I don't know." He rose in one subdued, brutal motion and dusted himself off with broad unnecessary whacks at the legs of his pants.

"Around you, I get these ideas." He tried to recover his dignity, folded his arms, then unfolded them, sat down, and rifled the desk for a cigarette. When he couldn't find one his threw up his hands as though to say, See? I can't get anything I want? And Delphine finally laughed.

MANY DAYS, they couldn't bear the tension and ignored each other entirely. They set a date four months away on which they would be married. At first it seemed a very long time to wait, and then it seemed to Delphine far too short a time and she thought maybe she would put it off. Fidelis bought their wedding license in the courthouse, showed her the paper casually, and they both signed their names with a dispassionate alacrity, as though they were signing banking documents. They were good at working together—quick and respectful and efficient. Delphine took over the bookkeeping and the ordering again, and she began to bring religion to the dusty office careening with papers.

One afternoon when Franz and Markus were eating in the kitchen, Delphine brought Fidelis in and pushed his shoulder. "Tell them," she commanded.

Franz paused, frozen, his hand to his mouth, waiting for his father's announcement. Markus continued eating, chewing serenely. Nodding, he said, "I already know what you're going to say." He took another bite, and asked the next important question.

"So does that mean Emil and Erich are coming home?"

"I wrote and sent money," said Fidelis, with assurance. "Tante will make the arrangements."

"Tell them," said Delphine, again, shaking his arm.

Fidelis gathered himself, but before he could open his mouth, Franz beat him.

"Oh, I get it," said Franz. "You two are getting married." He forked half of a baked apple into his mouth, chewed it all up. "And as long as we're making announcements, I'm going into the air corps. I'm enlisting."

"There is no war!" Fidelis's low voice nearly cracked with intensity— he still had his hopes. But Franz didn't seem to notice.

"Oh, there will be," said Franz. "Just you wait. I see it coming, and

308

when it does I'm . . ." He made a skimming motion with his hand, like an airplane taking off. He buzzed his hand into the wild blue yonder and then he grinned at them all, nodding to encourage their approval. Fidelis hunched his shoulders in distress and left the room.

"Do you have to be so happy about it?" said Delphine, annoyed with Franz for spoiling the announcement, but also suddenly aghast at his thirst for war.

"I'm happy about it," said Markus. "It's like you already live here."

"Oh, that," Franz said. "He can do what he wants."

"You know what I'm talking about!" said Delphine. "Can you go and sit with him at least?"

"Dad wouldn't want that." Franz took a walnut from the bowl on the table, cracked it with his fingers, just like Fidelis. He tossed the meats up in the air and caught them on his tongue. "I'll fly a Spitfire! We won't get anywhere near German territory. I'll be fighting other pilots—not Dad's people. He knows that."

"You have no idea what a war means!" Delphine tried not to raise her voice or drive him off. But his willful ignorance was making her passionate. "Forget that I'm marrying your father. Be realistic, Franz. They could put you in the infantry."

"Me?" He looked incredulous, pityingly, at Delphine. "A bomber, maybe. But no. I'll be a fighter pilot." He made noises with his mouth and pretended to machine-gun Markus, who popped his lips back at him.

"God, you're a hard soul!" Delphine cried, overcome.

"What do you want? The marriage is your business," said Franz. He sulked. "It doesn't matter what I think."

"Of course it matters," said Delphine coaxingly.

"Well then, I think I'm leaving," said Franz. "Don't take this personal, but I don't want to think about it." He got up and sauntered away, shoved his fists in the pockets of his poor, tattered, imitation flight jacket. As he passed out of Delphine's sight, he swore hard, kicked the dust. His eyes watered. Then he laughed sarcastically at himself. He had never been so miserable in his life.

* * *

WHENEVER FRANZ passed the place where he and Mazarine had swung from the road to enter their special place underneath the pine, his throat burned. A tension collected around his heart. For hours after, he would think about the pine tree, his ribs tightening and his chest shutting out the air. It was hard to take a breath. And yet suddenly his breath came out in huge, deep, surprising sighs. Food went dry in his throat and the weight dropped off him. The bones of his wrists jutted out, his cheekbones sharpened. Nor could he sleep right. His dreams were of reckless bargains. Torrents of water swept him from Mazarine or tumbled her over cliffs and through culverts, just out of reach. Things had only gotten worse as it became apparent that Mazarine Shimek truly meant her *no* and would not have him back. Mazarine, in the new clothing he had never touched.

She wore a soft plaid kilt of rust brown to school now—even Franz could tell that it was perfectly sewn. The hem swished just the right way around her legs when she walked, whirled softly when she turned. The colors of her pleated skirt were the browns and golds of the light that used to fall upon the two of them underneath the great pine tree. She wore crisp blouses that managed somehow to drape, as well, across her bird's collarbone. The fabric joined across her chest with rich, glazed, mother-of-pearl buttons. She wore her hair in a braid now, twined through with a ribbon of heavy satin—sometimes blue, sometimes yellow. He could not help recording a list of these details—they were all he had of her right now. But Mazarine didn't in any way return his regard. She didn't speak to him, much less let him take her books from her arms and strap them onto her bicycle and give her rides, as though she were a much younger girl. He missed that the most, he thought. Even more than touching her he longed for the weight of her wobbling between his arms on the bicycle. Him steering and her laughing as she tried to balance. The farther away she kept herself, the more he knew this: he loved Mazarine—to the death, he thought wildly, beyond death.

How stupid! He crashed his fists on his temples. At night, he thought of and rejected ways to make it up to her, ways to draw her to him. He would throw himself upon her mercy. Waylay her. Beg her. Buy her a hothouse rose and lay it on her bed at night. She needed him, didn't she? Anyone could tell she was unhappy. Look how quiet she was, walking the school hallways, how serious. Look how her slender grace had become an alarming thinness. How she kept her hair, which had always swirled with her movements, stiffly locked into that one thick braid.

The only thing that really diverted him was the airfield. Sometimes, Franz looked at the other men who worked around him, and wondered if they'd ever had such feelings. He doubted it—none of them looked as if they could ever have been in love with anything but their machines. At first he scorned such limitations. Then they made sense to him. To actually fix a touchy engine was a relief. So whenever Fidelis let him out of the shop, Franz worked on airplanes. In payment, Pouty Mannheim began to teach him how to fly.

Each time they went up, Franz felt the same roaring physical release from the earth that had charmed him when he first watched, from the field behind the house, the plane take off and lift over the windbreak. Only it was better to be in the plane itself. Better now as he understood exactly how to control the flight, read the wind, the signs in the clouds small and large. On their eighth flight, Pouty let him have a chance at the controls. For weeks, they practiced taking off, touching down, and then gradually added a beginning barnstormer's repertoire of stalls, spins, easy wingovers and gentle loops. When Pouty finally let him take the plane up solo, Franz experienced a startling lightness. The plane flew at a touchy and thrilling balance with just him in it. He focused on the town grain elevator, a thin mark on the horizon, kept his nose directed at it and did a slow point roll. Then a more complicated hesitation roll, a loop, a difficult spin. The earth tipped over him. Concentrate, or die. Things were simple upside down. By the time he landed, he was absolutely at peace. After that, he thought that maybe he would survive the loss of Mazarine if only he could spend his life up in the air.

NO GUESTS, no cake, no flowers. After she married Fidelis and Franz left to start his tests for the air corps, Delphine continued to divide her time between the butcher shop and her house, nursing Roy. She kept part of her filing job, kept reading her books, tried to keep as much of her old routine as she could. Still, the past with its horrors, complexities, and incompletions intruded. Although she was married, the background to her new life seemed unfinished, like a jumbled stage set. She wished that she could file her past the way she filed the papers at the courthouse. Then Cyprian returned.

He was sitting on the front steps of Delphine's house one early evening, wearing a hat. He squinted out at the road and nodded, cool and self-contained, as Delphine drove the car into the yard. Then he took off the hat, and Delphine saw that he was utterly bald. He looked even more attractive, exotic, like someone from a prehistoric world jolted into pants and shirt and shoes. The head made you think of him naked. Her heart jolted when she saw him. She took a deep, ragged breath to calm herself as she stopped the car and took in his presence through the windshield. So here he was. She smiled, an involuntary reflex, before she thought of Clarisse, then realized that she could find out what happened to Clarisse. The smile altered but stayed on her face. In spite of everything, she was glad to see Cyprian.

As she opened the driver's door, jumped out, and nearly ran toward him, Delphine was surprised to experience a sudden uncomfortable pang. Was Fidelis watching? Irrationally, she glanced to all sides. She tried to shrug the discomfort off her shoulders like a cape, but her uneasiness persisted. Her greeting was tentative, and she stood before Cyprian in the bent sun of early dusk, shifting her weight, hoping he'd not come into the house with her. Again, this sense that she was doing something wrong although there was no wrong in it, but there was the intimidating certainty of Fidelis. The realization that she was now susceptible to a man's jealousy irritated her. From under the porch and the stillness of the grass, mosquitoes started to whine. Cyprian tipped his head to the side and fanned away the bugs with his hat. They sat down on the porch steps.

"Light up a cigarette, will you, to keep off the bloodsuckers?" She accepted a cigarette from Cyprian and allowed it to burn down between her fingers.

"I'm not even going to talk to you," she said in a low voice, finally, "until you tell me what happened to Clarisse."

"I didn't know about Hock," Cyprian offered.

"I know what the hell happened to Hock. I asked you what happened to *her*."

"All she said to me was this: 'I'll go where my work is necessary, and appreciated.'"

"That actually sounds like her," said Delphine. "I'll bet she went south, New Orleans . . . no, farther. The Yucatan or maybe even farther down, Brazil. I can see it." She sighed and shook herself. She couldn't see it. Missing Clarisse was still a daily habit, like drinking coffee or turning on the radio. She didn't stop to ache or wonder or brood over Clarisse anymore. She just missed her and then was done with it and went on to the next thing. And that is the kindness of time, she thought.

She looked at Cyprian. "So you didn't know about Hock. Until when?"

"Until she told me."

"Which was *when*?"

"Right away, on the trip to Minneapolis."

"Didn't it occur to you, then, that somebody might connect the two of you? Think you were in on it?"

"Sure it did," said Cyprian, "which is one reason why I parted ways with her."

"Why did you come back here?"

Cyprian turned his hat around and around in his hands—it was a smooth clay brown fedora with a wide brown grosgrain band. Expensive looking. He pinched the brim, his fingers careful, choosing his words.

"I'm passing through," he said finally. "But I just had to see if you love him."

"Of course I do."

"The hell you do!"

Suddenly they turned, their eyes locked in outrage, and they stared at each other. Their exasperation was so exactly matched that it struck them both, at the same time, as ludicrous. They turned away, each unwilling to let the other see any softening, or smile. Delphine fiddled with the cigarette, sharpening its ash on the wood of the steps, waving it slowly around her to make a smoke barrier.

"So you came back not knowing if you'd get picked up for murder, just to see if I love Fidelis."

Cyprian didn't answer for a moment, then he nicked his head. "Like I said, I have other reasons." He shrugged and raised his eyebrows. His eyes were sharply lovely.

"Come in then," she said at last. "Roy's in bed. He needs a good laugh."

Cyprian jammed his hat on his head, then took it off, and followed her across the bare porch and into the house. Inside, he took off his hat and held it over his stomach as he walked into the kitchen, where Roy slept. Cyprian sat down by the bed and waited for Roy to wake. For a long time, Roy lay still, hands on the quilt, eyes shut. Eventually, he opened one eye just a crack, took in Cyprian's presence, and shut his eyes again with an elaborate fluttering of lids. Delphine was surprised to find that she was cheered to see this deception, this hint of the old Roy, and she pulled her chair up, too.

"Hey, Dad," she said softly, "you have a visitor."

Roy lay mum, deciding whether to retreat from consciousness or seek out communion with the living. His brows knit and he worked his jaws in little chewing motions. Finally, he gave a decisive jerk and let his eyelids flap up to display great, staring, milky-blue rounds of iris.

"Cyprian! Cyprian the Bald!"

Cyprian grasped Roy's bony, spectral, age-freckled hand. Once he'd decided to join the living, Roy became energized by possibilities.

"Oh for a beer," he cried. "A little sip of schnapps. Could you see your way clear to wet my whistle?'

"Dad . . ."

"Yes, yes, assuredly, I know there is compelling evidence that it might kill me." Roy made brushing motions in the air as if swiping off the warnings. "But a very tiny amount might actually be beneficial, serve as an inoculation, if you will."

"We're down to a teaspoon or two every few hours," said Delphine. "I guess it wouldn't hurt to have your teaspoon."

"Now we're talking!" crowed Roy. He patted Cyprian's arm. "Would you care to join me? Give this man a teaspoon!" Roy swept his arm grandly toward the little cutlery drawer.

"He can have a glass, Dad." She unclipped a set of keys from her belt, took a glass outside to the car. She unlocked the trunk and then used another key to unlock a toolbox padlocked into the trunk. From the box, she removed a pint bottle of brandy. She poured the glass half full, set the glass on the roof of the car, locked everything back up, and brought the glass of brandy back to Roy's bedside. She poured a bit of the glass into a bottle cap and dipped in a teaspoon.

"Salut!" Roy opened his mouth and then closing it around the spoon.

Cyprian nicked his glass at the old man.

"What are you up to now?" Roy's tone was convivial, but his eyes glittered, full of sudden tears. "Are you casting around for a job and looking for a wife? Did you come here as a dog returns to a place it's once been fed?"

Cyprian took a large swallow of the brandy, and Roy went on speculating. "There's always farmwork around here, of course, but that is both brutal and seasonal. I speak from much experience. Now there's our thriving main street, all those shops lined up raking in cash. Clerking. Perhaps you could learn to barber. Oly Myhra's getting old. His pole needs painting. Hah hah! His pole needs painting! My pole"—he nudged Cyprian—"hasn't been painted for the last twenty-six years. What about yours?"

Cyprian looked at Delphine. She raised her eyebrows but kept her face impassive.

"The paint's fresh on mine," said Cyprian. "What do you hear from the rest of the club?"

"Mannheim is still aloft," said Roy. "And Fidelis married the woman you skipped out on, that is"—he nodded at Delphine with affection—

"her Royal Obstinacy. Once again, she has nursed me back from the brink of the abyss. I had flung myself headlong into the drink, you know, and made of myself something of an embarrassment to her. Still, she loves her old dad. She tapered me off. How about that second tea-spoon?"

"Live it up," said Delphine. Roy closed his eyes and opened his mouth. She put the spoon in.

"I didn't run out on her," said Cyprian, giving Delphine a meaning-ful look. "I offered her an engagement ring. A real nice one. She turned me down."

"Watch out," said Delphine. "I know all about where that ring ended up."

"Ah," gasped Roy. He had taken the spoon from Delphine's fingers and was sucking on it like a happy child. "The disappointments of love lie heavier each year. Time does not, as the philosopher's wishful think-ing goes, time does not heal all wounds. When I fell, I fell hard," said Roy proudly. "I fell through the center of the world."

"You've milked your love martyrdom far enough," said Delphine. "I'm tired of it. She was my mother you know, I'm the one who really got the raw deal here. And ended up taking care of you, you booze hound, all of these years!"

"And hasn't it been a grand old time!" cried Roy. He was always en-couraged and cheered when Delphine joined him in his bantering. "I believe that the sacred love I have borne these many years is a love that has sucked me straight into the vortex, the omphalos of the universe, and there I have seen such things my friends. Such things! . . ." Roy let his voice trail off and his gaze unfocus, as though he were reliving a vision. "Mostly though"—he shook his head, jolting back—"I have seen a lot of hooch disappear."

"Dad's mistaken the navel of the universe," said Delphine, "for the dimple at the bottom of the schnapps bottle."

"Well, be that as it may, I am actually here," said Cyprian, with an air of setting things right at last, "to play an engagement."

"A what?" Roy's mouth dropped in delight.

"That's right," said Cyprian. "I'm not really looking for a job. I'm part of the lyceum series. I travel with the Snake Man now." He reached into his pocket and drew out a roll of pink cardboard tickets. "How many would you like?"

"The Snake Man?" said Delphine, a little wounded somehow, maybe even a bit jealous. "You could have written. Does he double as your human table?"

"It didn't have the same effect," said Cyprian, "with two men, though we did work out a few other balancing tricks. He owns his own python, brings it onstage in a leather case on wheels. He's got an assortment of reptiles," Cyprian paused, "and one arachnid."

"What's his name?" said Delphine.

"Mighty Tom."

"A good name for a performer."

"No, that's the spider. My partner's name is Vilhus Gast."

So that, thought Delphine, was that.

"What's he like?" she asked.

"Well, he's a lot like me," said Cyprian. "A performer, you know. He made it over here from Lithuania and he's a Jew. I was a real curiosity to him at first. I took him home with me." Cyprian laughed. "Boy was he surprised."

"How come?"

"There's no Jews on the reservation, I mean to speak of. I never knew one when I was growing up, any more than he'd know an Indian. Except he did know about us and said he believed we were one of the lost tribes of Israel doomed to wander, too, like his people. Always to be on the edge of things. Hounded and hunted, he said. 'Well, okay,' I said. 'So let's roam around together.' So we got this act up and since then we've been playing it steady."

DELPHINE AND MARKUS arrived early at the school gymnasium the next night and took a seat in the first row of creaky wooden folding chairs. There would be talk. Cyprian would be recognized and his shaven head remarked with wonder, maybe derision. People, customers, old schoolmates, would turn to crane at Delphine. If she sat in the back, she would have to endure their shielded or open curiosity. Sitting in the first row, she had her back to them. They could gawk and whisper to their heart's content. Delphine would ignore them. She intended to enjoy the show.

The curtains parted. Cyprian and his partner stood barefooted, clad in tight black gymnasium suits, on great red rubber balls. Pedaling their feet, they do-si-doed around each other, speeding up until to much applause they hopped high in the air and exchanged places on the spinning balls. Vilhus Gast was very like in size and shape to Cyprian, though nondescript of feature, and he wore a very bad toupee that shifted as he moved.

Suddenly, Gast stood quite still, precisely balanced, hands raised like a ballerina's, and Cyprian began to bounce, the ball caught between his feet. With a giant catlike effort, Cyprian sprang off the ball and into the air, upended, coming down exactly in position to lock hands with Vilhus Gast. The men swayed, each powerful muscle defined, and nearly toppled. Amazingly, they righted themselves and balanced.

Now, Gast began to dance the ball back and forth across the stage. To shouts and laughter, he pretended to have trouble holding Cyprian aloft. They balanced one-armed, one-legged, and then something wonderful and awful happened. The unattractive toupee that Vilhus Gast wore crept slowly off his head. To the delight of boys and the shrieks of ladies, the bad wig revealed itself to be a giant spider. Gingerly, horribly, the thing eased itself up Gast's arm, felt its way to Cyprian's elbow, and then, as Cyprian lowered himself, the spider embraced his bare skull and remained there. The men stood, pranced, held their arms out to receive mad clapping, hoots, and whistles. From a box on a small stand, then, Gast shook loose another, smaller, but equally hairy spider. The audience hushed. He coaxed it along his arm with a feather, then helped it up Cyprian's throat. Delicately, the creature felt its way up the cliff of Cyprian's chin and over his mouth. The spider curled into a square black mustache on Cyprian's upper lip, in the warm breath from his nose.

Along with the spiders, Cyprian also donned a swallowtail suit coat and polished black leather boots. His legs were still comically bare. He was Adolf Hitler, with intestinal gas. Every time an offstage tuba sounded, Cyprian's muscular ass end popped between the tails of his formal jacket, danced, jigged, reacted with a life apart from the absurdly stern and hypnotic features of the Fuehrer, whose attempt to inspire the howling crowd was undone. Every time he called for the Nazi salute, the tuba squawked and his rear end explosively twitched. The spiders stayed attached to Cyprian's head somehow. The audience discovered that they could make the Fuehrer fart by giving the salute themselves. They straight-armed, uproariously, until the tuba was one long groan and Hitler went zinging all around the stage like a flea on a hot griddle. The curtains shut to roars and howls. The first act was finished.

Laughter hadn't even died down when the curtains were flung wide again. An eight- or nine-foot leather valise with several handles was displayed upon four sawhorses. Cyprian and Vilhus Gast appeared, wearing jeweled turbans and dressed in strange and delicate transparent veils of fabric that ballooned around their legs, floated in the air beneath their arms, and drifted behind them as they walked. A tinny phonograph record played exotic whining music as the two men unlatched the valise and displayed something live, mottled, and very quiet, but with a vibrating energy that made people catch their breaths. The men coaxed the enormous snake from the case into their arms and announced the Dance of Death. They wound and unwound with the snake as it became more alert, tried to curl them into its coils and draw them close. Their dance was impromptu, graceful, and sensuously peaceful. Every member of the audience, believing that the python meant to devour the two men, was mesmerized with interest. Cyprian and Vilhus Gast danced the python down the center aisle. The crowd was allowed to touch the dry, charged skin. All saw the incongruously small head, an evil wedge of muscle. Its brilliant, cold, criminal's eyes made them shudder so they were glad when Cyprian and Vilhus returned the snake to its leather case, resnapped the locks, and produced two sharp-toothed, gleaming handsaws, with which they proposed to reduce the python into stove lengths.

"Is there a butcher in the house?" called Cyprian. Pete Kozka was given the saws to test. He pronounced them keen and effective. The men sawed up the python. It writhed horribly in the valise, its tail whipping through the unlatched end. Then they burned a fragrant substance and began to chant portentous syllables, made some signs over a pot of school glue, and stuck the python back together. The show continued. They put away the python and juggled lizards. Displayed a huge iguana still and blinkless as a stone carving. Once again introduced the talented arachnid, Mighty Tom, who played the part of Vilhus Gast's toupee. They brought him down the aisle in a great round candy jar so that people could look aghast at him and marvel. They balanced cups, plates, and their curly-toed shoes on pates and noses. They did a few more acrobatic tricks and then bounced off, to wild applause and shrieks of encore! They came back out as twin Hitlers on unicycles that they rode while breaking wind and saluting and from which they nearly toppled when their farts grew boisterous. They juggled swastikas set on fire. They juggled hatchets, cleavers, knives. They juggled apples and snatched great bites from them until they juggled only cores. They were an enormous hit.

For weeks after Cyprian and the Snake Man had vanished, Markus talked of nothing but the show, and people stopped Delphine in the street. They treated her with shy admiration. She received the deference of one who knows, or has access to, a great artist. They addressed her with respect. They wanted details, secrets.

"The python, has it eaten anyone?"

"Has the spider underneath Cyprian's nose ever caused him to sneeze? If he did, what would happen?"

"Where did he learn to juggle? To ride a unicycle?"

"Will he return? Ever again?"

Delphine couldn't answer any of the questions except the last one. And she only answered it on instinct, though she was proved right.

"No," she said, "he won't come back here." And he never did.

ROY SEEMED CONTENT to stay in bed next to the stove most of the day, courting sleep, soaked in sleep, washed in the pleasant duty of it.

Because Doctor Heech had prescribed a prolonged rest in order to relieve his liver and keep his cough from turning to pneumonia, at first both Roy and Delphine counted each hour of his loss of consciousness as a healing virtue. However, after a time, she understood that it was something more. She could tell this sleep was different for Roy, not restorative, but some final preparation. He slept so earnestly. It was as though he was practicing. She began to fear he would die when she was out at work, and she put her hand on his face first thing when she returned every day, and first thing when she rose in the morning. Along with the overpowering sleep, he hardly ate. He swallowed a few mouthfuls of soup, then lay back and let sleep take him once again. She had to watch him. He was shrinking. Growing weaker and quieter. He'd asked for the pictures of her mother, Minnie, and set them on a shelf of the spice and flour counter, where he could see them from his bed.

Delphine had asked Roy to tell her about Minnie, but he had surprisingly little information for one who so flamboyantly existed in a state of destructive long-term grief. She didn't even have a gravestone to visit, and Roy would not say why that was or where she was buried. All Roy would say was that Minnie was the only one left to tell the tale.

"What tale?" Delphine had always asked, but Roy had kept his mouth shut.

Now that his tongue was somewhat loosened by the codeine, and he was bored, Delphine thought she might have better luck with her questions. One night she sat with him, speechlessly tending a little fire in the stove, lost in her own brooding. She slowly became aware that she was waiting for something, she was not even sure of what. Perhaps Roy was going to die this night. Her thoughts had become dispassionate, and she regarded him with detached affection. Poor Roy. He looked weary and his skin had gone fragile, soft, almost translucent. Blue blotches came up on his forearms, bruises that seemed to have surfaced from deep, invisible, interior blows. It was as though he was finally showing all the knocks life had dealt him. Delphine suddenly decided not to let him die with all of the secrets that she had a perfect right to know.

"All right. I want answers. Where was she from?" Delphine asked, pointing to Minnie's picture.

"She was from down there." He waved vaguely south. "Then she came up here."

As usual, thought Delphine, he would give her nothing. But when she stared at him and said, "More. I want to know it all," he seemed to reconsider, and spoke more alertly. "Actually, she was originally from *way, way* up there." Roy rolled his eyes northward until the whites showed, then stared at Delphine in concentration, frowning. Perhaps he understood that in Delphine right now he had the perfect audience. The vagueness of sleep in his face cleared. As if an electrical wire was spliced, the old Roy came on, the one who told stories in bars and eased Eva Waldvogel into death by talking the secret language of wolves. Delphine hunched close to hear it all, and held her breath until he started speaking with such an eager intensity that she knew she was finally getting the story.

"You want to know? Of course you want to know. I'll tell you, too. So go on, take notes. Put these things down for posterity or posteriority, what have you. Minnie. She wasn't no ordinary, everyday, woman. She wasn't just a person you would walk past. She wasn't forgettable. Not Minnie. She had something else in her—the blood of her forefathers, and foremothers, too, and that blood was not just any blood either, but I'm telling you she was of the great nation of the Indians up north called the Crees and Ojibways who mixed with the French, of whom she was descended of kings. That's right. Her great grandpa was the bastard of the Sun King himself, or so he said, and had escaped across the ocean to lead a clean life skinning pelts. While from the south, she was an adopted second cousin to old Crazy Horse or could have been, though she was almost tragically destroyed. I set this up so you'll realize that from all sides and all directions there was royal lines simmering and boiling and knocking up against one another in the blood of this woman, your mother. And don't, no, don't start diverting me with other questions. Let me go on. Let me speak. For what you now will hear I've told no other, and for good reason. It is a story so sad and incredible I don't like to think of it myself. It is better forgot. It is the story of who your mother became at the age of eight years and why thereafter she grew into someone who could never be tamed by the likes of old Roy Watzka, not me!"

Roy sat up, gestured for some pillows to prop at his back, took a sip of the water into which Delphine had mixed a bit of ginger to calm his stomach and help the blood flow quicker to his heart.

"Picture a Christmas service in a snug built church deep in the heart of plains country!" Roy spread his fingers wide before him. Eyes narrowing, he stared into the back of his hand as though it were made of prophesying crystal. "A ragtag bunch of starved and freezing Minneconjou Lakotas—what the layman will call Siouxs—rap humbly at the door of this Christian house of worship. They're on the run, mostly women and little children, and a few wore-down warriors half mad from their strivings and their defeats. Their chief is dying in a wagon they got dragged by two racks of horse bones that used to be war ponies. They have seen Sitting Bull betrayed and their everyday survival shot to hell. They have this idea they can dance the world back, sing to the dead and the dead will hear them and all will rise and live. They are very lonesome people, is all, and I know about lonesome. Just ask me. They want to see the faces of the ones they love. It is Christmas on the plains, mind you. These poor folks come begging for a handout, a little mercy. And do they get it?" Roy glared blindly at the scene in his head. "What do you think?"

"Well from how you set it up," said Delphine, "no."

"No," said Roy. "It's the God's truth. They were turned away." He was breathing quickly, his storytelling tongue on fire. "Among them there is a girl from the Indians I have mentioned, those Indians up north who blended with the French. Her daddy is a Cree who was sent down by his people to learn of this new method of dancing to bring back the dead. He is supposed to report back and tell the old people of his own tribe if it works—so far, he has seen no resurrections. On this trip, he took his favorite, his youngest, his daughter. The others are left behind. This girl and her father traveled first to the camp of the Hunkpapa Lakota, where folks are leaving for the village of Chief Hump, to the south. They meet up with a Minneconjou bunch there and walk deeper into the Badlands territory with the remnants of the believers, who at this point are just trying to go home. Pretty soon they got nothing, food nor shelter, except the steep bluffs of a place called Medicine Root Creek. It is there that they entertain an army major of the notorious, inglorious, Seventh Cavalry, Major Samuel M. Whitside. At Porcupine Butte he convinces them to follow underneath the white flag of surrender to a military camp near a place called in Lakota something unpronounceable by me, and in the English language, Wounded Knee."

Roy paused for a long moment, squinting into the darkest corner of the room, moving his tongue across his lips as if to find a word or two caught there like a crumb. With a jerk of energy, he roused himself and continued.

"Camped at this place they are headed for is an army of men which has declared themselves a shelter for the Lakota, the Siouxs if you will, should they be so desperate as to approach. With their chief, old Big Foot, dying of pneumonia in that wagon bed and with no food, starving mainly, these people beg protection. They give up their guns and set up camp where they are told. Minnie's father has an old piece of bannock in his pocket, their last food, which he shares with a woman who has invited them into her tent. She has a baby tied to her and no man in sight. After it is eaten, they have nothing. But the woman picked up something thrown to her by a member of the congregation in the church way back there. It is a tough one-legged gingerbread figure. This, she offers to share with them. She divides it crumb by crumb. They eat it, and fall asleep in her tent. That next morning, the woman fills a pot with snow and puts the little pot upon a fire of twigs. The woman takes a bundle of roots from the bodice of her dress and she stews one of those roots in the pot of melted snow. She tends the pot with the root like it was something special, watching it so careful, hushing her baby, testing the potency of her brew with a finger, withdrawing the root and examining it from time to time. She removes the little pot from the fire, eventually, and she allows the tea to cool just enough. Then she motions to Minnie to drink it. And just as she is drinking this tea, there is a shot fired outside the tent.

"Well, you can read about this in the history books if you want to, though rarely is the full extent of its pity told or believed. Minnie's father, running out of the tent, is gunned down right off, for that accidental shot brings down thunder. A great, crackling ripple of sound! Smoke and brimstone! Bullets ripping through the cloth, Minnie plunges from the tent with this woman, who grabs her arm and steers her for the white peace flag of surrender. They stand underneath it, shots whizzing and whining in swarms. The woman still has her baby at her breast, tucked in a tied shawl, at her nipple. Again, that thunder rolls! It is Hotchkiss guns trained down straight on the camp of women and on the children and on the white flag of surrender, too. This lady, she keeps nursing. Even as she's struck and killed, she slumps down with that baby still drinking and now covered in its own mother's blood. And Minnie's father, she curls next to him a moment, just in time to receive his last words, a message, and to feel the life go out of him. Which is when Minnie walks right off, through it all, just mystified. She scrambles down a ravine, where she sees sights that she never can get out of her mind. She sees grown soldiers ride down women and then fire their guns point-blank as the women hold their little babies in the air. She climbs out of the dry wash and under a wire fence. From there, she watches a grown soldier on horseback chase down a skinny, weeping, stumbling boy. Another strips a dead girl naked for her figured shirt. The soldiers leave Minnie alone, maybe because she wears a farmer dress and farmer coat, not a blanket, or maybe they see her lighter brownish hair or her skin paler than the skin of those Lakota or they see her French eyes. She walks out of there and zigzags behind some others who are fleeing too. She walks through snow, following the tracks of those others when she falls too far behind to see them anymore. Their tracks save her. She puts her feet in them and never quits walking until she reaches a mission run by an old priest named Jutz. That's all that happens. I can't tell you no more."

*   *   *

DELPHINE STARED at Roy in a fit of skepticism. There was suddenly a big noise in her head. It was too much, and just like Roy to give her this strange and terrible information, and then to quit just as soon as the scene had unrolled in her mind. She thought she'd heard of the place he mentioned, but had long forgotten the how and why of what happened there. She hadn't known any Indians well, except Cyprian, to whom, if she believed Roy, she might now be related.

Delphine's suspicious reception of his story disappointed Roy. He waited for some sign of appreciation for his efforts and lost interest when Delphine continued blinking at him and drumming at her lips with a finger, deciding whether or not to believe the story. He shut up, turned away, and stared at Minnie's blurred photograph. His eyes glazed over, his face grew peaceful.

After a while Delphine knew it was no use to gather herself, to ask anything else. Real questions sat on her heart. Simple, undramatic. What was Minnie like? Had she been happy to have a daughter? Had she loved her? Loved Roy? Had he really felt such an extraordinary happiness with Minnie? Why had he used his loss of joy as a sorry excuse to make his daughter's life miserable, not to mention waste his own? Would he now die happy, living on memory—was that his booze now? Was he telling the truth?

He told her nothing else. When she asked him why he'd loved Minnie so much, what made her so wonderful that he still looked at her fuzzy pictures after all these years, or even what her personality was like, his answers were so general as to give her nothing. Or maybe he was selfish, maybe those private memories were all he had, and he couldn't give them up, not even to her.

Still, there were things he needed to say.

Day by day, as he weakened, his voice softened to a fragile whisper. To hear him, Delphine always had to lean close, into the circle of his breath, which was not the sour alcohol rankness she had been familiar with all of her life, but a childish scent, milky and pure. His gaze was owlish, bewildered. He wanted to talk all the time, and his speech was often garbled—tenses collided, main facts were missing, characters loomed large but with no reference. He seemed to have lost the ability to sustain narrative, as though his lifetime of booze had eaten into every other cell of his brain and made his mind skip like a scratched record. There were occasional times, too, when he spoke with great clarity out of some protected corner of his thoughts. Delphine was never sure which it would be from one sentence to the next.

"Stop looking at me," he frowned at her one afternoon.

She'd had her back turned, and now she did look at him.

"Or I mean," he sighed, "stop looking like you're looking at me. I don't know which. I never sang your part, you know, Chavers. Shut your damn trap." He sighed calmly and then seemed to recognize Delphine. "I've had enough of him knocking on the floor. He's never quit, you know. Banging, banging. I suppose he's waiting for me on the other side. Him with his whole damn family—and I never knew they were there!"

Roy's voice was the frightened whine of a four-year-old.

"I know you didn't, Dad, you were looped out of your mind," said Delphine in some annoyance. She didn't want him to slide onto this mental track of self-pity and comfortable blame. She'd heard his lament many times. But then he said something different. His face grew solemn, then both crafty and confiding. "I could have justified Porky, though it took me a lifetime."

"What?" Delphine peered into the vague, watery, washed-out blue of his eyes. "Justified?"

Roy grabbed her hand and spoke urgently. "I told him to get the ginger beer out of the cellar. And while he was at it, hunt around for the good stuff. And take a candle or two so you can read the French labels! Maybe old Chavers was looking for the king's wine."

Roy twisted uncomfortably, winced, shut his eyes and continued then to speak with his eyes shut, perhaps to keep from seeing the effect of his words on Delphine. "Who knew the wife and kid went down there with him?"

Delphine bent over and shook him lightly, but his body flopped like an old dog's and she released him and he groaned on.

"The kid, Ruthie. I don't remember what happened, but it could be I shut the hatch! *Maybe I shut the hatch.* I remember what I yelled down at him. 'Hey, Chavers, you can come up again after you quit singing over me in practice!' You know, he was always puffing his chest and inching forward, singing over me."

Roy was silent, raptly watching the air between them.

"You went away for three weeks. A long drunk," said Delphine, her face stiff. A wave of sick unbelief dragged over her.

"Longer," Roy said in the faintest whisper. He went silent for several moments in which the wind boomed in the box elders and the windows shook lightly in their frames. Then he coughed a deep hacking cough, spoke clearly. "I came back to get the liquor in the cellar, went to find it. Saw them. After that, I stayed drunk until you showed up. You and Cyprian." He looked up at her, his eyes glazed in hopeless appeal, then shut them when he saw her face and turned away. Drew the blanket over his head.

Delphine got up and walked from the house, out onto the small front porch. She sat down on the top step and folded her arms around herself. From time to time, she slapped away mosquitoes or shook from her hair the seeds falling from the trees in a gentle snow. They were delicate, tiny beads sealed in a papery, brown, transparent case. She brushed the seeds off her skirt. Occasionally, she felt the zing of a mosquito bite, but she didn't want to go back indoors. As soon as Roy died, she would sell the house, she decided. She would leave the butcher shop and Fidelis and move away to the city. Chicago. Get a job in the theater even if it was only selling tickets. I won't think about Markus. Ruthie! She touched her fingers to her temples, then clenched her fists and kneaded her forehead with her knuckles. She pictured the apartment she would live in, small and efficient. Near a park where she could take short walks, a library, maybe an art museum. She'd learn everything, stuff her brain, become a teacher. Write for a newspaper. She pictured herself at a typewriter, a cigarette burning at one elbow.

She was wearing a crisp white blouse and a tight gray skirt, heels. Or no, one shoe was off. She was thinking.

She pictured herself thinking.

I'll never do it, she thought. I'll never really think. I'm not thinking now, I'm just fantasizing. That's a much different thing than to play in the free openness of your own mind. She felt the keen sense of something escaping, bright as silver. Then she couldn't remember the last thing she'd held in her mind, just the sharpness of it. Who gives a damn anyway, she went on. What's done is finished, and Roy's his own punishment. I should not hold myself responsible for his drunk sins. And oh yes, I'm a married woman. I'm good at doing business, at holding up my end of the bargain. I'm good at taking care of kids that aren't even mine. She felt her mind stuttering, searching a way out of guilt and horror. She closed her eyes and saw the hulks in the cellar. One resolved and became an immaculately dressed little girl with a shrewd mouth and snapping eyes. She wore a small, round hat and stood with her fists on her hips, frowning. Her eyes opened slightly, as though she'd noticed Delphine watching her. Tossing her chin up, the little girl laughed in a mocking, unpleasant way. Her laugh was acid with sarcasm and when she turned away Delphine saw snakes twirling off her shoulders and down her arms and the backs of her legs.

"Leave me alone," Delphine whispered.

You are alone, the snake child mocked, more alone than you know. Your husband's from a foreign country and you haven't got a child. Your father's dying and you don't know the face of your mother. You are different from everyone else living in the town. You think you're smarter, that you read more. The truth is you just feel sorrier for yourself. Poor Delphine. Poor girl Polack. Poor butcher's wife!

Poor me, poor me, Delphine started to laugh and it felt so good that she didn't stop even when Roy called out in a hopeful voice for his teaspoon of whiskey.

THE COUNTY VISITING NURSE found Roy Watzka, wide-awake dead sitting up and staring at the obscure and illegible pictures of Minnie placed just before him on the counter edge of the flour cupboard. She set down her bag on the kitchen floor, opened it, put on her stethoscope, and listened for a heartbeat. There was none so she took off the instrument, folded it back into the bag. She uncapped a pen, next, wrote down the exact time of day, and a sentence or two about the condition of the body and her own conjecture on the reason for his death. She recorded the eerie, composed death stare that compounded the legendary nature of his love. The nurse composed his limbs, shut his eyes, lay him down, and contacted Delphine. While waiting, she used the telephone and broadcast the news of Roy's stare all around the town.

Roy's funeral was well attended. The wives of the bankers and landowners came, those who perhaps longed for similar devotion to the very death. There were fragile rafts of flowers in the church, many flourishes of hankies, and a general clucking at the photographs laid facedown in the coffin, over his heart as he had instructed. There was a dinner afterward in the church hall, a gymnasium that had been the scene of a basketball game the night before.

Delphine walked over once Roy was buried, and stood in the corner of the gym. The place smelled faintly of stale excitement, old sweat, and salted popcorn. The tables set up for the funeral dinner were decorated with small pots of flowers—African violets, ferns, sweet potato sprouts, taken off the windowsills of the parish ladies' homes. There was creamed chicken, creamed corn and spinach, mashed potatoes with butter and cream, and just plain cream for coffee. Pies and cookies were set out on doilies cut of white paper. The dinner was served by an interdenominational bunch who for the first time seemed to Delphine more kind than curious, more eager to please than to gawk, somehow of slightly more genuine feeling. Still, their solicitous care overwhelmed Delphine with a simple claustrophobia.

In the swirl of food and sympathy, Delphine abruptly stood with Mazarine Shimek.

"Come with me," she said to the girl. And they left the church hall to stand in a little plot of blistered grass behind the church kitchen.

"If I smoked anymore, I'd smoke now," said Delphine, pushing her hair away from her face. She'd had it trimmed and set, but the curls wouldn't mind her brush and sprang out every which way. Another thing she had in common with Mazarine, whose hair possessed so much unruly life.

Mazarine told her that she was sorry.

"Me too," Delphine muttered, but actually she was very tired, and hopelessly angry. She was mad at the long waste of his life and his waste of her affection. As soon as Roy died, she had experienced the stupid and desperate love she'd had for him as a child. Tears suddenly choked her and she tried to wave them off. She'd prepared herself for years to lose him and when he'd exasperated her, had even looked forward to the day. She couldn't explain just why she felt such a deep, blind, stirring of emotion. This is not grief, she said to herself, this is not fear of loneliness, this is not even exhaustion or relief. It's existential, she decided, and straightened her back, taking courage from the word. Mazarine was standing next to her, one hand on the brick wall, patient and humble.

"I want to tell you something," said Delphine, recovering her voice. Without knowing exactly what it was she wanted to say, she realized that she had something urgent to impart to the young girl, something that her father's death, embroidered though it was by wishful romance, made plain. "We all die," she found herself saying to Mazarine. "Franz loves you. You love him. Why not write to him? Why not tell him?"

WHILE SHE WAS cleaning out the house a few days later, Delphine heard the familiar footsteps and opened the door. A shaft of light fell out on the grass and Fidelis walked into it, shuffling at the threshold, stamping his feet as he entered. Delphine brought beer and then sat with him. He took the wooden rocking chair across from her reading chair. "I'm going to keep my house," she said. "Sometimes I'll stay here." Fidelis opened his fist and closed it, but said nothing. They sat in silence for a long while, listening to the wind sweep and groan in the eaves of the house. Tree branches scraped together and tapped the roof. All of a sudden, Fidelis rose and in one motion picked up Delphine from the chair and carried her into her bedroom.

He carefully pushed the door closed after them, with his heel, and then lowered her onto the cold, slippery, yellow-gold bedcover. He hadn't known that he was going to bring her there and now she lay before him in the light of a bedside lamp, staring at him with a cat's self-possession, her eyes the same color as the fabric behind her. The small glass clock on the dresser ticked with a simple insistence. Above her bed, there was a clumsily painted picture of waves bursting over rocks. Draped on the bedside table, an orange velvet scarf. His blood roared in his ears. The wood of the bed was recently polished with beeswax. He could smell sun on the bedsheets as he leaned down toward her. He breathed an earthen scent of her warm skin as she moved toward him, just a fraction, but then all of a sudden she rolled away. She sat on the edge of the bed.

"Listen," she said, and then she felt her heart pumping too quickly, "I've got to tell you something." Her mouth went dry and she tasted rust. She cast about for something else to say, nervous, wishing suddenly she hadn't thought that she must tell him about Roy. She had thought this out, imagined it, written it out in her mind. She winced and made herself blurt it out, no matter that it sounded like a false reading of a line in a play. "I am the daughter of a murderer!"

Bewildered at the sudden change in direction, he sat up, a little stunned, thinking maybe he'd gotten trapped and snarled in the English language. Maybe she'd said something very different. He waited, listened as she went on with a dramatic explanation and re-creation of all Roy had admitted to before his death, and how she had reacted to his revelation. As she spoke, agonizing over what was or was not in her father's mind, and taking on blame, then rejecting it, he could not help his own pictures from appearing.

One after the other, Fidelis saw the faces of the men he'd destroyed, as in an album or a keepsake book of death. He could no more stop his brain from paging through them, once it started, than he could stop the wind from blowing across the plains. As Delphine's voice surged around him, he lay back on the bed, closed his eyes against their banal formality, but the pictures invaded his darkness and grew more detailed. He opened his eyes and focused on Delphine's face, but now he couldn't hear a word she spoke. He saw his fifth kill. A blond man who looked a lot like Pouty Mannheim reached across a sandbag for what . . . a cup of tea maybe . . . a tin cup in a friend's hand. Then he'd opened his mouth and thrown back his head as if to belt out the beginning of a song. The bullet had smashed into his face and now Fidelis saw that face, as he did so often. Blond hair, a dark red hole, a nothing. Ears. He saw that no-face. It lived on. The no-face knew him and it never died. The others, too. He saw them all whenever the album opened.

Sometimes in his mind it worked for Fidelis to stand on the black cover and hold the book shut underneath the same hobnailed boots he had worn then. He tried closing the book, now, concentrating until he sweat. Muck oozed up around his boots. He smelled shit and death. He'd been cold-blooded, invincible, bringing down the enemy's personal, vengeful fire upon himself and everyone around him. No wonder the other men had hated him and feared him, except Johannes.

"Are you all right?" Delphine was shaken. He knew she had told him something that she felt was terribly important, but he didn't remember much of what she'd said. He must divert her. He took her face in his hands and concentrated fiercely upon her features.

"*Es macht nichts,*" he said, speaking German in the hope that Delphine would interpret what he said in the way most comforting to her. Then he stilled his heart, his breath, his thoughts, and leaned into her until his heart knocked hard and his breath tore through his lungs and thoughts turned into shifting colors that ripped softly into many pieces and rained down all around them as ordinary light.

WALKING AWAY FROM the little house much later, in the middle of the night, through the brilliant blue air, Fidelis knew that something had shifted. Up and down the center of his body he could feel the movement of his blood for the first time, as though agitated molecules boiled slowly top to bottom. Several times, as though drunk, he nearly lost his footing. The strange inclination took him at one point to shout aloud, and he did, in the booming dark wind, the cropped black wheat stubble stretching for miles around him. New wheat coming up. There was nothing to throw back his voice, no echo, only blurred horizon. He imagined that perhaps the sound traveled all the way around the world, the faded vowels bouncing back on his shoulders before he moved, and he laughed. It was the shout, the sound, that told him later as he entered the lights of the town's outskirts and drew near to his own door, what had happened to him. He'd lost his stillness, his capacity for utter cessation, the talent he'd once possessed for slowing his heart and drawing only the slightest breath. That was disarranged. He couldn't do it anymore. That was finished. And yet it didn't matter, he thought, there was no need anymore for that sort of quiet, that stillness, that absence, to survive.

THE WALLS OF THE bedroom Fidelis had shared with Eva were a pale maple-colored plaster. After Eva died, Tante had taken her clothes to distribute among the needy. She had claimed Eva's porcelain figurines, her jewelry, and packed away what was worthless, too personal, or even sinister: Eva's tortoiseshell combs, letters from her family, a few books interleaved with personal notes, holy cards of angels, virgins, saints, and Catholic martyrs. After it was cleared out, Fidelis had slept in the bedroom. But it was clear that he had just endured the space, used it only because there was nowhere else to sleep. He'd gone unconscious there and then awakened with little interest in his surroundings. The one deep, long window's sill was piled with motor parts, beer bottles, broken cups, full ashtrays, and dead plants.

One day when things at the shop were slow, Delphine cleaned out the room. She divided the junk into piles that she would deposit in proper places or discard. There were still a few things of Eva's—a jacket, a forgotten shoe, some powder and a drawer of underslips that she packed carefully away into a cardboard carton. Fidelis had put the old bed he'd shared with Eva in the boys' room and bought a new one, in a plainer style, and a dresser to match it, both stained a deep cherry red-brown. Delphine had bought a bedcover for the bed, and now she spread it across. It was woven with intense red and purple threads, deep and beautiful colors. She stood back, looked at the bed glowing in the room. She rubbed almond oil into the wood of the new dresser and polished the mirror. When she met her own eyes in the mirror, though, she had to stop and sit down on the side of the bed. She was breathing quickly, in a panic, not at all from exertion. Her heart surged and her chest tightened. Did she love Fidelis too much or did she love him at all? Her eyes looked hollow with greed. No good would come of it. She had no control over what he could do to her and where it would end. And what if he should die someday—that would be the limit! Her throat burned. Tears ached behind her eyes. She put her face into her hands and breathed the blackness behind her palms. When she lifted her face, she thought she might tell him that they should not have married. She could still go away. The thought loosened the tightness in her chest and she breathed more easily. Yes, she could walk straight out of his life! But all she did was walk out of the bedroom into a slightly longer hallway, and then down that hall toward the shop.

As she walked the brown and white tiles, toward the door of stained pine that divided the shop from the rest of the house, she had the odd sense that the walls had squeezed slightly in and the passageway was longer than she remembered. All along the walls the stuff of running a business was hung on iron hooks or stuffed in cupboards. Stained aprons, towels, wooden bins of screws and bolts and extra nails. Tools for fixing the coolers and building new shelves. Catalogues and flyers and price lists. Samples and trial labels. Invoice forms and rolls of waxed paper. Halfway down the corridor, in the dimmest part of the hall, she stopped and took a deep breath of air scented with dried blood and old paper. Spices, hair oil, fresh milk, clean floor. It was all there. She breathed the peace of the order she'd achieved. A powerful wave of pleasure filled her. And then the customer bell rang out front, and she walked swiftly forward to take her place behind the counter.

THE SCHMIDTS had already changed their name to Smith and the Buchers were now Mr. and Mrs. Book. The Germans hung American flags by their doorways or in their windows, and they spoke as much English as they knew. Into the joking fellowship of the singers there entered an uneasiness. The men were out back of Fidelis's kitchen, sitting around a rough wood table on the pounded grass underneath the clothesline. A galvanized tin washtub held ice and cold beer. A shallow barrel held warm. Fidelis thought cold beer was bad for the stomach, and he drank his only after the sun had thoroughly caressed the bottle. He opened one bottle now as he listened. Chester Zumbrugge was concerned that the singing in German might be construed as treasonous activity.

"Not that it could be considered a real crime. Not that we'd be prosecuted! However, I think we've got town sentiment to consider."

"Those Krauts beat the beans out of the damn Polacks," said Newhall. "I don't care what you say, they're a war machine."

"They're a bunch of damn butchers," said Fidelis, and the others laughed. Fidelis tried to crack a walnut between his fingers, but his fingers slipped. He tried three times before he shelled the nut and tossed the meat into his mouth. He cracked another walnut, this time with a swift crunch of his fingers. But he said nothing else. Pete Kozka walked into the yard.

"Look who's here!" said Pouty. He handed Kozka a beer with one hand and shook Kozka's hand with the other. Sal Birdy slapped him on the back. Newhall nodded happily, and pulled a chair out. They'd lost Chavers, and then Sheriff Hock. Not that long ago Roy Watzka. Their number was dwindling and it was good when one of their old company appeared. The men cleared their throats, found their pitch, smoothed their way into the songs with beer. They leaned toward one another in concentration and let the music carry them.

I was standing by my window in the early morning
Feeling no worry and feeling no care
I greeted the postman who smiled with no warning
And told me the day would be fair.

The air glowing warm on the grass of the lawn
He handed me the mail in a stack

Little did he know as he turned and was gone
He had brought me a letter edged in black.

Oh mother, mother, I am coming . . .

"Do we have to sing that one? I call it morbid, and I think that we should be singing more uplifting tunes," said Newhall.

"For instance?" said Zumbrugge. "Name me one uplifting song that isn't a dirty drinking song."

"America songs," said Fidelis, uncapping another bottle of beer. They sang every patriotic song they knew, but these were getting boring now that they sang them over and over at every meeting. Roy's legacy of songs he'd learned in the hobo jungle usually saved them, and now they started on the one that began "When I was single my pockets did jingle," and moved on to a series of murdered-girl ballads that they accomplished in a moving and lugubrious harmony, which gave them enormous satisfaction, and always made Delphine laugh. IWW songs that Roy had taught them ran out well before the beer and they moved on to what Kozka called the Polish national anthem, but had become an American song, the favorite song of troops on the move: "Roll Out the Barrel." Then to a song that they had learned from Cyprian, a métis waltzing tune called "The Bottle Song" that they always sang with huge gusts of imitation French eye rolling and fake savoir faire.

Je suis le garcon moins heureux moins dans ce monde.
J'ai ma brune. Je ne peux pas lui parler.
Je m'en irai dans un bois solitaire finir mes jours à l'abris d'un
*   rocher.*
Dans ce rocher avec une haie, claire fontaine . . .
J'avais bon dieu, j'avais bon.
Ah! mon enfant, j'aimerais ton coeur si je savais être aimé.
Ah! amis, buvons. Caressons la bouteille.
Non. Personne ne peut prédire l'amour.

I am the unhappiest fellow in this world.
I have a girlfriend to whom I cannot speak.
I am going to go away to a hidden woods to finish my days in
    the shelter of a rock
with a hedge and a quiet spring.
There I will be all right.
Ah! my child, I would love your heart if I knew
how to be loved.
Ah! friends, let's drink and lift our bottles.
No. No one can predict love.

After the men left, Fidelis sat alone in the yard. As the dark came down he finished off the beer and sang to himself, practicing old tunes that no one else knew, all in German. The moon came up, a brilliant gold disk that slowly tarnished to silver and brightened again as it moved upward. His voice melted to a growling croon. The garden, Eva's overgrown garden half tended by Delphine, whispered and rustled all around him. Grasshopper music surged on and off in waves. Somewhere a frog croaked, hoarse with longing. Pigs mumbled in the killing pen. He thought of Franz, Markus, Erich, Emil, recalled the moments he had held each boy for the first time in his arms. He was going soft on himself. Sobs tightened his lungs and his eyes burned. His voice trembled as he sang the reproachful song of the enemy, "Lili Marlene," and he grew angry. They were his enemies and his sons would fight them and rescue their brothers. "Lili Marlene." Even the tune of the sentimental old piece of tripe filled him with shame. A disastrous need to see the faces of his parents took hold of him and he carefully quashed the feelings with a deep gulp of beer.

FOURTEEN

The Army of
the Silver Firs

DELPHINE HAD always known that her body would not be inclined to grant her children, not after what she'd seen in the cellar of her father's house. She felt the lack less than other women might, perhaps, because she'd helped raise Eva's boys. Markus especially bore the force of her maternal attention. Delphine had observed that after his resurrection from the earth, Markus was a very different boy from the one who had dug the tunnels and fought ecstatic boy wars and smashed himself into trees in go-carts and tumbled off sleds. Lying in the grip of earth had quieted his mind and cooled his blood. He became a reader, developed a studious quiz-bowl intelligence, bought himself a record player. Squeaking horns, the human moans of saxophones, smooth backwards scrolls of music spurted from his room. Some of his teachers sent home glowing reports and others said that he was arrogant, lipped off, and was a troublemaker in the classroom with all of his criticisms and his questions.

When he was younger, Delphine scolded Markus for losing mittens, and then knit him new pairs. Developed strategies of feeding to combat his thinness, which did not work. As he grew older, she helped him study and celebrated the awards that he won in school. Consoled him when he was forced into eyeglasses and made him wear them, hoping secretly that they would keep him from acceptance into the army. By cheating on the vision tests (she was sure) he schemed his way in anyhow.

The day he told her, she was prepared.

"Markus, sit down with me."

He sat down eagerly at the kitchen table, confident and excited, indulging her. Delphine knew already that he wasn't going to listen to her or believe her, but she was determined to make some impression.

"Markus, it's not like in the movies where they shoot you in the shoulder or even if you die it is neat. Drilled through the heart. Men get ripped limb from limb. Torn up like so many pieces of paper. And half the time it's out of some mistake and our own side kills its men by accident. Whatever you do, Markus, I am begging you, for Eva's sake and your father's sake and even though I'm not your blood mother, my own sake, too. Don't get yourself put in the thick of it. Nobody says what it's really like, Markus, to the young men. No one says boys get mangled."

"Mangled!" Markus looked at her in patronizing surprise. "Where did you learn all this?"

"Reading, and common sense." She could feel herself becoming desperate with irritation at his superior attitude. "What do you think bombs do? Pick out the Germans and Japanese? Make distinctions when they fall close to our lines? And then neatly and invisibly do away with you? They're meat grinders."

"Mom," said Markus, "calm down." As if he were dealing with a crazy person.

"Are we all a bunch of stupid suckers?" Delphine burst out passionately. It wasn't even the war that made her so angry, it was the hypocrisy, the cheerful façade, the lies. She grabbed a magazine and leafed to an ad for toothpaste that exhorted the reader to send a tube to their boys in the front lines. "As if the worst you'll suffer is a toothache! And this!" An ad for gum implying that a stick in every letter would counter loneliness and even sharpen the troops' observational skills.

"That's how we are in this country," she cried. "Destruction is a way to sell gum!" She put the magazine down, nearly weeping.

"I know, Mom." Markus put his hands on her shoulders now and patted gingerly. He spoke quietly, dropping the cocksure tone. "I'll be careful. I won't let anybody shoot me or mangle me. I'm not like Franz, you know. He was a trained pilot when he went in. Me . . . they probably won't even ship me overseas." He said this kindly, to comfort her, but although she was grateful she could tell he both thought and hoped otherwise.

She put her face in her hands as Markus continued to pat her, awkwardly. She knew he wished that he were somewhere else. She felt her heart splitting right in her chest. "Go, get out of here. It's your last night home," she finally said, wiping her face with her apron. "Go tear up the town."

"There's nobody here to tear it up with anymore," he said. "I'm gonna take a walk, buy a newspaper. Then I'm reading myself to sleep."

HIS BROTHERS' ARMIES still ranged across the room, along the top of the dresser, on the windowsill. Markus had long outgrown the set, but he didn't take down the display. In fact, after he'd taken his walk, unable to sleep, he spent his last evening at home perfecting the battle. Even though it was stupid, sentimental, Markus righted the tiny horses and toppled lieutenants, rearranged a charge and fortified a stand. As he fiddled around, he grew absorbed by the boy's play. He surrounded a motley reconnaissance group with the wooden rocks and trees the twins had sawed of lumberyard scraps and painted in crude woodland colors years ago. He arranged the armored vehicles, with real rubber treads and tin flags. The soldiers had tiny helmets that could be blown right off their heads. And the horses, and the cavalry, they were obviously no match and easily reared over backward, hit, when, in a moment of fascination, Markus ranged their homemade machine-gun nests before them and made a sweep, and then sent in the tanks. Anyone could see that it was romantically insane to send mounted horsemen against armored divisions, as the Poles did when Blaskowitz's Eighth Army drove eastward against Lodz, but Markus meticulously arranged the seated horsemen with the rearing officer at their head.

When Delphine and his father first married, Markus had hidden behind the door of the office listening to his father on the telephone. From thinly disguised talk between Fidelis and Delphine, he understood the truth that his brothers weren't coming home. That was when he decided that he wouldn't put the toy soldiers away. He would never put them away. He would have to keep their toys prepared. And so, as though the passionate games they'd played for hours, lost in their careful arrangements, would of their own force and incompletion draw his brothers back home, Markus had wiped the dust off the infantry and set them into a new and stricter formation. He'd kept them looking sharp ever since. Now, he took a step backward, frowned, then swept some down with a finger to lie with their rifles pointing at the ceiling. His action suddenly frightened him. Superstitious, he set the soldiers up again.

THE NEXT DAY, MARKUS left on the bus to Fort Snelling and Delphine baked until midnight. Then she sat at the table, reading mindlessly down a stack of popular novels she'd lugged home from the town library and eating half the cookies she meant to send in his first package. At two A.M. she baked another batch and when she finally fell asleep she dreamed, for the first time in many years, of those dead in her cellar, of Ruthie, who rose toward her spitting clouds of white moths.

When she woke in the streaming light, Delphine knew that she'd have to take unusual measures to ensure her sanity and contain her anxious grief. An assessment was in order. She must be strict with herself. She was thirty-five years old and the one she'd called her son was grown and gone. What had happened to the two younger boys in Germany was quite unknown. Her husband had dragged from her a sort of love. Not romance, after all. The weight of it once all their feelings had settled was enormous, like a rug to sleep beneath instead of a goose-down quilt. It was a love full of everyday business, full of selling and killing and hemming pants. They slept heavily, deeply, and probably both snored. He still ironed his own shirts. She bought a sharp French perfume and badgered him about his touchy digestion. Theirs was a tolerable and functional love, and precious to her because it did not have the power over her that she had feared.

More and more, Delphine liked the work of grocering and butchering and figuring accounts. Keeping track of the store's inventory satisfied a streak of mania for detail. And then there were civic duties that befit her position. To her bewilderment, by simply marrying, following a daily schedule, attending to details and minding her own business, she became one of the town's most stable and respected women. Her advice was asked. Her solutions were quoted. Her sagacity with cheap cuts of meat and her saving ways with money were admired. She knew when to spend a dime on advertising or equipment and when to save it or buy a war bond. And she read—that was something, too. People followed her appraisals or withdrew books from the library that displayed her neat and forthright signature on the cards tucked into cardboard pockets inside the back cover.

Lately, she had less time to read, less time for everything. The war was changing the business in a startling rush. Suddenly, they were behind orders. Customers came out of nowhere. Jewish synagogues from Minneapolis sought out Fidelis for custom kosher work. At the same time as business boomed, shortages plagued them. Although Fidelis possessed a much coveted C sticker for the delivery truck, they were always low on gasoline. Coffee disappeared. The government requisitioned butter from the dairies, so she sold blocks of oleomargarine with little pats of yellow dye. Her distributor could supply only the lowest grade of canned goods, then none. No eggs. They were all being powdered for the soldiers, apparently, as Markus wrote to say that powdered eggs were their breakfast staple. He lived for Clark candy bars and any fresh fruit he could get, and he was desperately bored. Delphine bought a dozen Modern Library paperbacks and mailed them two by two. Dos Passos. Faulkner. Cather. She seemed busier than ever, and yet the restlessness that had assailed her as soon as Markus left continued.

Delphine wrangled with suppliers, argued about rationing, made up clever advertisements containing jokes, like the picture of the cow and its slogan, "Our Only Dissatisfied Customer." She worked long hours in the shop, hoping to exhaust herself. But every night she woke at precisely four and could not still her brain. Sometimes she felt Fidelis awake beside her, thinking about the twins. "They're too young," she said to him, thousands of times. She waited until he slept again, and as soon as his breathing deepened, she tossed and turned. She tried to write, to keep a diary, but her attempts irritated and then bored her. For a while she took up sewing and then grew impatient with seams and patterns. At last, she began taking night walks before bedtime.

While Fidelis prepared himself for sleep by listening to the radio and soaking his feet in a hot Epsom salt bath that she prepared for him after he drank his first highball, Delphine walked the town streets. Passing the serenely lighted houses in the cool of dark, she wondered whether she had absorbed the insomniacal heron-stride of Step-and-a-Half. Perhaps she would be known as similarly eccentric. Perhaps at night, people in their houses would hear her pass by and say, "There goes that old Delphine."

As she passed by the graveyard where her father lay, and Eva too, she often turned through the gate to visit. Even at night, the cemetery with its blunt square stones was a welcoming and ordinary place with nothing of death's majesty or mess. All was neatly laid out, measured inch by inch. Hock's grave with its severe black spike of granite (he'd already picked it out, way back then) was no more than a sad curiosity. Roy's grave smelled to her faintly of schnapps. Eva had chosen to be buried in Argus and not shipped back to Germany. But it had pained her sometimes to think of staying forever in such a new country, far from her mother and father's graves, parentless. Delphine had planted a small pine tree behind Eva's gravestone, leaving room for it to grow. She found comfort in imagining that by now the roots had twined down to cradle her friend. One night, although the ground was cold, Delphine wrapped her coat around herself and sat beneath the pine. She listened to the soft wind rushing in its needles, and pretended that the sound traveled down the long roots so that Eva could hear the beauty of it, too.

"If I hadn't met you," she told Eva, "maybe I'd have moved on. But now, the strange thing is, you took my ambitions and left me with your life. I have your life now. I kept on running things."

Fidelis had bought a large cemetery plot, and he would lie next to Eva. Although Delphine had claimed his other side, she thought now that she would rather if Eva lay between the two of them. Beyond her was Roy's place. At least I'll have Roy at my shoulder for eternity, Delphine thought, telling rough jokes in my ear. But in that cool, rushing darkness she also felt the bottomless loneliness one can only feel from a childhood loss. That mother loss had made Delphine strong, but also caused her to live as a damaged person, a searcher with a hopeless quest, a practical-minded woman with a streak of dismay. Even now that she could count herself close to middle age, she missed her mother. Stroking the icy blades of grass over Eva's grave with her hands, she had the sudden urge to lie down and listen to the ground, as if she would hear a great heart beating beneath her ear, as if she would be tranced like a baby by the humming of her mother's blood.

ENTERING THE WARM KITCHEN, Delphine found her husband reading the paper, sitting in a chair with his feet in the bath. She'd made the water as hot as he would tolerate, but now the foot bath was cooled. She looked at him—he'd grown a mustache and it came out entirely pale gray, although his hair was the same roan as when she first knew him, shot only here and there with strands of age. She touched her own hair, just a little duller, thinner, in spite of the rich black walnut shampoo she bought from the supplier. Yet she had kept her looks—she knew that from the exasperation of the female customers who declared themselves jealous and then, she imagined, went off uttering words of condescending pity for the inability to conceive that enabled Delphine to stay so young, and was not worth it, in their opinion, given the joys they experienced with their children.

Delphine sat down on a little stool before Fidelis and took his feet into a towel on her lap. Fidelis's feet were white and heavy as sink porcelain. The butcher's defenselessness lay in the tender skin, the surprising arch, the square vulnerability of his toes. Delphine poured eucalyptus liniment into her hands from a big brown bottle, and rubbed her husband's feet to aid the circulation, then she pared the nails, salted his feet with coarse sea salt and rubbed again to smooth their calluses. At last, she poured more liniment on her hands and rubbed harder. He put the paper down and groaned with relief as her hands worked, and he thanked her in a sheepish voice. This attention always slightly embarrassed him, but he couldn't resist it. He had never recovered from the old war-time frostbite, and lately cramping pains and a numbness of the toes had begun to plague him.

When his feet were safely stuffed in woolen socks, he poured another highball, made with rum. He was trying to get used to it as whiskey from overseas was scarce. Delphine put away the foot bath, sat next to him. I've missed out on God, she thought. Still, I haven't fooled myself. I still think God's a drunken lout who hasn't given the world a second thought since making it. Formerly a genius, yes, I'll give God that, but a supremely careless artist who casts His most extraordinary paintings and sculptures and exquisite live works to hell and lets the devil shit on them.

"Just read between the lines," she slapped the Fargo newspaper headlines. Guadalcanal. Stalingrad. "No divine presence would allow such evil mayhem. What kind of God is that?" she asked Fidelis.

Fidelis didn't answer because he was used to her noisy newspaper reading, where she made anguished replies to the lists of the North Dakota fallen. He never minded her shooting wild ideas, funny stories, sorrows, and irritated opinions at him out of nowhere. Besides, when it came to God he agreed even though he prayed every night for his sons, just as he had prayed when under fire, knowing it was useless but having no other option but to apply to God for help. He bent across the space between himself and Delphine and kissed her forehead. It was a rare tenderness. His hands drifted down her neck. He tipped his face sideways and kissed her again, slowly, then drew away. She looked straight on at him and the knifepoint dimples on either side of her smile deepened. They got up. Ceremoniously, the dog trailing after them, they made the rounds of the house and shop testing door locks and dousing lights. Somewhere in the front of the shop Fidelis took her hand. Gouged, ripped, healed, their hands fit together like pieces of old pottery. They held hands as they walked down the hallway into their bedroom and closed the door behind them.

Left outside, the white dog moved up the hall with an old dog's lumbering aches, and stood in the gloom of the shop, half blind, nose high, making certain that all was as it should be. When she was satisfied, she turned back down the hallway, nails clicking slowly on the linoleum tiles. At the bedroom door she paused a moment, and her ears, large points delicately furred inside, cocked forward with a concerned attention, and then relaxed. She turned around twice and lay down in a cool spot she cherished, shifted onto her side, her legs stretched in a running bound.

EMIL'S WAR WAS VERY SHORT. He didn't have to lie about his age because the army became desperate for reinforcements and took the entire class from his Adolf Hitler Schule, including the teachers and platoon leaders. Both Emil and Erich were highly praised and singled out at the selection camp as officer material. They had planned to join the Hitler Jugend division of the Waffen SS and spend the whole war shoulder to shoulder. But Emil stepped on a mine planted in a sheep pasture, early on. His new uniform was blown apart before it was ever stained or dirtied. A swirl of green passed before his eyes, and he realized with wonder that he was upside-down in the air, looking down at the grass. He was dead before he landed on it. A picture of Tante soaked up blood in his pocket and a piece of honey candy cooled in his mouth. His grandmother made him bring the honey candy. Recalling that his father had survived the great war on honey, she'd hoped it would similarly protect the son.

Erich walked on though he was half gone, blown away from himself with his twin. He had vowed to fight to the death, and his expression never faltered, but he found that when the shelling was constant his bowels disobeyed him. His arms froze around a sandbag. His fingers numbed and locked into fists. The sacred oath he had sworn and the *Kameradschaft* he lived by were useless shelter from the rain of blood, guts, brains, and undifferentiated bits of meat or even, once, the marvel of a boy turned into a burst of red vapor. He hadn't slept for four days and nights when he was captured, but he still, by some instinct, kept himself from croaking an answer in English when the GI who disarmed him said, "This one's just a kid, probably doesn't have fuzz on his balls yet." What would he have said, anyway, he wondered, as the soldier was more or less right?

Later, he'd made a vague grab for the GI's rifle and crumpled instantly when he was bashed over with a curse. "I hate these baby storm troopers. Bunch of little rattlesnakes."

"They're goddamn poison," said another soldier. "We should kill 'em. Save the trouble. Where the hell, anyway, are we going to march them to?"

The first one stepped back, raised his M-1 and just as he might have fired Erich was horrified to hear himself scream, "Jesus Christ, sir, please don't shoot me."

"What the fuck?"

"I was born in North Dakota," Erich choked out. "My dad still lives there."

"I'll be fucked. What are you doing here, you little pissant?"

"I got sent here before the war."

"What the fuck are you then, a fucking Nazi or a fucking American?"

Erich was further shocked at his sudden yell. "I don't know what the hell I am, sir, but I've got no hair on my balls!"

The Americans went crazy with laughing and his fellow Hitler Schule classmates, the two who were left, looked at Erich in mystified and sober wonder, deciding that he either possessed a hitherto unknown brilliance or had, under the pressure of battle, entirely lost his mind.

*　　*　　*

PERHAPS IT WORKED. Maybe the lead armies that Markus carefully arranged before he left drew Erich back. Of course, Erich couldn't have known it. He did think of his toys, as he thought of every aspect of his childhood, when the stripped-down American train car within which he and two hundred other prisoners rode, went north, as well as he could make out, because it was nighttime, toward somewhere around the Great Lakes, maybe Wisconsin or Michigan. He couldn't remember anything about the map—he'd forgotten all he could about the States. After the shocking ignominy of his surrender, Erich had hidden that he knew and understood English perfectly. There were fervent Nazis in his group who'd vowed to punish any of the prisoners who collaborated. So he continued to affect a suspicious, withdrawn silence. All the way across the country he'd been nearly struck dumb anyway just looking out the train windows. So were the others. They were all waiting to gloat over the miles and miles of bombed-out cities, the devastated countryside, blackened crops, dead farms they were promised by the radio reports back in Germany. And yet, they had penetrated farther and farther into a curious, cheerful, teeming, spectacularly untouched country. The prisoners were tragically awed, bewildered. Later, some would feel betrayed. Others would choose excuses of their own invention. Erich did neither, for his brain was too busy, too desperate, too crammed with excited memories and despair.

They kept traveling north, and north, into the pine forests. Here, those from the southwest of Germany felt at home and pointed and nodded at the great, dark, revolving stands of fir that shifted and bristled in the blue light of dawn. The train veered deeper into the trees and the forest seemed to close behind them. At a small station, their hands were linked to a chain and they filed out of the train cars and then walked a muddy road for miles. It was early summer and the blackflies were out. When one man reached for a stinging fly with his chain arm, the whole chain clanked and the others' hands jerked, but the flies were so bad that the men couldn't help swatting.

"Where the hell are they gonna go?" said an American soldier guarding them. There were six guards altogether. "Let them off the chain."

"Nah," said the officer, but not with much conviction. German prisoners of war did not escape in this country, they found cousins. Former village neighbors. They worked on farms and were paid good money for it. Nobody was supposed to talk with them, take their pictures, give them food, or even notice they were there, but plenty of people did.

The line of prisoners kept moving, clanking and jerking, but the men were speechless until they reached an enclosure deep in the woods. Pine logs were stuck all around the camp, anchored deeply into the earth, and several different thicknesses of wire were nailed onto the logs. Barbed-wire rolls were set on the ground to either side. Yet because of the surrounding trees and the blue light of the sky, the place was not all that forbidding. They'd live in simple barracks cabins. In spite of his confusion and the burden of his memories, Erich entered with a lightness of feeling that nearly choked him. They lined up for blue work outfits emblazoned with PW. They were given overcoats, shoes, four pairs of socks, undershirts, drawers, even a wool shirt and a raincoat. They were given two blankets, toothbrushes, soap, one tiny towel each. Erich accepted each item and frowned at the involuntary satisfaction that he felt. Maybe it was the fresh air, he thought, working on his brain. Or the fact they were going to do forestry work—good hard mindless work, a thing his body craved. And then the food, served at once and ladled hot into their tin pans from great cauldrons in the central log house, was sweetly familiar. There were baked beans—he hadn't tasted the tang of molasses, the heat of the powdered mustard, the smoked fat of pork, in this particular combination since he was a child. He suddenly thought of Delphine. Although famished, he ate slowly, with a combination of reverence and shame, wiping the plate with white bread sliced into a soft, square page.

There was no meat but the fatback, but there was for each man a mound of creamed corn and a huge baked potato. Onto each plate, a slug of lard was tapped. There was a two-inch square of white cornbread with Karo syrup poured over it. Each man received the food, staring at it as though it would vanish. Some pocketed their potatoes, inhaled the sweet cornbread, or cleaned their whole plates before they even got to the tables. Inside the great hall there was utter silence from the men. Only the scrape of tin spoons. The animal wetness of their chewing. They were silent not only because they were famished but because, from the quality of the food, the amount, and that it was somehow carried to this remarkably remote place and actually fed to them—dregs, prisoners—they knew that Germany had lost the war.

THEY USED crosscut saws for the big trees, Swedish saws to trim the branches on the trails. They used chain drags, a couple of heavy trucks, and for the remote trees they had two mules they named Max and Moritz. One of the supervising soldiers spoke passable German and had the job of censoring the little newspaper that the men put together on a handset printing press. Although years before it was thought that none of the Waldvogel boys had inherited their father's voice, Erich's had developed once he hit adolescence. He'd opened his mouth one day to hum tunelessly, then snapped his jaws shut in surprise when a rich sound boomed forth. To kill time now, in that beautiful place, he began to sing and soon others sang with him, swapped the words to songs, made of the singing a nightly event to cut the tedium.

The songs acted on their emotions, entered their dreams. At night in the bunkhouses, men cried out in their sleep, coughed, farted, snored, snuffled, and sometimes moaned tunelessly into the darkness. Erich heard them every night, since he was wakeful, as he listened to the sounds from the outside. The smooth mutter of pines, the owls calling back and forth, curious and hollow. He longed to go back to Ludwigsruhe, wondered if he'd ever see his grandfather, whom he adored, or eat the sausages he'd stolen at night to share with Emil in their bed. He thought of his brother, but with dispassion. He'd made his heart numb. He avoided and then shut out all thoughts of his family here. It might have cost him his life to make the specifics of his identity known, or take advantage of his American upbringing. There were rumors of German POWs sawed to bits and burned and scattered through the woods by the *Heiligen Geist*. They disappeared if they got too friendly with the Americans, it was said. No one had actually known, or seen, or spoken with anyone who knew this for certain. But some of the older prisoners put dread into the hearts of those who weren't loyal enough to Germany. As for Erich, in a fierce crush of training and in the years of his formation, he had become in his deepest person thoroughly German. Or what he thought of as German. That is, he'd replaced his childhood with a new wash of purity. Belief, death loyalty, hatred of the weak. He lived simply, by one great consuming oath.

MAZARINE WENT OUT behind the house and emptied her mother's night bucket, then walked slowly back and set the galvanized pail on the broken back stairway. The unpainted wood of the little house still sagged, and great clumps of thistle and burdock had thrust up around the outhouse. That didn't matter. The weeds were full of twittering birds—tiny golden throated warblers, green finches, drab sparrows. Let it just cave in, thought Mazarine. Who cared? Certainly not her mother, who now called weakly from her bed for a cup of water. Mazarine ignored her. Growing against the side of the teetering steps a lilac bush, one she'd planted herself from a tiny sprig long ago, lifted a fat cone of fragrance. Mazarine pulled the branch against her face, breathed the sweetness that always filled her with a sweeping nostalgia. Lilac dew crawled down her neck. The sun was already warm in the grass. Mazarine wasn't much good with a hammer and nails, but the day before she'd found both and now she turned and fit the snow-warped boards into place and attempted, as best she could, to repair the winter's damage. She hammered over her mother's repetitive cries, over the creak of protest as her mother rose and began to move about in the kitchen, drawing her own water from the indoor pump, perhaps even stirring up a little fire to cook herself some oatmeal.

Mazarine had gone to teacher's training college in Moorhead, and now she had a grade school certification. She had returned when Roman was wounded in the war and got his medals. Her mother took to bed and did not rise, so Mazarine stayed. The Argus school needed her to fill a temporary position anyway, so she'd taken over a fourth-grade class. It had been six months now and Mazarine thought that her mother would probably stay in bed until the house collapsed all around her. She could see it happening—the mice chewing down the flimsy walls, the lilacs growing up to her bedside, painted swallows and wood-peckers nesting just over her mother's head and learning instead of their own bird calls to imitate her mother's faint cries, *Mazarine? Mazarine?* as the light sifted through the tattered shingles.

She steadied the lowest step with a rock lugged from against the side of the house, and then sat down again on the weathered wood. The smell of sun on the wood reminded her of the salty, dusty, summer boy smell of her brother's hair. She pulled down a bunch of flowers and breathed deep. The lilac had benefited from her mother's laziness—she tossed her wash water out the window instead of walking to the door. As the spring sun rose the fragrance intensified. Mazarine touched the side of her skirt and stirred the crackle of the letter in her pocket.

> *Delphine told me that you are back in town and didn't get*
> *married yet out in the wide world, which is good. I didn't either.*
> *I'm coming home pretty soon and you're going to see me whether*
> *you like it or not because I have never forgotten one single*
> *moment and I still love you.*
>
> *Franz*

I shouldn't see him, Mazarine thought. I lost him once already and I do not want to lose him all over again. But Franz must have written something about his intentions and feelings to Delphine, because as school was letting out that afternoon, Delphine drove up beside the school in the meat truck. She got out, and walked up to the playground where Mazarine was standing, her dress and hair in a whirl, laughing at some children's games.

"Well, he's going to be here tomorrow or the next day," Delphine said. "We even got a phone call."

Mazarine didn't pretend even a moment of ignorance, although they'd never spoken of Franz since the day of Roy Watzka's funeral, years ago.

"You look good," said Delphine, a little critically, as though she was appraising Mazarine on her stepson's behalf. Then she laughed and waved away her scrutiny. She was slightly embarrassed at her assessment of every girl her boys took an interest in—she hadn't liked that Zumbrugge girl way back. It was a good thing she had no idea about the women Franz probably met on his furloughs. And of course she'd always liked Mazarine, though she still had the nagging feeling that she had to save the girl from the situation with her mother. But then, Delphine herself recognized that she hadn't exactly found a way of handling her own father when he was alive. And Mazarine did look as though she was surviving fairly well. She hadn't cut her hair or permanented it, as so many of the girls did now, and a thick fall still flowed around her shoulders, lighter from the sun in the schoolyard. She was one of those teachers little boys fell in love with. Her cheeks were rose red from running with the children, and her brown eyes, always lush and expressive, had lost that hungry look she'd had as a skinny girl. Though she was anxious, thought Delphine, about Roman's difficult recovery and she was still probably drained by her mother.

How is she, the big slug? Delphine wanted to ask. Instead, she said, "I hear your mother's back in bed."

Mazarine gave a cool nod, neutral. She was sensitive about her mother's reputation. She asked if Franz was going to take the train or the bus. Delphine said the train and that, if she were Mazarine, she would be looking for Fidelis's car and Franz driving it, shortly after she heard the train whistle.

"If not before," said Delphine, her voice deadpan amused. "He sounds ready to jump off and get a running start."

THE SUN FELL thick along the banks of the river and heated the scored gray trunks of trees that swayed out over the driving spring current. The air was dry and the old leftover grass, packed by snow, a haylike and dusty padding on the ground. Mazarine settled herself, pulling a huge old brown woolen coat around her knees. Franz, in his father's borrowed clothes but wearing the heavy Christmas coat he'd received from Germany so long ago, sat beside her on the tough, dead grass. He was close enough to touch her hand, but he didn't. Anyway, she soon wrapped her fingers in the folds of her sleeves and stared away from him, at the opposite bank.

Across the boil of water the trees were loaded with last year's brittle wild cucumber vines—the strings and suckers drooped off the limbs like hair. Here and there, within the fresh wounds in the bank where a tree was torn out by the spring breakup, or where the ice had gouged a wedge of earth clear, dirty pockets of snow still lingered. Crows, the first birds to return, wheeled raucously through the skim of branches. They hurtled past one another like black stars and crosses, and their cries seemed to hold a fever of meaning.

"I suppose we should talk," said Franz, at last.

"All right," said Mazarine.

"Not that I know exactly where to start," he said with an uncomfortable laugh. He had forgotten how quiet she was, and how composed. She met him with the same gravity with which they had parted. She didn't fidget about, finger her hair and retouch her lipstick, or make any sort of small talk, and for that he felt grateful. Yet he missed those things that other women did. Those gestures made it easier for him to maintain a simple gloss of conversation. To attend to himself was an uncomfortable task. So much had happened to him. Returning from the war, he felt tremendously strange, dislocated, even menacing, like a ghost that comes to spy on the living.

"I thought about you all the time," he said, helplessly.

She nodded, still regarding the veiled trees and the shouting crows. "And what did you think?"

"I wronged you." He was tentative, thinking that he must revisit his old transgression first and apologize, just in case it was required of him.

"No, don't." She withdrew her hand from the sleeve, waved it, and put it back. "None of that's important, not anymore."

He knew very well that that was true, they had certainly grown past those times, but he had expected that he would be required to pay some homage to her old misery. He had expected that she might even exact some sort of humiliation from him. Any other woman would have, he thought, probably any man. But she was not interested, he saw now, and although he admired her disregard for the past it also confused him. Where were they, then, if they could not go back in time and make repairs?

"You wrote," she said, "but you didn't say what really happened to you. You've been all over. You've been through things." She turned to him, and her eyes were very clear, so that it was simple to look straight back at her. "You think I don't want to know. But I do want to know," she said. "I can't know unless you tell me, and if I don't know . . ."

She left off, her voice trembling slightly in the liquid spring air, her face suffused not with pity but with an intimate calm that left him slightly breathless. ". . . where do we go?" They were already at the heart of things and Franz was panicked. He could not answer at first.

"Anyway, I won't be in the worst of it now," he said to her, finally, his voice so low it blended with the mutter of the icy river. "I'll drop paratroopers or tow gliders and release them. I'm not a fighter pilot anymore, not with a heavy bombardment group, either. I fly a C-47. That's a transport plane. I evacuate the wounded, drop supplies—food, clothes, medicine, stuff like that."

She nodded, letting the silence yawn between them, hoping he would continue.

"I was reassigned," said Franz, "I was . . ." He searched for the word, but there really wasn't one. "Tired out, I guess."

Mazarine was silent, knowing that was not it. Her breath stilled, her heart squeezed painfully, her skin burned, and she couldn't help imagining herself lunging toward him, dizzily. She had to close her eyes and turn away. She knew that she shouldn't have agreed to see him. His presence leveled the defenses she'd put up and made her wretchedly alive with longings, thoughts, hopes.

"I want to hear what's happened to you," she said evenly after a while. She gestured in the direction, down river, of the butcher shop. "It's just that there is nowhere else to start," she said gently. "Neither of us is the same. But I'm different because of small, good, manageable things. You're different because . . . things I don't know."

She looked at him so long, her eyes so still and warm, that Franz turned to her. She opened her arms and then shook him, lightly, with an angry tenderness. He was panting, his breath squeezed by the effort of not remembering. He was extremely cold. Ashamed of his shaking hands, he pressed his fingers between his knees. He bit his lips, gray as the tree bark, and he tried to control the absurd urge he had to tear off his clothing and dive into the slush, swollen river. She saw that he was in the grip of an unbearable need for flight, and she kissed him to change, if she could with one sudden gesture, the character of his fear.

"I was shot down," said Franz suddenly, as if the kiss unstopped his tongue. "That was the first time. The next time, my engine quit on me. The worst of it was seeing my friends die—I saw Schumacher dragged onto a black reef off Corsica. He'd parachuted out. Another time, I saw Tom Simms go . . . his parachute was ripped apart by flak but he didn't know it until the chute opened and then disintegrated above him. He gave two little kicks, as if to try and jump himself into the air, and then he just surrendered. It must have felt like a dream, I don't know."

Mazarine pulled his hand into the sleeve of her coat to warm it. He reached his other hand along her arm, up her other sleeve, then knelt before her holding her by the elbows and staring into her face. "I hope it felt like a dream," she said.

A huge baffle of sorrow penned him. He hated that he nearly wept, a sob of hoarse anger that he choked back. He made his mouth move and talked quickly, his voice neutral.

"I could see spouts of light just below, the second time, but there was no sound to the fire so I knew I was deaf. My legs gave out on me, and I probably wouldn't have had the strength to get out of my harness if I hadn't . . ." But here Franz had to struggle for words, and stopped.

"Hadn't what?"

Franz's breath came harsh and he tried to slow his heart. He didn't dare tell even Mazarine. He'd heard a woman's voice that filled him with a powerful assurance. Eva's voice. He'd put his arms out and was not surprised to feel her in front of him. He tucked his arms tight, closed his embrace around the waist of his mother. As he stepped into the air his eyes filled with blood. Blind, he held her. Falling, he heard her counting, low and musical, in German as she had when he was little, first on his fingers and then on her fingers, until his parachute opened and the earth swerved up to meet them.

"Part of the design," he said, weary now, slumping.

Mazarine kissed him again and folded him down carefully next to her, wrapped him in the huge folds of coat that swathed her like a blanket. They lay back against a great root that had pulled itself from the ground like a damaged foot.

Holding on to Mazarine, Franz breathed the old crush of pine needles, the innocence of breakfast cooking. I'll never get enough of her scent, he thought, I'll never. He smelled her teacherliness, the waxen crayons and stiff, new paper, the same blue powdered soap that had always poured in a tiny stream from the metal dispensers above the Argus school sinks. She smelled of milk cartons, chalk dust, and tulips. She made him think of safety rules and clean hands and politeness to your neighbor. Franz felt himself floating off into a mesmerized half-sleep. He relaxed against her and she continued to hold him, stroking his hair, looking upward, listening to his heavily drawn breathing, to the greedy wash of the river and the hectoring and bitter arguments of crows as they wheeled among the whips and flails of spring branches.

FROM THE WAY Franz and Mazarine moved around each other, it was obvious to Delphine that they were lovers. Nothing most people would have caught—they were still too shy to even hold hands in front of their parents. It was more an awareness, as if they were two dancers carving lines in ordinary rooms. They leaned toward each other no matter what they were doing. Dazzled, electric, they laughed too quickly, ran out of breath, made gestures unexpectedly clumsy. The day after Franz left, Mazarine came to visit Delphine. The two women worked side by side, hands moving, desperate. They hardly spoke. They couldn't sleep. It took days for them to even say his name.

It had been a dizzying relief to Delphine when Markus wrote to say he'd flunked the vision test and that he was probably going to be doing some sort of desk job at the OCS for the duration. Delphine was elated—it felt to her as though some reparation had been granted to them in the design of things—and she began at last to sleep. Markus wrote about ten or twenty times as many letters as Franz did, and later on he was able to talk about his job, which included writing other letters. Ghost letters by ghosts, written for ghosts, about ghosts. Those were the kinds of letters he composed. Delphine didn't understand a word of it until he came home.

Markus had become a spare, thoughtful, professorial young man. Still, he had a quick laugh and a wicked talent for mimicry. Of course, she had expected that he would be very different. He was neat. A square package of cigarettes jutted from his breast pocket, and he was extraordinarily well groomed. The starch hadn't wilted from the press of his pants and shirt. His face was meager and tired but his eyes were still Eva's, filled with a penetrating sadness and rich good humor. He walked toward his father and without embracing the two sat to drink beer. From time to time they exchanged short and half-meaningless blurts of sound. They were so awkward at talking to each other that they were lost without Delphine. So she joined them, with her own beer, asked Markus what the letters he wrote were all about.

"Dead boys, Mom," he told her. "I'm good at condolence and the commanding officers give me lists of names to write the letters to their parents. Of course, I never knew these guys. I never know how they lived or who they were or how they died. I'm becoming quite adept at the art of creative fiction, I guess you could say, but I hate it."

He took a long drink of cold beer and the three let a quietness collect at the table. Then Markus abruptly set his bottle down, and said, "I'm here for something else . . . I wasn't sure that I would tell you because it might just be a wild hair. But here's the thing . . ." Markus squared his shoulders, folded his hands. Then he unfolded his hands, drummed his fingers on his knees, and addressed the tabletop, frowning as though he wasn't sure he should say what he had to say.

"There's this guy," he finally told them. "I ran across him and we were having a smoke because he's from the Midwest anyway, Illinois, right, and he's been transferred. Anyway, we swap our names and when he hears mine, my last name, he makes me repeat it twice and he gets this look on his face, like he's remembering something. All of a sudden he snaps his fingers and he says, 'I know why you look familiar . . . and that name. There is this guy looks kinda like you and he's got the same name Waldsomething in the camp where I was a guard way up north.' His first name? He didn't know. He's a POW."

Fidelis put his beer down with slow precision. He adjusted the glass on the table, then raised his head. He stared quizzically at Markus, and when his son looked back at him, biting his lip, nodding slightly, Fidelis hid his face in his hands. For a long time no one said a thing. There was a fuzzy quiet in the kitchen, and the cranking whine and then roar of the cooler generators across the yard underneath the wild grape vines. Schatzie appeared at the door and Delphine rose and let her in. Everyone watched the dog walk calmly through the room, straight to her post in the hall. Markus took a sip of his beer again, and then he spoke. "The guy said one other thing . . . I should tell you. He said this prisoner . . . he never talks, but sings. The guy can sing, this Waldvogel."

Fidelis gripped his fingers together now, and his head began to nod up and down as he glared before him.

"I got us a clearance. It took some doing, but I've got the papers right here." Markus patted his breast pocket. "So I'm heading up there tomorrow," he said, very softly.

"I am going with you," said Fidelis. "Can we get him released from this place? *Er ist ein Junge.*"

"I know," said Markus, "but I doubt they'll let him go. To tell the truth, I know they won't, Dad, but we can visit him. That's something. It's a big thing, Dad—you don't know how hard I worked, how many strings I pulled."

Together, unspeaking, the two went out front to close the shop. They worked side by side, washing down equipment, checking the coolers, counting and securing the cash from the drawer.

Delphine let them go and stayed in the kitchen, began to clatter dishes, wash pots. As she always did when things were troubled, she started to bake. Cookies, she thought distractedly, pouring out ingredients, sifting flour. Gingersnaps. Measuring and stirring helped her make sense of things. Going up there—she didn't want to do it, just an instinct. She didn't want to see the men shattered if the boy wasn't Erich or Emil and also she didn't even want to see if the boy was one of them. There was too much that would be answered, in too short a time. How he'd changed and how he had survived. How he got into the war in the first place, so young. And would he have news about his twin? Perhaps she was just protecting herself, she thought, putting the cookies in the oven. And she thought that again, the next morning, as she watched Markus and Fidelis drive out of the yard and down the road. Protecting herself. Perhaps her place was really to be sitting next to her husband, to hold his hand in the car as they drove along. But she couldn't. For all those reasons. And then, too, there was a voice in her that asked a small and terrible question, a quiet question, one she would not ever speak aloud. For the news was all over the place, rumors and horrors coming out, and she had to wonder knowing what she read in magazines and papers if they had killed any . . . in her mind she said *innocent people*, or *civilians*, but in her heart she thought Jews.

AS THEY CLEARED the flat North Dakota prairie and entered sandy pinelands and rolling prairie of central Minnesota, which they would drive all day, Markus had the childish urge to ask his father to sing to him in the car. His father had the side vent open and was smoking but letting the smoke out into the rush of air. Markus would have begun to sing himself, as a way of starting without directly asking his father, but he was embarrassed about the quality of his voice, the scratchy thin tunelessness of it, no melody, a talent he wished he'd inherited. Instead, he got his mother's curious mind, he guessed, her drive to learn things and her oversensitive nature. He would have had a hard time of it in training if he hadn't also learned from Delphine to talk back smart and keep his eye out for bullshit. If he hadn't learned from his father's friends how to play a good game of poker. Thank God he played cards, kept himself in a man's game, otherwise they would have stepped all over him.

The roadway was narrow, with potholes and near washouts, and the two traveled slowly north and then due east into the deepening forest. The former prison guard had drawn a map of the location, which he maybe thought he shouldn't have done. Markus knew just about what he was looking for anyway. It wouldn't be some big secret. The camp was set on the edge of state forest lands, which were marked. And there was just one fairly obvious train track that the highway followed for a long time.

They reached the place in the late afternoon, drove down the simple rut of a logging road, and parked at the barbed-wire-and-log entrance. There was just one man on duty, too casual in a rumpled uniform. He stopped them, took the papers from Markus, and shot a few questions at them. Nodded in surprised intrigue when he found out one of the prisoners might actually be American born.

"You gotta wait, they're out burning slash," he told them.

So Markus and Fidelis sat in the car, the doors open, breathing the green air of pines and eating some chocolate bars Markus had bought back at his PX. They weren't the kind that could be bought almost anywhere else. They saved one. Then they tried not to smoke too many cigarettes or to say too many times, "I wonder if it's one of them," or "it's probably not." They tried to keep a lucid conversation going, but without Delphine their meanings tangled and finally it was best to simply sit there, silently, letting their thoughts drift, lighting and stubbing out cigarettes.

They tried not to jump up when the men came back, but couldn't help it, and stood on one side of the car scanning the men intently as the work crew neared from down the road. At once, they recognized Erich. He was still strong, bull-chested, ruddy, and had the same gold lights in brown hair. He was wearing an old rumpled uniform jacket, the blue POW clothing, and a pair of washed-out dungarees. He saw them too, right away, startled by their shouts. They could tell he knew them from the involuntary wildness in his eyes, a shock he covered as he looked away from them both. Erich gazed straight ahead at the entrance, kept a rigid profile as they rushed toward him, didn't turn when they were held away from the men by the American guards. As Erich passed, they talked to him, called out to him, names and anxious questions. But he locked his features, narrowed his stony eyes, jammed his hands in his pockets when they started to shake.

Something in Erich's boy stubbornness, so like his own, sent Fidelis over the slippery edge of worry and relief into a blood bent rage. So immediate was his anger that he opened his mouth and roared, at the back of his retreating son, an old threat he'd used when Erich was a child. Then he swore his full swear, which always stopped everyone around him and made the boys shrink away and go still. *HeilundKreuzmillionenDonnerwetternocheinmal!*

Some of the other prisoners did stop, and one or two of them smiled in startled recognition, as though at their own fathers' oath, but Erich did not turn to look. He kept on walking. His hands hardened and his mouth twitched slightly with derision. He gathered himself, his thoughts. He wasn't about to put himself in danger for reasons of mere sentiment. Besides, he was not who they thought he was, not at all. His father was an old man now and ruined, lost, foolish to have come here looking for someone whom he thought was Erich. This man who had sold his sausage all the way to North Dakota—now he looked bony and defeated. Not heroic or even strong. What he'd come to here was nothing, and the man was nothing, thought Erich. What absurd threats, too, as though he could hurt a trained soldier far more powerful in body and cunning in mind than Erich believed Fidelis Waldvogel ever had been in his life. As though anything that Fidelis roared could possibly affect Erich. He almost laughed, thinking of the bull's pizzle hung on a nail behind the door—that used to frighten him. Now it seemed stupid, almost benign. His father's arm had once been hot iron. His father's blue glare had ruled him. And the gentleness, occasionally, that his father showed had made his sons slaves to its possibility. No more. Erich strode on, did not even turn when they cried out Emil's name again. So they didn't know yet! *Ist gestorben*, he thought angrily. Killed by one of your land mines. *Leck' mich am Arsch*, he wanted to scream. They'd killed his brother, the other half of him. What did they want now? But after all he had been trained not to show his reaction and reminded himself that this was still war. Unlike most of the other men around him, Erich hadn't swallowed Germany's defeat with either the abundance of food or the friendliness of the people in the nearby town or even the American guards, with whom they spoke German. Erich's fanaticism was that of the culturally insecure. He'd struggled to be a German, and not even captivity was going to destroy what he'd gone through when shipped off to Ludwigsruhe. Erich's new father was a boundary on a map, a feeling for a certain song, a scrap of forest, a street. It was a romance as enduring as the spilled blood of his brother or the longing of Fidelis or the pains of this war. It was an idea that kept him walking through the prison gates.

FIDELIS WAS SILENT as Markus backed the car into the road, then turned around and steered down the way they had come. They drove south through the pine and then the mixed birch, maple, and popple groves of second- and third-growth trees. They passed through the small towns, each with its orderly main street layout of church, post office, grocery, hardware store, and café. Once or twice, Markus opened his mouth to say something to his father, but then lost the impulse and continued on and on in a meditative state of sadness, until they were low on gas.

He pulled into a rowdy-looking little station attached to a tavern. The attendant came out to pump the gas, and Markus and his father looked at the doorway of the bar. It was a battered red door surrounded by a bristling trim of deer antlers. There were no windows in the place.

"Let's get ourselves a drink," said Fidelis.

Markus parked the car and then the two walked through the odd, fanged door, into a dark little bar of wooden booths. Amber light glowed in the early evening calm from small candle-shaped wall lamps. Each ordered an expensive whiskey. Fidelis tossed his back and put out his shot glass for another. Markus asked for a ham sandwich and gestured for the bartender to bring one to his father, who was frowning at the tabletop and taking his second whiskey and then his third drink, a cheaper beer, more slowly. They still hadn't said a word about the visit. Maybe they wouldn't, thought Markus. The comforting darkness of the bar enveloped them. There were no other customers, and no sounds except for the soothing, muted clink of dishes and glasses being washed out in back. Markus looked steadily at his father, then looked away. Fidelis's hands, cupping the glass between them, were startlingly pale in the barlight, and Markus had noticed that under all the nicks and roped scars and red callus those hands were rebelling from Fidelis's control. He was careful not to show any sign of clumsiness, and firmly steadied his fingers on the table. Still, at one point he nearly knocked the glass over. Another time, he absently grasped at his drink and missed—the sight filled Markus with a stricken awe and he was glad when the sandwiches came to occupy their hands and mouths.

It was a beautiful, prewar sandwich. The bread was fresh and heavy, just baked. Country bread thickly spread with real sweet butter. The ham was perfectly smoked, cured, and cut fresh in a generous slab. There was a plate of crisp dill pickles alongside, sliced into thin green spears. They ate with slow gratitude. Fidelis said, "He must have thought he lost his mind when he saw the two of us."

"I bet," said Markus.

"We should write him, get him used to the idea," Fidelis went on, growing optimistic as the beer and whiskey smoothed his thoughts. "Let him know we're coming back."

"We're coming back?"

"He's stubborn, but we'll break his stubborn."

Now that Markus knew how to play it, he laughed a little. "He thinks he can play stubborn. Well, fine. We'll play stubborn, too."

Fidelis asked for another beer now and drank it with a pleasantly congenial air now, addressing his son like a conspirator.

"We'll kidnap the little son of a bitch."

"Damn right," said Markus.

His father drank the rest of the beer in a long, smooth gulp, and then he rose to find the men's room and take a piss. He had to steady himself on the booth's table as he cleared the space. Markus noticed that his father's hand groped for the backs of the chairs as he passed among the tables, and that, as he reached the end of the bar, he staggered and righted himself, then proceeded with a slow formality that nearly hid the fact that he was drunk.

"FRANZ WROTE MORE than a page—that proves he's crazy for you," said Delphine to Mazarine, who came by to sit with her in the store. "In fact, six whole pages."

"Well, actually, it's seven," said Mazarine, only a bit self-conscious. Her baby curved seven months over her thighs now, underneath a flowered and foolish maternity dress top with a spanking white bow. She had taught school up until the previous week, and there were some who said that she should not be seen in that condition, not be influencing children. At least they couldn't say all they would have liked to include in the gossip. Early on, when Mazarine had told her about the baby, Delphine had taken care of things. She'd gone to a jeweler up in Fargo, bought a wedding ring in Mazarine's size, and gave it to her, saying, "This will shut them up." And then Franz had an engagement diamond delivered to her, so she had one for either hand. She wore them both and let people speculate, though who cared, thought Mazarine, when there was the war. Wasn't it enough that there be one new life?

Delphine raised her eyebrows. "And you kept the last page in your pocket."

Mazarine had brought the long letter from Franz—all except the last page, in which he concentrated all that was private between them. He knew that Mazarine and his parents shared all of the letters they received from Franz because he couldn't write often. They existed in a state of suspense that wore into months and showed mostly in Mazarine's eyes.

"It's going to be over soon," said Mazarine. "I can feel it. Just read between the lines."

As Delphine sat with her now, poring over the latest letter, the younger

366

woman rested her hand on the swell of her baby. The capacity of her thin body to expand so shockingly was alternately thrilling and tedious. Women told her horror stories of their pregnancies and she was grateful that she suffered only the normal discomforts—a boring nausea, stinging nipples, sleeplessness, backache. Harder for her than the physical changes were the unexpected sweeps of emotion. When she was caught up in those great nets of feeling, tears poured from her eyes. Ashamed of her uncontrollable weeping, she rushed to be alone and found relief in walking to the edge of town, where she stood in the presence of a raw sweep of sky. She checked on its changing incarnations. Great thunderclouds had piled darkly over the horizon that very morning, but although she could see the sheets of rain sweeping in a smokelike blur to the west, not a drop had yet fallen upon the town.

Mazarine touched the page in her pocket. Franz existed around the corner of each thought or occurrence. She tried to discipline herself to give in to her extremes of feeling only twice a day. At morning and in the evening, she gave herself leave to exist in the sharp reality of memory. Then, she would put away her wild imaginings about his safety. She would make imaginary love with him or reexchange their first words of truth or reargue the foolish arguments or resay their anguished, sexual, good-bye. At all other times, when he entered her mind, she tried to concentrate on anything else—on the housework or her mother or the classroom before her, or now, on sitting here in the sunlight with Delphine. Slowly, as Delphine read, Mazarine smoothed both hands over the flowers of her wide blouse. The baby rippled and rolled underneath her fingers and knocked its fist against her heart.

At last, Delphine folded the letter back into its envelope, and then rose and went to the refrigerated case, withdrew a half quart of milk and came back to sit with Mazarine. She put the bottle of milk on the table between them and pointed at it. Mazarine removed the cap and grinned at Delphine before she raised the bottle in a mocking toast.

"Where's yours?" she asked, meaning of course the milk, but then she saw a thread of shadow pass behind the honey gold of Delphine's eyes, and with a shock understood that Delphine was hurt, recovered, went on, all in an instant. Mazarine might easily have missed this, were she not acutely tuned to that moment and to Delphine's emotions. She saw a tiny flash of darkness, an intimate admission.

"I always hated milk," said Mazarine.

Delphine just nodded, watching her drink it, stirred by satisfaction at providing nourishment, and desolation that she herself had never needed to take such pains.

FRANZ WAS ASSIGNED to the 439th Troop Carrier Group. The fighters wore insignia patches embroidered with eagles, wolves, lions, lightning bolts and broken chains. Franz's carrier group rallied behind the sign of an angry beaver. He wrote:

> *You have to wonder who the hell makes up the insignia—maybe someone like Markus. I like my beaver, though, he's mean looking and has transport wings growing out of his shoulder blades. We fly under the sign of the Beaver Volant Proper, Incensed (holding a missile in his right paw). Mazarine, I go over that long ago time in my mind you know which time. I do not understand myself. She meant nothing to me, but you knew that. It was my weakness you could not endure. I suppose you could say of this man that he's toughened up some but the beauty of it is that he looks upon the world from far above and it is a calm world, not a tortured one. He acknowledges a surrender in his heart. It is like the innocent love of a small boy. He was a youth when first he knew you. Flying is forever mixed with those mysterious hours.*
>
> *Now we'll have a boy or girl to tell that we loved each other ever since school days.*
>
> *The war here is over and we are doing cleanup so don't worry, the major peril we face is sunburn.*

DELPHINE HEARD IT first from a customer who got it from the radio that morning. By that night they had the evening edition out of Fargo with the headline ATOM BOMB HITS NIPS. They spread the paper out on the kitchen table and pored over all the front-page stories. Terror Missile Has 2,000 Times More Blast Than Blockbuster. Sun Power Holds Key to Explosive. Churchill Says Germans Had Some Secrets. Kitchen Dream a Reality—Combined Clothes, Dishwasher, Potato Peeler Due in 1946. Quadruple Amputee PFC James Wilson Uses Artificial Limbs. Husband Shoots Wife, Kills Self While They Are Dancing. Delphine read: "'Truman revealed this great scientific achievement today and warned the Japanese that they now face "a rain of ruin from the air the like of which has never been seen on this earth."'"

Fidelis leaned forward in his chair. "Read everything," he said. "Everything on the page." So Delphine continued: "'Mr. Truman said that despite the vast multiplied potency of the bomb, "the physical size of the explosive charge is exceedingly small. It is an atomic bomb," he said. "It is harnessing the basic power of the universe."'

"And over here," said Delphine, "right beside that story, listen to this. 'Realization of a housewife's dream—a combination clothes washer, potato peeler and dishwasher, with the addition of a butter churn and ice cream freezer—was near today.'"

"Just near?" said Mazarine. Dazed, she was dancing her baby back and forth in the bouncing sway new mothers automatically acquire. "You mean we've harnessed the power of the universe and not perfected the potato peeler?"

"Apparently," Delphine said. "And listen to this. 'Friends told police the tragedy occurred in the dimly lit basement of Mr. and Mrs. Michael Wojcik, who were giving a homecoming party for their son, Edwin, an army sergeant back from England. Other guests said three couples were dancing when two shots echoed through the apartment. "Are you shot, honey," Rzeazutko was heard to ask. "Yes," his wife replied. "Then, I might as well finish the job," he said, and fired a third bullet into his head.'"

"Oh Christ, read back to that stuff about the bomb," said Fidelis.

"One bomb equals 1,228 pounds of TNT for every man, woman, and child living in Fargo," Delphine reported.

"Stop reading," said Mazarine.

"The war's over," said Fidelis, very softly and with a surge of emotion in his voice that was startling to the others.

Delphine put down the paper and the three sat absorbed in their own thoughts and listening intensely. The refrigerator hummed on, and a fly threw itself against the outside door screen. The water ticked, dripping into the sink strainer. Sparrows argued in the grape arbor, twittering, busy. These ordinary sounds provoked great feeling in Delphine. It was as though they held a meaning, representing a cipher of daily pursuits. A script emblematic of a greater whole. If she could only read the pattern, if she could discover more, if she could force her mind to thread the connections. But her thoughts swung disturbingly between horror and relief. She thought she should weep. She wanted to shout. She left the others, walked outside, and worked for a long while in the hot and ordered chaos of the garden, pulling and piling great handfuls of rag- and pigweed until her brain was filled with the fresh acid fragrance of broken stems and crushed leaves. Screwing her fingers deep to tug the taproot of a vigorous dandelion, she touched the knob end of what she knew was a bone. They were all down there, still, the ones the dog hid, the bones that Eva buried, the mice, snails, birds that died there on their own, the tiny deaths and the huge deaths, all the swirl and complexity of life, one feeding on the other. Forever and ever amen, she thought, dragging out the root with the bone. Both were thick, stained, vigorous, brown. She tossed them into her weed pile and continued until her hands hurt and her thoughts were no more than a weary hum. *They will be safe now. Coming home.*

AS A BOY, Franz always pictured himself dying heroically, if he had to die at all, in a Spitfire, after a thrilling battle to the death, shot down by a German Focke-Wulf 190, his favorite enemy craft—dark blue as a lightning storm and pale as sunrise, with virgin yellow cowling, deadly and sunny and fair. He would, of course, shoot the Focke-Wulf down, too, as he chose to face vengeful immolation in a final burst of fire. They'd salute each other as they spiraled straight down, together. In some corner of his mind he'd held on to some childish vision of triumph through the boredom, terror, the tedium of daily survival in the real war. He would have been surprised that it came down to a stupid mistake of timing. A hungover mechanic. A snapped cable.

Franz was walking into a supply locker, a kind of big metal closet, when the plane took off behind him. One of the ground crew had forgotten to unhook a heavy steel cable and it played out behind the plane as it lifted. The other men ducked and scattered. If Franz had walked just a little faster, or even slower, he would have been out of reach when the cable flicked out like a bullwhip. With its last touch before it was dragged into the air, it caught Franz neatly across the side of the head. It tapped like a finger, neatly brushing his temple. His hand kept opening the door, but the rest of him couldn't step through it. He had no thought. No moment of surprise. He hadn't the faintest notion. He was still looking at the scarred steel frame of the door.

MAZARINE HAD ALWAYS hated the smell of hospitals. They were no different in New York state. When she walked into the lobby, there was the staleness of cigarette smoke, and then the grim, overpowering scent of rubbing alcohol. The nurse came, and she stood up too quickly, juggling her baby's diaper bag as he shifted in her embrace. Her purse spilled, but there was only a tube of lipstick, the train ticket, a neat little wallet, and a booklet of ration coupons stuck in the teeth of a comb. Mazarine wished there were more to pick up. She was trying to hold herself together, but parts of her took turns shaking, her hands, her knees, her heart. Delphine had accompanied her across the country on the train to help her with the baby but when they stood before the double doors of Franz's ward, she had stepped to one side and remained in the hall.

"You should see him first," Delphine said, taking the baby from Mazarine's arms. Her chest hurt with the tension. She could hardly breathe. "I'll come in later."

She prodded Mazarine forward, and the younger woman entered the doors behind the wide, swishing businesslike white rear of the nurse. She walked toward Franz. Halfway down the row of men, some surrounded by curtains, some incurious, others whose glances clung to her, Mazarine realized that she was holding her breath. She gasped dizzily and took in too much air. The odor was worse here because it included everything that the disinfectants and germ-killing alcohol was meant to eradicate: the gamey-sweet smell of slowly healing flesh, the sharp scent of old piss, the sweat of desperation, the vinegar bleakness of resignation. And yet, she knew—for this was the reason she was here—these were the rescued. These were the men who would probably live. And then the nurse examined a chart and stopped before a bed. She drew open a curtain on a hoop around the bed to allow Mazarine to enter the makeshift room.

As she passed between the folds of the curtain around Franz's bed, Mazarine knew that she was leaving the before—where Franz existed in her memory and imagination—and entering the after. Until she looked directly at him, until her eyes took in the damage, he would still be perfect, a boy, a young man, and they would not have entered the world of grown-up love, with all of its terrible compromises. I can't do this, she thought. But she knew what she could or could not do didn't matter. The man who inhabited the bed was lost in a drugged sleep. Her eyes began at the bottom of the tucked-in sheet and traveled slowly up the blanketed form, noting every detail, until she could no longer avoid his face.

The man in the bed was still Franz while he was asleep, and so she sat with him tasting the illusion until it became unbearable. Still, she could not wake him. Franz breathed so slowly and slightly that she could not see his chest move. The hurt side of his head was swathed, and dark bruises flowed down his neck. There was no telling what would happen, how much would return, the doctor had said. Mazarine held Franz's wrist, tightening and loosening her grip as if she could pump her own strength into him. She sat there, and she sat there. Around them the blank curtains were a closed screen upon which, more wrenching and more complex than death, their future spilled.

FIFTEEN

The Master Butchers
Singing Club

*T*HE MONUMENT to the victims of the bombing of Ludwigsruhe was to be unveiled that afternoon, and all of the master butchers were gathering from the outlying villages and even more distant towns to sing. It was 1954, and all flesh of the war dead was earth. During the month of their visit to his hometown, Fidelis had been practicing with the ones who were left, those few men who had survived. While he was practicing, Delphine went walking through the town cemeteries, famous for their beauty, or she strolled along the charmless streets of blocky Marshall Plan stores and apartment houses, in and out of jewelry shops where imitation gold lockets could be had so cheaply, but were so finely made, and at last to the garden where her husband had played as a child and where the statue now stood wrapped in canvas and roped carefully so that the town officials could drop the veil in one tug.

She sat in the audience, alongside Tante, who craned stiffly toward the speakers and ignored her. All that Delphine could see of her was her foot, still elegant, cased now in a finely made blond leather pump. On the other side of Tante sat Fidelis's brother and sister-in-law and their two grown children, and on the other side of them Erich with his new bride. When she and Fidelis had planned this visit, it was to be something of a much delayed honeymoon, but the trip had turned out very differently. Fidelis had suffered mysterious pains on the way across, and an X ray told them of an enlarged liver and a threatened heart. Chronic constipation had plagued them both, though they ate buckets of fresh strawberries to try to obtain relief. Delphine could understand nothing of the fast floods of language. Her mouth hurt from smiling, and she was tired of her own amiable nodding. Her isolation had become tedious. Yet some of the relatives would, it seemed, do anything for them—people from her husband's past planned picnics and camping trips, hikes all through the forests, lavish dinners of wild game and local mushrooms, gave them handmade gifts, and kissed and hugged Fidelis with frantic joy.

And yet Delphine felt bewildered, darkly helpless. What kind of people were these? Delphine looked around at the crowd seated expectantly, and watched them as the speeches rolled over, waves of language, sounds on sounds. Women wore small hats and drab gray or tan suits of outdated style, thick heels, rubbery stockings, no gloves. They wore dresses made of somber flowery material—purples and browns. Handbags were in their laps, the leather softly tanned, the colors muted and glowing. She put her own hand above her eyes, to view the scene. The sun moved in and out of puffy clouds. Everyone cast sharp, distinct shadows. The shadows cut across the women's faces and lay hard beneath their hands and pooled under their feet. There were shadows around their purses and shadows glancing down the legs of the chairs. Cast by the backdrop of paper streamers, shadows striped the town officials. Germany was all darkness and light, bright flowers and drab summer gabardine. Delphine breathed the sweetness of a hothouse gardenia on some woman's bosom, the sizzling fat fragrance of a portable wurst stand just behind the gathering. Below the thick German language sweeping over the crowd, she caught undertones and strained to hear what seemed a murmuring hum, the curious singing of some other crowd.

That low sound became almost overpowering and then the butchers filed from their front seats to the podium, stepped into their formation, and began their songs. Most were large men, but not all. Some were thin and wiry. Their voices surged out, over the crowd. Sound sprang from their great chests and bellies. The music unsheaved out from the tight-muscled small men in a pour of energy. Those instruments, their voices, built a solid wall of melody. Delphine watched them, thoughts drifting. She began to listen past the singing. She didn't hear singing, soon, at all, but only saw the mouths of the men opening and shutting in unison, in a roar, like some collection of animals in a zoo. For some reason, she saw her mother's indistinct photograph, large and flickering, imposed on the cheerful scene. She thought of all that had happened here, the burning and the marching, an enormity beyond her, a terrible strangeness in which things unbelievable were done. And yet, now, here were these butchers singing. And the songs were lovely to the ear. Her own husband's voice soared in German air.

Delphine's vision receded, she blinked dizzily. A sense of unreality was stealing over her, a ringing in which all sound was one. Then her eyelids were knocked upright. She saw what was really happening. As the veil was torn away, as the statue of the burned stood washed in pleasant sunlight, as the master butchers parted their lips in song, smoke and ash poured out of their mouth holes like chimneys. Their hearts were smoldering, she thought, disoriented. Their guts were on fire. Their lungs were hot bellows. Yet they kept on singing as though nothing was wrong at all. Nobody pointed, no children cried. Darkness continued to spiral up out of the men's oven-box chests. Smoke swirled, ash drifted. Finally the singing ended. All the cloudy dark the men had belched disintegrated and was gone, except for the tarry residues of the shadows. People surrounding her smiled and nodded. Clapped their hands with a solid racking clatter that went on and on. So, thought Delphine, very tired, throwing her hands together along with everyone else, it was normal for black plumes to rise from the mouths of the singing butchers into the brilliant air of the garden. It was an ordinary thing to witness here.

THERE WAS A knocking in Delphine's dream. Loud, whispery, rapid. Then more urgent, tapping knocks, as though from just beyond a wall. Impatient knocks. When she woke, still in Germany and fitted beside her husband upon a narrow mattress of soft sheep's wool, Delphine knew these sounds. She understood that Eva was asking for Fidelis. Delphine would have to return him very soon. Delphine knew that the knocking was Eva because she had heard the exact sound before. Long ago, the same tapping knocks had occurred in Delphine's dream, and when she had awakened, back then, in Argus, she had known that Eva was dying.

Now, as Delphine woke again to that rapid knocking, she knew that Fidelis was hiding his illness. Time was an army marching like the butchers onto the stage. Time was a singing club whose music was smoke and ash. Delphine moved close to Fidelis and held him in his sleep, felt the even sigh of breath, the humming blood, the troubled beating of his heart.

In her last letter from Europe to North Dakota, she wrote Markus:

He is not very well and I think we should get the doctor to give him a good once-over. Please watch our new help and take note of when they arrive at work. We are too well fed (sauerbraten everywhere we go, or forest venison, pastry like I never knew about) and I can't wait to get home for good. Tell Mazarine to kiss Johannes, if he'll stand still long enough, and to give her mother charcoal pills for the gas.

STEPPING FROM the USS *Bremen* into the milling New York crowd, Fidelis ached with the unfamiliar exhaustion he had battled all the way across the ocean, sleeping twelve, fourteen hours at a stretch, napping in the afternoons, too. The tiredness was bewildering—it had come upon him gradually and now it was beyond his control. He didn't know it, but his heart had begun to fail ten years before. When his son had marched past him in the woods of Minnesota, choosing a gated prison house rather than his father, Fidelis had felt the first intimations of the weakening disease that would eventually clog and then destroy his heart. When he received the telegram telling of Franz's injury and then the letter about Emil, he had felt his heart shredding. He tore up the papers, roaring. When Franz had come home only to fade from life in bewildered anger, part of Fidelis had gone out raging with him. But to one born in the phenomenon of strength, weakness is an alien lie. Fidelis would not accept the news that he was ill. He ignored his body, despised its needs, kept his old habits as though they would bring back his power.

Now, although his lungs were tight and aching, he lighted a Turkish cigarette, one of those he'd bought in Germany. As he breathed out the smoke and waited at the customs gate for their clearance, shuffling slowly behind Delphine, toward the officer's booth, he remembered standing in the same line those many years before. He recalled how the memory of his father had come to him then—his father boiling the sausages in the great copper sausage kettle, his heavy red forearms lifting the links in and out of the steam. Again, Fidelis saw his father's huge face above it all, calm and disciplined and sweating. He mopped his brow with a heavy cotton handkerchief and braced his feet so that he could continue to stand there unsteadily, feeling heavier, growing slightly dizzy. The tailored coat he had bought in Ludwigsruhe was too heavy for this weather. The now and then of things was colliding. The days between his first arrival and this one were like an innumerable pack of cards laid out upon a great table, each of a predictable suit and color. Suddenly they were swept up in a stern hand and tapped neatly into a suffocating deck. The days collapsed, one on the next.

The cigarette dropped from his numb fingers. He followed its curious trajectory as it bounced, still lit, off his shoe. And then, he did not know how, he smelled the rich smoke of it burning just under his nose, and he was looking at a floor of stained and smeared tan linoleum that reached to either side of him forever. As when he had first come home from the war, he experienced, once again, the strange singing of the light. It gleamed in fragments of a rich song off the floor's farther reaches, where no one was allowed, and the tiles still bore their original morning polish. Fidelis wondered at the music, the familiar croon of voices. He was on his hands and knees, kneeling there on the floor like an animal. This was the way the animals suddenly collapsed, but, he thought, wearily, this is an arrival gate and not a killing chute. He felt himself rising and dusting off his coat, walking a few steps forward, and so he was surprised to find that he had not moved at all, and was still looking at the floor.

All his life, the day for slaughter had arrived every week, and Fidelis had always been there to carry out death's chores. Now it was his time—he knew that when he looked into the swirl of the grimy floor. Who was there to do the same for him? His arms splayed out, his legs stiffened, he went down flat. Someone turned him on his side. Someone took his hand. Delphine's face wavered into his line of vision and she bent over him, crouching, looking down at him and moving her mouth in a familiar pattern. He knew what she was saying and wanted to respond, but he couldn't. To his surprise, his mouth wouldn't open. His hands wouldn't move. Nothing about him would do his bidding. His heart seized. A stunning rip of anguish widened his eyes in shock. Delphine's face blurred. The light dimmed, the singing stopped.

SIXTEEN

Step-and-a-Half

WHEN STEP-AND-A-HALF was a
very old woman she at last became beautiful, in the way a wind-shaped
rock or the whitened bones of deer are beautiful. The starkness of age
revealed the underlying symmetry of the planes of her face, the antique
but sturdy ivory of her teeth, her graceful hands and straight legs and
arms. Even her hair turned to a whiteness of unusual purity and formed
two majestic waves that vaulted off her smooth forehead. Age, the own-
ership of her junk store, and the insomnia that still plagued Step-and-
a-Half forced her often into a state of reflection that she had been able
to avoid when in motion. Before she came to Argus, she had wandered
the long North Dakota roads. She had slept in the ditches and the fringes
of trees along the rivers, in the occasional barn or porch. She'd walked.
Nobody knew how far she walked—she didn't know herself. Her long
stride ate up twenty, thirty miles a day, and the distances were easy, the
space a soothing mesmerization. Once she'd arrived at a place she often

couldn't remember getting there. Arrival was its own enigma—how did she know she'd arrived when she had nowhere to go? Yet Argus had long ago become an arrival. And because she began to arrive there more and more often, and then to stay in that town, she began to collect its truth.

Now, when she looked at the streets around her and all the people, she saw them from a junker's point of view. She saw them from the alleys where they burned their garbage and from the back porches of their houses, where they left rags—not the front steps, kept so tidy. She knew them not from what they wore or the façade they showed to the world, but from what they tossed out, discarded, thought worthless. She knew them by their scraps, and their scraps told their stories.

The bottles in Gus Newhall's trash bin told the common secret of his income back in the bootleg days. The Bouchards had a habit of throwing plates when they fought, and were a source of shards that often could be fitted back together with more success, as it happened, than their marriage, which fell apart. Pouty Mannheim threw out both socks when one toe frayed—he never darned them, being a bachelor, and he didn't keep the widowed sock, for which he earned her respect. Yet his proud and profligate sock habit also told her that he would one day fail in business. As for his mother, candy wrappers told her secret vice. Though she remained slim enough, her teeth dropped out. Step-and-a-Half was not surprised. She found awful things—pet carcasses, ripped-up love letters, bedding soaked with death, blood, illness, waste. She found good things—books and sheet music, which she kept though she did not read, toys that children had accidentally lost, which she cleaned and set on windowsills. She found a prosthetic wooden hand and an eyeball made of glass. A tin filled with weird blue seeds, all of which she planted in a coffee can of dirt, one of which sprouted a fat white flower shaped like a comical soldier's helmet and smelling of sex and cinnamon. Razors to sharpen, tires that could be mended, engine parts as well as the stacks of clothing the resale of which as rags bought the flour that made her bread, and sometimes grease to butter it. She'd found a gold pocket watch, a radio, a music box that played a few bars of an elusive tune that Eva once told her was composed by Mozart.

She'd found a perfectly good pot roast, a box of foil-wrapped chocolates, six bars of brand-new fragrant pink soap. She'd found peppermints and crackers and fancy stuffed pillows that suffered only from a bit of mildew. She found these things in trash heaps and burning barrels and along the river, down the sides of ditches, in the street and here and there. There was no question, however, that her most spectacular find was fished from the hole of Mrs. Shimek's outhouse.

It was a find that had defined her life, a discovery that had circumscribed her wanderings, given shape to her thoughts, and provided her with an emotion that she never quite recognized but upon which she acted, again and again. Although it had happened more than forty years ago, the drama of it was still with her, and the consequences, which she'd seen played out before her as on a mystery stage.

THAT NIGHT, long ago, was still and deeply cold. The moon was a brilliant and distant polished disk. That October, there had been an early bitterness in the air, but deadly temperatures had never bothered Step-and-a-Half. The walking solved that. She generated her own warmth and knew how to wrap her limbs to conserve heat and repel the wind. She had stayed in Argus long enough then to know its routine. After all the taverns closed, after the doors in the town had banged shut, the fires in the stoves were damped, the curtains drawn, the dogs silenced, she walked. In time, she passed behind the Shimeks', a place she rarely stopped, as it was merely the source of boiled-out bones and hairballs and stained newspapers. She would have passed by as usual on that night, had she not heard from the shut and weathered outhouse, a single groan. The sound arrested her. It was somehow familiar. She waited. The sound made her terribly uneasy, yet she could not leave. Four more times it sounded, and with an increased and animal intensity that made her certain that the person needed help. She had just made up her mind to violate the shack's privacy when Mrs. Shimek, at the time a large young bride of a vacant innocence, a harmless bovine type of woman, red-cheeked and incurious, burst from the outhouse door and staggered away like a drunk farmer.

In the shadows of scrub box elders, Step-and-a-Half watched the woman pass into her darkened house, and Step-and-a-Half would have moved on herself, relieved, had she not heard from within the outhouse one more sound—a single, scratchy, outraged squawl. Enough moonlight fell through the door when she opened it for her to see that the seat and floor of the outhouse were slippery with a darkness of blood. That Mrs. Shimek's husband was a lazy man, and hadn't dug a deep new winter's outhouse hole and moved the outhouse according to the autumn custom, was on that night a fortunate thing. For Step-and-a-Half's arm was just long enough so that by reaching down and straining against the wood of the toilet hole, groping through the unfrozen filth, she was able to grasp the heel of the infant. The baby had dragged its own afterbirth up with it by the umbilical cord, and Step-and-a-Half severed the cord with nothing other than her own sharp teeth. With a finger, she cleaned out the baby's mouth. She puffed a little air into its face, then opened her coat and pulled up the knitted vest underneath and unbuttoned the three dresses she wore one over the other. She pressed the convulsed thing hard against her flesh and inside her clothing, then she covered it with the dresses and the knitted vest and held it tightly. She had heard its one cry before it sank the incremental inch that covered up its mouth. And it was always, she thought, watching Delphine grow up, exactly the margin by which the girl escaped one dirty fate after the next.

Those thoughts came later, though, and after Step-and-a-Half had time to regret and wonder at the choice of where she left the child. She took the baby with her, of course, to the place she considered her den the way a roaming wolf will put itself up temporarily. For a few weeks only, she'd come to the barn and then the door itself of a bachelor farmer on the edge of Argus. Roy Watzka was shorter than she was by nearly half a foot, but he had fallen in love with Step-and-a-Half anyway. He declared that he would marry her. He made all sorts of plans. He'd buy her a milk cow and a golden ring. A wagon would be hers, and a strong gray horse to draw it. A chicken coop, which he would build, with fine piles of straw for the chicks and hens. He would learn to play the hand organ, to amuse her on winter nights. But she would have to stop wandering, he said. She would have to settle down with him.

Those settling qualities, which he claimed at the time, had fooled her. She had known she would take the baby back there right from the first. As she started to walk, she felt it move, clenched silently at first, and then, dragging somehow a bit of air into its miniature lungs, it gave a shorter, deeper, ragged cry so sad that it seemed to know, as Step-and-a-Half herself knew, it was now doomed to life.

By the time Step-and-a-Half came to the house—boards and tarpaper, but of a solid and thorough construction—the baby was most definitely alive and rooting desperately for a nipple. Roy had a goat, whose mild milk she thought would do. She banged on the door and when he let her in she told him to stoke up the fire and go milk the goat. She'd wakened him, of course, and he stood mystified in his baggy cream-white long johns as she unbuttoned her coat and lifted the vest and rummaged in her three bodices. Her finds interested and sometimes embarrassed him. This one frightened him.

"Holy Jesus!" he cried out, flapping his hands in the air and then wringing them together, "you've got a baby there, Minnie."

Both the baby and the woman who held it eyed him fiercely. The baby was covered with patches of dried and reeking stuff, and it began to tremble and bleat in the cold of the room. The woman Roy had nicknamed Minnie, in a romantic fit, quickly returned the baby to her chest and covered it.

"Quick, it's in tough shape."

He threw two logs in the barrel of the stove and jumped into his overalls, shot out the door with the small pail. Surprised the goat, who sleepily butted him at first and then gave up and tiredly let him milk her. When he came back into the house he saw that Minnie was boiling pots of water. In one, she was sterilizing a rag. The other water she was warming to wash the baby. After it was fed with the rag twisted into a teat and dipped in the milk over and over, a tedious process, Minnie wiped the tiny girl clean, pinched a clothespin onto the stub of her navel cord, and swaddled her tightly in a ripped flannel pillowcase.

"Let me hold her," said Roy. Although he felt a little stupid at first, trying to arrange himself into the proper angles to support the baby against him, it all worked out. He even had a rocking chair, although its joints needed to be reset with glue. As he sat there going back and forth, the rocker creaking high and the floorboards beneath creaking in a lower register, he watched Minnie in the kerosene lamp light as she shed her knitted vest and peeled off two layers of her dresses, and then began to wash within the folds of the dress closest to her skin.

She made a businesslike job of it, soaping and scrubbing and then rinsing. She washed her face, the sides and back of her neck, then she twisted up the rag and washed her ears. She washed the slope of her throat and underneath the collar of the dress. Then she wrung the rag out and resoaped it and pulled the dress off her shoulders a bit, turned to unbutton it and washed each of her breasts, which he'd never seen yet, and never would see, as it turned out. She buttoned up and then, still turned away from him, set one leg on a chair and peeled off her sock. She washed up the inside of that leg and then washed between, lifted the other leg, pulled off its sock and washed along that leg as well. She added the last of the hot water to the basin on the floor and sat in the chair across from him, set her feet inside to soak. She sat there steadily, watching him rock the baby. Her eyes were intent and slanted, un-blinking, steady as a hawk's. He wondered what she was thinking, but he didn't dare to ask because he was afraid that she was thinking that she had to walk.

And it was true. He didn't understand—none of them did. She looked on most other people as upon a species different from herself. For cer-tain, she knew, they couldn't experience what she did inside and live one day, the next and the next, without needing to outwalk their thoughts. If she stopped for very long she might see the trust of the baby, eyes shut, nursing faithfully at the breast of its killed mother. She might see the lit-tle boy throw his arms to his face, a toddler who thought the gesture would make him invisible. The gunfire cut him in half. Later on she'd heard that there was one baby who had lived three days, lived through a blizzard, and been rescued although frozen in a sheet of its mother's blood. It wore a tiny cap beaded with a bright American flag. Who wouldn't try, for a whole life, to walk off such memories? For that was what it came to and why she did it—walking was the only way to outdistance all that she remembered and did not remember, and the space into which she walked was comfortingly empty of human cruelty. An unfeeling sky, brutal wind, cold, and the indifferent broil of the sun she could accept. The rush of wind in her ears drowned out the sounds of that fizzling and sifting Lakota language, and the other language, her first language, which she spoke with her father. Into her old age she still saw his surprising smile, as they looked into each other's eyes, where they lay on that snow-hard ground, beneath a roof of bullets. She heard his words, "Go home, gewehn, n'dawnis. Tell them it is over." The roar of clouds drowned out his silence after that as well as the silence of unspirited bodies sprawling in the slippery gullies, where the wind boomed for days until its voice, too, was gradually choked with snow.

Who wouldn't walk? Who could ever stay in one place?

Ever since, she had paced the earth. Roy couldn't expect her not to walk. She knew that eventually she'd leave him with the baby, but she didn't know that she'd feel compelled to return, again and again, that she'd give him her money to keep the child secure and that, at times, she'd attempt to tend the growing girl in small and clumsy ways. She didn't yet know that Roy had taken her own picture. She hardly knew what a photograph was. Nor did she understand that she was beautiful, at that time, as she would be again when old and remembering.

NOW, IN THE LITTLE ROOM behind her small shop on an Argus side street, she could seldom muster more than the strength to travel in and out onto the ground before the windows. Only occasionally did she walk the roads, and then the miles that melted away her flesh still temporarily soothed her old torment and put off her reflections. More and more, she rested. Every afternoon she crept upstairs to nap in a bed with blankets quilted out of her best finds of fabrics—thick and figured velvets, heavy satins and fragile silk. Before she fell asleep underneath that crazy quilt of all her pickings and wanderings, scenes assembled. Her brain bothered her back into startling and vivid moments that she'd already lived through and thought she'd finished with in memory.

Again she passed the butcher, Fidelis, whose suitcase she'd imagined entirely empty from the way he tossed it hand to hand as he walked into town, way back then, looking for work. She found out later it held his fancy knives. The suitcase would be filled again, though not with knives or sausages either. The suitcase would go back to Germany. She saw the tender arrangement of boys belonging to Eva, and lived again the surprise and the sorrow of her friend's death. She saw the boy unsealed from the hill of dirt. The boy who climbed into the clouds, then fell in love with Delphine's little sister. She saw Roy, and was glad he'd taken those pictures of her to the grave with him, so that there would be nothing left of her to walk upon this earth. She remembered how he'd claimed, early on, that he drank to show her that he couldn't live without her. To which she answered, "That's a load of bull crap," and stepped out the door.

Step-and-a-Half remembered Delphine playing in the dirt that day, swirling it into piles as she passed her, and then the girl, too small to recall this, toddling after her and calling out, just that once, *Mama?* And Step-and-a-Half remembered breaking her stride at that and kneeling down so that she could look directly into the child's face, the eyes too beautiful to meet, the cheeks fresh and open, blazing with purity. Step-and-a-Half's heart squeezed in fear, and then she heard herself saying to the child, "Your mother is dead." The little face, only beginning to know what dead was, had frozen shut suddenly, then recovered and looked straight at Step-and-a-Half with kindred, bold, shrewd, survivor's eyes. Delphine then had reached out a swift small fist and rapped Step-and-a-Half on the forehead with her knuckles, as hard as she could. Step-and-a-Half rubbed her head and said, "Good. The tough ones live."

"My mother will come back," Delphine stated, as though *dead* were a place just like *heaven* or *road* and she had convinced herself that her mother would return.

Well, dead *is* a place right around the corner, but she didn't have to convince herself of anything, thought Step-and-a-Half. Delphine's mother had never left. She persisted right down the road from Delphine even now. She would live forever, messy as a haystack, her shack outlined against the huge and lowering clouds. But Delphine would live forever, too. Step-and-a-Half took pleasure from the picture of Delphine and her sister in the plant shop they had renovated. Two curly-headed old women surrounded by hothouse trees, refrigerated flowers, and bedding plants grown in the rich stockyard dirt. Sleep tugged Step-and-a-Half underneath the quilted scraps of Argus days and Argus years. She gave up and entered the wide pull of dreams. She could see one square of sky from her window. Step-and-a-Half slowly released her weight into the mattress and let herself be carried into that blueness. The blanket was comforting and familiar against her face. One of the pieces sewed into the quilt was a piece of ragged shirt the good Sioux lady had given her to wear beneath her coat, so long ago.

Step-and-a-Half had kept a scrap of the ghost shirt ever since, a bit of yellowed muslin and tattered fringe. She touched its faded painting of a crow, eyes bright, beak open, and pressed her cheek to the horned white moon. Some said the ghost dancers believed that those shirts would protect them against bullets, but Step-and-a-Half knew the dancers were neither stupid nor deluded. They just knew something that is, from time to time, forgotten except by the wind. How close the dead are. One song away from the living. She had heard the soldiers bawl their drinking songs the night before the great guns sounded. Sometimes rough, sometimes smooth as whiskey, the harmonies of male voices had seemed mellow and oval in the freezing December air. "Aura Lee." "Auld Lang Syne." "Calpurnia, the Faithful." From across the tent, she had heard the mournful sweetness of the lullaby that the mother crooned into her baby's soft swirl of black hair. No, the dancers understood just what was happening. They were told. The cloth of the shirt allowed the wearer to visit the dead and to draw comfort from their singing.

From underneath the crazy quilt now, Step-and-a-Half heard them, outside. Wild keening of women. Men exercising their voices. Up and down the scales. La-la-la. Foghorns of chords. *Adeline est morte. Elle est morte et enterrée.* Ina'he'kuwo' Ina'he'kuwo'. *Ich weiss nicht was soll es bedeuten.* The air scoured the fields, then hit the telephone wires and trees. It entered and was funneled through the streets and around the sides of buildings in Argus. The singing flowed over rooftops and rammed down chimneys, trapped itself in alleys or bent the tree branches in a muted off-key roar. Sometimes it was all joy and bluster! Foolish ballads, strict anthems, German sailor's songs and the paddling songs of voyageurs, patriotic American songs. Other times, Cree lullabies, sweat lodge summons, lost ghost dance songs, counting rhymes, and hymns to the snow. Our songs travel the earth. We sing to one another. Not a single note is ever lost and no song is original. They all come from the same place and go back to a time when only the stones howled. Step-and-a-Half hummed in her sleep and sank deeper into her own tune, a junker's pile of tattered courting verse and hunter's wisdom and the utterances of itinerants or words that sprang from a bit of grass or a scrap of cloud or a prophetic pig's knuckle, in a world where butchers sing like angels.

ACKNOWLEDGMENTS

THANK YOU Diane Reverand, Andrew Wylie, Trent Duffy, Terry Karten, Lisa Record, Jen Mundt—and most of all, Ralph Erdrich, my dad.

In the oral history of the massacre at Wounded Knee it is said two people from the north, Cree or Ojibwe, died with Bigfoot's people. I have always wondered about them.

The picture of the young butcher on the cover of this book is of my grandfather Ludwig Erdrich. He fought in the trenches on the German side in World War I. His sons served on the American side in World War II. This book is fiction except for snout salad, the bull's pizzle, and my grandmother's short stint as a human table in a vaudeville act.